THE PRICE OF GLORY

Other Nathan Peake novels by Seth Hunter

The Time of Terror
The Tide of War

THE PRICE OF GLORY

a Nathan Peake novel

Seth Hunter

McBooks Press, Inc.
www.mcbooks.com
Ithaca, New York

Published by McBooks Press 2011
First published in Great Britain by Headline Review,
an imprint of Headline Publishing Group, a Hachette UK company, 2010
This McBooks Press edition of the work has been revised from the original U.K. edition by the author's request.

Cover illustration © 1971, licensed from Shutterstock.com, 2010.
Cover and interior design by Panda Musgrove.

Library of Congress Cataloging-in-Publication Data

Hunter, Seth.
  The price of glory : a Nathan Peake novel / Seth Hunter.
     p. cm.
  ISBN 978-1-59013-625-6 (alk. paper)
  1. Great Britain. Royal Navy--Officers--Fiction. I. Title.
  PR6108.U59P75 2011
  823'.92--dc23

                        2011030524

        Visit the McBooks Press website at www.mcbooks.com.

            Printed in the United States of America
                9 8 7 6 5 4 3 2 1

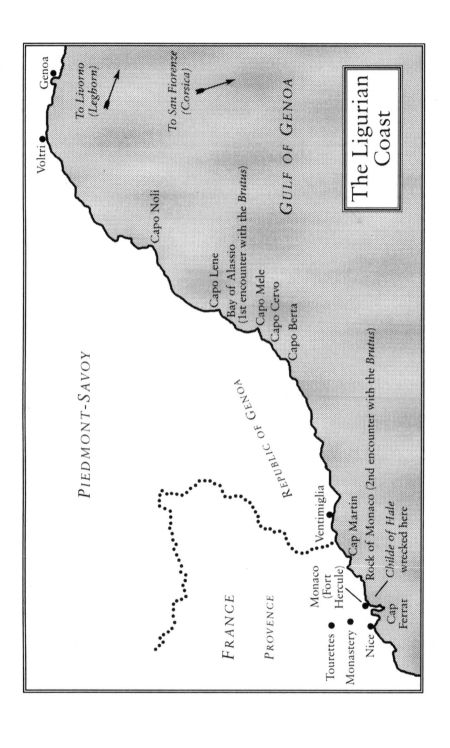

The Ligurian Coast

Genoa

Voltri

To Livorno (Leghorn)

To San Fiorenzo (Corsica)

GULF OF GENOA

Capo Noli

Capo Lene

Bay of Alassio (1st encounter with the *Brutus*)

Capo Mele

Capo Cervo

Capo Berta

PIEDMONT-SAVOY

REPUBLIC OF GENOA

Ventimiglia

Cap Martin

Rock of Monaco (2nd encounter with the *Brutus*)

Childe of Hale wrecked here

Monaco (Fort Hercule)

Cap Ferrat

FRANCE

PROVENCE

Tourettes

Monastery

Nice

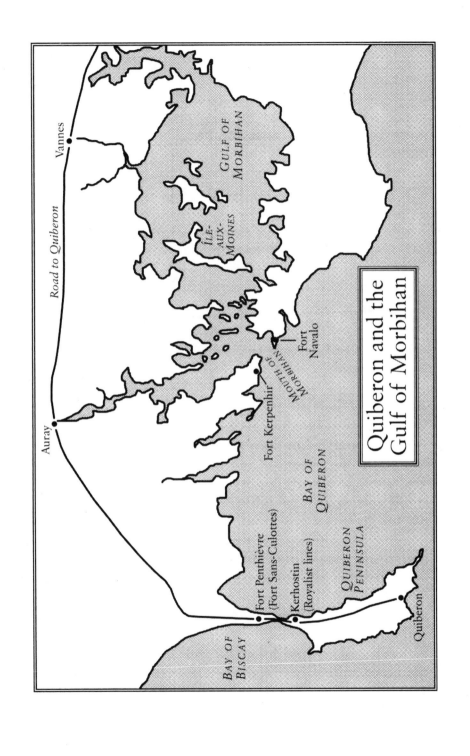

Quiberon and the
Gulf of Morbihan

Vannes

Road to Quiberon

Auray

GULF OF
MORBIHAN

ÎLE-
AUX-
MOINES

Fort
Navalo

Fort Kerpenhir

MOUTH OF
MORBIHAN

BAY OF
QUIBERON

Fort Penthièvre
(Fort Sans-Culottes)

Kerhostin
(Royalist lines)

QUIBERON
PENINSULA

BAY OF
BISCAY

Quiberon

PROLOGUE

the Throne of Death

YOU WILL FEEL NO PAIN," they said. "It is like the tickle of a feather or a lover's kiss."

They had cut her hair and torn her chemise to expose her neck and breasts. To make her ready, they said, like a bride for her groom.

"He is waiting for you," they told her, "in the Place du Trône."

They were drunk, which was not uncommon when they had a new cargo to prepare for the machine, but there was uncertainty in their eyes, verging on fear, for rumours of unrest were circulating among the people, rumours of conspiracy in high places. And on the way through the city, a mob surrounded the carts shouting that it was all over, that the tyrant Robespierre was overthrown and the executions must stop. But the guards did not heed them.

And now they were here and there it was, waiting for them, the Scientific and Humane Execution Machine. The cure for all ills. Dr. Guillotine.

Some of the prisoners began to weep and wail; others sang hymns or songs of love.

"Courage, my friend." Sara felt the soft breath in her ear and the strong fingers at her wrist, tugging at the rope that bound her. She turned and met the eyes of the stranger sitting beside her in the cart.

She had told Sara she was the Princess of Monaco but she was probably mad. They had their share of madwomen in the cart. There was
one who said she was Queen Marie Antoinette and another who
spat upon her and said she was the late King's mistress and the only
woman he had ever loved. Yet another who claimed to be the bride
of Satan, three who said they were nuns, and two confessed whores.

But then they were all whores to the people who had sent them
here. Nuns were whores of God. Marie Antoinette was the Austrian
whore. And Sara was a noble whore. Sara de la Tour d'Auvergne,
Countess of Turenne. And they would all die together in the Place
du Trône.

But she must not think of that, the unthinkable that. So she turned
her head away and having no future, she thought of the past.

She had been born not too far from Monaco. In the mountains
above the coast, near the border between France and Genoa. Her father was one of the local *seigneurs*, Scottish by birth, and a soldier.
But he was an old man by then and on market days, having nothing
better to do, he would take her into Tourettes-de-Vence and they
would sit at a café in the square, the old man and his little girl, and
the *patron's* wife would bring them drinks: wine for the *seigneur*,
lemonade for his daughter, and little golden cakes made of oranges,
and they would sit together in the shade of an umbrella pine and
watch the world go by.

The guards were letting down the sides of the carts and helping
the prisoners to descend, for they had their hands tied behind them
and it would not do to let them fall and hurt themselves at the foot
of the machine. But Sara's hands were loose now. One tug and they
would be free—much good it would do her. Save to seize a bayonet
from one of the guards and slit her throat. And cheat Dr. Guillotine
at the last.

She began to tremble, her whole body shaking in the sweating air.

"Courage, my friend." Those words again; the soft breath at Sara's
neck.

Like the tickle of a feather or a lover's kiss.

She had a lover. An Englishman. The love of her life. But where was he now? And she had a son, a little boy.

But she must not think of this.

They lined them up, facing the guillotine. This was not right. They should be facing the other way, so they would not see the full horror that awaited them up there on the scaffold. As if they could not imagine it. But still, it was not right. They knew the rules. It was spoken of all the time in the prisons. People even rehearsed for this moment, the crowning moment of their lives. In the Place du Trône.

But the guards were nervous. The crowd was not with them for once; people were hurling insults at them, spitting and cursing. Others tried to reason with them. They said that as citizen soldiers—servants of the people—they should abide by the will of the people. And the will of the people, expressed in the National Convention, was that the executions must stop. But then Hanriot, commander of the Garde Parisienne came charging up on his horse, waving his sword and urging them to carry on and be damned to the lot of them. Sanson, the executioner, was already up there on the scaffold with his valets, checking that the ropes ran free in the runnels, chewing on a straw like a farmer going about his business—and behind the scaffold stood a large, low-slung farm cart with its interior painted red, waiting to take the bodies away when the job was done.

They were buried in the catacombs, Sara had been told: the labyrinth of tunnels under the streets of Paris. All thrown together, the bones all jumbled up in the dark, with no stone to say who they were or how they had died. The only record was kept by the two *huissiers,* the officials appointed by the Revolutionary Tribunal who sat at a table beneath the scaffold, like waiting carrion, with their black robes and plumed hats, the silver chains of office around their necks and the death warrants in front of them. When they signed them on the back, the warrants became death certificates to be handed back to the Tribunal as proof that the sentence of the court had been carried out.

And Sara's would be among them.

The executioner was nearly ready. He pulled a blood-stained smock over his head and signalled to his valets, who laid hold of the first victim and half-dragged, half-carried her up the steps. She was a woman Sara knew. They had spent several hours in the same cell, awaiting trial at the Palais de Justice. She was a prostitute called Catherine Halbourg, nicknamed "Egle," who had been arrested with one of her friends in the Rue Fromenteau just before the trial of the Queen—the *real* Queen, who the Revolutionists called the Austrian whore. The way Egle told it, some of the men from the Commune had suggested putting a couple of real whores in the dock with her, to make a point. But the idea was vetoed by a superior authority and Queen Marie Antoinette was tried and executed alone. Not that this helped poor Egle. They kept her in prison, not knowing what to do with her, and then someone decided to kill her anyway, for being an enemy of Virtue.

"I am ready," she had told Sara. "I have been rehearsing."

They had held mock executions in the prison, she said, practising with their hands tied behind their backs, laid out on a plank.

And they held séances, when they conjured the Devil.

"He is not like the priests say he is," she had assured Sara earnestly. "He is very handsome and wise and rich. And he has chosen me as his bride. He has many brides in Hell but I am the only one that is French. 'Believe in me,' he said, 'and you will be saved.'"

But now she did not seem so sure of herself. She was shaking and crying and she ran around the scaffold like a hen in the farmyard but the two valets seized her, one by the arms and one by the feet, and threw her down on her belly along the plank, sliding it forward under the blade and clamping her neck in a vice. And then Sanson pulled upon his rope and it was all over.

Sara, who had shut her eyes, heard a swish as the blade fell and then the thud.

Like the tickle of a feather or a lover's kiss.

The crowd, that had held its breath for this moment, now broke into a new chorus of booing and yelling, calling the guards cowards and traitors, and surging almost to the foot of the scaffold. And the guards fell back and the drummer beat his drum and Hanriot waved his sword and the horse reared and plunged, foaming at the mouth where he had raked it with the bit, showing the whites of its eyes as it smelled the blood.

And then it slipped.

Horse and rider sprawling together on the blood-wet cobbles and the horse up first, panicking, wild with fear, and bolting straight into the line of guards.

Who went down like wooden soldiers in a skittle alley.

And the woman who called herself Princess of Monaco grabbed Sara by the arm and said: "Run!"

They ran straight into the crowd and the crowd opened before them and let them through. There were shouts. Then shots. Sara fell, slipping in her wooden *sabots*, and the woman came back for her. The woman came back for her and reached out a hand and then went down herself and Sara saw the black, smoking hole in her chemise and then the blood. She pulled at her, regardless, trying to haul her up. But there were others pulling at Sara.

"Run!" they said. "They have killed her. Run!"

And Sara saw that it was true, and so she ran. And the crowd closed after her until she was running alone through empty streets; running she knew not where, but with one overriding thought: to put as much distance as possible between herself and the groom who was waiting for her on the Place du Trône. The machine with a lover's kiss.

And she was running still.

PART ONE: THE DEADLY SHORE

CHAPTER ONE

the Fog of War

THE BAY OF QUIBERON, off the south coast of Brittany, the 27th day of June in the Year of Our Lord 1795—or Year 3 of the Revolution, according to the system prevailing in these more enlightened climes: the month of Messidor, the day of Garlic.

A day of fog, in fact, and the frigate *Unicorn* floating upon a flat calm, her people standing listless at the guns which had been run out as a precaution, so close to these hostile, bristling shores of France, though they had to take this in good faith from their captain and he from the sailing master, for the fog hung so heavily about the ship it was difficult to discern the forecastle from the quarterdeck and caused the lookouts in the tops to suppose they were cut off entirely from all human contact and become a species of ghoul that dwelt in clouds. A nasty, brutish, troublesome fog; a Republican fog. A wet blanket draped over history: the glorious day that was to turn back the tide of Revolution.

Mr. Graham, the ship's master and a loyal subject of King George, glared out upon it from under the battered brim of his hat, as if he would seize it by the throat and throttle the life out of it, or blast it into Kingdom Come with a double broadside.

It had crept upon them in the dark and now they were halfway through the morning watch and still it would not lift, and they could be anywhere between Belle Isle and the wicked claw of Quiberon, with its shoal waters and its savage rocks and its treacherous tides.

Not that the master would have admitted publicly to so imprecise a knowledge, for he knew that the captain had his eye upon him, and that it was a cold and speculative eye, for Mr. Graham was new to the ship, having joined her less than a week ago at Portsmouth upon her return from the Caribbean, and he had yet to win the confidence of either captain or crew.

The *Unicorn* was a new ship, launched a little over a year ago: one of a new class of heavy frigates with thirty-two long guns, 18-pounders for the most part, and six 32-pounder carronades. But she had taken some hard knocks on her first commission, harder knocks than many an older ship. She had endured mutiny, hurricane, yellow fever and battle, losing many of her crew and most of her officers in the process, and the replacements who had come aboard at Portsmouth were as yet unproven, and in the case of Mr. Graham not popular. It was not only her captain who looked upon their new master with mistrust, for it had been observed on the lower deck that he had an eye for the young gentlemen and exorcised his demons with the bottle.

Four bells in the morning watch, tolling in the muffled air like a funeral dirge in a country churchyard. And as if in reply, a distant keening away to starboard and then again, closer, off the larboard bow. Some of the newcomers, mostly landsmen taken by the press, looked wildly about them, fearing Sirens or other ill-intentioned spirits of the sea, and the older hands looked grim knowing it to be the shrill alarum of boatswains' pipes from at least two other ships, warning the unwary to keep their distance.

"I think we must shorten sail, Mr. Graham," said the captain, "to be on the safe side. And let us sound a warning." Then, raising his voice a little: "Mr. Holroyd there!"

One of the young gentlemen came scurrying aft, eager with nervous importance for he had recently been raised to acting lieutenant, a promotion that more than compensated, to his mind, for the loss of an ear on their last commission. "Sir?"

"Have some of your people line the rail with sweeps, if you will, Mr. Holroyd, and stand by to fend away."

A rush of feet along the decks and up into the forecastle. The gun crews fidgeting at their guns and the lookouts peering from the tops, questing for some substance to these eerie, spectral wails. The captain rejoined his first lieutenant at the rail.

"I think we have found our squadron," he mused.

"Unless it be the French."

"We should smell them, surely."

"Of what does a Frenchman smell that is distinct from the human?"

"I have not been able to elicit a precise account, but I am told you know it when you smell it."

There was irony in these remarks, for both men had a large dose of French blood in their veins, sufficient, as they said, to make one whole Frenchman between them. The captain was descended on his mother's side from a distinguished line of Huguenots whilst his companion hailed from the Channel Isles—the illicit progeny of a fisherman and the daughter of a local *seigneur*. In fact, they shared rather more respect for the traditional enemy than was deemed natural or seemly in an officer of the King's Navy, though they tended to keep it to themselves in company.

The two men were roughly of an age, which was somewhat between twenty-five and thirty: one dark, one fair, both tall and personable if a little scarred here and there, as if they had been in the wars—which they had. They wore identical tarpaulins buttoned up to the throat and might have passed for midshipmen, the lowest form of marine life to bear the king's commission, had it not been for a certain authority in their bearing and from the way the true midshipmen that were about the quarterdeck kept their distance as if there was an invisible line drawn upon it—which there was.

The captain, Nathaniel Peake, had attained these lofty heights on the untimely demise of his predecessor, who had suffered the indignity of having his throat cut by former members of the ship's crew off the Floridas. The first lieutenant, Mr. Tully, had been assisted in his rise to greatness by the enemy, who had obligingly knocked his rivals on the head, one by one, in the waters of the Caribbean. Indeed, the two men had shared enough perils and privations to form a kind of friendship, inasmuch as that relationship could prevail between the captain of a King's ship and a mere mortal.

The sharp report of a cannon from somewhere off to starboard. A signal gun, in all probability, but the gun crews tensed and the captain cursed, betraying the unease beneath his banter, not so much at the prospect of an engagement as from the fear of a collision, for the tide was running swiftly enough to promise he would lose more than his dignity and his ship a little paint if such a misfortune were to occur. He had been ordered to join Sir John Borlase Warren off Quiberon "with the utmost haste," but his great fear was that the *Unicorn* should prove too hasty and announce her arrival by running upon one of Sir John's squadron in the mist, adding to a growing, if in his view unwarranted, reputation for recklessness.

The signal gun again—and as if it had awoken Aeolus from his slumbers, they felt the first real breath of wind that morning: a mere zephyr that barely stirred the sodden canvas, and faded . . . only to return stronger and more confident, and the sails filled, flattened and filled, and the frigate shied like a colt so that Nathan was moved to utter another curse and instruct the sailing master to back the fore course.

Then, all of a sudden, the fog lifted. And there were the spectres that had haunted them: one, two, three stately ships of war, the nearest about a cable's length to leeward. Nathan could see the white ensign at her stern and the officers about her quarterdeck and he was about to touch his hat to them, with that nonchalance to which he always aspired, for he could see she was on a parallel course and posed no immediate threat, when an urgent commotion forward alerted him to the greater danger: a brute of a two-decker, dead ahead, and so close it seemed impossible they would not run aboard her. He was at the con in an instant with a stream of orders, the helmsmen frantically spinning the wheel. Slowly, slowly the bows came round. Nathan watched in an agony of helpless apprehension as the *Unicorn*'s long lance of a bowsprit advanced upon the stern windows with all the jaunty confidence of a charging knight. He braced himself for the splintering, wrenching shock and the retribution that would surely follow . . . And then they were clear. Clear by a good six feet and drawing away, leaving an enduring memory of the double band of broad white stripes and the pale, astonished faces on the rail above and one, more ruddy and in the uniform of an officer, shaking his fist and bellowing a terrible curse.

"Captain Peake—so here you are at last. I had given you up for lost."

Sir John Borlase Warren, the expedition commander, was seated in the day cabin of the flagship *Pomone* with a white cloth spread over his shoulders whilst his barber, or one of the many servants available to supply that function, applied an even sprinkling of powder to his ample brown locks. Behind him, through the stern windows, Nathan could see one of the three 74s of the squadron and beyond that, several of the fifty transports that made up the bulk of Sir John's command, the steam rising from their decks as the June sun mopped up what remained of the morning mist.

The commodore was in his early forties: keen-eyed and noble-browed, possessed of a long straight nose, a firm chin and an excellent tailor. He had two claims to distinction, both of which made him an unusual member of the species of naval officer. He possessed a university degree—an MA from Emmanuel College, Cambridge—and he had entered the service as an able seaman. His admirers proposed that, by sheer energy and application, he had succeeded in combining a life upon the lower deck with the life of a Cambridge scholar; his detractors that he had contrived through the influence of friends in high places to have his name entered on the books of HMS *Marlborough,* then serving as guard ship on the Medway, in order to secure valuable years of sea time without the inconvenience of spending years at sea. He had compounded this crime, in the eyes of these cynics, by entering Parliament, within a year of gaining his degree, as the member for Marlow in Buckinghamshire, a constituency in the gift of his family. And though this imposed even fewer restrictions upon his time than a university education, he had not properly entered the service until the venerable age of twenty-seven. Two years later he had been made post captain of a frigate.

Nathan had reason to acknowledge the value of patronage but he had served as midshipman and lieutenant for ten years before his first command and he was not disposed to admire a man whose ambition had been considerably aided by his political connections.

Just as he resented the implication that he had taken his time getting here.

He felt obliged to point out, with respect, that he had left Portsmouth within a few hours of receiving the order and proceeded as fast as the winds would allow.

"Well, well, you are here now and no harm done," conceded the commodore, "for we have given the French a bloody nose in your absence and have them bottled up in L'Orient."

So Nathan had heard from the commander of a sloop he had encountered off Ushant, though he might possibly have disputed the use of the pronoun "we," had he valued his career less than he did. Warren's convoy had been attacked by the French off the Île de Groix, but the rapid intercession of the Channel Fleet had caused the enemy to run for L'Orient with the loss of three ships of the line.

Nathan said that he was sorry to have missed it. And he meant it. The prize money would have been useful, for his circumstances were unusually straitened.

"Well, it has eased our situation somewhat," agreed Sir John complacently. He considered his appearance in the mirror that was raised for his inspection before dismissing the menial with a languid hand. "And now all that is left for us to do is to put our eager fellows ashore with as much haste as we can muster."

Nathan had seen a selection of these eager fellows lining the rails of the transports on his way from the *Unicorn* and would not have said they displayed any more signs of haste than the commodore. Though they wore the red coats of British regular infantry, they were French émigrés who had fled to England in the years since the Revolution and were now being sent back courtesy of the British government and at the expense of the British taxpayer, to restore the Bourbons to the throne of France. Judging from the scowls Nathan had observed as he was rowed past them in his barge they were by no means as fervent to accomplish that feat as those who had despatched them hither.

"And what force is at our disposal, sir?" Nathan enquired, "if it is not to betray a confidence."

"Well, it is to be hoped the French remain in ignorance for a while longer but I believe we may share the secret with you, Captain, as you must play your part in ensuring our success. The first contingent consists of above two thousand infantry—but doubtless Mr. Finch will have a more precise figure to hand."

Mr. Finch was the Commodore's political adviser: a man of indeterminate years, but no longer youthful—if indeed he had ever enjoyed that state—with a long, thin face and the sober dress of a clergyman or a banker. Being an appointee of the First Lord of the Treasury, it was probably the latter. Mr. Pitt must have dipped heavily into the public purse to finance the expedition and Mr. Finch was doubtless expected to account for every penny upon his return—and the value derived thereof.

He attached a pair of spectacles to the end of his long, thin nose and began to read from one of the many documents on the table before him: "Four regiments of foot under d'Hervilly, Dudresmay, d'Hector and La Chartre, each comprising between 300 and 340 muskets. Rotalier's artillery regiment comprising 60 guns and 720 men. Some 80 additional officers to command volunteers from the local population. And 50 priests under the Archbishop of Dol."

Sir John noted Nathan's surprise at this latter provision and was moved to explain.

"The local populace having a great respect for their priests, not dissimilar to that of the King's Catholic subjects in Ireland. Despite the efforts of the Republican authorities to persuade them otherwise." His tone remained sardonic. "Doubtless they will perform miracles."

They would have to if such a miserly force were to turn back the tide of Revolution, Nathan thought. Possibly this heresy conveyed itself to Mr. Finch who added: "This being the composition of the *first* division. The second, of approximately equal number, has been assembled in the Channel Isles and is to join us presently. And of course we anticipate considerable reinforcement from the Royalist rebels currently active in the Vendée."

Warren arched a thin brow in Nathan's direction. "I take it you are familiar with the situation in the Vendée, Captain?"

"I have not made it my particular study," Nathan temporised, carefully.

In fact the present company might have been surprised to know just how much the situation in the Vendée interested him, and why.

"I am sure Mr. Finch will supply any deficiency in that respect," the commodore murmured.

Mr. Finch required no further prompting. "I think it is fair to say that the whole of Brittany and much of the country south to the Gironde is united in its opposition to the current regime in Paris," he announced confidently. "Many have risen in open rebellion, led by their nobles and their priests, calling themselves the Catholic and Royalist Army—otherwise known as the Chouans, a term derived from the French word for the hooting of an owl which they employ as a signal to attack, usually by night."

"I think we may assume that Captain Peake needs no tuition in the French language, whatever his appreciation of the strategic situation," Sir John proposed, "or of the local wildlife."

Despite the flippancy of his tone, Nathan wondered if the remark betrayed a greater insight than he would have thought possible in the circumstances. The only man he had told of his interest in the Vendée was Martin Tully and he was confident he could rely upon his discretion. But there had been the letter to his mother . . . Pitt's agents were perfectly capable of intercepting correspondence between private individuals and might, indeed, be expected to do so if it originated in France. Besides, she had been under surveillance for her Republican sympathies since before the war. Could this be why he had been sent to join the expedition, so soon after his return from the West Indies? But for what purpose?

"They are, of course, irregulars," Mr. Finch continued, "but they have enjoyed some success over the National Guard and we hope to increase this by furnishing them with a sufficiency of weapons and equipment. To wit . . ."

"To woo," murmured the commodore as his secretary dipped his nose once more into the papers. He looked to Nathan for appreciation and allowed a small but petulant frown to cross his noble features when he observed none.

Mr. Finch summoned up a thin smile before reading on: "Eighty thousand stand of arms, clothing and shoes, horses and saddlery, food, wine, brandy, and several tons of gunpowder . . ."

"I believe you may spare the captain a more detailed inventory," interrupted the commodore. "However, it is imperative that this equipment is put ashore as quickly as possible and finds its way to the right people, which is where your expertise will come in useful, Captain."

It seemed to Nathan that the expertise of a good army quartermaster would be of more use. Or a pilot with intimate knowledge of the Bay of Quiberon. But he proposed neither of these solutions.

"If you will oblige me by considering the charts." The commodore levered himself from his chair, brushed an imagined speck of powder from his shoulder, and crossed to the table. "Here is our present position." He drew an invisible circle with his finger just off the long crab's claw of Quiberon, projecting some nine or ten miles out into the Bay of Biscay. "And here is the Gulf of Morbihan." He moved his finger to the mainland and indicated a narrow gap in the coastline opening into what appeared to be a large inland sea. Nathan noted a great many islands and almost as many rivers or inlets extending deep into the surrounding countryside.

"Morbihan," repeated Warren, "from the Breton, *Ar Mor Bihan*, meaning 'the Little Sea.'" He traced a winding trail along the northern edge of the Gulf. "And this is the only road to Quiberon from the interior which—as you can see—gives the Morbihan a wide berth until it reaches the River Auray." His finger paused at the longest of the several rivers flowing into the Gulf. "And here it is obliged to employ the use of a bridge." He tapped upon the chart several times for emphasis. "The bridge at Auray. Mark it well, Captain. The only bridge I am assured, for some fifty miles. Now if our information is correct . . ." he rolled a leery eye in the direction of Mr. Finch, "there is a large contingent of Chouans investing the town, doubtless practising their owl hoots upon the Republican garrison therein. If one were to land a quantity of arms within their grasp they may aspire to greater things. If they were to *take* Auray—and hold it for us—then as you will see it will prevent the approach of Republican forces from the interior."

But Nathan's practised eye was taking in other details of the map, most especially the batteries marked at the mouth of the Gulf and the depths within. These were shallow waters, even at high tide, and at low tide they would be mostly mud. But Warren had anticipated these problems and had the solutions to hand.

"I am assured the batteries look more impressive on the chart than they are in reality. The guns are old and have not been fired in anger for many years. You should be able to silence them easily enough with your 18-pounders."

"But I cannot take the *Unicorn* into the Gulf, sir, not with her draught."

"No, sir, and only a fool would suppose it. You will command a fleet of smaller vessels that are being assembled as we speak, with as many seamen and marines as I can spare for the enterprise. And you may, of course, avail yourself of your own marines and crew. That is," he raised a mocking brow, "if you have no objection to the commission."

Nathan ran his eye once more across the chart. A labyrinth of small islands, mud banks and creeks, beset by perverse currents and washed by wayward tides. And no clear idea of what force the enemy could muster against him or of what help to expect from the Chouans, if any.

He inclined his head in a polite bow. "No objection at all, sir. Indeed, I thank you for giving me the honour."

"My pleasure, Captain," replied the commodore, with a smile.

CHAPTER TWO

the Mouth of Morbihan

WELL," DECLARED NATHAN lowering his Dolland glass but keeping his observation for Tully's private ear, "if those guns have not been fired in anger for as long as the commodore believes, it can only be because no one has been fool enough to provoke them."

The entrance to the Gulf of Morbihan was every bit as bad as he had feared from his consideration of the charts: a nightmare of currents and eddies, girt about with rocks and shoals—and barely a thousand yards across. According to Monsieur Calvez, the old fisherman who had been recruited as guide—and official Jonah—to the expedition, the flood ran at between 6 and 8 knots; he did not mention the ebb as it was clearly impossible to enter the Gulf whilst it was running. In fact, you did not *enter* the Gulf of Morbihan at all; you were either sucked in or spat out, depending upon the tide.

But the natural hazards were as nothing compared to those contrived by man, for on each side of this channel were the batteries the commodore had dismissed with such nonchalance. The one on the western flank was at the end of Point Kerpenhir, slightly into the mouth of the Gulf not much above sea level; the eastern on a gentle slope above the fishing village of Port-Navalo. The guns might well be as old as Warren said they were but they appeared to be in excellent condition: a dozen 12-pounders to each battery, protected by a stone palisade and angled so as to sweep the mouth of Morbihan in a murderous crossfire. From the amount of smoke in the air, Nathan judged that the gunners possessed braziers in which to heat the shot, which would make life even more interesting for any vessel that tried to run the gauntlet.

A sudden flash, closely followed by the report rolling out across the water: a ranging shot from the battery on Point Kerpenhir. Nathan marked the splash, some three or four hundred yards off their larboard bow, the shot skipping over the flattish waves towards them before sinking well short. He felt confident that he could stand off and pound either position with impunity, though he doubted he would achieve much by the manoeuvre for the batteries were hunkered down behind steeply sloping banks of earth, each topped by a stone parapet. He might have shelled them into submission had he possessed that option—a bomb ketch would have changed the situation greatly in his favour—but the commodore had not thought to provide him with such an object. The fleet he *had* provided stood well out into the bay: a motley collection of gunboats and barges and the gun brig *Conquest,* which unlike the *Unicorn* could operate in the shallow waters of the Gulf. If she survived the hazards of entering them.

"Major Howard. Good morning to you, sir. Perhaps you would care to take a look at our objective."

This to the officer of marines who had just appeared upon the quarterdeck, yawning and stretching and looking about him as if dawn was a new experience to him, which it possibly was.

Major the Honourable William Howard commanded a force of just over two hundred marines, presently distributed about the smaller boats of the squadron. He had not previously been to sea, he had confided to Nathan shortly after coming aboard, and had been frightfully sick upon the voyage from England. The calmer waters of the Bay of Quiberon suited him better and he was able to put his eye to the glass with equanimity, bracing himself against the rail.

Nathan waited patiently while the major exposed the two batteries to a lengthy study and then transferred his attention to the slope beyond Port-Navalo on the eastern flank. Nathan had also given this some scrutiny. It was open heath for the most part with no cover save for a small patch of brushwood and a few ancient dolmens—the peculiar stone monuments that littered the region, about the size of a man. A small cove lay about half a mile further along the coast to the east, with a sandy beach which would make a perfect landing place—well out of sight of the guns—but Nathan doubted if much could be accomplished with a couple of hundred men. And nor did Howard judging from the thoughtful expression on his face when he handed back the glass.

"Anything spring to mind?" Nathan enquired, more in jest than hope.

"A hornet's nest, is what springs to mind, sir. Best avoided."

"Best avoided," Nathan nodded. "Thank you, Major, I shall put that in my report."

"Well, I suppose under cover of darkness and with some kind of a diversion . . ."

"What do you think?" asked Nathan of his first lieutenant in the privacy of his cabin while the *Unicorn* and her little squadron cruised off the Morbihan, waiting for dark.

Tully studied the chart as if it might tell them something they did not already know.

"Well, if the marines can take the fort on the eastern approach under cover of darkness, and we bring the fleet in close to the eastern shore—and the guns on the western approach cannot sight us against the land—then it might be possible." His tone was not encouraging. "But to sail so close to the shore in the darkness and then into Morbihan itself when the tide is low . . ." He shook his head. "Is there no other way?"

"None that I can think of." Nathan flopped down in his chair. "To hell with it. I shall go back and tell him it can't be done."

Tully's silence was eloquent.

"You think I would not do it?" Nathan demanded, considerably vexed. "The whole strategy is flawed, Martin. We are landing in the wrong part of France with soldiers I would not trust to tie their own bootstraps, and in the hope of support from men who are fighting their own war fifty miles from here and who are, according to the information *I* have received, already beaten."

"You mean the Chouans?"

"That is exactly who I mean."

"Why are they called that?"

"Ah, that is another thing. Mr. Finch would have us believe it derives from their practice of hooting like an owl as their signal for an attack. He is wrong. It comes from their leader in the early days of the rebellion, Jean Cottereau, who was known as Jean Chouan, after the local name for a screech owl, because he would often mimic its cry as it swoops upon its prey."

"Why?" enquired Tully with a frown.

"Why?" Nathan gave it some thought. "Well, perhaps it amused him. I, as a child, used to make the sound of a cockerel when I was particularly pleased with myself."

Tully regarded him with interest. "Really?"

"Usually when I had put one over those who considered themselves in authority over me. I was much inclined to rebellion in my youth."

"But you have stopped now? Making the sound of a cockerel that is."

"Yes. I sometimes feel the inclination but I suppress it, in the interests of discipline." Tully conceded the wisdom of this decision. "And of course, I am not so often pleased with myself." They brooded upon this in silence for a moment.

"Quite possibly he used it as a rallying cry," Nathan reflected. "But I cannot believe it was in general use as a signal for a night attack—for once the story became widely known it would serve to warn the defenders, would it not, that they were about to come under attack."

"This is true." Tully acknowledged. "But perhaps that is why they were defeated."

Nathan frowned. "My point is that Mr. Finch—like other political advisers of our acquaintance—does not know his arse from his elbow. Unless he deliberately seeks to misinform us as to the true situation."

"Why should he wish to do that?"

Nathan shrugged. "Possibly because he is long accustomed to telling his masters what it is they wish to hear, not what they should rightly know."

"And what is the true situation—as you have heard it described? Can we expect any support from the Chouans, or none at all?"

"Well, they are still active in the Vendée," Nathan allowed. "But in small groups, I am told, fighting in the forests, like Robin Hood and his Merry Men. The days when they could put a large army into the field are long gone. Jean Chouan was killed at Nantes in '92 and since then they have suffered a series of defeats. The government has sent death squads from village to village burning, raping, killing. The whole land has been laid waste from the Loire to the Charente."

Tully gave him an odd look. "You appear to have made this your particular study," he remarked lightly, but in a way that invited further confidence.

"I knew someone in Paris who fled to join them," Nathan admitted cautiously.

He had never told Tully about Sara. It was too painful, too secret. Even now, a year later, there were some things he could barely bring himself to contemplate.

He had met her on his first visit to Paris, on a confidential mission for William Pitt. Sara de la Tour d'Auvergne, Countess of Turenne. Not that she called herself that, for it was the time of the Terror when even a minor title secured its holder the privilege of death by guillotine, and Sara had married into one of the noblest families in France. Her husband, a much older man, had died in exile with the French Royalists in Koblenz, and Sara lived quietly in Paris, with her young son, Alex. She used her own family name of Seton, which was sufficiently obscure to evade the attentions of the authorities or the local informers, though her father had been a noble of the sword, a Scottish soldier in the service of the King of France.

Sara. Nathan lapsed into an unhappy silence, lost in his memories, while Tully stood uneasily beside him. She was the only woman he had ever truly loved. He would have married her if he could. He had wanted to take her back with him to England. Even at the last, when they were both in prison, he had plotted and contrived to that end. Until her own brutal ending on the guillotine.

So he had taken her young son and gone to England without her.

In time the pain had lost its edge, replaced by a melancholy sadness that he knew he would carry with him to the grave. But then he had received the letter, telling him that Sara was still alive and had fled to the Vendée to seek refuge among the Chouans.

Nathan did not know if he could believe it—and there had been no way of checking. Until now.

"And this friend of yours, is she with them still?" enquired Tully, who could be disturbingly perceptive at times, for Nathan had noted his use of gender.

"I have no way of knowing," he confessed. "The situation there has been worse than in Paris at the time of the Terror. Whole communities have been massacred, shot in the churches while at prayer. Sometimes, to save on ammunition they drive the people on to barges, shoot holes in the bottom and push them out into a river to sink. Or bind them in couples, a man and a woman, and throw them from a bridge—and call it a Republican wedding."

He caught Tully's eye and detected a hint of disbelief.

"Well, that is what I heard," he added defensively. Then, after a moment: "It may well be a biased view for my chief informant was a friend of my mother's." Tully nodded understandingly. Many of Nathan's more surprising political insights were derived from friends of his mother, who kept a famous salon in London, though now in reduced circumstances. "He was a member of the Girondin party, forced to flee France during the Terror, and one would not expect him to speak favourably of those who have, in his opinion, betrayed the Revolution. However, we both know that when the Jacobins were in power there were terrible atrocities committed against those who did not share their own narrow view of progress. Unhappily, their excesses appear to have caused a general revulsion against any progressive movement, anywhere in the world."

Tully offered no opinion on the matter. Politics, religion, and to some extent sex, were not proper subjects for discussion in the King's Service, even in the dubious privacy of the captain's cabin where the marine sentry at the door or an idle midshipman leaning over the stern rail might easily pick up a whisper of dissent. Contrary to the view propagated by the government and their hacks in the journals, not all officers in the King's Service were entirely devoted to the King's interest, or that of his Tory ministers. Many were Whigs, vaguely aligned to principles of liberty, reform and freedom of expression. A lesser number even believed in them. And although Nathan had not discussed it, other than in a passing aside, he suspected his friend and fellow officer shared opinions that would be considered dangerously radical by their superiors, had they known of them.

This was partly attributable to temperament; partly to their unorthodox backgrounds. Though Tully had been raised as a gentleman in his grandfather's house on Guernsey, he retained many of the degenerate instincts of his fisherman father who, like every second man on Guernsey, supplemented his meagre income from fishing by running sought-after goods from France to England without troubling to cut the government in for a share of the profit. At the first opportunity Tully had run away to sea and allied himself to these free traders, as they called themselves, though the government, less tolerantly, called them smugglers and hanged them whenever they could, or packed them off to Botany Bay—or, in extreme circumstances, obliged them to join the Navy. This latter fate had befallen Tully and though he had profited by the move, he still favoured the independent spirit and opinions of the free traders, a notoriously dissident profession.

Nathan was infected by an even more deplorable heritage. His father was a good English Tory but his mother's family were French Huguenots—Calvinist dissenters—whose independent views had led to their persecution and exile to New York where, in the course of time, they had joined the rebellion against King George. While, as an Englishman, Nathan regretted the loss of the American colonies, he could not bring himself to deplore the birth of the United States and the values enshrined in their Constitution. Nor, indeed, was he opposed to the ideas advanced by the Revolution in France.

All of this combined to make him wonder, at times, quite what he was fighting for. Promotion and plunder were considerations, of course, and the prospect of Glory. As a schoolboy Nathan had been much exposed to the exploits of Francis Drake and Walter Raleigh, of Admirals Blake and Anson and Hawke. He craved the victor's laurels as much as any true Englishman, even one of his own dubious inheritance. His present difficulty was in reconciling his concept of Glory with his government's determination to restore the Bourbons to the throne of France with all the flies and hornets that buzzed around their honeyed court. There were worthier causes to fight and die for.

Then of a sudden, and in this most pessimistic of moods, it came to him.

"Why, that is it!" he exclaimed. "Major Howard has given us the answer."

Tully gazed at him without comprehension.

"'A hornet's nest,'" he said, "'best avoided.' But in Sussex, when I was a boy, they had a way of dealing with hornets."

"I believe the major may be obliged to get his feet wet," remarked Tully as he watched the first of the ship's boats ground on the shingle of the small cove.

"Well, let us hope he knows how to light a fire," Nathan replied a little tensely. He had watched the officer climb into the ship's launch and then, before the astonished gaze of the crew, spread a linen kerchief upon the sternsheets where he was obliged to sit. Nathan hoped this was mere affectation and not an indication of his fighting spirit. He consoled himself with the thought that he was accompanied by Lieutenant Whiteley, who commanded the thirty-four marines aboard the *Unicorn*.

"Look there!" exclaimed Tully, pointing toward the distant headland where a small troop of horsemen had appeared. Nathan inspected them through the glass. There were six of them, not enough to contest the landing, though there might be more hidden from sight beyond the ridge. But they looked more like artillery officers than cavalry and it seemed their purpose was strictly observational, for as soon as the marines began to advance across the beach they turned and cantered back in the direction of the fort. They could have seen little to concern them for it was designed to withstand an assault from either land or sea. It was in the shape of a diamond perched on the edge of the headland: the larger cannon ranged along the two walls facing the channel, but the walls on the landward side equipped with swivel guns and mortars and with loopholes for muskets. The garrison was probably small but a hundred men could have held it against ten times that number as long as they had sufficient supplies and munitions.

Nathan lowered the telescope and addressed the sailing master whose glum expression reflected his disapproval of the entire enterprise. "Very well, Mr. Graham."

There was a rush of men to the braces as Graham set sail on a course that would carry them parallel to the coast at a distance of a little over a mile, with the rest of the flotilla following at regular intervals, or as regular as their poor sailing qualities would allow.

Nathan joined the pilot, Monsieur Calvez, at the rail and addressed him in his native tongue. Or French, rather, for the man was a Breton, born and bred: "Well, sir, it is to be hoped your eddies do not fail us."

The pilot rewarded this observation with a shrug, but he stood high in Nathan's estimation at present, having assured the war council hastily convened aboard the *Unicorn* that, although the tide could reach up to eight knots in the mouth of the Gulf, the very speed of the flow created powerful back-eddies—*tourbillons*—at either side so that, in effect, it flowed the opposite way at each of the points. This was vital information, if only it could be relied upon.

They would soon know. They were nearing the eastern point near the village of Port-Navalo. Now they could see the guns of the fort, a hint of dragon's breath coiling from the black muzzles.

"Keep your distance, Mr. Graham," Nathan instructed him tersely, for the ship's head was drifting noticeably toward the shore.

"Aye, aye, sir."

Nathan wished he had more confidence in his own sailing master, but he always had to keep his eye upon him. He knew it made the man nervous, but there it was. The slightest error of judgement, the slightest delay in carrying out his orders, and they were lost.

There was a sudden eruption from the battery and the first shot came skipping over the waves towards them before sinking off their starboard bow.

Nathan caught Tully's eye. "We may see your fire engine in action before the day is out," he remarked, lightly, knowing he did not fool Tully for an instant.

Tully was an admirer of all things mechanical and the fire engine had become his personal concern. It was standing by in the waist, just abaft the mainmast: a wonder of gleaming brass and canvas hose, ready to pump a stream of water over rigging and decks. But the wonder of the world would not save a ship composed almost wholly of timber, hemp and canvas once a fire took hold. Nathan saw the bows shift a trifle to windward, felt the movement through his feet and raised his voice to reach Lieutenant Holroyd on the gundeck.

"Stand by, Mr. Holroyd."

"Aye, aye, sir."

Holroyd had bound a bandana tight about his ears—or rather the one ear he had left and the hole that was the other, the missing organ having been detached by a cutlass on their first commission. He had persuaded the ship's doctor, McLeish, to sew it back on again but the graft had become infected and the ear had been cut off a second time, with surgical precision. Normally he let his hair hang unbound to cover the mutilation, but the bandana gave him a bold, buccaneering air, even without an earring. He had come on greatly since Nathan had first met him at the Havana nine months ago: a spotty-faced snotty, not yet twenty. But he had fought in three battles since and the spots had quite vanished from his complexion, though the loss of the ear was to be regretted.

Nearer still. And now Nathan could see the smoke—not from the battery now, but from beyond, rolling across the headland from the burning brushwood that Howard's marines had set alight: thick black smoke, as dense as the morning fog.

That is what you did with a hornet's nest: you smoked them out.

"Very well, Mr. Holroyd, fire as you bear."

"Fire as you bear!"

The broadside rippled along the deck and Nathan leaped up into the shrouds to watch the fall of shot: most of it kicking up dirt from the escarpment but at least two striking the stone ramparts above—ramparts that suddenly blossomed in orange flame as the battery replied. The sea erupted in a series of waterspouts, the nearest so close, Nathan felt the spray on his cheek. One ball skipped clear across the waist, another announced its arrival by knocking loudly upon the hull. They were out in mid-channel now and Nathan could feel the full force of the flood, pushing them into the Gulf beyond with its shallows and its shoals—and the waiting guns on the opposite point.

He turned to watch the *Conquest* as she bore away, following the curve of the coast and leading the smaller craft in a long line behind her, like a flock of nervous ducklings, close under the guns of the battery. Guns he could no longer see for thick black smoke.

They were still firing blindly through it but Nathan could see no obvious damage to his little fleet of gunboats and barges that were even now scuttling through the gap. Judging from the waterspouts flung up by the falling shot, the French gunners were aiming far too high. He thought he could hear the sharper crack of musket fire, too, which could indicate the marines were in action on the farther side of the fort—but he had warned Howard not to persist with his attack if he met with any serious resistance.

It was time to look to his own affairs. They were on a course now that would take them within range of the guns on the opposite point. He saw Graham shoot him a look, impatient for the order to bear away, but it was far too soon, for they must draw their fire from the craft on the far side of the channel. He saw the multiple flash of fire from the distant muzzles and a series of waterspouts erupted just off their starboard bow. Seconds later the *Unicorn* replied and Nathan marked the fall of shot against the embankment. Far too low. Holroyd roared out instructions, running from cannon to cannon, the gun crews heaving on crowbars and slamming in quoins to bring the muzzles up as high as they would bear.

But they were fairly rushing down upon the battery now and the French gunners had their own problems, for their next salvo was aimed far too high. Nathan could see them through the embrasures, frantically swabbing and worming the smoking barrels. He might have as much as two minutes now, before they fired again, for they were no great shakes as gunners. Thus he comforted himself as they drew ever closer to the point and the promised *tourbillons*. Monsieur Calvez was looking thoughtful. Nathan hoped to God he knew what he was talking about. Closer still. He could see faces peering down at them through the embrasures and the black muzzles of the guns as they were trundled back in place.

And then he felt it. The sudden tremor as the bows bit into the counter current.

"Hard a larboard, Mr. Graham!" Nathan roared, loud enough for the helmsmen to start spinning the wheel long before the master's order.

"She does not answer!" Graham wailed, watching the helmsmen in anguish. For a moment their fate hung in the balance and then the bows came round to face the open sea and Nathan felt the full force of the *tourbillons* pushing them round against the tide and he grinned at the pilot who rewarded him with another careless shrug and a lugubrious pout of the lower lip as if to say, what did you expect?

And now a string of orders as the *Unicorn* worked her way to windward, clawing away from that terrible shore. A flash and a bang from the fort. Fired too low now, for the shot fell just short of their stern as they clawed away. And another, with the same result. The French were firing singly now, perhaps to mark the fall of shot. The next smashed into the stern rail, showering the quarterdeck with deadly splinters. Men were down, some screaming, some silent. Kendrick, one of the new midshipmen who had joined them at Portsmouth, a boy of thirteen, had a great shard of wood sticking out of his arm. He was clutching it with the other, white-faced, biting his lip and he looked at Nathan, as if for reassurance. It took all Nathan's will not to run to him. "Get him below," he snapped to his steward Gabriel, who was in his usual position at his side, and he turned abruptly away, looking aloft as the weather leeches began to flutter and lift. They were close-hauled now, jammed as close to the wind as she would lie. If they were taken aback now, so close to shore . . .

"Mr. Graham!" The master appeared hypnotised, gazing aloft. "Ease off a point, sir, ease her off."

A shot struck the muzzle of the 18-pounder nearest the quarterdeck and shattered, dismounting the gun and spraying hot metal over the crew. One man was on fire. A trail of powder ignited and flared across the deck. Tully left the helm and ran forward. His fire engine sprayed water in a great arc across the waist.

But the sails were filled and drawing well. Too well, for they were drawing away from the shore and losing the back current; they must not stray too far from the shore. Why in God's name could the master not see that?

"A point more, Mr. Graham, if you will," Nathan commanded,

struggling to keep his voice calm, for the sails were feathering and they were losing way as they felt the pull of the tide once more. No response. Nathan whirled upon him but before he could damn his eyes, or give the order himself, a direct hit shattered the helm, killing or maiming both helmsmen and sending Graham flying to the deck. Worse, the foretopmast began to sway forward until with a terrible deliberation it came crashing down across the bows, bringing the foresails with it in an impossible tangle of canvas and rigging and spars—and at once the head dropped off from the wind and the frigate was swept back into the mouth of Morbihan.

Nathan met Tully's appalled gaze and knew with an awful certainty that they were lost, but he began to shout orders in a desperate bid to stave off disaster. One party was sent below to man the tiller ropes, and Holroyd and his people were fighting to clear the tangle of wreckage up forward, but the frigate was now firmly in the grip of the tide and it was moving them remorselessly back down the channel into the Morbihan and the guns on Point Kerpenhir. Every shot was hitting home now and several fires had started on the gundeck. It seemed a question only of whether they would be burned or battered to death. Bodies sprawled among a shambles of rigging and dismounted guns, the wounded crying out piteously but there were hardly any men spare to carry them below. Those men who were not hacking at the rigging or working the guns were fighting fires. Then, with shocking suddenness, they struck. Struck with such force that not a man was left on his feet, and with a groan like a tree crashing in the forest, the foretop came down to join the chaos on the deck below.

CHAPTER THREE

Fire and Shot

NATHAN STAGGERED TO HIS FEET, dazed and bloodied from his violent contact with the deck, and gazed wildly about him but even in the extremity of his anguish and pain, he knew they had struck sand and not rock, that the bottom had not been torn from the hull and that with the tide still rising there was a reasonable chance of floating free. But not at once. Not at once, and every minute they waited they would take another pounding from the guns on Point Kerpenhir—and at such close range they could hardly miss. The *Unicorn* was being battered to death before his eyes. He had no option but to strike.

He looked to the stern where the white ensign flapped lazily in the warm summer breeze and called for Mr. Lamb. He appeared to be scrambling around behind the starboard carronade. Why? Was he trying to hide? No, he had simply lost his hat. He crammed it on his head and came running aft.

"Sir?"

But no. He could not ask a boy to haul down their colours, nor any of the crew. This was something he had to do himself. He moved over to the halyard but paused a moment, searching for some reason to put off the inevitable. He looked back over the stern towards the flotilla, now safe inside the waters of the Gulf, but what comfort was that when he had lost the *Unicorn?* He raised his eyes toward the fort above Port-Navalo. It was no longer wreathed in smoke. Then, to his astonishment, he saw the tricolour coming down from the flagstaff. And after a moment, when time seemed to stand still for him, the Union flag was run up in its place. Howard's marines had taken the fort! And now Nathan could see them, in their red coats, standing up on the ramparts waving their black shakoes, oblivious for the moment to the fate that had befallen the *Unicorn.* But their success gave him heart—and pointed to the one hope he had of saving his ship. If Howard could take one fort with a parcel of marines, Nathan could surely take the other with his battle-hardened veterans of the *Unicorn.*

He sought out Tully amid the confusion on the quarterdeck. He seemed dazed, a thin stream of blood running down the side of his face. Nathan gripped him by the arm and stared hard into his eyes. "Martin, are you hurt?"

Tully shook his head but his gaze was strangely vacant.

"We must try to take the fort," Nathan insisted. "I am going to take as many men as I can in the ship's boats. Martin? Do you hear me?"

"Yes, sir. The ship's boats . . ." Tully looked uncertainly to their stern. The four boats had been lowered before the *Unicorn* went into action and the tide had dragged them far out to starboard but at least they had escaped the mayhem on the frigate's decks.

"If I succeed you will be able to float her off on the rising tide but if I fail . . . Martin, if I fail, you must strike, do you understand me?"

"Aye, aye, sir." Tully half turned to go but then checked himself and turned back. "Good luck," he said, with a shaky grin. Nathan wondered if he meant "Goodbye."

Another salvo from the fort, most of the rounds smashing into the hull so that Nathan swore he felt the vessel shudder at the blows she was taking and there were fires breaking out all over the deck, most of the gun crews running about with buckets of water while the guns stood abandoned, unable to bear. Fire and shot were destroying the only ship he had ever come to love, for all the troubles she had brought him.

"Gabriel! Gilbert Gabriel there!" Nathan turned to look for his servant, but he was there already, at his shoulder. The Angel Gabriel he was called by the hands, in irony, for his character was by no means virtuous. He had been a highwayman—and destined for the rope—before Nathan's father had snatched him from the jailhouse and borne him off to sea.

"Bring my pistols from the cabin," Nathan instructed him. Then, after a moment's pause, to his retreating back: "And the letter from my desk."

Gabriel would know what letter he meant, though he checked a moment in his stride and Nathan knew what he must be thinking. That Nathan meant to have it with him when he died, his last word of Sara.

Holroyd and Lamb were leading their divisions aft, pitifully thinned now and barely a hundred strong. Nathan ran his eye over them, seeing men he knew and liked, and whose lives were now forfeit to his blundering conceit, and not for the first time. Jacob Young, his coxswain, a young man of almost the same age as he but with a cheerful vitality that often made Nathan feel as old as his father; Dermot Quinn, the only survivor of the mutineers, pardoned by Nathan in flagrant abuse of his powers and now rated Volunteer, First Class; George Banjo, the leader of the African slaves Nathan had freed in the Americas . . . He had been called Jorge then—at least by his owner—but the hands had anglicised this to George. How the name Banjo had been added was still a mystery to Nathan. He had enquired once and been told it was his Yoruba name, but this seemed unlikely, unless it was an approximation. Michael Connor, the biggest man in the crew, who had been in shackles when Nathan had first encountered him on the orlop deck of the *Unicorn,* though it seemed the only offence he could reasonably be charged with was pissing upon the deck, whilst drunk. He still had a fondness for liquor, though he appeared to have been cured of his more noxious habit.

Most of these men had followed Nathan into battle before in the Caribbean and it had been bad then but never as bad as this and doubtless they knew it as well as he but he told them what he required of them as if it was a perfectly reasonable option. He thought of adding something more appropriate to the occasion, some stirring words on Death or Glory, but they did not need that, and nor did he.

Gabriel was back with his pistols, the pair Nathan had taken from the armoury in the Palace of the Tuileries just over a year ago—on the day the tribunes of the people had finally found the courage to rise up against Robespierre and put an end to the Terror. The same day he learned that Sara had been sent to her death on the guillotine.

He took the letter and folded it into an inside pocket. Then he made his way to the larboard rail where his barge was waiting, filled already with above a score of men, and nodded to his coxswain to cast off.

The tide now worked in their favour for the *Unicorn* had grounded some three or four hundred yards seaward of the battery and the four boats swept rapidly down upon it. The guns ceased their remorseless pounding of the frigate and sought out these new, more elusive targets, but they were moving so fast and so close to shore the gunners were having problems finding the range. Even so, they tried, and the water erupted in their wake and all but swamped the jolly boat as it came clear of the stricken frigate. Nathan's barge drew swiftly level with the battery, but they were still some way off the shore and it was a desperate struggle now, for the tide threatened to carry them beyond the point and on into the Gulf. Somehow they gained the shallows under the redoubt but here was another problem: a frenzy of white water breaking over half-submerged rocks and more of Jonah's *tourbillons* that threatened to drive them back into midstream and the fire of the guns. There were more than twenty men crammed into Nathan's barge and the water was breaking over the gunwales, but with over a dozen pulling on the oars and the rest bailing furiously, they finally ground on the shingle.

Nathan left the crew to drag the boat ashore and stumbled across the narrow strand to the cover of the rocks where he could take stock of their situation. It did not improve with proximity. The fort appeared to be built to the exact design and dimensions of its neighbour on the opposite point. A gentle slope of sandy soil and sea grass rose to the foot of the battery and though the cannon could not be depressed low enough to sweep this rise there was not a scrap of cover to shield an attacker from the inevitable musket fire. Then there was a ditch, doubtless filled with the steel spikes the French called *fleur de lys* and other pleasantries to impede their progress, and then a steep earthen embankment, topped by the stone ramparts. The guns had ceased firing for some reason—though it could only be that the gunners had taken up their muskets to await this new attack. Which was clearly suicidal. Under cover of smoke, or darkness, they might achieve something, but there was no prospect of the former and though the sun was now quite low in the sky it would stay light for two hours or more. And if Nathan delayed more than a few minutes the guns would inevitably resume their pounding of the *Unicorn*.

He looked back at her: a sorry sight with her stumps of foremast and mainmast and the wreckage of canvas and rigging draped over her bows—and the wounds she had taken from the heated shot all along her hull. He could see some of the hands hacking away with axes to clear the debris from her forecastle and even as he watched a mass of it fell into the sea and was swept away by the current. Moments later there was a flash of flame from the 6-pounder in the starboard bow and the shot whistled high above their heads to smash into the stone ramparts above: a splendid act of defiance that cheered him a little even though he knew it could achieve nothing; not even to provide them with decent covering fire.

He glanced along the ragged line of men crouched among the rocks with pistols and cutlasses, axes, even belaying pins, fired up, eager to go. How many of them would make it to the redoubt? Perhaps half if they were lucky, and the defenders less practised with their muskets than they were with their cannon. It was said that musket fire was so inaccurate it took the weight of a man in lead balls to kill him. Nathan had not believed this when he first heard it, in a Sussex tavern; and he certainly did not believe it now. He touched the letter in his pocket—for luck, or for the last time—drew his sword, and stepped out from behind the rock.

He was not immediately cut down in a hail of fire. In fact there was not a single shot aimed at him so far as he could tell, though he could hear the sharp crack of musketry from above. As he scrambled over the rocks and started up the slope, he could see the cannon in the embrasures, smoke drifting out from the muzzles, but no sign of movement. A glance to left and right: Gilbert Gabriel at his side, Michael Connor and George Banjo a step or two behind, with Young and the boat crew close on their heels; Holroyd and Lamb with their two divisions in a long straggling line on each flank. It was hard going up the slope for there was very little purchase in the soft ground and he was breathing heavily, a roaring in his ears. But no roaring from the men. They advanced in an almost eerie silence, so unlike their usual tigerish charge across a deck, as if they feared to rouse the defenders from their inexplicable slumber.

They were three-quarters there and still the gunners did not fire. For a moment Nathan wondered if their attention was so fixed upon the *Unicorn* they had not perceived the danger advancing from below. But if this was so why were they not firing upon the ship? No, it had to be from a perverted sense of amusement: waiting until their attackers were almost upon them before obliterating them with one devastating volley.

Yet still he could not see their muskets.

They reached the ditch. Nathan paused, every nerve tensed for an eruption of flame and smoke all along the ramparts and the terrible impact of a musket ball at close quarters. But still the French held their fire. Dimly he heard the sound of shots, even shouts and the clash of steel, but wherever they were coming from it was not from the battery.

The ditch was too wide to jump. But it contained no mantraps, no steel spikes, nothing more alarming than mud and nettles. Down they went in an untidy wave and up the other side, breathing heavily, even growling a little now, like a great predator closing in on its kill. But still no roar. Now the embankment, steeper, much steeper than the slope leading to it, so they were forced to scramble on all fours, pistols in their belts, knives, even cutlasses clenched between their teeth.

Nathan felt a sudden fierce exultation, fed by the impossible belief that they had taken the defenders by surprise. Smoke still drifted from the mouths of the cannon that had played such havoc with his ship and he wondered if the gunners possessed no other means of defence and were waiting for the moment the attackers appeared in the embrasures before they blew them apart with 12-pound heated shot. But for all the damage they had inflicted on the poor *Unicorn*, they could only destroy a dozen or so at such close range—one of whom would be him, of course, for he was a pace ahead of Connor and the Angel Gabriel. And now came the roar as the wave broke upon the parapet and they were clambering through the gaps, climbing over the cannon, cracking shins, burning hands and legs on the searing hot metal.

And the roar dying in their throats as they saw what awaited them on the other side.

The interior of the redoubt was filled with a struggling mass of men, fighting hand to hand with swords, pikes, axes and muskets, even a few pitchforks: fighting with a deadly, furious intensity over the bloody corpses of the fallen, and not a one of them aware of the attackers pouring through the gaps in the walls. Nathan paused on the gun platform, staring in wonder at this bizarre spectacle. Had the defenders fallen out among themselves? But what could possibly have provoked such a fratricidal bloodbath? There was little to distinguish the combatants: most were fighting in their shirt-sleeves, some stripped to the waist, though there were a few blue uniforms here and there, similar to those worn by the French National Guard—the citizen soldiers of the Republic—so it might reasonably be supposed that whoever was fighting them must be his allies. Yet he was loath to pitch his own men into such an affray when they might so easily be attacked by both parties, simply on the grounds that they were unknown to either, as happened in many a waterfront brawl. He glanced down the line of ordnance: all in good order with powder and shot beside each gun, braziers glowing in the fading light; rammers and swabs and all the other tools of the gunner's trade lying abandoned in their midst.

He sought out his two subordinates, Holroyd and Lamb, and instructed them to select a sufficient number of the hands and turn two of the cannon upon the warring parties.

"And load with canister," he added, for he could see this commodity stacked up in quantity next to the powder kegs and the neat piles of round shot.

While a score or so of the hands devoted themselves to this enterprise, Nathan gave his attention once more to the battle. The Blues, heavily outnumbered, were fighting in small groups, back to back, though still giving a good account of themselves and clearly determined to fight to the death. And judging from the number of corpses strewn across the further ramparts, this had been the fate of a good many of their number. Nathan deduced that the attackers had stormed the fort by that particular route and that the gunners had ceased pounding the *Unicorn* to take up their swords and muskets to confront this new threat at their rear. Their best course now, it appeared to him, was surrender but they were obviously made of sterner stuff than he for even as he watched, one of their number began to call out: "*A moi, mes enfants . . .*" and the other groups began to fight their way through to him to make a kind of phalanx in the centre.

Nathan looked to his own *enfants* and saw that Banjo had taken Connor's place at his back in some unspoken, or at least unofficial role as bodyguard.

"George," he addressed him self-consciously, for though he did not normally call the hands by their first names, he could not bring himself to utter the name Banjo in civilised converse with a fellow human being, "do you see the flag there?"

Banjo saw the flag there. The Republican tricolour flapping limply from the flagstaff halfway along the battery.

"Would you be so good as to haul it down for me?"

Nathan had neglected to bring a Union flag to haul in its place. It would have required a greater degree of composure—and optimism—than he possessed. But it would serve to inform Tully and anyone else who might be watching that the fort had fallen.

The two cannon had been redeployed as Nathan suggested, but here was Michael Connor knuckling his forehead with an apologetic crouch that brought him to near human dimensions.

"Mr. Holroyd's compliments, sir, but he begs to report that the guns is already loaded, sir, with round shot, and wishes to know if your honour is still desirous of loading them with grape?"

Nathan shook his head. "It is no matter," he said. "Round shot will do."

He drew one of his pistols from his belt, cocked it and fired into the air. The battle continued unabated. He summoned Connor again.

"My compliments to Mr. Holroyd, and would he be so good as to fire a round—above their heads."

The roar of the cannon succeeded where the pistol had failed. The warring parties stopped fighting and stared in their direction, but instead of waiting respectfully for Nathan to address them, as he had vaguely surmised, the men of the Blue party, apparently acting upon instruction from their officer, broke away and rushed en masse towards this new adversary. Nathan wished now that he had insisted upon loading the cannon with grape, but he had near a hundred armed men at his disposal and though he scarce had time to make a proper tally, his attackers could not have exceeded a score. He raised the still loaded pistol with the intention of discharging it at the officer and unleashing a more general slaughter, when to his further confusion, the men stopped just a few yards in front of him and turned to face their former opponents; all save the officer who approached Nathan and asked him, somewhat breathlessly but in a calm enough voice, if he spoke French.

"I do," Nathan assured him, lowering his pistol, but frowning a little as he wondered what was coming next and whether it would inconvenience him at all.

"Then permit me to present myself . . ." the fellow made a small bow. "I am Captain Le Goff, of the Republican Guard, and to prevent further bloodshed I am obliged to offer you my sword."

Which object he presented to Nathan, hilt first.

Nathan regarded it with concern, for it was dripping with blood from the captain's recent exertions and he was not aware of the proper form on such an occasion. Men had surrendered to him before, but they had never offered him their swords and he was somewhat touched, though aware that there could be complications.

They were not long in making themselves known to him.

"We are your prisoners, sir," the captain insisted, "and I would be obliged if you would inform these animals of that fact before they make you an accomplice in their atrocities."

Indeed the animals appeared to be gathering themselves for a rush. They certainly looked capable of atrocities, Nathan thought, if indulged.

"Who are they?" he enquired of his apparent prisoner.

"These ones?" The officer made a contemptuous gesture of his chin in their general direction. "They are the ones that call themselves the Chouans." He smiled a crooked smile and added, with a sneer: "Your allies."

Nathan regarded them with new interest. The Screech Owls. They had a look of a peasant army, he supposed, taken as a whole.

"Very well." Nathan took the proffered sword and gave it to the Angel Gabriel. "Instruct your men to lay down their arms."

The captain frowned. He was a man of middling years with a grizzled jaw and a long drooping moustache, greying a little at the edges. Le Goff—the blacksmith. And possibly that is what he was, in his civilian capacity, though it was more likely, if he was an artilleryman, that he was a professional soldier, a veteran. Certainly he spoke like one. "I beg you to first make yourself known to these pigs," he implored Nathan, "and inform them we are your prisoners and under your protection, or I fear there will be a massacre."

In this supposition he was undoubtedly correct, for the pigs had taken the opportunity to reload their weapons and were clearly preparing to resume hostilities. Nathan viewed them with a stern eye and asked who was their commander.

One of the herd, more elegantly groomed than his associates, stepped forward and executed a bow that might have been reassuring, had it not been so clearly mocking. He was a small man, almost childlike in stature, though there was nothing childish about his face, its wolfish features flecked with blood, and he carried a sword that had seen some service.

"I have that privilege," he announced. "And who have I the honour of addressing?"

Nathan told him, and the fellow had the courtesy to remove his hat. "Then permit me to present myself. I am the Chevalier de Batz, in the service of His Most Christian Majesty King Louis of France, and these sons of whores are my prisoners."

Nathan took in the long lean jaw and the wide mouth—and the mad, cruel savagery in the eyes. He acknowledged the man's title with a polite inclination of the head, but not his claim.

"I am desolated to have to disagree with you, sir," he replied, "for I have just accepted their surrender and they are under my protection."

The whole situation was taking on the nature of farce, and though it was preferable to the outcome Nathan had anticipated earlier, he felt it necessary to assert his authority. Unhappily, so did the chevalier and his manner of doing so was rather more to the point, and considerably less polite. With a sigh of one exposed to intolerable boredom he removed his sword from the right to the left hand, extended the empty palm to one of his obedient vassals, who stepped forward to place a pistol into it, and before Nathan had grasped the significance of this gesture, much less made any move to counter it, he coolly aimed it at Captain Le Goff and shot him through the head.

Nathan was shocked into immobility, his brain unable to

comprehend the enormity of the deed, even while it registered the spatter of blood and other gruesome material on his cheek. God knows, he had seen enough of violent death in his time but this was beyond anything he had witnessed on the deck of ship of war or even at the foot of the guillotine. This was callous, cruel—and most shocking of all—*casual* violence, and for a moment he could neither move nor speak. But he could hear; and though the count spoke softly, and as nonchalantly as if he was ordering the eradication of vermin, Nathan distinctly heard him say: "Kill them. Kill them all."

CHAPTER FOUR

the Screech Owls

NATHAN LIKED TO THINK that he was a reasonable man. Slow to anger. Cool-headed in a crisis.

His mother had always refuted this.

"You have always been emotional," she had informed him on more than one occasion and to his profound irritation. "Just like your father. Though he, too, would have it otherwise. You suffer from a rush of blood to the head. Or a red mist, descending."

Certainly, it was one or the other that saved him now. Without considering the consequences, let alone the danger, Nathan strode forward, grabbed the chevalier by the throat and pressed his pistol into the man's cheek with such force he heard something crack.

"Get back," he ordered the others, who in truth had scarcely had a chance to move. "Back—or by God I'll blow his head off."

He felt de Batz trying to pull away and he shifted his grip to the collar and lifted him from the ground, shaking him like a rat, whatever his title, for he was a small man and inconsequential in weight.

"You don't think I mean it? By Christ, only tempt me." He cocked the pistol with his thumb, though a part of his mind registered that he had neglected to slide back the metal cap that kept the powder dry, a frequent mistake that one day would be the death of him. Too late, now, for he did not have a free hand, but he doubted anyone had noticed, least of all the man in his grip. The blood had drained from the chevalier's face and his eyes were as venomous as a snake's, but there was fear there, too, and pain, for Nathan had pressed the pistol so hard into his cheek he had broken the flesh and possibly one or two of his teeth.

The seamen had advanced in a long menacing line, clearly ready to resume the slaughter they had so lately interrupted. Gilbert Gabriel was at his captain's side, Connor too, eager to knock heads.

"Steady boys, steady" Nathan admonished them, for he did not want to have another fight on his hands. He heard the echo of the lines from "Hearts of Oak," the battle hymn of the King's Navy, and he laughed aloud, laughed with a half-crazed delight at the absurdity of it all; laughed in the chevalier's face which stopped his capers as effectively as if Nathan had brained him with his pistol, for if he had not known his assailant was mad before, he did now. Nathan whirled him round like a partner in a dance, and called out for William Brown, the *Unicorn*'s master at arms, a hulking turnkey of a brute with a pistol in one hand and a tomahawk in the other, which he had acquired in the swamps about New Orleans during a similar engagement. Nathan threw the chevalier in his direction, so violently he sprawled in the dust.

"Take this thing and keep him under close guard and if he gives you abuse, gag him."

But now he had to calm down; now he had to take control of the situation before it got entirely out of hand. He faced the enemy again—the enemy, his allies—and one of them stepped forward: a youngish man who, to confuse matters further, wore a blue jacket, though not the uniform of the National Guard. In fact, unless Nathan was much mistaken, it was the uniform of a warrant officer in the British navy. This was not the only surprise.

"I guess this is what you might call a stand off," the fellow observed in an amiable drawl and in perfect English—or as near perfect as a citizen of the United States would ever achieve. "But perhaps I can be of assistance."

There were questions to be asked of this, but they would keep.

"Stand these men down," Nathan instructed him firmly. "For I am under orders to assist the forces of King Louis of France which I believe places us upon the same side in this quarrel and it would be folly to fall out among ourselves."

"I'm with you there, sir," agreed the American equably, "though we were doing well enough, I believe, without your assistance. However, stand down it is."

He instructed the men accordingly—in passable if by no means fluent French—and though there was some reluctance and a few fierce looks towards their late commander, the majority seemed relieved to accept the arrangement. Lowering their weapons, they began to move away, looking to their wounds and their wounded.

"And when you have tended to your people, report back to me."

This was received with a jaunty tip of the hat which, though it had altogether too much of the New England about it to pass muster in the King's Navy, encouraged Nathan to believe he could safely stand his own men down.

"Mr. Lamb!"

"Here, sir." The midshipman was still at his post beside the loaded cannon, swinging his sword about as if he were mowing grass. Nathan pointed to the Republican soldiers who had retired to the rear and were huddled in a sullen group about their abandoned guns. "Take a dozen hands and make those men secure." Secure was not quite the word but it was to be hoped Lamb would interpret it adequately.

"And Mr. Brown . . ."

"Sir?"

Nathan glanced towards de Batz, now in the grip of one of Brown's bullies. What on earth was to be done with him? The sensible thing would be to send him back to his men; accept his offence as a moment of madness committed in the heat of battle. Except that it had not been in the heat of battle. He had murdered a prisoner in cold blood—Nathan's prisoner and therefore a prisoner of His Britannic

Majesty—and besides, there had been that soft-spoken command: *Kill them. Kill them all.*

Had he meant only the Republican guards? But even if he had, it would have been a flagrant abuse of the unwritten rules of war between civilised nations.

By God, he was rehearsing his defence already.

The chevalier returned his scrutiny with a look of such pure hatred, Nathan knew he had made an enemy for life. Walking over to the ramparts, he peered through one of the embrasures toward where he had left the *Unicorn*. The light was fading fast and he could not see her at first, and for one awful moment he thought she had foundered. But no, there she was, some distance from where he had left her—and by God, she was afloat! The rising tide had lifted her off the sandbank, moored by the head in mid-Channel. Nathan looked to the sun, an immense red buoy on the horizon, marking its own demise. Two hours to the turn of the tide. He glanced up at the Union flag flapping at the masthead. The wind held steady from sou'-sou'-east. His brain struggled with the calculations. Others could do this as easily as read the time but for Nathan it was always an effort, like assembling some gigantic, moving puzzle and forever losing the pieces. He switched his thoughts to another problem, somewhat easier to resolve.

"Mr. Brown?"

"Sir?"

"Take the prisoner back to the ship and clap him in irons."

"Clap him in irons it is, sir."

Joyous words to Brown's ears; he liked nothing better than to clap a man in irons, lest it was to see him lashed up to a grating for a good flogging. The last captain of the *Unicorn* had been more to his taste in this regard; though he had finished up with his throat cut.

"And let Mr. Tully know what has happened here."

Brown frowned. This was more difficult. Nathan wondered if he should send Holroyd or Lamb. He tried once more.

"Tell him we have taken the fort and made contact with our allies."

The frown cleared a little.

"Aye aye, sir."

And now for their allies. And the American in the British naval jacket.

"Bennett, sir. Benjamin Bennett."

He removed his hat, a large, sloppy, black affair such as a Sussex drover might wear on a weekday. Save that there was a feather in it and a humorous look in his eye that Nathan had not seen in many drovers, not mocking as the chevalier's had been, too good-humoured for that, but as if they were playing a game.

They stood on the ramparts of the redoubt in the light of a lantern, for it was properly dark now in the shadows of the fort. Nathan's men sprawled comfortably about the guns and their allies comported themselves in a like manner on the far side of the redoubt. Out to sea he could see the broken masts of the *Unicorn* against the paler sky and if he looked the other way, the lights of the smaller vessels moored off Long Island, in the mouth of the Auray, just inside the Gulf.

"Well, Bennett, I take it you are an American."

"From Nantucket, sir, Rhode Island."

So not Boston. Much superior to Boston, at least in the view of the residents of Nantucket.

"A seafaring man."

"I am, sir, as are most men from Nantucket."

"And once in the King's Navy, I think, by the coat you are wearing, unless you acquired it by other means."

Bennett glanced down at it with a look of surprise as if he had quite forgotten that he was wearing it, and what it might signify.

"Ah yes, sir, the coat. I fear it needs a good wash and a bit of make and mend." He flicked at some particular blemish that had caught his eye, remarkably given the state it was in, for even by the poor light of the lantern it was apparent that it needed a good deal more than a wash; it needed burning. But it still had most of its brass buttons, if a little tarnished, and Nathan could make out what had once been white edging on the fall-down collar. "I served aboard the brig sloop *Phoebe* for a year or so, in the squadron of Admiral Saumarez, off the Isle of Oberon."

"You were a volunteer?"

"Ah, well as to that, only in a manner of speaking, sir, being as I was pressed into the service."

Nathan nodded understandingly. It did happen.

"I was second mate on the *Tristan* barque out of Nantucket and bound for Bristol on our usual run when we ran foul of the *Phoebe*, so to speak, in the Bay of Biscay and I was among those that was took. I was rated able seaman but the captain allowed as how I might assist the master, seeing as I possessed some small skill in navigation."

Nathan understood this, too. Not many captains would relish having a man on the lower deck who could read a chart and a sextant, not if he had the slightest fear of the hands seizing the ship. Men had been hanged for less.

"And now you are a deserter," he said, with just enough menace in his voice to remind him of the consequences thereof, and that this was not a conversation between equals.

The head came up, the eyes sharp. "A deserter? Never say that, sir. Never say that. We was chasing a blockade runner into La Rochelle when we grounded—aye sir, as you did, but on a falling tide—and the gunboats came out and pounded us so bad we was forced to strike."

Nathan frowned, as much for his ignorance of the event as the ignominy of a King's ship forced to strike her colours. He followed the news of nautical encounters as rigorously as any officer in the service and felt sure he must have read of such an incident in the *Gazette*. However, a brig was not the greatest of the King's ships and it was possible the journal had dealt somewhat sketchily with the affair, especially as it had involved surrender.

"So you were taken prisoner?"

"I was, sir, with all the officers and crew, but seeing as I was American, and a pressed man at that, they reckoned I was no more eager to serve King George than they and might be willing to sling my hook in a French ship. I told them I'd as soon not, begging their pardons, which I fear they took ill, but they allowed I was not so great a menace to the Republic as to be shut up with the rest of the crew and they might save themselves the expense of accommodating me. So I was left to make my own arrangements, along with the rest of lads from home."

It was a plausible if garrulous explanation. Nathan had heard that there were more than a hundred American ships locked up in La Rochelle by the British blockade and most of their crews with them. But it did not explain how he came to be serving with the Chouans.

"Ah, well, that is a longer story," he began, when Nathan put this question to him, "but in short, after I had been there a few days I had seen enough of the place, not having the means to make my stay there a little more pleasurable, so I took it into my head to move along the coast a bit, in the hope of maybe stealing a boat and making my way back to the squadron."

"Your zeal does you credit," murmured Nathan, who did not believe a word of it.

"Well, a man can do worse than a life at sea, even in a King's ship," the reprobate assured him, as if Nathan looked a man of promise and should give it some consideration. "And I was never going to get back to Nantucket on my own, was I? Not in the kind of tub I might pick up in a French fishing port."

There was that.

"And you did not fear to be taken up by the authorities as an Englishman and a spy?"

"It was a risk, sure, but I spoke enough of the language to get by, I reckoned." He noted Nathan's frown, for this was unusual, and grinned. "I had a girl once from Louisiana—Creole—who taught me the lingo."

Nathan wondered at that, but did not challenge him. "So, you made your way up the coast . . ."

"I did. But before I had got very far, I fell in with a band of Chouans who had other plans for me and were as persuasive, you might say, as an English press gang."

"This is the band you are with now?"

"Smaller, no more than a score or so—but we encountered a good few more on our travels. We were more than five thousand strong at one point but we took some hard knocks. Very hard." A grim look came over him and he fell silent for a moment.

"So you were with them for some while?"

"Almost a year now. With the rank of sergeant."

"I will bear that in mind, Bennett, when you are restored to the lower deck," Nathan assured him ironically. "But tell me about them. As soldiers."

"Well they are not the foot guards, sir. Nor even the marines. I guess you would say they was lacking in discipline. But they know how to fight."

"And who is their leader, since Jean Chouan was killed?"

He looked surprised at Nathan's knowledge. "They are several. Sombreuil, Stofflet, Charette . . ."

"And de Batz?"

Bennett nodded, but reflectively. "Yes. Though he is not as high in their ranks as he should be, in his own estimation."

Clearly Bennett was not one of the chevalier's greatest admirers.

"And how is it you came to Morbihan?"

"We had orders to march north, almost a week ago."

"Then you knew there was to be a landing?"

"There was talk. We were to make for Quiberon so it seemed possible."

"This is not Quiberon."

"No, sir, but we had orders to take the battery here, which was in our rear. Fortunately for you, I think."

"And for you, Mr. Bennett," Nathan replied evenly, "for you have achieved your ambition to rejoin the service at last, and have no need to steal a boat."

If Nathan had thought to discomfort him by this, he had

misjudged the man. The only response was a wide grin and a slight duck of the head.

"Would that be as able seaman, sir, or master's mate?"

"We will rate you able seaman, Bennett, for the time being and see how you go on." But this would not do, this would not do at all. The American was a godsend and could not be so lightly consigned to the lower deck. "However, for the moment I believe you must continue to lead your Chouans, for they seem to heed you well enough."

The eyes wary now, the grin a little exposed.

"And where am I to lead them, sir? If I might ask."

Nathan hesitated. But if he was to make use of the man he could not let him remain in ignorance.

"I am commanded to link up with the Chouans in this region," he confided, "provide them with arms and supplies and lead them against the Republican forces in Auray."

Bennett looked surprised. "Oh, but we took Auray the day before yesterday."

"You took Auray?" Nathan was astonished. "With these few?"

"Oh, we had a good few more than this. Over a thousand, under General Charette. And they surrendered without a shot. Near two hundred of them. They had marched out on the road to Quiberon and engaged with some of the Royalists that was landed and come off the worse for it, so they was in no state for another mauling."

Nathan considered what this meant for him. With Auray in the hands of the Chouans, half his objective was accomplished already. Now he had only to land the weapons and supplies. The town was some fifteen miles upriver but from his memory of the charts it looked navigable, at least to some of the smaller boats, and it would make life a great deal easier if he could deliver his cargo directly to where it was most needed—and by river.

Bennett was confident it could be done and that with the tide they could reach Auray in three or four hours.

"And, in your opinion, can Charette hold the town, with the forces he has at his command?"

"Well, that depends what is disposed against him, sir. But long enough, I reckon, if his men were better armed and provisioned."

But Nathan could not take Bennett's word for this.

"That can be done," he assured him. "If you are willing to go back there with one of my officers to arrange for their distribution."

"I'm your man there, sir—most willing."

It occurred to Nathan that as a pressed man in the King's Service it did not matter if he were willing or not.

"You are back in the service now," he reminded him, "and answerable to me and any other officer, not to any Tom, Dick—or de Batz."

"Aye, aye, sir." The grin again. "So I am to act as quartermaster."

"In a manner of speaking," Nathan replied cautiously, "but you will be entered on the ship's books as able seaman and you are not to forget it and take it into your head to go wandering about the countryside again."

"Would that be dated back, sir, to when I was took?"

Nathan reminded himself that the fellow was from Nantucket and certain allowances must be made.

"I will instruct the purser accordingly. Is that to your satisfaction, Bennett?"

If Bennett noted the sarcasm he did not let it trouble him. "Well, I guess I am in no position to haggle," he conceded cheerfully.

"No, you are not," Nathan assured him. "And you will remember that you are subject to the Articles of War—and the penalties for breaking them. Now get back to your men."

But there were other questions preying on his mind and for once time was not so pressing. The men were hunkered down for the night, the *Unicorn* as secure as she could be with half her masts down and the rest of his little fleet moored in the sheltered waters of the Gulf of Morbihan.

"Wait," he called out, as the man turned away, pulling down his hat. "You have served the Chevalier de Batz for long?"

"A few months, I reckon."

"And what impression did you form of his character?"

"His character?"

"His character, Bennett. As an officer and a gentleman."

The American turned his head aside and for a moment Nathan thought he was going to spit, but he only smiled grimly and said, "He's a brutal swine of a man and incompetent with it. Whatever his title." This was reassuring. What came next was not. "However, he is kin to the Comte de Puisaye who commands the Royalist troops at Quiberon."

"I see."

"Will that be all, sir?"

"Just a moment. You heard his order—before I was obliged to . . . to seize him up?"

"Yes, sir." Bennett had stepped a little away from the light and it was impossible to read his expression but his tone was cautious.

"And what did you hear?"

A moment before the answer came. "He ordered us to kill them."

"Kill them. Kill them all."

"I believe that was the gist of it."

"And what did you take him to mean by that?"

"That we was to kill the Blues."

"The prisoners?"

"Yes, sir."

"And what of the rest of us?"

Bennett frowned. "Well, truly I did not really give that much thought. It was all so quick—and then you had him by the throat."

"Very well, Bennett." But there was another question he had to ask. He put his hand up to his breast pocket to check he still had the letter. "There is one more thing."

"Sir?"

"You saw a great deal of the Vendée, I suppose, on your travels."

"More than I wished, sir, the state it was in."

"There is a woman I have been asked to seek out. She was said to have escaped the guillotine almost a year ago in Paris and fled south, to seek refuge among the Chouans."

He was aware of Bennett's scrutiny, even in the dark. His own face was in the light and he moved away from it a little before he continued.

"Her name is Sara, Countess of Turenne, but she may be calling herself Seton, or some other name." It was absurd. Even if she had lived, how could Bennett have met her, or even heard of her? And why the Vendée? She was from Provence, in the deep South, half Irish, half Italian, born into a land of sunshine and wine and song, and she always said she would go back there, if she ever had the chance. He could hear her now, her soft voice in his ear, as they lay together in her apartment in Paris.

"There is a little town called Tourettes, near where we lived in Provence. I used to go there as a child, with my father. A walled town on top of a hill. There is a café in the square where I drank lemonade and ate the little cakes made of oranges and watched the people coming to market. If I leave Paris, that is where I will go, to Tourettes—that is where you will find me, drinking lemonade and eating little cakes made of oranges and waiting for you there."

"The Countess of Turenne?" There was surprise in the man's voice, but not the expected ignorance. "Yes, I have heard of her. I have even met her. They call her La Renarde. The Vixen. She is the mistress of François de Charette and fights at his side. She is there now—at Auray."

CHAPTER FIVE

the Vixen

NATHAN STRUGGLED OUT OF A TROUBLED SLEEP, stiff-limbed, parched, his brain chasing the fleeing remnants of a dream. Sara was in it somewhere and the guillotine . . . and a dark catacomb lined with skulls. He lay on his back staring up at one. There were sounds, too, of rats . . .

Then he was awake, properly awake, in the stern cabin of the gun brig *Conquest*, riding at anchor in the Gulf of Morbihan, and gazing up at the dawn, weakly filtered through a murky skylight. And what he could hear was the sound of the watch changing.

The morning watch. He closed his eyes again with a sigh. He could sleep for at least two hours yet without troubling his conscience. But his restless mind would not let him. How could he be sure the woman Bennett had spoken of was Sara? She would not be the first to pluck a title from the bloody pile left at the foot of the guillotine.

But he had asked Bennett to describe her to him. A beauty he had said, a dark-haired, dark-eyed beauty, "like the women of Spain or southern Italy."

And the lover of a Chouan general whose men called her La Renarde.

The Vixen. With its connotations of promiscuity and lust. Was it the bestial screaming they made whilst coupling? He had heard that whores in London used to wear a fox's tail stitched to the rear of their skirts to denote their profession . . .

Did he think her a whore?

That would be absurd. Unjustified. He had no claim on her. Yet the thought of her with another man disturbed him more than he could ever say.

He should not be thinking of this. There were more important things to think of than this. Clambering out of the narrow cot, he dressed clumsily, forced into an ungainly crouch by the meagre proportions of the cabin, more suited to a child of ten than a man over two yards tall. Though they were into the first week of July, the air felt unusually chill and a violent flurry of rain on the skylight persuaded him to reach for his heavy boat cloak before climbing the short companionway to the deck.

A huddle of officers in tarps and tricorn hats, like wet owls, grudging the dawn. Balfour, the brig's commander, an elderly lieutenant, past forty with the face of a Scots pastor, nursing the moral certainty of everyone's damnation but his own; the master, Rigsby, who had the morning watch, older still, damned already; a couple of midshipmen, Foley and Stamp, mere boys, faces tearful with rain or rebuke. Lamb, the young gentleman from the *Unicorn* Nathan had brought as his courier, trying by his expression and a certain stance of his still childlike body to distance himself from the rest. There appeared to be some kind of conference in progress, hastily adjourned at Nathan's emergence. He sniffed the air and found it resentful, but he gave them a brisk "Good morning," and surveyed the now drearily familiar surroundings of the Little Sea.

They were moored in the mouth of the Auray, in the lee of Point Kerpenhir, with the smaller boats of the squadron curving away in a long line astern. Beyond, at a distance of about half a mile, was the fort they had taken, with the Union flag now hanging limply from its battlements in the rain. Little had changed since their fortuitous victory over three days before, apart from the weather which had taken a turn for the worse. The wind had shifted to the north-west and the black clouds rolling in from the Bay of Biscay promised more rain to come and possibly storms.

"No news, I suppose?" He cocked his head at the lieutenant, but without expectation.

"None, sir." Balfour would probably have sent to wake him if there was, though you could not count on it for he was a man of few words and less imagination. Any news, even bad, would have been welcome to Nathan. He sniffed again—and smelled coffee. _His_ coffee. The Angel Gabriel working miracles in the galley. So, that was something at least. In an hour or so he would have breakfast to look forward to. Then a long gap until dinner.

"I tell you what," he remarked, to no-one in particular, "if this goes on much longer I shall begin to feel the war is ended and no-one has bothered to inform us."

The ghost of a smile from Balfour. Nathan felt guilty for taking the man's cabin from him but he could not be stationed aboard the _Unicorn,_ forced by its draught to moor well out in the bay, nor did he care to be on land—and he did not feel so guilty as to seek accommodation aboard one of the smaller vessels. It was bad enough coping with the cramped accommodation aboard the _Conquest._

She was an odd hybrid of a vessel, the only one of her class, though Nathan had heard there were others being built to the same draught, their lordships being desirous of something with a bit more clout than your average gunboat and able to travel an appreciable distance to deliver it. Clout she certainly had, with a broadside of ten 18-pounders and two 32-pounder carronades firing fore and aft. It was the delivery that was questionable, for though she was rigged as a brig she was a notoriously poor sailor. She rolled alarmingly with any kind of a sea running, and even in the sheltered waters of Morbihan she shied at the merest gust of wind and tended to drift with the slightest current so that her forward progress more often resembled that of a crab on a beach than a respectable man-o'-war. She was equipped with eighteen sweeps so that she might operate as a galley in calm waters, without the assistance of slaves—though slaves could hardly have been worse accommodated than the crew of the *Conquest*. Or flogged as often, for from what he had heard, Mr. Balfour believed that the damned need not wait for Death or the Devil to receive just recompense for a life of sin: not when *he* was conveniently to hand.

Gilbert Gabriel came aft with Nathan's coffee. He took it gratefully and carried it over to the rail. It was almost low tide and the waters had retreated from the shores of the gulf to expose a large quantity of mud, among which a number of wading birds picked their delicate feet and grubbed for sustenance. He turned his face into the rain, squinting up the length of the river, a long finger pointing north. He had sent Howard and Whiteley up there three days ago in one of the cutters, with a quantity of marines and Bennett as their guide and translator, to make contact with the Chouans at Auray and report on the situation there. Since then, not a word. He anguished now that he had placed too much reliance on the American's version of events in the town and that it might still be in Republican hands. But it was hard to know what else he could have done. He could hardly have gone charging up there with the whole squadron, not knowing what he might find at the end of it.

He missed Tully, who made a perfect sounding board for his anxieties, though on this occasion there were certain of them he might wish to keep to himself for all Tully's discretion. Certainly, in his own mind, Nathan knew he was shy of meeting with the Chouan leader, Charette, and thereby confirming without a shadow of doubt that the woman who fought by his side was Sara—*his* Sara. La Renarde.

A sudden flash from out of the darkening sky, followed after a few moments by a clap of thunder. And now the rain came down in earnest, dancing upon the deck and churning the waters of the Gulf into a violent froth. Nathan turned from the rail.

"I am going below to write up my journal," he informed Lieutenant Balfour, for want of a better excuse, though neither excuse nor explanation were needed. "*I am going below to cut my throat,*" he might have said, and Balfour would have responded with the same indifferent nod, touching his hat.

Yet even in the depths of his misery he could not help but wonder what was for breakfast and whether it would be long in coming. He raised his voice.

"Gabriel! Gilbert Gabriel there!"

The presence loomed, never far from his side.

"Sir?"

Gabriel had been his father's servant when Nathan was a boy. He had taught him to load and fire his first fowling piece and tanned his hide on more than one occasion for some mischief considerably less ambitious than highway robbery.

"Would you have another coffee on the go, Gabriel? And I believe I will have breakfast now rather than later."

Nathan turned guiltily away, not wishing to consider the negotiations that were sure to be involved in fulfilling such an outrageous request. Back in the privacy of Balfour's cabin, he seated himself at the tiny desk, rolled back his cuff, and took up his pen:

Friday, July 3rd. Rain.

He stared at this startling revelation for some considerable time without adding to it. He felt like a schoolboy compelled to write some dreary composition. Verse was more appropriate to his present mood.

Rain, tippling from the morning sky
And drumming upon the taut canvas
Of my vexéd mind
As dimly I hear the vixen's love-tortured cry . . .

Love-tortured. No. Something else, something less maudlin yet expressive of sexual anguish and grief . . . He set it aside for future consideration and returned to the more mundane matter of his journal. Their lordships, who might one day read it, were not, as a general rule, enamoured of verse, not in a captain's journal. Nor, so far as he was aware, of sexual anguish.

Light wind NNW.

It was the duty of every officer in the service, above the rank of midshipman, to keep a record of their commission. Indeed, the lieutenants were obliged to satisfy their lordships, or at least their lordships' underlings, that they had fulfilled their obligations in this regard, and have it attested by signature, before they were permitted to draw their pay. So the voyages of the *Unicorn* were documented severally beside the official version recorded in the ship's log, which was kept by the ship's master and tended to be less imaginative: though in truth imagination did not figure largely in any of them. Nor, as general rule, were they ever read. They were only read if something exceptional occurred, such as victory, or defeat, or mutiny. But then the journals were transformed from essays in banality to loaded weapons that could be used against one's fellow officers. Or oneself.

Naturally, when anything untoward did occur, there was a degree of collusion in their composition: a collective instinct to tell the same tale, based on the principle that they either stood—or hanged—together. Nathan did not encourage this propensity but nor was he averse to it, if it was to his own advantage. And there was the rub. He could not bring himself to examine his officers' reports before they were submitted; nor influence them, as he knew other commanders did. He knew he might already be facing serious charges for his conduct in the Caribbean. He was accused of recklessness, of endangering his ship. And now there was this business in the mouth of Morbihan: the grounding of the *Unicorn* and the "arrest" of the Chevalier de Batz . . . cousin to the Comte de Puisaye, commander of the Royalist troops at Quiberon.

Nathan put his hand to his head and massaged the ache about his temples. He had already written up a report of the incident and sent it by the *Unicorn*'s cutter to Commodore Warren—considerably sweetened, of course, by news of the taking of the two forts. But he wondered what his own officers would have to say about it in their individual reports.

It was unlike him to be so anxious. He shook his head to dismiss the demons that lurked there and dipped the pen once more into the ink.

Only to be saved by the clatter of feet down the ladder in the companionway and the rapping of a midshipman's knuckle—it was odd how you always knew it was a midshipman—upon the panels of the door.

Midshipman Lamb, to be precise, with Mr. Balfour's respects and the news that the cutter was sighted, bearing down upon them under full sail from out of the Auray.

"So what kept you?" Nathan demanded as he scrutinised the faces of the two officers in the privacy of his cabin. "It cannot be more than four hours to Auray with the tide."

"I beg your pardon, sir, but we were detained by the enemy." Major Howard was as laconic as ever, if a mite less dapper. His uniform was soiled and rent and he did not look to have washed or shaved for several days. Whiteley looked dead on his feet.

Nathan gestured for them to be seated and they sank wearily into the cushions of the bench under the stern window.

"Bennett reported that Auray had fallen to the Chouans," Nathan began.

Howard nodded. "So it had, but we had not been there above an hour when we came under fire from a strong force of Republicans that had marched up from Vannes. We were under siege for two days." He drew a hand over his unshaven jaw. "Finally, the Chouans decided to make a break to the west, towards Quiberon, and we fought our way out by the river."

"But . . ." Nathan struggled to make sense of this. "What of the invasion force? Has it not advanced inland?"

The two officers exchanged glances.

"We are informed not."

"Informed?"

"By Charette—the Chouan commander at Auray."

"But what—" It came out as a croak, his mouth was so dry. He cleared his throat and started again. "But why have the Royalists not advanced inland? We were informed the enemy had very little force in the region."

Howard seemed unusually reticent. Nathan glanced at Whiteley. He wished he could have talked with him privately for there was some mystery here and Whiteley would have been less cautious about revealing it.

"Tell me what you know," he instructed Howard. "At least, what you have heard. I will make no report of it unless it is necessary. But it is important I know exactly what is happening so far as the land operations are concerned."

"Well," Howard assembled his thoughts. You could almost hear them creaking. "This came from Charette and I am not sure he is to be trusted. He has . . . well, he is a man of strong opinions and his political views, that is . . . I believe he is not entirely in sympathy with the Royalist cause—at least as it is represented at Quiberon."

Nathan waited patiently.

"However, he reports that there is dissent in the Royalist command. Some are for marching inland; others for remaining at Quiberon until there is more welcome news."

"News?" Nathan screwed up his face. "News of what?"

"Of what is happening elsewhere. In Paris, in particular."

"In Paris? Paris is two hundred miles from here and unless I am misinformed it is ruled by the Republicans. What has Paris to do with the situation here in Brittany?"

"I am only reporting what we heard, sir."

"I am sorry. Go on."

"We were told that the invasion was timed to coincide with an uprising in Paris, and the overthrow of the Republican government by Royalists in the capital."

"I see." Nathan wondered if he did. Was the invasion meant to draw troops from the capital? A mere diversion to the main thrust of the attack? But this was political work and it was too much to expect that the people fighting on the ground would be informed of it.

"I take it nothing further has been heard of this 'uprising'?'"

"No, sir. Charette—and those of his followers we spoke with— I had the impression they do not look to Paris for relief. Or much else in this world. For them, Paris is the source of all evil. A Hell on Earth, entirely occupied by demons."

A knock came upon the door and Gabriel entered with two of his lackeys bearing coffee and a large skillet of ham and eggs, pork sausage and hunks of fresh-baked bread. At Nathan's invitation the two officers fell upon it as if they had not eaten for days. Nathan held back though his stomach growled wolfishly.

"So." He was battling to come to terms with all of this, and what it meant for him and his small force in the Gulf of Morbihan. "Tell me about the situation in Auray, when you arrived?"

Howard paused in the act of forking half a sausage into his mouth and laid it down with reluctance. "The Chouans held the town right enough. I would say there were above a thousand of them posted about the place." He looked to Whiteley who confirmed this estimate with a nod. "But no more than half were armed. That is, with proper weapons: muskets or fowling pieces. Most had no more than a scythe or a pitchfork. Or a sling. We saw a lot of slings. They are very good at using them. They can bring down a bird in flight." His voice had resumed its familiar sardonic tone but he caught Nathan's eye and changed his tune. "They are not lacking in spirit, though they could use a little discipline. I would not care to lead them on an open field but I understand that is not their way, to fight in the open."

Nor would it be mine, reflected Nathan privately, if all I had to fight with was a sling and a scythe. He thought with regret of all the modern muskets stored in the holds of his gunboats.

"Well, they are a peasant army," he reminded Howard. "We knew this—that is why we came here. And what of the force that is opposed to them?"

"About twice that number. Well-armed and equipped. And well-disciplined so far as we could tell. They have a number of field pieces. And they say more troops, including regulars, are closing in from Vannes."

"Who says?"

"Well, the Republicans. They sent a deputation, under flag of truce, to demand the town's surrender. On terms. Or there would be no quarter, they said. Charette declined. Just after that he made the decision to break out—and we took our chance on the river."

"So Auray is not cut off entirely?"

"They had covered the river with field pieces but it was dark and we went with the current. And they were somewhat distracted by Charette and his men."

"Even so, you did well," Nathan assured him. He had changed his mind about Howard. "Now you had better finish eating and then look to your men while I consider what is to be done here."

When they had gone, Nathan sent for Bennett. He looked as dishevelled and as weary as the two officers but there was something else in his expression. An element of defiance—and barely constrained anger.

"Well," Nathan began, uneasily, "this is a fine kettle of fish."

"You could say that."

Whatever else the service had taught Bennett, it was not how to address an officer. Nathan tried not to resent it. He rather doubted if Bennett would give a damn if he did.

"Did you speak with Charette?"

"I did."

"And what did he make of the situation? I mean with the Royalists at Quiberon."

"You want me to give you his exact words?"

"A summary will do."

"He thought them a bunch of cowards and whoresons."

"I see. And the talk of an uprising in Paris?"

"Hogwash. Besides, even if it were true, why should it stop them marching inland?" Nathan had no answer to that. "Except that they have no stomach for a fight and wish to stay as close to the sea as they can—and the ships that will take them back to England."

"But it makes no sense," Nathan protested. "Why would they come all this way to sit around on the shores of Quiberon until we take them off again?"

"Maybe they thought to hear the government had fallen and they could march to Paris like conquering heroes." Bennett wiped a grimy hand over his face. It did nothing to improve his looks or his temper. Exhaustion was etched in every feature. "Only it has not happened and now they are shitting their pants at the thought of Hoche heading their way."

"Hoche?"

"Lazare Hoche. Republican general. Best they've got. Ex-corporal. Beat the Prussians on the Rhine in '93. Now he is on his way here— with the Army of the West."

"You appear remarkably well informed."

"Charette told me."

Charette again.

"Then Charette is remarkably well informed."

"He keeps an ear to the ground. He has to, being allied to traitors and scoundrels who are as much enemies to each other as they are to the Republic."

This was true. And certainly there was a strong whiff of betrayal in the air. But Nathan had other things on his mind. He broke the awkward silence that had fallen between them. "This Charette, what is he like?"

A shrug. "I am not sure I am the right man to tell you. I have only met him twice and both times he was, one might say, preoccupied."

"Young or old? Soldier or civilian?"

"In his middle thirties, I would say. He comes from La Garnache— on the coast, not far south of here. A nobleman. Old family. A good soldier, I think, though he was a naval officer before the Revolution. He served in the American War, fighting the British."

"A naval officer?" But why should that surprise him? Perhaps she had a taste for naval officers.

"After the Revolution he emigrated to Germany. He was at Koblenz, with the royal court in exile."

As was Sara's former husband, the Count of Turenne. They must have known each other. Was this the connection? Useless to speculate. But self-torture once begun was never easy to stop.

"Handsome, brave, dashing . . . ?"

Bennett shot him a puzzled look. "Well he is not ugly and certainly no coward. He confronted the mob when they stormed the Palace of the Tuileries. Saved the Queen's life, according to some accounts."

"Marie Antoinette?"

"I believe she was Queen at the time."

"So he was in Paris in '92 . . ."

Had Sara met him there? Had they been lovers, even then?

"Strange that he was not arrested."

"He had connections, I believe. Service friends, men he had fought with in America and were in favour with the Republicans. He was allowed to live on his estates in the Vendée but when the peasants rose up they asked him to lead them. And he agreed, though from what I have heard he had no great hopes of them."

"Then why . . . ?"

"If you saw what was happening in the Vendée at that time, you would not need to ask. It was a charnel house. He had no choice."

"So what are his chances of breaking out of Auray?"

Bennett considered. "Better than his chances of staying alive if he remains there."

"And this woman—who calls herself the Countess of Turenne—was she with him?" He tried to keep his voice casual.

"La Renarde? No, she was not. She had been, but she left the day we arrived. For Quiberon."

"For Quiberon?" There was hope then for all he tried to suppress it.

"To carry a message from Charette to the Royalist commanders—and the British. So I was told."

Nathan frowned. "Is that not extraordinary, to give such a task to a woman?"

"She is an extraordinary woman." He regarded Nathan curiously. "You have never met her?" Then he shook his head. "But how could you?"

"I told you, Bennett, I was asked to make enquiry of her—by friends of hers that are in England. She has a son there, a young boy. She will be concerned to know that he is safe and well and with . . . with friends."

"Well, maybe you will find her in Quiberon," said Bennett, "for that is where this business will end, I think. In Quiberon, with their backs to the sea. And God help them, if your ships do not take them off."

CHAPTER SIX

Apocalypse

NATHAN BRACED HIMSELF against the mizzen shrouds of the *Unicorn* and stared, appalled, at the unfolding tragedy on the shores of Quiberon. Here were all the ingredients of Chaos, plundered from the Book of Revelations. Thunder, lightning, strong winds and driving rain; the sea a raging fury and a sky like the wrath of God. And all a mere backdrop to the real drama enacted upon the storm-lashed beaches: the struggling, surging, desperate mass of people: men, women, children, babes in arms, wounded soldiers, half-drowned sailors; ten, twenty, maybe thirty thousand or more, fighting, squabbling, lying down to die or stretching out their arms in supplication to the unrelenting sea.

And the English ships that were their only hope of salvation.

Nathan had taken the *Unicorn* as close in as he dared under her jury rig, for even here in the bay, with the long claw of Quiberon providing some shelter from the pounding seas of Biscay, there was a great risk of shipwreck. He could see the shattered remains of several small boats on the beach and others foundering in the breakers, their timbers stove in, tossed this way and that, the playthings of the waves. The tide was out and much of the shore bristled with rocks, the angry waves crashing against them and exploding high into the air as if in fury at the helpless prey just beyond their reach; and yet

Nathan could see people clinging there, others wading out breast-high through the foam: women with babies held high above their heads as the sea broke over them and the lightning flashed and the clouds rolled in from the west. And all around the carnage and debris of defeat: clothing and timber and all the accoutrements of war and its victims: horses, mules and men, floating lifeless upon that terrible tide, like a rehearsal for the Apocalypse.

The *Unicorn* was lying to with her topyards backed and all four of her boats out—it was for this reason Nathan had brought the frigate so close to shore—and he watched anxiously as they heaved and plunged in the breakers just off the reefs, trying to pluck a few souls from the water. Their orders were to take off only the fighting men, so that they might be landed further down the coast to pursue what was clearly a lost cause, but it was impossible to stop the sailors from trying to rescue women and children who had advanced towards them through the waves. The gig found a gap in the rocks and was immediately assailed by a floundering rush from the shore and Nathan watched in anguish as the crew was forced to beat off their helpless supplicants with oars and cutlasses.

"Dear God, how has it come to this?" he shouted to Tully, braced beside him at the rail. But Tully could only shake his head, as perplexed and helpless as he. It was the storm that answered, with a great flash of lightning and the almost instantaneous roar of thunder, mocking the puny belligerence of the guns of Fort Penthièvre on the narrow strip of sand linking the peninsula to the mainland. In the past few days the fort had twice changed hands—and names, for it had been called Fort Sans Culottes by the Republicans in honour of the Paris mob. Held briefly by the Royalists, it had been recaptured in the last twenty-four hours, thanks in large part to the treachery of the very troops sent to defend it.

Treachery, Nathan had learned within hours of his return, was as rife among the Royalists as Bennett had proposed. And the British were not without blame in this regard, for it transpired that the King's chief minister, William Pitt, had ordered the release of over a thousand Republican prisoners to swell the Royalist ranks. Possibly he had imagined that they would uphold the allied cause out of simple gratitude. More likely, that complicated abacus of a brain thought only to save the expense of their accommodation in the prison hulks. Either way, it had been a disastrous decision, for most had waited only until the moment they were set ashore before deserting to the enemy while others, more cunning, had waited until they were installed at Fort Penthièvre before sneaking out after dark and leading the Republicans back along the shore at low tide to take the position where it was least defended. And now General Hoche had his foot firmly planted upon the neck of Quiberon, with the rest of the peninsula at his mercy—and all that were lodged upon it.

On that slender strip of land, barely eight miles long and less than three at its widest point, were huddled an estimated 30,000 souls: the émigrés landed from England, the Chouans who had joined them, and those locals who had reason to fear the Republicans' revenge. Most without food, or water, or shelter. And all looking to God or the British fleet to save them.

From his present perspective Nathan had little faith in either.

"Mr. Holroyd's respects, sir, and *Pomone* is signalling."

Nathan followed the messenger across the canting deck to where Holroyd and Lamb were huddled, heads together over the signal book. Some short distance to leeward he could see the signals flying from the gaff halyard of the *Pomone* and he waited impatiently for the two officers to agree on a translation. It was not long in coming for the order was a simple one. He was to report aboard the flagship. Its execution, however, was another matter.

"How am I to report," he complained peevishly to Tully, "when all our boats are out? Would he have me walk on water?"

"I expect he would be content if you were to swim," Tully assured him and though he smiled his eyes expressed a lively concern, for the Chevalier de Batz was still confined below decks, no longer in chains, but with a marine sentry posted at the door—and there had been no reply, as yet, to Nathan's report on the matter.

•   •   •

"Ah Captain Peake, here you are at last. I believe you have already met Mr. Finch."

The commodore's greeting was not so very different from when they had last met, but his appearance had changed very much for the worse. His hair hung lank and unpowdered, his jaw was unshaven and there was a hint of desperation in his eyes. Nathan was not at all surprised. Hardly a thing had gone right for him since the fog had lifted on the morning of the *Unicorn*'s arrival.

If Sir John Borlase Warren had thought to find glory in his appointment his hopes had been cruelly dashed—and he must surely fear that he would be held accountable for the failure of the enterprise. It occurred to Nathan that his main concern must be to spread the blame as generously as possible and indeed, the commodore's next words confirmed him in this opinion.

"I have read your report on the venture into the Gulf of Morbihan. A pity. A great pity. Had we been able to hold on to Auray for a few days all this might have been avoided." The commodore gestured vaguely towards the stern windows and the obscure view it provided of the chaos on the beaches. "However, it may not be too late to save the day, if we are prepared to put our duty before any other considerations. Now if I may draw your attention to the chart." He returned his gaze to the object in question while Nathan considered how he might be held responsible for the fall of Auray. If there was a way, he was sure the commodore would find it. He was clearly out of favour with Mr. Finch, who had not bothered to rise from his chair at Nathan's entrance or return his bow though now he looked more closely this appeared to be prompted by reasons other than discourtesy. Indeed, he rather thought the man was dead until he noted the sheen of sweat upon his pale countenance.

"Good day to you, Mr. Finch," he greeted him cheerfully as he made his way over to the table, and was rewarded with a glazed eye and something very like a death rattle.

"Here is Penthièvre, or Fort Sans Culottes as the Republicans call it." Warren indicated the fort at the narrow neck of the peninsula. "Its loss is a grave blow and I fear that until we receive the promised reinforcement from England we are in no position to take it back. Indeed, our main concern at present is that General Hoche will use the fort as a forward base to attack the Royalist lines here at Kerhostin."

He drew an imaginary line with his finger across the peninsula at a point a little south of the fort. As imaginary as the Royalist lines, so far as Nathan was concerned, for he had seen no physical sign of them.

"I am assured by the Comte de Puisaye that he has sufficient men to mount a creditable defence," the commodore continued, "and I have no reason to doubt his estimation." Nathan blinked a little but said nothing in contradiction of this astonishing statement. "However, you will have noticed that at low tide a considerable amount of beach is exposed on the eastern side of the peninsula." Nathan had. "The concern is that the French—the Republicans— will take advantage of this to outflank de Puisaye's defences, just as they did at Penthièvre. And he has insufficient resource to extend his lines. So—we must provide cover from the sea."

Which made some sort of sense—if there had been any sea. But at low tide, as Warren must know, it retreated some considerable distance from the land. And with the shoals and rocks it would be impossible to sail a vessel of any size, or weight of broadside, to within a mile of the coast in that vicinity. Add to that the difficulty of operating so close to shore in a near gale and the impossibility of firing the guns with any degree of accuracy . . . Nathan began to point out some of these difficulties to the commodore but had scarcely begun when he was tersely interrupted.

"What of the *Conquest*—and the squadron you led into Morbihan?"

Nathan looked at the chart again, noting the depths of water at the landward end of the peninsula.

"It might be possible," he conceded. "If the weather abates somewhat and we can find a pilot who knows the shoals about that point."

"And the pilot who guided you into the Morbihan?"

"I would have to enquire." Nathan frowned, disadvantaged.

"Then please do, as soon as you feel ready to broach the subject." Whatever he had lost in elegance, the commodore's sarcasm was sharp as it ever was. "But I fear we cannot wait upon the weather, for I am persuaded General Hoche will permit himself no such luxury. You will have to put on your tarpaulin and your southwester and make the best of things."

Nathan prepared to make his leave, but Warren had not finished with him yet.

"I understand from your report that you have a number of Chouans aboard."

"Yes, sir. I thought they would be of more use here than in the Gulf of Morbihan."

"Then let us make use of them. Put them ashore to reinforce de Puisaye. The *Unicorn* may provide support at whatever distance you consider will not put her at risk. We do not want you running aground again, as you did in the mouth of Morbihan."

Nathan swallowed his anger and his pride.

"Will that be all, sir?"

"No, it is not all. Before you go, this business of the Chevalier de Batz . . ." Nathan braced himself. "Regrettable. Most regrettable."

"Indeed, sir." Nathan composed his features into a suitable expression of gravity.

"You know who he is, of course."

"I was informed by his lieutenant, after the event, that he is cousin to the Comte de Puisaye."

"Quite. And held in considerable regard by the count and his circle."

Nathan chose his words with care. "I acted upon the spur of the moment, sir, with a pistol to my head, so to speak."

The commodore raised his brow. "I understood, from your own report, that the pistol was held to the head of the Chevalier de Batz."

Nathan flushed. "It was a figure of speech, sir. However, he ordered his men to fire upon us—and I took such action as I deemed to be necessary at the time."

"Indeed? You are quite sure he meant to launch an attack upon you and your men? Not upon the Republicans?"

"That was the impression I formed, sir. But even had he meant the Republicans, they were prisoners, in my charge. The officer had given me his sword."

The commodore glanced at Finch to ascertain if he had any opinion on the matter. He did not.

"In the heat of battle, Captain Peake, could it not have been that the chevalier considered they were still a danger to his men, and indeed to yours?"

. "I do not believe that was in his mind, sir."

A heavy sigh. "Well, it is most unfortunate. There have been enough problems with our allies without this." The sound of the ship's bell recalled him to his other considerations. "I propose you send the chevalier over to the flagship and we will accommodate him here until such time as we can arrange a full enquiry into the matter."

Nathan kept his expression carefully blank but this was not what he had wanted to hear. A full enquiry—in the wake of what looked like being one of the worst disasters to befall the Navy since Byng lost Minorca. And Byng had faced a British firing squad.

"Will that be all, sir?"

"Yes, Captain, and let us hope you can render such assistance to the Comte de Puisaye as to make him feel obliged to you."

It took Nathan the best part of an hour to assemble his scattered flotilla, and another to cover the short distance to Penthièvre for there was a very real danger they would be carried on to the shore at Carnac. He was obliged to lead them well out to sea and then come about and stand on the wind, close-hauled on the starboard tack under double-reefed topsails. Now they stood about a mile out from the shore, the *Unicorn* hove to with her main topsail to the mast and the gunboats working closer to shore with their sweeps, though he very much doubted if they could achieve much with the kind of sea that was running. The *Conquest* in particular was making such heavy weather of it, he did not think she would be able to open her gunports, much less fire her broadside. Which was probably just as well for she was rolling so badly the shot could go anywhere. The beach here was strangely empty after the crowds they had seen further along the peninsula. A beach of startlingly white sand, even under the cloudy sky, but while he was looking, hundreds of ragged, scuttling figures emerged from the dunes and ran toward the water's edge, stretching out their hands imploringly.

Nathan sought out Tully on the weather rail to express his anguish: "How in God's name are we to provide support with that lot in the line of fire? And support what? Where are the Royalist lines; can *you* see them? For I am sure I cannot."

Tully was unable to enlighten him and Nathan went aloft in the hope of a better view but even braced against the topmast shrouds it was impossible to hold the glass steady enough for any detailed observation. He could see the fort plainly enough with his naked eye, a little over a mile to the north-west, but the Royalist lines the commodore had sketched so confidently on the map aboard the *Pomone* were nowhere to be seen. If they were there at all, they were well hidden among the dunes.

He wondered if it were possible to bring the frigate any closer to the shore. The wind had slackened somewhat and there was still a depth of water under her keel, but he was wary of performing what would necessarily be a complicated manoeuvre so close to the guns of Penthièvre, especially with Graham as his sailing master.

He looked again at the people on the beach.

"God help them," he murmured under his breath, though there was none to hear him. It was scarcely a prayer. He had lost what little faith he had in Paris during the time of the Terror. And yet he was shaken by this fresh evidence, to his mind, of the sheer randomness of fate that could cast so many defenceless people adrift, abandoned to the tide of war and politics. Did they believe their God would save them? God or Virgin or whatever Papist saints they prayed to in their churches and at their roadside shrines? Did they believe the Bishop of Rome would intercede for them with his prayers?

And yet for all of that, for all his scepticism and his deeply ingrained pessimism, he still needed to believe there was a greater power than his own puny endeavours, a benign presence to ward off the evil eye, even if you called it luck.

He was a man much inclined to Order—a student of astronomy who found comfort in the slightest evidence of some pattern to the universe and in the supposition that the planets moved according to certain rules and regulations, that all was not Chaos, as it so often appeared on Earth. He could not entirely dismiss the idea that behind this Order there was a force for good: call it God, or the Supreme Being, as Robespierre had, or something else, something no-one had yet discovered in the configuration of the planets. The Great Regulator. The Supreme Clockmaker (the divine twin of Mr. Harrison who had invented the marine chronometer, perhaps; it was a comforting image). He was perfectly aware that this belief—or whimsy, for it could not be compared to faith—was sustained in part by the terrible fear that there was nothing there. Nothing and no-one. That no amount of appeals to an unknown deity would make the slightest difference to the course of events, wherever they occurred.

Nathan had been led by his interest in astronomy to the work of a certain Persian astronomer, poet and mathematician called Omar Khayyam, translated by the English scholar Thomas Hyde who had travelled much in the East during the last century. Nathan had been much struck by a line of verse he had found in Hyde's translations:

> *The moving finger writes and having writ*
> *moves on: nor all your piety nor wit*
> *shall lure it back to cancel half a line;*
> *nor all your tears wash out a word of it.*

But if this was truth, need it be so cold? He longed for a more comforting philosophy, clung to the hope that the moving finger might pause a moment in its endless scribing and the divine hand soar from on high to pluck a single individual from the damned. Or in this case, the doomed horde that clung to the beaches of Quiberon like so many barnacles upon a rock. For surely Sara had not been saved from the guillotine only to die here on this wretched lump of rock and sand, while he looked helplessly on from his lofty perch.

He recalled another verse from a hymn often sung at his father's request at the family church in Windover. One of Cowper's, in fact, that reflected a more phlegmatic English philosophy than that of the Asian astronomer.

> *God moves in a mysterious way,*
> *His wonders to perform;*
> *He plants His footsteps in the sea,*
> *And rides upon the storm.*

He could see his father belting it out now, with more heart than harmony, knowing full well that for all his professed piety, when it came to storms at sea the old admiral had more faith in preventer stays than prayer, though he might try both at a pinch. And Cowper, he had heard, had been torn all his life by doubt and pessimism.

He came down from the mast and sent for Bennett who came staggering aft, too long ashore to have found his sea legs yet, though his complexion was ruddy enough. Nathan took him in the shelter of one of the tarpaulins stretched in the weather rigging to provide a little respite from the wind. He still had to raise his voice but was spared the effort of shouting in his ear, which was as well for some diplomacy was required.

"I have been ordered to set your Chouans ashore," he told him.

A diplomat might have put it better. Certainly it did not go down well with the man from Nantucket. His complexion grew a deal more flushed and his voice more heated.

"You might as well toss them overboard," he observed bitterly.

"The commodore is of the opinion that they may be of more use ashore," Nathan pointed out coldly. "Helping defend the women and children trapped upon Quiberon."

"Though the commodore is not himself able to defend them."

These were Nathan's sentiments precisely but they could not be expressed by a mere seaman.

"Bennett, if you cannot curb your tongue, we will have to see what a gag may achieve."

"I am sorry if it was impertinent, sir, but what would it achieve to send more men to their deaths?"

"It may not come to that, if Puisaye can hold the line."

Bennett regarded him evenly. "With your permission, sir, I would go with them."

"Nonsense. You will return to your duties."

"Sir, I am their leader, since you deprived them of de Batz. And, with respect, I fought at their side for over a year. They have risked their lives for me. How can I not go with them?"

"Bennett, you are not one of them. This is not your fight."

"It is as much my fight as any man's that is not French. And they trust me. They would fight better if I was with them. And what use am I to you here?"

Nathan wavered.

"Set me ashore with them." Bennett's eyes grew shrewd. "I will find La Renarde for you. And I swear to God, I will do my best to get her out of it."

Nathan stared at him, torn by conflicting emotions. His first passion was outrage, with some embarrassment that he had revealed more of his interest in the matter of La Renarde than he would have wished. But then, inspired perhaps by the confused theology of his lonely sojourn in the top, he recalled that line of Cowper's. Benjamin Bennett seemed an unlikely godsend but, as he had so clearly indicated, he was precious little use as anything else.

"Very well, Bennett. I will put you ashore with them. But you will wear a proper uniform so that we may pick you out of the crowd and take you off the beaches if it should come to that. And it may save you from a hanging if you are taken prisoner by the French."

Bennett frowned. "A proper uniform?"

"I mean a red coat. We have a stack of them in the hold to distribute to the Chouans. You may select your own rank, though you will have to apply to another authority for the pay," he added hastily.

"I am sorry, sir, to give offence, but I cannot wear a red coat."

Now Nathan, too, was frowning. "On what grounds?"

"I'd as soon not go into that, sir."

"For God's sake, Bennett, you wear the King's uniform."

"Even so, sir, it is not a red coat," he insisted doggedly. "My father would never forgive me."

Nathan shook his head. "Get out of my sight," he told him, "before I change my mind."

But Bennett had put another thought in his head and he was not to be shaken from it, not even by Tully's worried look when Nathan told him he was going ashore. It was his duty, he insisted, to ensure that the Comte de Puisaye had a proper line of defence before sending other men to join the chaos on the beaches.

He took Bennett, Whitely and six marines.

"Maintain your position as best you can," he instructed Tully, casting a guilty eye aloft. "And it might be as well to rig the fore topmast staysail when the tide turns to keep the head offshore. Though I should be back well before that." He was fussing unnecessarily, as Tully must surely be aware: the symptom of a troubled conscience for quitting the ship so close to a hostile shore but it was a virulent affliction and he could not help himself from glancing over towards the gunboats and adding: "And signal Mr. Balfour to give as close support as he is able."

He was to regret those words later, as much as any words he had spoken in his life, but they seemed insignificant at the time and his mind had already shifted to the practical problems of getting ashore.

He directed his coxswain to land as near to the fort as they dared, for the beach was quite deserted at this point and he trusted that the combination of spray from the breakers and blinding rain would sufficiently dissuade the gunners from trying their luck with a long shot. In this at least his faith was not misplaced and they landed without incident, though thoroughly soaked by the surf and with some misgivings that they would invite a sortie from the fort, for it looked a great deal further to the dunes than it had from the main-top of the *Unicorn*.

Nathan took Bennett and Whiteley with him, and the six marines, instructing Young to cast off if they came under fire and pick them up further down the shore. Then they ran for the dunes.

They were a little under halfway when a distant report indicated that they had tested the restraint of the gunners beyond endurance. The first shot ploughed into the sand some twenty or thirty yards ahead of them. The second was closer. Nathan shouted for the men to spread out to present less of a target but it seemed to him that the gunners then concentrated their fire upon him, which was as un-fair as it was unnerving. One ball hit the sand almost at his heels and he swore he felt the wind of another pass his head. He was not amused to note that a number of figures—Royalists, judging from their uniform—had appeared on the dunes ahead and a little to his left and appeared to be urging him on with broad grins and shouts of approval. Nevertheless he changed direction towards them and man-aged to reach shelter with nothing more serious to regret than the loss of his dignity.

The gleeful spectators turned out to be the extreme flank of de Puisaye's elusive lines which were scattered among the sand dunes to the west. They were in better spirits than Nathan had antici-pated, though they became somewhat less cheerful when he ex-plained that he had come to reinforce, rather than evacuate them. They had clearly been fortified by a quantity of wine—there were several empty bottles in the sand—and they had two small field pieces loaded with grape and rigged up under an awning to cover the beach. Which might have some effect, Nathan reflected, if they were sober enough to fire it and Hoche threw less than a dozen men against them.

They appeared to be under the command of a sergeant whose long moustaches were more impressive than his grasp of the military situation. Certainly he appeared to have no clear idea where his headquarters were situated, but after some discussion with his men he suggested that General de Puisaye might be found at the small chapel of Lotivy, whose crooked spire could be seen a few hundred yards further along the promontory. Nathan was about to lead his entourage off in that direction when Whiteley called urgently down to him from the top of one of the dunes. Nathan went up at a run and threw himself down amidst the swaying stalks of sea grass.

It was clear at once what had attracted Whiteley's attention. Advancing along the shore from the direction of the mainland was a long column of infantry.

CHAPTER SEVEN

the White Sands

NATHAN TRAINED HIS GLASS on the head of the advancing column. It was led by a single officer on a white horse but there was something odd about the rider's bearing. His shoulders were slumped, as if in the last stages of exhaustion, and the horse appeared to be led by a man on foot. Indeed, as Nathan moved the glass along the line, he found more anomalies. The slumped shoulders were fairly universal and many of the men appeared to be walking wounded. Head bandages were not uncommon and a number of men were being helped along by their companions. It looked more like an army in hopeless retreat than one embarking upon an attack.

Bennett threw himself down in the grass beside him and Nathan handed him the glass. He took one brief look and said, "It's Charette."

"The man on the white horse?"

"No. The man leading it. Charette and the remains of his army." He returned the glass with a bitter look. They were closer now and Nathan could see women and children marching among the men. They were almost level with the fort but the guns remained silent. Why did they not fire? Was it because of the nature of the target? It seemed unlikely, given the history of this brutal conflict, unless the Republicans were happy to add to the chaos on the beaches.

"Look to the rear!" Whiteley was staring through his own glass. "Coming up behind them."

Nathan looked and saw the long tailback of blue coats and the steely glint of bayonets. Republican infantry. Marching in a long, steady line at the rear of the retreating Chouans.

"They are using them as a shield!" he exclaimed. He looked searchingly at Bennett. "Does Charette not know they are there?"

The American shook his head, more in perplexity than denial. Nathan took up his glass again and studied the figure at the head of the column. He was much closer now and Nathan saw that he was staring straight ahead with what might be determination or indifference. And then with a shock he saw that the figure on the pony was a woman. Could she be Sara? She was slumped over the pony's neck and at this distance it was impossible to tell.

Nathan ran down the slope of the dune and found the sergeant commanding the battery. He was befuddled with drink and seemed to have difficulty in understanding what Nathan was trying to tell him. Finally Nathan dragged him bodily up the dune and made him look through the glass. He frowned in bemusement.

"Chouans," he said with a shrug. Nathan realised he must have seen thousands of them in the last few days, making their way on to the peninsula along the white sands.

"For God's sake, man, look behind them!" Nathan snatched back the glass and sighted it on the marching column of Blues, though you could see them now with the naked eye. He thrust it back. "Look there, to the rear. You must alert your commanders."

"I will do it," said Bennett—and before Nathan could stop him he was gone, off in a shambling run across the dunes toward the distant chapel.

"Bennett!" Nathan called after him but it was futile, his voice lost in the wind and he doubted the man would have heeded him anyway.

Nathan grabbed the sergeant by the arm, squeezing so hard he cried out in pain. "You must wait until the Chouans have passed before you open fire," he insisted. "Do you understand me?"

The man nodded but there was no comprehension in his eyes. Nathan shoved him back towards the guns and he lost his footing and rolled down the slope.

"There's more," Whiteley sang out, the glass still to his eye, and Nathan saw another long line of men marching out from the fort to join the back of the line. It was hard to calculate how many there were but he would not have said much less than five hundred. Quite enough to turn the Royalist lines if they were not stopped. He looked out to sea. Had Tully seen what was happening? Even if he had, he could do little about it at that range and with so many women and children in his line of fire. But the *Conquest* and the three smaller gunboats had come in close under their sweeps. And Balfour had his gunports open and the guns run out.

Nathan was filled with a sudden apprehension.

"He cannot mean . . ." he began tentatively. The answer came upon the instant. The starboard side of the brig erupted in a voluminous cloud of black smoke shot through with flame and the rippling thunder of her 18-pounders rolled back to him across the water as she discharged her entire broadside into the column of refugees.

For a moment Nathan stared as if stricken toward the murderous pall of smoke, swiftly shredded by the wind to reveal the little brig and the still smouldering row of black holes where her guns had been, before the recoil carried them back across her deck. Then his head whipped round to view the devastation she must have wrought upon that crowded shore. At first, it seemed there was none. The ragged column came marching on much as before and he dared hope the heavy seas had confused the gunners' aim or by some greater miracle they had found their true target among the Republican infantry. But then his eye travelled on toward the rear and he saw the terrible gaps torn in the Chouan ranks. And now the smaller gunboats were firing with the heavy 32-pounder carronades mounted in the bows: firing at musket range towards the rear of the column but with such wild imprecision they must have taken out at least as many women and children as the blue-coated infantry in their wake. They were firing grape, and from Nathan's vantage on top of the dune he could see the hideous damage it had inflicted, the tight-packed mass of lead spreading out over the distance to cut great swathes in its human target. There were at least a score of corpses scattered along the beach; others sitting wailing in the bloodied sand or dragging their shattered bodies away from the murdering sea. He saw mothers cradling the mangled remains of their children or standing shocked, their mouths forming a soundless scream as they viewed the horrors at their feet. And now the *Conquest* was coming round to expose her larboard broadside.

Nathan stood at the top of the dune, furiously waving his hat and yelling at the top of his voice for them to cease fire, but they could not possibly have heard him and if they saw him they took his wild capering for encouragement. Down she went in the trough, rolling so wildly he thought she must be swamped through the open ports, and then as she came up she fired, each gun within a half-second of her neighbour and another lethal hail of grape swept the beaches.

All but the head of the Chouan column now broke and scattered, running for the shelter of the dunes. This at least had the effect of isolating the Republican guards who came under fire from the gunboats. It also exposed the full extent of the carnage on the shore and Nathan sank to his knees as the enormity of the atrocity became apparent.

"Oh my God, oh dear God, oh dear God." He heard Whiteley's voice beside him, saw his shocked expression. "How can he have done that? How can he have done that?"

"Christ knows," said Nathan bitterly. He felt sure Balfour had intended to target the infantry but he must surely have known the risk he was taking in such a sea. Then in his numbed skull he heard the echo of his last command before he had left the *Unicorn*.

"Signal Mr. Balfour to give as close support as he is able."

Could those ill-considered words have contributed to the tragedy? Had Balfour felt pressured to take a greater risk than he would otherwise have contemplated?

At the very least Nathan felt certain they must have encouraged him to come much closer inshore than he would have dared if left to his own cautious devices.

The head of the Chouan column had halted and faced about, scattering across the beach as they deployed to face the enemy in their rear: all but the woman on the white horse who was riding at a gallop towards the *Conquest*, sitting upright in the saddle, her hair streaming out behind her like some pagan goddess as if she meant to ride across the waves to deliver some divine retribution. Nathan watched in astonishment as she rode straight into the surf, the horse rearing and plunging in the white breakers, and he saw her raise her arm and the flash of an explosion as she fired a pistol toward the brig, and in that gesture of defiance, in the wild dark hair flowing out behind her, he saw Sara.

He turned to Whiteley. "Take your men to the launch," he uttered hoarsely, "and wait for me there."

Then he was gone in an awkward stiff-legged run down the side of the dune towards the beach. He heard Whiteley calling after him but he was beyond reason or recall, intent only on reaching that distant figure on the white horse. He began to sprint in a diagonal line across the shore and as he ran he saw that her former escort was rallying the front rank of the Chouans, directing their fire at the Republican troops as they advanced. So, too, were the gunboats, though from his lower vantage Nathan could not see what effect they were having. And then the guns of the fort joined in and he saw the shot smash into the ranks of the Chouans; or rather the effect it had, hurling bodies this way and that. At least two shots ploughed into the sand in front of him but he ran on, regardless. Then a large wave broke over horse and rider and they both went under and only the horse came up, struggling through the white surf toward the shore and Nathan cried out her name, just once, before the cannon on the fort fired a second volley and he saw and felt no more.

PART TWO: THE COURTESANS

CHAPTER EIGHT

Hard Times

LADY CATHERINE PEAKE CROUCHED at the first floor window of her house on Soho Square and watched the two bailiffs retreating in the direction of Seven Dials, their loathsome hound at their heels.

On reflection, she decided that "retreating" was possibly an over-optimistic assumption: their swaggering, if somewhat bandy-legged, progress across the square suggesting rather a brief retirement to the nearest tavern before resuming the assault. Even the beast walked with a swagger, observed Lady Catherine, who was not a dog lover and reserved a particular dislike for the breed of bull terrier which it most resembled, though she was inclined from pure prejudice to doubt its legitimacy.

She felt a rare moment of despair. So it was come to this. A society beauty, a woman of substance, courted in her time by the rich and powerful, a noted feminist and champion of the oppressed, cowering on the floor of a rented house in Soho—which like herself had seen better days—for fear of the bailiffs.

Although she was still counted a beauty and prided herself that most of her acquaintance, even her intimates, would have been astonished to know she was much over forty, Lady Catherine was in fact fast approaching her half century and the future appeared bleak.

She made a brief but depressing tally of her current circumstances. She was estranged from her husband, her only son Nathan was in the navy and had not been heard of, at least by his mother, for several months, her once considerable fortune was buried in the ruins of her bank, her family in America was unable or unwilling to help her out—and the enemy was at the gates.

A tentative knock announced the arrival of reinforcements in the form of her companion and lodger, Mrs. Imlay—or rather the head and upper torso of this lady which were inserted into the small gap she had opened between door and frame, her normally handsome features contorted into an anxious frown.

"Have they gone?" she hissed, her eyes searching the room for evidence of the intruders, as if they might even now be concealed behind the Oriental settle before bearing it off to the debtor's prison, and all who sat upon it.

"They have gone," Lady Catherine assured her with a sigh. "Izzy has seen them off, for the time being. I believe it was in the nature of a 'softening up,' though it will take more than a couple of bully boys and a bulldog to discompose The Mountain . . ." Here referring to her maid who was built on the grand scale . . . "Unhappily I am made of less robust material and need to be fortified with a drink. Come and join me."

The newcomer advanced wholly into the room, revealing the winsome, if fractious figure of a young child carried upon her hip.

"Oh, Kitty, do not be dismayed," she ventured, "for you are a tower of strength to us all, and if you are to succumb to the vicissitudes of fortune, what will become of the rest of us?"

The child echoed this sentiment with a whimper.

"Oh for God's sake, Mary," Kitty replied with some heat, "you are far more able to withstand the 'vicissitudes of fortune' than I or anyone else of my acquaintance, and if there were the slightest danger that you would not, I am persuaded the Corresponding Societies would get up a petition to Parliament."

She regretted this outburst immediately, though the woman who now joined her at the window was singularly capable of exciting as much irritation as sympathy, or indeed admiration, in Kitty's volatile breast. Mary Imlay, née Wollstonecraft, was one of her oldest and most esteemed friends, whose book on the Rights of Women had raised her to the status of goddess in the progressive circles to which they were both attached, though more recent experiences had diminished her to a more human condition.

Kitty grimaced in the direction of the child. "Hello, Fanny," she ventured, with as much warmth as she could muster. The child answered with a sob and buried her face in her mother's shoulder, which, considering the amount of mucus that had lodged between her nose and upper lip, was probably not the best place for it. On the whole Kitty preferred small children to bulldogs but it was a close run thing. "Would you like a sweetmeat?" she enquired politely, recalling that they had a weakness for such delicacies. "You will find a bowl on the sideboard, I believe," she instructed its mother. "And also a bottle of gin unless Izzy has used it to unblock the drains. Pour two large glasses and let us drown our sorrows together. Fanny may play upon the floor," she added generously.

"Gin? Do you think we should?" her friend enquired with a resurrection of the worried frown, which had never entirely been laid to rest.

"What are your principle objections?" Kitty enquired dangerously.

"Oh, I did not mean to sound a prig but it is a bit early in the afternoon and people say it is bad for the com . . . com . . ." She caught her friend's eye. "Constitution," she finished lamely.

Kitty regarded her sorrowfully. This was the woman widely regarded by the Enlightened as the Inspiration of her Sex. "Oh for God's sake, Mary, we all know it is the ruin of expectant mothers and I doubt it would do a virgin much good if she splashed it about too freely but 'tis a bit late for you to worry about that on either score and there are worse things for the complexion, or 'constitution' as you care to put it: poverty and a visit from the bailiffs being one . . . or two. But if you are that bothered, suck on a sugared fruit and I'll take my chances with the gin."

Another knock came upon the door and a less comely counte-nance was thrust into the gap so recently vacated.

"Oh, Izzy," beamed Kitty. "Well done. A glorious victory—or hold-ing action, as I suppose we must call it. We were just about to hit the bottle, or at least I was. Will you join us?"

"Thank you, milady, but I won't, thank you very much, and nor should you this early in the afternoon, if you don't mind me say-ing so," announced this paragon with a fierce glance in the direc-tion of the sideboard as if it were personally at fault and would go the way of the rest of the furniture if it did not embark on a course of self-improvement.

"My goodness, what a pair of harridans!" exclaimed her mistress. "Goneril and Regan ain't in it. What time is it anyway?" She looked to the mantelpiece but the carriage clock had suffered in the general drive for economy and the single pewter candlestick provided no in-telligence on the subject.

"Time I was off to Berwick Street if I am to get the dinner in for I doubt your ladyship would thank me if I was to serve up chitlins, which is all that's in the larder at present, an' some mouldy cheese that I was saving for a rattrap. 'Specially if we have got company, which I expect we have and you forgot to tell me about."

Kitty regarded her thoughtfully. There had been a time when she had maintained a household of servants and not one of them would have addressed her in such a fashion, though she usually found it more of a diversion than not, there being little to rival it at present in the way of entertainment.

"Dear me, have we sunk so low?" she murmured. "Well, we have not 'got company,' so far as I know, more's the pity, but let us not deprive the rats of their cheese, I beg of you, and though I confess I am wholly ignorant as to the nature of 'chitlins' they do not sound at all appetis-ing. So let us 'eat ice and drink wine and be above vulgar economy,' as the Epicureans would say. And be damned to the consequence."

"And what am I to use for money?" demanded this amiable

servant, who occupied the role of housekeeper, cook and general fac-
totum in the much-reduced household, her considerable bulk and
proficiency going some way to compensate for the lack of numbers,
though her nickname—The Mountain—was derived less from her
proportions, which Kitty would have considered impolite, and more
in homage to La Montagne: the radical wing of the French National
Convention at the time of the Terror.

"Money?" Her employer appeared taken aback for a moment but
she quickly rallied. "Why, tell them you will pay them at the end of
the month," she suggested. "Is not that the way it is usually done?"

"And have them laugh in my face. This is Soho, milady. They don't
hold with credit round these parts. And I doubt I'd have much joy in
St James's neither, the way things is going," she added darkly, "'less
they take me for a harlot."

Kitty regarded her askance. "My dear Izzy, I do not suppose the
residents of St James's would take you for any such creature. I am
persuaded you are thinking of Haymarket. However, we shall not
put it to the test. Mary, my dear, lend us a shilling 'til the end of the
week, will you? So dearest Izzy may replenish the larder."

This with one of her brilliant smiles at "dearest Izzy" who responded with an even deeper scowl. "And how far do you think that
will go?" she demanded. "You know how much a standard loaf costs
these days?" Kitty shook her head wonderingly. "Three shillings and
thrippence. And if this war goes on much longer we'll be eating ur-
chins off the streets, like the Frenchies."

"I will go and get my purse," Mrs. Imlay assured her hastily, practically running from the room but returning immediately to scoop up
the child who had begun to howl alarmingly.

"Thank you, Mary," said Kitty when she returned and the servant
had departed on her mission with three silver half-crowns that she
said would *do to be going on with.* "I will pay you back as soon as I
have the money from Christie's. That should clear most of my debts,
though after that I fear I shall have to take in washing for we have
nothing else to sell."

She spoke lightly though she was more distressed by her present financial state than she was prepared to reveal in the face she presented to the public or even her closest friends. While her political views were widely regarded as radical, even Revolutionist, she had always lived in some style. Her family were Huguenots: French Protestants who had settled in New York and prospered there, largely in the shipping trade. As an only daughter she had been greatly indulged. Indeed, despite the failure of her marriage to an English naval officer, she had been sustained by the family wealth until almost a year ago, maintaining a large house in St James's and entertaining lavishly, but the collapse of her bank and other losses occasioned by the present war had caused a considerable reduction in her circumstance.

"Well, you still have a husband," her companion reminded her unwisely, "and a loyal, loving family that will support you."

"They have enough problems with the war," replied Kitty sharply. "And I would never ask Michael for money. Please do not look at me like that; it is not from pride, I do assure you." She considered. "Though it is possible shame comes into it somewhere. Besides he hasn't got any. None to spare, at any rate."

"Would you not consider living with him again?"

"What? In Sussex? With all those sheep? I'd rather cut my throat. In any case, I doubt he would have me." She paused for a moment and then added in a different voice. "I have not told anyone this, Mary, and I count on your discretion, but he is contemplating a divorce."

Her friend's eyes widened appreciably. "He told you that?"

"Not in so many words but I know it is in his mind."

"But, why?"

"Oh you are so kind, Mary. I positively blush."

"I do not mean that he would find it possible to live with you."

"Ah. Not so kind."

"I mean you already live apart. Why should he wish to contrive a divorce?"

"Because he may wish to remarry."

"Oh. And is that possible?"

"Well, it takes an Act of Parliament in England, I am told, which is an expensive procedure and causes a great scandal, as you might imagine, for the only grounds, other than consanguinity and attempted murder, appear to be the wife's adultery—male infidelity being considered perfectly acceptable from the legal point of view."

"But can adultery be proven?" Mary flushed deeply when she realised what she had said. "I mean, generally speaking."

Kitty regarded her friend archly. " *'Generally speaking,'* it is not beyond contrivance, if the husband has the means to purchase a good team of lawyers and a handful of plausible witnesses. Of course, the servants are always a good source of information on that score. I think I may rely on Izzy but there are others who might be tempted by the prospect of remuneration and a brief period of celebrity, for the proceedings are widely reported, I am assured."

"But that is despicable—and is there no other way?"

"Well, now I come to think of it I believe the wife can make a counter-claim of impotence. Of course, there being no other way of providing evidence, the husband would have to agree this to be the case and most men would rather have their tongues cut out or have hot coals applied to their private parts. However, there are precedents. A husband may, for instance, without the least dishonour, agree that he is impotent where his wife is concerned, but not with his mistress, or any other creature."

"Oh, Kitty. What vipers they are." The colour went from her face save for two small red spots high on her cheeks. She shuddered. "Is there no limit to the pain they will cause in the pursuit of their unbridled lusts?"

"Well, I am not sure lusts come into it, unbridled or otherwise, though I could be mistaken. The lady he has in mind comes with a not inconsiderable fortune attached. And he needs the money. For his sheep."

"Oh, that is all right, then. Dear God. Was there ever such a race of money-grubbing cowards and philanderers? Does Nathan know aught of this?"

Kitty grew more sombre for she had not seen her son in almost a year and had heard from him only fleetingly by letter. She was in constant fear of a message from the Admiralty informing her of his demise off some distant shore.

"I have no idea," she replied shortly. "But I expect he would not wish to take sides."

"Well, at least you do not have to support him as well as yourself," said Mary, glancing at her own child who was sucking at the tassels of the curtain for want of better nourishment. "And you still have your pride intact. Which is more than I can say."

"Oh Mary. What have you to be ashamed of? It is not your fault that . . . that . . ."

"That I married a scoundrel. A liar and a cheat. A mountebank. If, indeed, I did marry him for he now tells me it was not a proper ceremony at all but only a ruse to mislead the French authorities. And I have no more legitimacy than a mistress. An abandoned mistress at that."

"Oh, Mary, I am so sorry, I should never have mentioned it. Why did I? Only a moment ago we were talking about chitlins. What are chitlins, anyway, do you know?"

"Pig's entrails," Mary informed her wisely. "I had them as a child when we lived on the farm in Wales and had nothing else to eat."

"Oh." Kitty looked faint. "I have led such a sheltered life."

"You do not know the half of it. I thought then that I could never sink so low. And yet I tell you, Kitty, I was happier then than I am now."

"Oh, how can you say that, Mary, after all you have achieved?"

But this did nothing to cheer her. Indeed, she looked as desolate as Kitty had ever seen her.

"I have let myself down. I have let my friends down. I am so ashamed. I often wish I were dead."

Kitty regarded her worriedly but before she could compose a reply they heard the sound of the front doorbell.

"Oh God, are they back already?" She moved hastily away from the window.

"It is probably Izzy come back from the market," Mary answered dully. "I will go and let her in."

"No. It is too early. Besides she would not ring upon the front door." Kitty peered cautiously over the windowsill. And then she was running across the room and down the stairs leaving the trace of a scream in her wake and the baby's frightened howl lagging behind it.

CHAPTER NINE

the Fallen Woman

NATHAN SUCCUMBED TO THE INDIGNITY of having his chin grasped firmly in his mother's hand and twisted violently to the left so she could the better examine the livid gash above his right ear with the marks of McLeish's neat stitches still clearly visible in the shaven patch of scalp.

"It was a glancing blow," he assured her. "A spent round. Looks far worse than it is. The hair will grow over it in no time."

Nathan's account of his experiences on the shores of Quiberon was, of necessity, circumspect. His mother could, at times, be discreet but it would be unwise to count on it and she kept notoriously bad company.

"But what on earth were you doing on a beach in France?" she demanded indignantly. "Do you not know we are at war?"

Not for the first time in his life Nathan was rendered dumb by a logic that had confounded older and wiser minds than his own.

"You could have been killed," she admonished him, letting him have his chin back.

"Unhappily the government do not seem to be aware of this possibility," Nathan admitted. "Or else are indifferent to it. However, I was merely stunned and one of my officers insisted upon having me carried back to the ship."

"Then he showed more sense than you did," she informed him with a reproving slap upon the wrist. He reflected that if any of his officers or crew could have witnessed this iniquity he should have had to seek alternative employment. Fortunately they were alone. "So have they sent you home to convalesce?"

"What—for a scratch upon the head? That would be a fine thing. No, I am obliged to attend a meeting at the Admiralty."

"Why? Are you in disgrace, my pet?"

"Good God, Mother, you always look on the dark side. Why should I be in disgrace?" But he was sharply reminded that for all Lady Catherine's avowed naivety on certain subjects—naval and agricultural in particular—she had an unnerving way of divining the truth of the matter: the summons from the Admiralty being couched in a form that left him under no illusion that he was called to account for his several misdemeanours.

She regarded him shrewdly. "Well, I am sure I cannot tell what mischief you get up to when you are off on your adventures but I know from your manner—and the way you are slumped with that hangdog look about you—that there is something amiss. However, if you do not wish to tell me, so be it."

"Mother, I have just travelled up from Portsmouth in a rackety old chaise. I am sorry if I appear 'slumped.' I suspect it is because my arse is a few inches closer to my head than when we started out."

Her lips twitched. "Well, it is beyond wonderful, you vulgar specimen. I suppose I had better fetch you some refreshment. Would you like a gin?"

"No, I would not like a gin. When did you take to dispensing gin? I hope you are not drinking it," he added sternly. "It does no favours to the complexion, you know."

"So I have been informed."

"And what has happened to the servants?" He looked about him as if they might spring like genies from a bottle. Of gin, no doubt. "Where is Phipps?"

"I had to let Phipps go, and most of the others, for reasons of economy. There is just Izzy and she has gone to the market so we may have something to eat apart from chitlins."

Nathan stared at his mother in astonishment but resolved not to pursue the matter. He looked about him once more, this time more appraisingly.

"And I take it this is the reason you are living in Soho. For reasons of economy."

"Oh no, I just took a fancy to the area," she replied airily. "It is far more interesting than St James's, you know, with all the French that are living here. The pastry shops are quite wonderful and there is even a Huguenot church across the way, did you notice? I only have to walk there on Sundays and may leave the carriage in the mews."

"Well, I am glad you are making light of it," he assured her huffily.

"And what would you have me do—throw myself off London Bridge?"

"Is it really as bad as that?"

"Of course not. My goodness, if you think this is poverty, my lad, you need to look about you. It is not the rookeries, you know."

"Mother, a year ago you would not have known what the rookeries were, or chitlins."

"Nonsense. How dare you! I have always taken the liveliest interest in social conditions, as you very well know. A great deal more than you have, I might add."

He raised his hands in surrender. "All I am saying is that it must have been a great . . . *challenge* to you to make the . . . the *adjustments* that, that . . ." He gave up digging the hole. His mother's house in St James's had been one of the social landmarks of London and her salon quite notorious as the haunt of half the dissidents and degenerates in Europe. Even the Prince of Wales had been there. "And do you see many of your former friends?" he added lamely.

"If you mean am I abandoned by society, let me assure you that I do not lack for company and those that no longer count me a friend are not missed."

"I am sure there is no reason for you to fly into a temper," he soothed her. "I was merely enquiring after your welfare." He looked up at the ceiling. "And do you live here alone?"

This question, too, was loaded. There had sometimes been a gentleman in residence at the house in St James's and not always the same one.

"I do have one companion," she informed him, with a look that put him immediately upon his guard. He made a swift inventory of the most disreputable among his mother's acquaintance. "Her name is Mrs. Imlay, but you knew her as Mary Wollstonecraft."

Nathan was taken aback, for this was the last name he would have imagined. "Mary Wollstonecraft?" he repeated stupidly.

"Yes. You remember? The author of *A Vindication of the Rights of Women,* which you so much enjoyed reading."

"I know who you mean. But what is she doing in London?"

"Why should she not be in London? It is as much her home as anywhere, I believe."

"But, I had thought she was in France. At least . . ."

"She *was* in France and now she is in London."

Nathan was considerably agitated by this information, for he had known Mrs. Imlay in Paris during the Terror and was by no means sure he could count on her discretion, especially with his mother, whose methods of interrogation, though subtle, would have put the Spanish Inquisition to shame.

"And why is she staying with you?" he enquired with a frown.

"Why, where else should she stay in London? We were close friends when she was last here and corresponded even when she was in France, as you know, for I forwarded one of her letters to you. Concerning a mutual friend," she added slyly.

"Yes," he replied sharply. "Thank you for that."

"I suppose it is useless for me to ask how you became acquainted with the Countess of Turenne?"

"Quite useless," he assured her coolly, relieved to know that she had not already learned it from Mary.

"And was the rumour true, that she had escaped the guillotine?"

"I have no means of knowing. As you have explained, we are at war."

Her look was very like that of a cat contemplating a mouse that is altogether too assured for its own comfort. "So that was not why you were on a beach in France?"

"You have a very disconcerting way of putting two and two together and making five," he observed.

"Yes, and you know something? In the world of politics, of which you are not as ignorant as you would have me believe, five is very often the right number."

Finding himself unable to respond to this gibe as cleverly as he might have wished, Nathan contented himself with a shrug and the remark that there were some things she was better off not knowing.

"But that is exactly what the government thinks," she declared in mock surprise. "In fact, it might almost have come directly from one of their spokesmen in the *Morning Post*. If you should tire of the Navy, my dear, or they of you, I am assured you would find employment in the Ministry of Misinformation."

He regarded her warily. "Do they continue to trouble you?"

"Who?"

"The government. Or their agents. When I was last home you said they had you under surveillance and were making life difficult for your friends."

"Which you did not believe."

"I thought you might be exaggerating a little."

"Ha. There are none so blind as those that will not see. However, even you, child, must be aware of the measures taken by the government to suppress dissent. And they have grown far worse of late, with the war going so badly for them."

"Is the war going so badly? I had not realised. The last I heard was that we had won a great victory in the Bay of Quiberon."

"Pah. When only three French ships were took? I do not call that a great victory, whatever the government would make of it. But the expedition itself has been a disaster. Even their own hacks cannot disguise it. Surely you are aware of that." She fixed him again with her cat's eyes and he was assured she knew perfectly well that the beach he had been on was at Quiberon. "And it is the same everywhere. The Duke of York made an utter shambles of the expedition to Flanders and was forced to retreat almost to Scandinavia. The people have made up a rhyme about it. Since when the Dutch have been forced to surrender, the Prussians have made peace, and now it is said the Spanish want out. Soon your Mr. Pitt will not have a single ally in Europe."

"Well, that should content your friends in the Corresponding Societies," Nathan responded tartly.

"Those that are not in jail already," she whipped back at him. "I suppose you know you are taking a great risk being seen anywhere near me."

"Oh, they think you are mad, Mother, and quite harmless. Though having Mrs. Imlay under your roof will not please them."

"Oh and why is that?"

"Well, only that she has been in France for several years, moving about quite freely, though our two nations have been at war since '93. I am surprised she moves about quite so freely in London. Where is she now, anyway?"

Lady Catherine looked about the room as if surprised not to see her there. "She must have gone to her room. I wonder if she did not wish to see you. Can you imagine a reason why she should not?"

"None whatsoever," he assured her blithely, though there were many. "Save that my conversation might bore her."

"Well, perhaps she thought to leave us alone for a while, to renew our acquaintance, for I have been very worried about you." She regarded him fondly but the frown soon reappeared. "You look thin. When Izzy gets back from the market I will have her cook you a nice dinner. We usually dine late in Soho," she added airily, "but we will make an exception for you."

"That would be nice," he assured her, but it was impossible to shake off his general air of despondency. "And will Mrs. Imlay be dining with us?"

"I expect so. She usually does." They fell silent for a moment, each with their own thoughts on the subject. "Have you seen your father since you were back?" she enquired at length.

"No. I told you, I came straight up from Portsmouth."

"Oh. So you did. Well, and do you plan to visit him during what we must not call your convalescence?"

"Possibly. It rather depends what plans the Admiralty have for me."

Nathan wondered if she had been informed about his father's plans. Better not to say anything on that score, he thought. He might have dropped them. It was certainly to be hoped he had.

"How is Mary, anyway?" he persisted. "The last I heard she was with child."

"Well, she is now a mother. And the child is above a year old and quite a bonny creature, though Mary is not as well as I could have hoped." She dropped her voice. "Indeed I am quite worried about her."

"Oh, and why is that?"

"Well, you must keep this under your hat . . ."

Nathan lifted this item cautiously from the window-seat and peered under it as if to confirm that there was room.

"Well, if you do not wish to know . . ." his mother complained pettishly.

"I am sorry, Mother, do please continue."

"I was going to say, but why should I tell you, when you are so disagreeable and do not have the slightest concern for her?"

"I beg your pardon. It was remiss of me. Please. I am most concerned, for I have come to entertain the greatest respect for Mrs. Wollstonecraft, or Imlay, if that is what she wishes to be called."

"Oh, have you indeed? There is a wonder for you did not appear to be the least respectful when she was last a guest in my house and I seem to remember poured scorn upon her writing, not that you had read more than a page of it. And when did this occur?"

"Oh, it has just grown upon me, over the years," he remarked lightly. Clearly Mary had been discreet about the adventures they had shared in Paris—and the other friends he had made there.

His mother was regarding him with suspicion. "Well, as you appear to know a great deal more of her life than you are prepared to reveal to me, you probably know she has been crossed in love, as they say in the romantic novels."

He dealt easily with this. "I believe you told me when I last saw you that her husband was involved with an actress from a strolling theatre company."

"Did I tell you that? Yes, well, he still is, as Mary discovered upon her return from France. And what is more, he now maintains that their marriage was a sham. That is to say, in the legal sense, having been conducted by the American Minister in Paris and not a proper clergyman, though Imlay must have known this at the time, the rogue, even if poor Mary did not. And now he says that though he is prepared to give his name to the child he does not wish them to live as man and wife."

"Wait a moment." Nathan raised a hand in protest. "You are going too fast for me. When you say 'he still is,' what do you mean, precisely?"

"Well, I do not know how I can make it any clearer. I mean that he is still living with his actress."

"What—here in London?"

"Of course here in London. Where do you think I mean? In Eskimoland?"

It was quite possible, given Imlay's predilection for popping up in unexpected places. Certainly it would have been less alarming.

"Do you mean to say Imlay is here in London? Now?"

Lady Catherine raised her eyes to the ceiling. "Dear me. Am I expressing myself badly or has the blow to your head done more damage to your wits than you would have me believe?"

"I am sorry. I am confused." Having delivered Imlay into the custody of the authorities on a charge of spying for the French, he thought he had every right to be confused. But this was not something he wished to debate with his mother.

"So, he is seen walking about town, quite freely?"

"Why should he not be, there being no sanction in law to prevent a man forsaking his wife for another woman—and certainly he appears to have no shame at the plight he has put poor Mary in."

Nathan's head was spinning. Why had Imlay been released from custody? Had the charges against him been dropped or held in abeyance? Had he managed to talk himself out of the trouble he was in? This appeared only too likely. Imlay was nothing if not a plausible rogue.

"So poor Mary is now having to face up to the fact that the great love of her life, as she once described him, is a liar and a cheat," his mother continued, "and that she is cast in the light of the very creature she had always pitied and deplored: the victim, the abandoned mistress, the fallen woman. And I fear she has taken it very badly indeed. You would not know her for the woman you met in London before the war. She is a shadow of her former self, in looks and in spirits. Indeed, I confess I am more concerned than I can say." She hesitated a moment and then decided to say it anyway. "You really must not repeat this to anyone but shortly after she discovered the truth, she attempted to take her own life."

"You are not serious?" Nathan was genuinely shocked.

"I have it on good authority, though she thinks I do not know. She took an overdose of laudanum but was discovered in time by Imlay and brought to her senses. Well, I should not say her senses for she is still sadly lacking in those, but her life was saved. That is when he proposed they live together—with the other woman, I mean—though he has since thought better of it."

"What!"

"Did I not say? He proposed they should all live together as one happy family. All three of them." She did a quick sum in her head. "Four, counting the child. And Mary, poor fool that she is, agreed. She had some notion of 'reforming' the other woman, as she put it, but Imlay took fright and changed his mind."

"I am not surprised." Nathan shook his head wonderingly. The woman he had known in Paris had been a formidable creature and though she had clearly been in love with Imlay she was not so besotted that she would not express her disapprobation whenever he behaved in a way she considered beneath him. Which was quite often. She appeared to be unaware of his more clandestine activities but she had always been critical of his dealings in commerce. Perhaps too critical. Was this why he had chosen more tolerant company? Though it was no excuse for abandoning her—and with a child to boot.

They heard the sound of the bell at the front door.

"Oh, look out of the window, will you, and see if it is the bailiffs come back," his mother instructed him. "Let them see your uniform, it might intimidate them."

Nathan stared at her in astonishment. "The bailiffs?"

"Yes. They have been dunning me. It is more of a nuisance than anything but sometimes I feel besieged in my own home."

"Mother, I wish you would let me give you some money." In truth, he wished he had money to give her for he was quite short himself.

"Oh, I will soon be able to settle my debts, or most of them. But look out of the window, there's a good boy, and tell me if it is them."

Nathan twisted round in his seat and assumed his most ferocious quarterdeck expression.

"There is only one of them," he said. "And I do not think he looks like a bailiff."

Lady Catherine peered down over his shoulder just as the man in question looked up and saw that he was observed, whereupon he raised his hat to reveal a countenance that Nathan thought vaguely familiar.

"Oh, it is Mr. Blake," said Kitty. "You met him last time you were home, I recall, when he came to sell me some of his work. We have since become friends though I fear I am a poor patron. I will go and let him in."

"You will do no such thing," Nathan insisted. "I will go."

He returned shortly with a man of about forty whose imposing features were somewhat offset by a disconcertingly simple smile.

"I was in the neighbourhood," he announced, "and thought I should call on you, if it is not an intrusion. And now I have the double delight of meeting your son once more, though I am sorry to see he has been wounded."

"You are very welcome, Mr. Blake," Kitty assured him. "I expect you would like some tea."

"Only if it does not inconvenience you."

"It is no inconvenience at all. I will tell Mrs. Imlay you are here for I am assured she would not wish to miss you. Mr. Blake has illustrated one of Mrs. Imlay's books," she informed Nathan in the hope of providing them with something to talk about while she was absent from the room, for she did not think they would have a great deal in common, but she could not resist adding: "It is a book of fairy tales which should be more to your tastes than *A Vindication of the Rights of Women*."

"Oh, I do not think you will find her," declared Mr. Blake, "for I have just seen her at Westminster Stairs when I came over from Lambeth."

Kitty stopped in her tracks and regarded him warily for he was sometimes given to delusions.

"Are you positive?" she queried him. "I could have sworn she was in her room with her little girl."

"Well, I am almost positive," he insisted, "though when I called out to her she turned away as if she did not wish to acknowledge me. This happens from time to time," he informed Nathan engagingly. "I fear I sometimes embarrass people with my conversation."

"I am sure you do not," Nathan assured him politely, recalling that when last they had met, as strangers in St James's Park, he had been instructed on the subject of lepers and the exhumed body of King Edward the Confessor.

"I will go and fetch her," muttered Kitty, fleeing the room.

She was back within the minute looking strangely distraught and clutching a pair of letters, one opened and one not, and a number of banknotes.

"She is gone," she announced dramatically. "Leaving the child in its cot. And see what she has left me." She thrust the opened letter at Nathan but before he could read it she continued: "She says she can no longer bear to live with her shame and leaves the poor infant in my care with thirty pounds which is all she has in the world."

Nathan scanned the hastily scribbled words, snatching at a phrase here and there. *Yet having been so perpetually the sport of disappointment . . . what have I to fear who have so little to hope for! God bless you . . .*

"And here is another addressed to Imlay. I hardly know if I should open it."

Nathan had no such reservation. He took it from her and broke the seal.

My dear Imlay,

I write to you now on my knees imploring you to send my child and the maid to Paris to be consigned to the care of my very good friend Madame Farber, Rue Jacob, section du Theatre-Français. Should they be removed, their landlady, Madame Benoit, can give their direction. Let the maid have all my clothes, without distinction and do not mention the confession I forced from the cook—a little sooner or later is of no consequence. Nothing but my extreme stupidity could have rendered me blind so long. Yet whilst you assured me that you had no attachment, I thought we might still have lived together.

I shall make no comments on your conduct, or any appeal to the world. Let my wrongs sleep with me! Soon, very soon shall I be at peace. When you receive this my burning head will be cold.

I would encounter a thousand deaths rather than a night like the last. Your treatment has thrown my mind into a state of chaos yet I am serene. I go to find comfort and my only fear is that my poor body will be insulted by an endeavour to recall my hated existence. But I shall plunge into the Thames where there is the least chance of my being snatched from the death I seek.

God bless you! May you never know by experience what you have made me endure. Should your sensibility ever awake, remorse will find its way to your heart and in the midst of business and sensual pleasure, I shall appear before you, the victim of your deviation from rectitude.

Mary

Nathan turned on their discomforted visitor. "Where did you see her? Was it on the bridge?"

"No. The bridge is closed. She was waiting at the Stairs. I—I thought she was waiting for a boat."

Nathan snatched up his hat. "You had better come with me," he said to his mother.

"But do you think she means to harm herself?"

"I do," he said, handing her back the letter to Imlay.

"I will fetch my shawl," she said. "Mr. Blake, would you mind staying here to look after the child, until Izzy returns?"

"But . . ." Mr. Blake looked at them in bemusement. "Where are you going?"

"I think we must go down to the river," Nathan told him.

"Surely she will no longer be there. There were very few waiting."

But they were already out of the room.

"If the child cries, give her a candied fruit," Kitty called back over her shoulder. "You will find them on the sideboard."

They hurried down Frith Street in the direction of the Strand, Nathan looking back constantly for a cab and his mother half running and clutching her shawl to her bosom.

"He is right. We will never find her at Westminster," she lamented, "and then where shall we look?"

"She will make for one of the bridges," Nathan mused.

"But how can you know that? She could be anywhere on the river."

"No," he informed her with heavy patience. "Because then she would have to wade in from the shore and force her head under the water. And I assure you that is not easy, even for someone determined upon drowning."

"But could she not jump from a boat?"

"And have the boatman fish her out—if only to demand his fare? Dear God, when were you an expert on drowning? Though perhaps it is better not to enquire. Thank God, I do not have to tolerate this on my own ship."

And so they conversed pleasantly enough until they reached Westminster. There were several boatmen waiting at the Stairs but no sign of Mrs. Imlay and when Lady Catherine attempted somewhat excitedly to describe her to them, they only shook their heads and exchanged knowing glances as if they had found another fare to Bedlam.

"Which is the nearest bridge from here?" Nathan demanded tersely.

"Blackfriars," said one.

"Battersea," said another.

"Depending upon the tide," chimed a third.

"Oh, for Gods sake!" Lady Catherine raised her eyes to the heavens in hopes of more informed counsel.

Nathan looked, more calmly, to the river. "It will be Battersea," he said.

"Why?" demanded his mother, whose confidence in Nathan's judgement had not improved with age or his advancement through the naval hierarchy. "How can you possibly tell?"

"Because that is the way the tide is running," Nathan replied with heavy patience. "And I assume she would take the easier option. Will you take us to Battersea?" he addressed one of the boatmen.

With the tide in their favour, they reached the footbridge in a little more than twenty minutes, but the light was fast fading from the sky and it was threatening to rain. There were a number of people about the crossing, but they all seemed to be striding purposefully and none of them looked like Mrs. Imlay.

"Oh, I hope she did not go the other way," lamented Kitty, "for you are never right in your direction. And she will have thrown herself from Blackfriars or London Bridge. London Bridge is the most favoured, I am assured, since they took down the shops."

Nathan ignored her, but now the boatman had become interested and he offered to enquire among his associates on the shore. He returned with the news that a woman of Mrs. Imlay's age and description had disembarked on the northern shore but, after watching the people on the bridge for some minutes, had asked to be taken on to Putney.

"Then you must take us to Putney," Kitty instructed him urgently.

"Well I will an' all, but it will cost you another six shillin' for I am not a Samaritan."

"Nor would we have taken you for one," Nathan comforted him, "but I fail to see how it can be the same price from here to Putney as it was from Westminster to here."

"Ah well, there you go, guvnor, 'tis on account of the tide, d'you see, which is not so strong as 'tis dahn river an' I 'as to pull all the 'arder, d'you see? Add to that, when I drops you awf, I 'as to pull back agin' it, don't I?"

Nathan considered pointing out that the two statements ran counter to each other but his mother had begun to express her own feelings on the subject, saying that she found it impossible to believe he could resort to haggling at such a time, even going so far as to accuse him of being his father's son, which he much resented. With a sigh, he took out his purse and parted with another six shillings.

It had now begun to rain quite heavily and though the boatman provided a foul-smelling tarpaulin to shelter under, they were both thoroughly chilled by the time they sighted the next bridge.

"If I had known what I was letting myself in for I would have taken a room in a hotel," Nathan complained.

"Look! I am sure that is her!" Kitty pointed from under the

tarpaulin. A solitary figure was to be seen midway across the foot-bridge, walking in the direction of Putney village.

"You cannot possibly tell from here," Nathan objected, peering out into the rain.

"I assure you it is she. Quick," she urged the boatman, "set us down as close as you can."

"On the Fulham side," Nathan instructed him for the woman had turned and begun to walk in that direction. But as soon as the boatman began to pull for the Stairs, the figure turned again and began to head back towards Putney.

"What on earth is she doing?" Nathan demanded.

"She is agitated," his mother informed him. "See how she holds her face to the rain. Like King Lear."

Nathan stared at her in wonderment, shaking his head, but she grabbed him by the arm with a scream and when he looked back he saw that the woman had hauled herself up onto the rail. From whence, after pausing there a moment and stretching her arms to the heavens, she jumped.

CHAPTER TEN

the Secret Agent

"CAN YOU STILL SEE HER?" demanded Nathan, struggling to pull off his boots.

"No. I think she has gone under the arch," announced his mother as she peered into the darkness under the bridge. "Hurry," she implored the boatman, "or she will be gone."

"Which I am doing the best I can," this worthy assured her, manoeuvring to position himself for the mill-race in the centre of the arch.

"Let me take an oar," Nathan urged him. "We will be quicker."

"I doubt it, guvnor," the boatman replied disrespectfully, "'less I was to lose an arm. But if the lady was to sit down we would stand a better chance of not ending up in the water wiv the other wench."

Nathan instructed his mother accordingly and they shot through the arch at an impressive pace. He saw their quarry at once, floating face down in the water on the far side of the bridge.

"Hard a starboard," he instructed the boatman, who despite his confident assertion that he could manage better alone, was struggling against the turbulence beyond the bridge. Nathan saw that they would be swept well past the drowning woman, and heedless of the boatman's strenuous advice, he shrugged off his jacket and dived into the water, all but upsetting the boat.

It was a great deal cooler than he had imagined for the time of the year and he was shocked by the strength of the currents. But he was a powerful swimmer, having spent much of his early life in the Cuckmere or the waters off the Sussex coast, and he set off in a vigorous crawl towards the spot where he had last seen the inert figure. It shortly became apparent, however, that she was no longer there. Nor could he see where she had gone. He tried to raise himself in the water to look for her, but it was useless and the tide was carrying him into the darkness on the other side of Putney village. He had entirely lost her. He began to strike out for the nearest shore, but now he was caught up in so many back eddies and currents it was difficult to make any headway and the weight of his clothes seemed heavier by the minute. He reflected on the irony of being drowned in the Thames after his far more dangerous adventures in the Bay of Quiberon. It would not look good in the newspapers, he thought. Drowning in an attempt to rescue a woman who had thrown herself off a bridge might normally be expected to win the approval of the populace, even posthumously, but the woman in question being Mary Wollstonecraft, it would almost certainly detract from the value of the sacrifice, at least in the view of the more conservative journals.

He flopped over on to his back and let the tide take him as it was clearly useless to battle against it. He examined the night sky for a sympathetic star but it was entirely clouded over. Then he saw it—a solitary star. Without others to guide him, he was unable to place it but he was glad it was there, all the same. It was some comfort to him, though he wished he could have named it, his last star. A familiar voice jolted him out of this reverie.

"'Ere you are, guvnor, cop 'old o' that!" And an oar was thrust almost into his face. He rolled over and with some considerable effort, not unhindered by the attentions of his mother, he was hauled into the boat.

"I am sorry," he confessed as he lay panting in the thwarts, "but I fear we have lost her."

"No, but I think she is saved," his mother assured him, "for we saw another boat pulling her out of the water."

"Couple of fishing-men," the boatman elaborated for Nathan's benefit, "but I'd not go so far as to say 'saved' for she looked like a goner to me. But we'll find out soon enough."

He pulled them across the river to the Fulham side of the bridge where a group of boatmen and other interested parties had congregated to discuss the incident. But when he returned from interrogating them he had the sombre, though satisfied look of one whose worst predictions have been realised.

"They pulled her out, right enough," he announced, "but she was drownded. Kickerapoo. Dead in the water," he added for fear of being obtuse.

"Oh my poor Mary!" Kitty mourned. "Where have they taken her?"

"Duke's 'Ead Tavern," the boatman pronounced firmly, pointing to the lights of the inn, a little way downriver. "'Op back in and I'll 'ave you there in two shakes of a rat's tail."

"But why have they taken her to a tavern?"

"As good a place as any if you're a goner," replied their cheerful Samaritan, "an' I expect they needed to wet their whistles."

Having conveyed them thither, he graciously accepted two sovereigns from Nathan for services rendered and took his leave. They ran up the stairs to the inn. And there face down on the floor of the taproom, in a pool of Thames water, lay the body of Mary Wollstonecraft.

A man in his shirt sleeves was bent over her performing some bizarre ritual with her arms while a number of spectators gave encouragement or observed that it was a waste of time, mate, 'cos she was clearly beyond saving.

"Oh God, what is he doing to her?" demanded Kitty. "He is not a medical student, is he? This is just what she most dreaded. Please make them stop," she begged Nathan.

"I think you should leave her now," Nathan advised the man as he stepped from the shadows, and though his voice was moderate it had enough authority in it for the crowd to draw back a little and regard him attentively, marvelling at his waterlogged appearance, as if he were a species of river god come to claim her. The man on the floor continued with his exertions regardless.

"Just give 'im another minute or so, if you would, sir," implored one of the spectators, a be-whiskered gentleman in a waistcoat with a face like an otter. "'E knows what 'e is about. 'E's got certificates."

"But what *is* he about?" Nathan demanded, for the possessor of certificates was lifting the victim's arms above her head and bringing them down to her sides in a repeated action that appeared to be as bizarre as it was futile.

"'Tis the method taught by the Royal Humane Society," declared the Otter, impressively, "authorised by King George hisself."

"Well, I do not call it humane to treat a poor, drowned creature so," insisted Kitty, "whatever King George has to say about it. You are to stop it at once. Nathan, make him stop. It is disgusting."

"But 'tis the method they teaches 'em, ma'am, for the saving of lives. 'E calls it Hartificial Resuscitation—don't you, Jim?" The latter remaining intent upon the business in hand, the Otter took on the burden of explanation for himself. "It works like a pump, d'you see?"

To give credence to this description, a small deluge of water gushed from the dead woman's mouth and she began to retch violently.

The lifesaver continued to pump until he was satisfied there was no water left and then sat her upon a chair and recovered the beer that had been waiting for him on the bar whilst modestly receiving the plaudits of the crowd, his only detractor being the woman he had saved, who sat wrapped in a blanket shuddering violently and complaining to anyone who would listen that she had been better off left in the river.

"We will get you home now," Kitty soothed her, "before you catch your death of cold."

The general advice being against the river as a means of transport, given what had occurred, one of the customers offered to drive them back in his chaise which served the community in the nature of a hackney carriage: though he required ten shillings for going so far out of his way which would oblige him to lose a great deal of custom, he explained, as he was not allowed to pick up a return fare in the city. Nathan cashed another guinea at the bar, desiring the landlord to keep the change as recompense for any damage to the furnishings, and gave five more, which was all he had left in his purse, to the lifesaver, tactfully proposing it as a donation to the Royal Humane Society.

It had been an expensive evening.

"Do you know Imlay's address?" he enquired of his mother when she had returned from putting Mary to bed with several hot-water jars and Izzy to watch over her in case she contrived some other means of destruction.

"Why do you wish to know?" she enquired warily.

Nathan took Mary's letter down from the mantelpiece where it had been left. "Because we have this to deliver."

"But . . . I would have thought it was meant to be delivered in the event of her death," she pointed out.

"Even so, I think he should be informed of what he has brought her to."

"Nathan, you are not going to fight him."

"Would you object greatly if I did?"

"Well, that would depend on how certain I was that you would win," she confessed. "Would it be with swords or pistols?"

This was a reasonable enquiry for when she had been in funds she had paid for Nathan to be instructed in swordsmanship by Henry Angelo, a maestro of the Italian school whose fencing establishment in Soho was patronised by some of the most accomplished and aristocratic blades in England.

"The person challenged has the right to choose the weapon," Nathan explained, "but it is regarded as dishonourable in England to choose anything but a pistol."

"Well, how ridiculous! I never heard of such nonsense. Why would anyone make such a rule?"

"Because the sword, or knife, is the weapon of choice on the Continent," he replied, reasonably, "and deemed suitable therefore only for fops and assassins. But do not fret, I have no intention of fighting him. I much prefer him to be disgraced. Surely you would not wish him to remain in ignorance of the event, or to escape the calumny for it."

"Well, no," she replied uncertainly, "but as to calumny, you must remember, my dear, that if this became widely known Mary would suffer the consequence, and not only in terms of her reputation. Attempted suicide is against the law, I believe, in England. It is possible she might be imprisoned."

"I know that. But given the circumstances, I do not suppose the incident will go unreported, and I do not see why Imlay should be kept out of it and walk away scot free with not a stain on his character, which is his usual way. I am going to tell him what I think of him, that is all, and find out what recompense he is prepared to make. At the very least he can pay me back the ten guineas I have laid out in expenses this evening."

"Well, he took a furnished house at number 36 Charlotte Street," she told him, "but I am not sure if he lives there himself. Or whether it was for Mary—or his actress."

It was no more than a five minute walk from Soho Square to Charlotte Street and number 36 turned out to be a respectable-enough dwelling about halfway up. It was mostly in darkness save for a light in the basement and Nathan rang for some time before there was a response, if only it was the sound of the brass cap removed from the spy-hole. He smiled reassuringly. A female voice desired to know what he wanted.

"Mrs. Imlay?" Nathan enquired politely, though not without a degree of mischief.

A pause. Then: "Mrs. Imlay is not at home."

"Ah. Well, as a matter of fact it was with Mr. Imlay that I wished to speak."

"Well, Mr. Imlay is not at home, neither."

"I see." He had an inspiration. "Well, I am come from the Admiralty with an urgent message for him," he said, "which I must deliver this evening. To him personally. I assure you it is very much to his advantage."

He still wore his uniform jacket, which had avoided a ducking, with the gold epaulette clearly visible on the right shoulder.

"Well, he was planning to dine with some gentlemen at the Star in Covent Garden," she revealed doubtfully, "but I don't know if you will still find him there."

Nathan thanked her and took his leave. He suspected he was off on something of a wild-goose chase and not for the first time in the history of his dealings with Gilbert Imlay.

What Nathan knew of him came from a number of sources, none entirely trustworthy, including Imlay's own account which was probably the least reliable of them all. He was born in Philadelphia, he said, though his family was from New Jersey: Scottish immigrants who had prospered in business and bought land there. As a youth he had sailed to the West Indies and engaged in the rum trade, a euphemism, Nathan gathered, for smuggling. At the start of the American War he had volunteered to serve in Washington's army only to desert a few months later and return to New Jersey where he was suspected, even by members of his own family, of being a British agent. After the war he claimed to have been a frontiersman and explorer in the territories west of the Appalachians, though "land speculator" would probably have been a more accurate description of his activities as Nathan understood them. Facing arrest for debt he had fled to Spanish Louisiana and subsequently appeared in London with a book he said he had written—an account of the western territories aimed at encouraging immigration—which was published by Debrett with some considerable literary success. Another book had followed, less literary, less acclaimed, which was vaguely pornographic, modelled on the novels of the Marquis de Sade. Finding the air in England suddenly become rather chill, he had moved to

France, where he had established himself as a raffish man of letters.

Nathan had first met him in Paris during his brief stay there at the time of the Terror when both of them were obliged to conceal their true vocations. Imlay had by then set himself up as a shipping agent, running goods past the British blockade, but he had been willing to aid the British in smuggling millions of forged *assignats* into the country with a view to causing rampant inflation and ruining the French economy. At the same time he maintained excellent contacts in the Committee of Public Safety, the true rulers of France during the Terror, and appeared to be on good terms with Robespierre himself, though this had not prevented him from playing a key role in toppling the dictator.

Nathan had next encountered him in London, where he had been introduced to him by the First Lord of the Admiralty as a trusted political adviser. Imlay had accompanied him in this role on a voyage to the West Indies, where he had promptly decamped to the French. A Spanish agent in the Havana had informed Nathan that Imlay had once worked for them, though his true allegiance had always been to the government of the United States and that he was the member of an elite brotherhood of American agents known as "Washington's Boys," accountable only to the general and paid by him from his own secret funds.

Whether this was true or not, Nathan was persuaded that Imlay's true loyalties were first and foremost to himself, and that in pursuit of his own interests he would lie, cheat and if necessary kill. And yet he had charm. In fact, he would not have succeeded as well as he had without it. Mary was not the only woman, or man, to be taken in by him.

Somewhat to his surprise, after a long walk to Covent Garden, Nathan found his bird in residence, perched at a table in the window of the Star with a party that included almost as many ladies as gentlemen, though Lady Catherine would have considered both sexes to have been flattered by the description.

Nathan watched him through the part-misted window. Gilbert

Imlay was a little over forty years old, his thick brown hair looking a little grizzled now at the edges, but still in the best of health and ruggedly handsome. Someone had once told Nathan that he modelled himself on that great American pioneer and trail-blazer Daniel Boone of Kentucky, though as Nathan had never met the gentleman in question he could not give his opinion on the matter. His manner was that of a courteous and softly-spoken gentleman of New England with a raffish air of the American frontier about him; the look of a man who had gazed upon distant horizons and endured many hardships. In general, however, he was all things to all men—and women, too.

As for his relations with Mary Wollstonecraft, Nathan was convinced he had set out on a course of seduction partly because of the challenge she represented as the celebrated writer of *A Vindication of the Rights of Women*. What a triumph to add such a scalp to his belt—and not only to bed her, but to have her fall in love with him.

Of course it was entirely possible that he fell in love himself, if only with her image of him as a man of principle and high ideals, a true romantic and a child of nature: one of Rousseau's noble savages with the airs and graces of a gentleman. He had offered her the protection of his name and citizenship at a time when—as an Englishwoman living in Paris—she had faced arrest and imprisonment or worse. He had persuaded her that he wished only to make enough from commerce to buy a farm in Kentucky where they would live together as man and wife and raise six children. How Mary could have fallen for such tosh was beyond Nathan's powers to imagine, but then she was not the first woman, or man, to be fooled by Gilbert Imlay. He even fooled himself most of the time. But she had aspired to be the first of a new kind of woman, a new genus, proud, independent, free. How could she ever forgive herself?

Nathan stepped out of the shadows, crossed the street and entered the supper room.

Imlay saw him at once, his face betraying instant and considerable apprehension. He swiftly recovered his poise however and leaped to his feet with an expression of apparently unfeigned delight.

"Why Nathan, my dear fellow! Why, this is Captain Peake," he informed the company, who looked as reprobate a bunch of scoundrels and their attendants as Nathan had seen outside of Westminster. "A great friend of mine—we have shared many adventures together. You may have read of his exploits in the Caribbean." They did not look to be avid readers of the *Gazette* but they smiled indulgently, possibly taking him for a pirate. "Indeed, I was with him when he took the *Virginie* off Cuba." An astonishing piece of effrontery, even by Imlay's standards, for Nathan had discovered him aboard the *Virginie* when it was took, in the role of political agent for the French admiral. "A bumper of champagne for the captain!"

"I fear I cannot stay," Nathan declared. "I came only to give you this. It is from your wife." He presented Mary's letter. Imlay gazed at it for a moment blankly and Nathan saw his brain fighting its way through the haze of drink. An uncomfortable silence had fallen upon the company.

"But it has been opened," he said.

Nathan inclined his head without comment.

"Excuse me," Imlay addressed his companions embarrassedly. "I must . . ." He waved the letter vaguely. "An urgent missive . . ." He moved away from the table and Nathan followed him to the bar.

"What is this all about?" Imlay frowned.

"Why do you not read it and find out?"

He did. The frown deepened. He may have lost a little of the colour in his complexion.

"My God! She has killed herself!"

"Not quite. No thanks to you. She was fished out of the Thames more dead than alive, and she is now at my mother's house in Soho, wishing she had been left in the river."

"I must go to her!" Imlay chewed on his lip but this was the only motion he made. He glanced speculatively at the table he had recently vacated. His companions were looking back with bemusement. Nathan wondered if the actress was among them or whether she was the woman he had left behind in Charlotte Street.

Imlay looked at the letter again.

"This was addressed to me," he said. "Why was it opened?"

"Because you were not there at the time and had it not been opened she would now be at the bottom of the river—or in the morgue."

"I suppose you think me a scoundrel?"

Nathan shrugged. "I think you know my opinion of you very well from our previous dealings," he said.

Imlay glanced again at the letter in his hand, if only to avoid looking into Nathan's eyes. "Well, there are two sides to every story," he began.

"And I am sure yours would be the more entertaining, were I of a mind to hear it."

"By God, sir! What right have you to be so critical?"

Nathan said nothing but watched him carefully, for Imlay was as dangerous as he was slippery, especially when cornered, and he was clearly working himself into a temper.

"What part did you play in this," he demanded, thrusting the letter into Nathan's face. "Did you tell her of your . . . your unfounded suspicions, your biased view of my character?"

"The only part I have played was in helping to save her life," replied Nathan untruthfully, but there was no point in dwelling upon his own inadequacies in that regard. "And as to your character . . ."

"You were there?"

"I was."

"Well, I suppose I must thank you, though if you had been there for your own woman . . ."

He did not finish the sentence. Even had he known where it was going, he would not have been capable, for Nathan had him by the throat. He held him there a moment while their eyes met—Nathan's burning, Imlay's appalled—and then thrust him away with such violence he tripped over one of the bar stools and fell to the floor.

He was up in an instant, his face red and his hand to his throat, but for all his apparent eagerness, Nathan knew he was calculating his options. He glanced towards his companions, several of whom were moving in their direction, and shook his head. There was no way out. It had been too public a humiliation, too many people had seen it.

"You will answer for that," he said. "Danvers, may I rely upon you?"

"Willingly," replied one of his companions, glaring at Nathan. "Name your second, sir."

Name your second. Possibly, for the first time, Nathan became aware of the consequences of an action which had been as little calculated as when he had held his pistol to the head of the Chevalier de Batz. But the reference to Sara had been too much for him. He was too vulnerable on that score.

"You will find me at Number 2, Soho Square, whenever you care to enquire," he said.

Who on earth could he name? The only friends he had were aboard the *Unicorn* or other ships of His Majesty's.

He bowed once more, to the entire room now, for every eye was fixed upon him, and took his leave. It was raining again but he walked home regardless, almost welcoming it. He really must stop this, he thought; he was become as reckless as an Irishman.

CHAPTER ELEVEN

Pistols at Dawn

NATHAN SAT IN AN EASY CHAIR by his bedroom window, nursing a glass of wine and looking out at the night sky over London. It was a clear night and the moon almost full. From this height he could see clear across the rooftops towards Lincoln's Inn Fields where he was to meet Imlay in the morning. It was now well after midnight but he had never been able to sleep on the eve of a fight, unlike the cool character upon whom he tried to model himself, who would have slept like a babe whatever crisis lay before him. But this was a character of fiction. Besides, he could not afford to sleep for there was no one to wake him at the required hour; he could hardly have told his mother about the duel and if he had told Izzy she would have informed upon him.

He looked about the room—*his* room—reflecting that his first night here might well be his last. All of his possessions from the house in St James's had been moved here, though mostly stored in cupboards, waiting upon his return. In some ways he preferred it to his old room. It was more homely and had more character. The house, according to his mother, had once been the residence of the Venetian envoy to London, in the early part of the century when the area was still fashionable. But the rich had moved to Mayfair and the square was in genteel decline. Several of the houses were badly in need of renovation, the gardens in the centre of the square neglected and the statue of Charles II in the middle a disgrace that should be removed by the authorities, his mother said—though her objections, Nathan gathered, were more political than aesthetic. But time was slowly eroding the Merry Monarch, his libertine features so worn it looked as if he had syphilis. In a century or so he would be unrecognisable. People would wonder who he was—if they had not carted him away by then to the graveyard of old statues.

A distant bell chimed the half hour. St Anne's most likely. Nathan wondered if he should have gone to church. Composed himself for death. As it was, he would die unshriven. The phrase played on his mind, in harmony with the melancholy of his thoughts.

He was too restless to sit still. He heaved himself up from the chair and crossed to his bed, treading lightly on the bare floorboards so he would not be heard by his mother who was sleeping below. He had not told her about the fight. He supposed he should leave a letter for her but it seemed melodramatic. Besides, he did not expect to be killed. It would cause Imlay too many problems.

Was he sure about that?

No, he was not at all sure. Imlay would do a runner, as he always did when things became a little difficult for him. He had probably made his preparations already. A smuggling vessel waiting off the Kent coast, most likely. He would be in Calais by nightfall if the wind was right.

So was he going to kill Imlay?

He had been thinking about that, off and on, since he had walked away from the Star. His first thought had been that he would shoot to miss. But then, if Imlay did not shoot at the same time . . . The rules were quite clear on the issue. He would have to stand until Imlay had fired. And he did not at all like the thought of that. He could shoot him in the right arm, if he was a good enough shot. But he did not think he was. Not that good. And he did not suppose the pistols were that accurate, despite the assurances he had received on the issue.

He lifted himself off the bed and crossed to the wardrobe. Most of his personal effects were at his father's house in Sussex: the place he had always thought of as home until his father had confessed his plans to remarry. But there were a few clothes here that he had left in St James's and the case containing his flute, which for some reason he had brought up to London. And next to it was the case of pistols he had borrowed from Mr. Whitbread, a friend of his mother's who had agreed to be his second: a fine pair of duelling pistols, made by Mortimers of London, for Mr. Whitbread despite being a radical, was a brewer and a wealthy man.

Nathan lifted one of them out of the velvet-lined case and weighed it in his hand. It was the standard .58 calibre with a 10-inch barrel—a good two inches longer than the Belgian pistols he had left on the *Unicorn*. A much better pistol all round for a duel, if not for a fight on the crowded deck of a man-o'-war.

Whitbread had never fired them in anger, he had told Nathan, though he confessed there were a few Tories he would like to meet some day. He seemed to be rather looking forward to the event. But Nathan didn't envy him having to tell his mother if it ended badly.

He removed the safety and pulled back the hammer. Very easy. The mechanism had been well oiled, probably by Whitbread himself, dreaming of shooting Tories. The butt was carved with a number of pie-shaped segments which made for a good grip and the words H.W. MORTIMER LONDON GUNMAKER TO HIS MAJESTY were engraved along the top of the octagonal barrel, which inspired confidence. He selected one of the flints from the case and screwed it in. Then he stood sideways, opposite his own reflection in the window, swung up his arm straight from the shoulder and pressed the trigger. There was a loud, clean click and a satisfactory spark as the flint struck the iron. The touchhole, he observed, was lined with platinum. Nothing but the best for Mr. Whitbread. He reversed the pistol and looked down the barrel. Too dark, though, to see anything. Smooth bore, of course. It was held to be dishonourable for a gentleman to use a rifled pistol for a duel: it fired too straight. Practising was also frowned upon.

But of course it would be entirely out of character for Imlay to obey the rules. He would find them absurd. And he was probably right.

Nathan laid the pistol back in its case, next to its twin, and put the case back in the wardrobe until he needed it. He took out the flute instead. No dishonour in practising upon the flute, so far as he knew, though it might wake the rest of the house.

He leafed through the sheet music that was there and after some thought he chose the "Aria of the Shepherd" from La Liberazione di Ruggiero by Francesca Caccini, the only female composer he knew.

Unfortunately there was no music-stand but he laid the sheets on the small table by the window and weighted them with the glass of wine and the half-empty bottle. Then he assembled the flute. He had not played for some time and there were several false starts, but after a while he felt his old skills return to him, though in truth he had never entirely mastered the instrument. He aimed it at the window out of consideration for the sleeping women in the rooms below, though he flattered himself that the music was so enchanting it would not awaken them. Indeed, he did not think he had ever played better. After a few minutes a dog began to howl mournfully from the darkness in the streets below and soon it was joined by another, but he took this rather as a compliment than a criticism. Then a drunken voice was raised in angry rebuke—at the dogs, he thought, rather than his playing—but it rather spoiled his mood so he set the flute down and sat in the armchair dozing a little or looking out at the stars. And surprisingly he drifted into a heavy sleep, waking with a start to find the sky had turned from black to grey.

He moved quickly then, fearing to hear the doorbell, dressing in a clean shirt and stock with a plain black jacket instead of his uniform coat. Then he crept down the creaking stairs with his boots in his hand and the case of pistols tucked under his arm.

The brewer was waiting for him in his carriage across the square but he climbed down at Nathan's approach and looked him over.

"I was about to come for you," he said. And then doubtless

realising that this might imply reluctance on Nathan's part, he added hastily: "You slept well I trust?"

"Overslept," Nathan could not resist informing him. He yawned, though not from affectation—he always yawned when nervous. The brewer's face was composed with care, as if he had dressed it for the occasion, following the guidelines in the Code Duello. They climbed into the carriage and Nathan gave him back his pistols.

"You have tested them? I mean, the weight."

Nathan nodded silently and his companion rushed on again as if to disguise some error of etiquette. He was more nervous than Nathan. "A fine pair. Very well balanced. Good grip. Did you find?"

"Very good."

"And a sound lock. I have never known them misfire."

How often had he fired them?

"They were a gift from my father."

"I will try not to return them in as pristine a condition as they are now."

"Ha, ha. Quite. Quite. Let us hope it."

But this seemed to quieten him and they drove the rest of the journey in silence.

There was a fog upon the fields, rising from the wet grass and climbing a little way up the trees so they appeared to be rising out of a bog. It was still not quite light and the fog blurred the edges of things but Nathan discovered his senses to be remarkably alert. Every sound appeared exaggerated. When the coach stopped he heard the creaking of the harness and the springs as they settled, the horses chewing upon their bits, the slow drip of water from the trees. They climbed out of the coach and he noticed an extraordinary number of magpies strutting about the grass and quarrelling shrewishly, clacking their beaks. He did not count them but there were more than in the verse: a multitude of sorrows. A squirrel looked down at him from a low branch and appeared to be studying him intently. The sky was brighter and he heard the first birdsong, tentative at first and then, as if in response to some hidden heavenly baton, swelling to the full dawn chorus. It sounded too loud to Nathan—frantic, almost hysterical.

The other coaches were there already. One for Imlay and his second; the other for the referee and another man, presumably the doctor. There was some conferring. They began to load and check the weapons. Imlay stood a little apart, looking back towards the city as if he were expecting someone, but most likely lost in his thoughts.

Did he deserve to die? Probably not. Not for what he had brought Mary to, for it was impossible to tell what had happened between them.

There are two sides to every story.

For being a French spy, then?

Well, yes, for it would have served to hang him, if proven, or have him shot before a firing squad. But *was* he a French spy? Nathan was no longer sure. Certainly the Admiralty appeared to have given him the benefit of the doubt, else he would not be walking freely about the streets of London.

It occurred to Nathan now that if he was a double agent, which seemed likely, it would go some way towards explaining his difficulties with Mary, for how could he have an honest relationship with someone when his entire character was cloaked in deception.

He was getting nowhere with this. He had killed many who did not deserve to die. Why make an exception for Imlay?

Save that the others had been in the heat of battle and this was in cold blood.

And he had never really thought of himself as a cold-blooded killer.

Whitbread was coming back with the referee, Colonel Dowling, a retired officer of marines. They had brought Imlay's pistols for Nathan to examine. He took one of them from the case. It was heavier than his own, made by Samuel Nock of Fleet Street. Probably .75 calibre, which would make a sizeable hole in him if he was hit. He noted that it was fitted with sights but doubted if it would make much difference given the range and the size of the targets, unless Imlay intended to take his time and aim for something in particular.

He looked down the bore but knew before he did so that it would not be rifled; nor was it. He handed it back.

"One thing you may not have noticed," murmured Whitbread, "is that it has a hair trigger."

Nathan inclined his head courteously, but he was more interested than he appeared. If you were the slightest bit nervous a hair trigger could be far more dangerous to the man who fired as he who was fired upon. A man had been known to shoot his own foot off with a hair trigger. Nathan suddenly found the possibility of Imlay's shooting off his own foot quite hilarious and he felt the first bubbling of an unforgivable mirth. He recognised the symptoms for this had been a familiar affliction since childhood. Whenever it was least appropriate, he would be seized by an irresistible fit of the giggles. It had been an agony for him at many a church service for the slightest thing could set him off and he would be reduced to a helpless quivering bundle of weeping laughter during a sermon, despite the certain knowledge that he would be punished by going without his dinner or handed over to the Angel Gabriel for more physical chastisement. It would certainly be inappropriate now and he choked it back by reflecting that the choice of a hair trigger indicated that Imlay was a cool customer who had fought many a duel in the past, though it was far more likely that he had borrowed the pistols, sight unseen, as had Nathan.

He tried to concentrate as Colonel Dowling explained the rules of engagement but his mind kept wandering. He was impatient to get on with it. And indeed the instructions seemed unnecessarily complicated.

"Should one person fire and miss, or hit and injure the other duellist before that duellist has also fired, then the person who has so fired must wait, without moving, until his fellow has also fired, if he is capable of so firing. Is that clear to you, sir?"

Nathan nodded but he was not really taking it all in.

"If both shots miss, Captain Imlay as the offended party, will be asked if he is satisfied. If he is not, I will instruct your seconds to hand you the other pistol and you will be invited to fire again. And so on, until Mr. Imlay announces that he has had satisfaction—or one or other of you is incapable of continuing."

Captain Imlay? But of course, it was the rank he claimed he had attained in Washington's army, in the first year of the Independence War. Captain and paymaster in Colonel Forman's regiment of the Continental Line, though Nathan had been informed that he had never advanced beyond the rank of lieutenant before finding employment that was more to his taste, doubtless taking the regimental funds with him.

"Very well. Then take up your positions."

And so the farce began in earnest, if you could have an earnest farce. The two men stood back to back, pistols at the ready. Suddenly it came upon Nathan that within the next half minute he stood a very good chance of being killed or maimed, and to his intense alarm he felt a stirring in his bowels. By God, he was never going to fart, not while standing back to back with Imlay! He was able to check the process before he was disgraced but the thought of it, and Imlay's reaction, brought a return of the earlier affliction. And this time he was unable to suppress a snort of laughter.

"Excuse me," he said, wiping his nose with his free hand.

"Are you ready, Captain?"

"I beg your pardon," said Nathan, "but I think I am about to sneeze. May I trouble someone for a handkerchief?"

This caused something of a problem. They had pistols, powder and shot, bandages, sutures, probes, but not, it appeared, a handkerchief; until Imlay, who had clearly been holding himself back, reluctantly produced one from his sleeve.

Nathan wiped his nose. "Thank you," he said, handing it back. Imlay took it with distaste and handed it to his second.

"You are quite ready now, Captain?"

"I am," said Nathan. "I do beg your pardon."

And so once more they took up their positions back to back, and this time Nathan managed to control both extremities of his anatomy for the ten paces necessary to reach the firing position.

He turned, still holding his pistol at his cheek, and for the first time that morning looked Imlay straight in the eye.

"Take aim!" the colonel announced.

Nathan stretched out his arm and aimed at Imlay's head. He thought that he saw a flicker of alarm cross Imlay's face but it might have been in his imagining. He felt nothing now but a deadly calm.

"Fire!"

Very deliberately, Nathan swung his arm to the right and fired. High and wide. He did not know until that instant that this was what he was going to do. When the smoke cleared he saw that Imlay was still standing motionless, his pistol at the ready. He still had not fired. This surprised Nathan. It seemed to surprise Imlay too, for he looked upon Nathan as if he had not expected to see him there. And so they stood, in this same identical pose, for a second or two. It cannot have been longer. The smoke from Nathan's pistol still hung in the air, mingling with the mist from the ground. The magpies had risen from the ground in a patchwork quilt of white and black. Nathan's arm still pointed at an angle from his body, like a frozen lookout, four points off the starboard bow. He gazed steadily back at his opponent, partly in defiance, but mostly by way of a challenge. *Kill me and see how it will profit you.* And it was possible that this thought also occurred to Imlay: that it would not profit him at all and might even occasion a serious loss. Or possibly, he had made his mind up long before, for he too fired wide. Though not so wide that Nathan did not feel the wind of its passing and to his eternal shame flinched, though the ball had long gone.

"Are you satisfied, sir?" the referee called out to Imlay.

Nathan did not hear the reply, his ears being slightly deafened by the report of the pistol, but it must have been in the affirmative, for the seconds were nodding as if they, at least, were satisfied, and shaking each other's hands and taking turns to shake hands with the referee, and the doctor was packing up his bags and the magpies were swooping back to earth with ribald cries, as if they had seen it all before and would again and it never amounted to much more than this, for all the arduous preparation, and the squirrel had resumed its diligent accumulation of wealth among the branches of the trees, or more likely had never ceased. And Nathan sighed.

But the farce was not yet over. For from out of the mist, hanging still in the direction of the city, came another coach. And although it might have been the continuing problem with his ears, it seemed to Nathan that it travelled in a ghostly silence, the rags of mist parting before it. A black coach with four black horses. He half expected it to contain the spectre of Death, come to complain that he was robbed and to insist the duel continued until *he* had satisfaction and at least one corpse to take away with him. But it was only the gentlemen of the Watch—the Holborn Day Watch in their smart blue coats and their black hats, come to bring a halt to the proceedings, though as usual far too late, and to arrest Captain Peake on a warrant for disturbing the peace.

CHAPTER TWELVE

Atonement

I FIND IT REMARKABLE, quite remarkable, that having a great many charges and complaints levelled against you . . ." his lordship consulted the list that lay before him and blinked in affected wonderment at its length and variety, "and being summoned to answer for them to your superiors, you embarked upon a course of action which, had it proved fatal, would have rendered your country and your sovereign an even greater disservice than anything you had previously contemplated." He raised his eyes from the multitude of reports and regarded their subject coolly. "And when I say fatal, I mean, of course, to your adversary."

Nathan acknowledged this distinction with a small bow and pointed out that he had not meant to kill, or indeed, even wound, his opponent; that he had, in fact, deliberately fired wide.

"Did you indeed? Well, I can only say that this shows a more mature judgement than is your normal practice; the one consistent theme in this wretched miscellany of error and miscalculation being that you invariably act upon an impulse as hazardous to our friends as it is to our enemies."

Earl Spencer spoke in the dry, confident tones of a man who has been used for the greater part of his life to saying very much what he liked to whomsoever he pleased without regard for the consequence.

A descendant of the great Duke of Marlborough and one of the first lords of the land, he had now added to that distinction by being made First Lord of the Admiralty, though to Nathan's knowledge he had as much understanding of the sea and those who sailed upon it as any politician. But Nathan had been in the Gulf of Mexico when the appointment was made and his views on the appointment had not been sought.

"I was not inclined to think of Mr. Imlay as a friend, either to my sovereign, myself or the country at large," he remarked, in a tone very like that of his superior, though without the authority to support it.

Clearly this deficiency had occurred to his superior.

"Your opinion, sir, is of no consequence and you would do better to keep it to yourself," Earl Spencer informed him briskly, "unless you are asked for it, which is unlikely."

Nathan was not used to being addressed as a midshipman, not at least since he had occupied that lowly status, and was disposed to resent it. With difficulty he curbed this inclination and lapsed into an indifferent disdain, an offshoot of the fatalistic mood that had crept upon him during his brief internment in the Holborn Bridewell when he found he cared very little what became of him; or perhaps before that, when he had watched the *Conquest* fire upon the crowds at Quiberon and the woman he loved vanish beneath the hungry waves: for he was convinced now that the rider on the white horse had been Sara. And with this indifference came an inclination to find some other means of employment, less taxing upon the sinews and the spirit. In truth, Nathan felt ill used. The Earl Spencer's contempt—and apparent concern for Imlay above one of his own captains—much increased this inclination. He had always loved the sea far more than the service. It would not grieve him overmuch to be done with it.

But he admitted to a certain curiosity. Why would Imlay's death have done a *"great disservice"* to King George? It was partly in the hope of receiving an answer to this question that he stifled the desire to counter his lordship's pleasantries with some choice observations of his own.

"I beg your pardon, my lord," he replied, "but after witnessing Imlay's perfidy at first hand, it is difficult for me to comprehend why he continues to be held in such high esteem. Or why, indeed, it is not *he* who is brought to answer charges, rather than myself."

"That is none of your business, sir," his lordship replied sharply, but it seemed to Nathan that behind Spencer's cool manner there was something very close to embarrassment.

During his recent dealings with Whitbread, Nathan had asked the brewer what he knew of the man, for both had been members of the Whig faction in Parliament and had shared the same broadly liberal views, before the war with France had propelled them to opposite extremes of the political divide. Whitbread had initially condemned him as a turncoat but on reflection, he moderated this view somewhat, describing him as "torn by conflicting loyalties." He advised Nathan not to be taken in by his pose of patrician languor and indifference which, he said, disguised an active and intelligent brain. A graduate of Trinity College and a Fellow of the Royal Society, Spencer had been Member of Parliament for Surrey before inheriting his peerage and had served briefly as a Lord of the Treasury. He was one of the many Whigs who had rejected the somewhat erratic leadership of Charles James Fox when the French declared war, and had "gone over" to the government, for which Mr. Pitt had rewarded him by first making him ambassador to Vienna and then recalling him to take over from Pitt's own brother at the Admiralty. He had been here too short a time to be judged, Nathan supposed, and though the disastrous landings at Quiberon were not an auspicious beginning to his new career, they could largely be blamed upon the divisions in the Royalist command and, of course, William Pitt, who had encouraged the venture.

"So, do you have any answer to these charges?" his lordship enquired, with a mild display of interest, "or do you intend to challenge every one of those who have made them, including the acting governor of Jamaica?"

Nathan ignored the sarcasm. "As to my conduct in the Caribbean," he replied, "I believe every one of my duties was accomplished satisfactorily, even despite the attempts of Mr. Imlay to frustrate them."

"I am inclined to agree with you," replied the earl, surprisingly, "and would have been ready to dismiss the charges and commend you upon your achievements, had it not been for the more recent complaints from Sir John Warren and the Chevalier de Batz, and your public assault upon a trusted agent of the government . . ." Nathan opened his mouth to protest but the First Lord stilled him with a gesture, ". . . the which have disposed me to agree with your detractors, for you do indeed appear to be something of a hothead, sir—a loose cannon who does more damage to your own reputation and that of the service than he does to the enemy."

"Though I venture there are a number of Frenchmen who would disagree, my lord," Nathan pointed out, provoked into a manner he would normally have despised.

"Would it concern you to be dismissed the service?" his lordship enquired with dangerous composure.

"It would concern me that I was unable to serve my country at a time of war," Nathan replied carefully.

"But not enough to moderate your behaviour?"

"I am not sure that moderation in time of war . . ."

"Do not bandy words with me, sir. The fact is you are very close to being court-martialled and at the very least relieved of your command, a disgrace that would considerably distress your father and doubtless add to your mother's current financial liabilities." Nathan felt the blood rush to his face. "And do not glare at me, sir. I speak as an admirer of both, though Lady Catherine, I must say, is her own worst enemy, a feature you appear to have inherited. However, you seem to have your own admirers. Or at least, those who urge me to consider your more useful attributes. Mr. Pitt, for one."

Nathan was stunned into silence, for he had met the King's chief minister only once, an encounter which had led directly to his employment as a government agent in Paris.

"Yes, I thought that would give you pause for thought. Mr. Pitt is of the opinion that you might yet do your country a service. You appear to have that facility, rare in one of your rank, for sailing a lone furrow—is that the word? And, one might say, under false colours."

Nathan remained silent, though his mind was racing.

"Indeed, it is the opinion of Mr. Pitt, and some of his associates, that you are ideally suited for such an enterprise. So much so that he has asked me to propose a return to your former occupation. Temporarily, that is, before resuming command of the *Unicorn*."

"He wants me to go back to France?"

"That would appear to be the gist of it."

"For what purpose?"

Spencer inclined his head. "I must first ask you how you are disposed to respond to such a proposal?"

Nathan was surprised to register a quickening of the pulse, not entirely unpleasant. A surge of excitement almost. For despite his ordeals in Paris during the time of the Terror, he knew that Pitt was right and that something in him was drawn to the life of the secret agent. Operating independently behind enemy lines, "sailing a lone furrow," as the First Lord had put it, "under false colours." He wondered sometimes if it had originated in his peculiar childhood, as a boy born in America, living in England during the War of Independence, the son of an English father and an American mother, who had been parted almost since his birth. Divided loyalties had been bred in his very constitution. As a child he was used to wearing different masks. And growing up in Sussex he had liked nothing better than to trespass on forbidden territory.

But in those days all he had risked was a beating.

"I am not averse to the proposal," he replied guardedly, "but I was summoned here, I believe, to answer certain charges."

"Quite. Well, let me put it to you quite candidly, Captain. There are also certain charges against Mr. Imlay—charges made by yourself among others—the which, as you have pointed out, have been strangely overlooked by those in authority. There are reasons for this.

Reasons that involve the services Mr. Imlay has done us in the past and may continue to do in the future. The same would, of course, apply to you."

"And yet I would not wish the charges against me to be overlooked," Nathan replied, "when I believe I have a very good case to have them dismissed entirely. In all instances."

All but one. The instance of the *Conquest* firing upon the crowd of women and children on the Beach of the White Sands. For it weighed heavily upon his conscience and there was a price to be paid for it, even in blood.

Spencer shook his head wearily. "My dear sir, if the First Lord of the Treasury and the First Lord of the Admiralty are both satisfied with your conduct—indeed, if they approve it on all counts—then they will most certainly be dismissed. If you wish to counter them however, to call for a full investigation, perhaps, then, so be it. But I must advise you that it will take a great deal of your time—and money—and that in the meantime I will be obliged to suspend you from command."

So there it was. Blackmail, pure and simple.

Nathan made a slight, but not unappreciative bow.

"Very well, my lord, I am not at all averse to the proposal."

The First Lord returned the courtesy.

"Very good," he said, "then there is someone I wish you to meet."

CHAPTER THIRTEEN

the Madonna and the Rose

MR. BICKNELL CONEY was introduced to Nathan as a banker—a director of the Bank of England, no less— though he looked to Nathan very like one of those exponents of Three-card Monte at the Epsom Derby who invite you to find the Dirty Lady and depart the proceedings very much to their advantage. An ill-favoured fellow with something of the ferret or the fox about him, his most notable feature was a long, sharp nose that listed visibly to starboard, possibly from the constant tapping upon it of a lean and prescient forefinger. His beady eyes betrayed a lively concern for his own interest and he carried about him a great air of secret knowledge.

"Mr. Coney is a man of singular ability," Earl Spencer informed Nathan with apparent sincerity, "upon whose insights His Majesty's Government have come very much to rely."

Which was possibly why it was so very much out of pocket, Nathan reflected privately.

Mr. Coney's insights, in this particular instance, were more political than financial, and concerned the present composition of the government in France.

"Since the demise of Robespierre, it has been dominated by two men, Tallien and Barras" he began, "both of whom are, I believe, known to the captain."

The captain demurred. He had met them but once, he insisted, and that only briefly, on the day of Robespierre's overthrow. "Imlay knows them rather better," he assured the First Lord meaningfully.

"Indeed," acknowledged the banker, before his lordship could comment, "but before we move on to Mr. Imlay, let me say that behind these two gentlemen stand, or perhaps one should say, lie . . ." his smirk did nothing to improve the beauty of his appearance, ". . . two very interesting women. You will have heard, perhaps, of Thérésa Cabarrus?"

"Our Lady of Thermidor," Nathan murmured.

"Quite. The new Madonna—at least in the eyes of her admirers. It is widely believed that she played a significant part in the coup against Robespierre during the month of Thermidor, as the Revolutionists insist upon calling the high months of summer. The story goes that she persuaded her lover, Tallien, to speak out against him in the Convention and even provided him with the knife with which he was to stab the tyrant, threatening to stab herself if he failed in the venture; though as she was in prison at the time, awaiting execution, I think this is another example of the French passion for dramatics."

Again that horrible smirk, though his lordship smiled with what appeared to be genuine enjoyment. It occurred to Nathan that despite the large gulf in their station, the peer was somewhat in thrall to the banker, but perhaps this was not so very remarkable. He was doubtless in his debt for a few house improvements.

"Be that as it may," Coney continued, "it served to convert the condemned prisoner into Our Lady of Thermidor, the heroine of the hour, the saviour of France who brought an end to the Terror. And so she has remained, despite the charges of corruption and dissidence levelled against the current regime. Married now to her lover and more correctly addressed as Madame Tallien, the paramount leader of French society whose influence over her husband and his partner Barras—who is very much the senior partner, by the by—is considerable. In another age I would say she was the power behind the throne."

"I think you said there were two women," Nathan reminded him, for his informant had sunk into reflection.

"Ah yes. Thank you for reminding me. The other—somewhat in her shadow but no less important for our purposes—is Josephine de Beauharnais, known as Rose to her intimates, of which there are not a few. Interestingly, she is a Creole: the daughter of a sugar planter from the French colony of Martinique and the widow of General de Beauharnais, who was beheaded during the Terror. As his wife, she was condemned to suffer the same fate and was incarcerated for many months in what had, until the time of the Terror, been a convent of the Carmelite Order. During which time she became the good friend of Thérésa Cabarrus and the lover, by the by, of General Hoche, with whom you very nearly became acquainted on the shores of Quiberon." The knowing smirk crept out, once more, from beneath the long, sharp nose. "Now she is the lover of Barras, though it is said he would willingly exchange her for her great friend Thérésa, the wife of his junior partner. So there you have it, the Madonna and the Rose. 'A fine pair of tarts,' as they would say in Wapping, though a less vulgar term would be 'courtesans.' These two women have, in a very short time, re-established Paris as the capital of fashion, indulgence and scandal—and themselves as its reigning deities. They are rather more interested in their amusements than they are in politics, but their paramount interest, I can confidently assure you, is in money. And money, as usual, is at the heart of what I am about to tell you. I can, of course, count on your absolute discretion?"

"The captain's discretion is legendary," murmured his lordship, with a return to his customary humour.

"Rose, if I may call her that, is practically a pauper, though you would never know it from her style of living, while Thérésa is the daughter of Count François Cabarrus, financial adviser to the King of Spain and a man of considerable wealth. But both women are ever in need of the means to finance the daily grind, as it were. And both are known to take bribes from those who think it may buy them an advantage with the current government of France." The small pause that followed might have been for effect or from a natural revulsion to such alien practices, as might be expected of a director of the Bank of England. "And more to the point, both have invested heavily in the speculations of one Gilbert Imlay. A gentleman with whom, I understand, you are well acquainted."

So, here it comes, Nathan thought: another of Imlay's intrigues. And the way the conversation was going, he was destined to become as involved in this one as he had been in the last, though it had come close to killing him on occasion. That, too, he recalled, had begun with a conversation at the Admiralty.

"You knew him in Paris, I believe, and then in the Caribbean?" The banker did not wait for Nathan's reply. "And he may have told you of his investments in the western territories of the United States."

Now he did wait, his head inclined to an angle and his eyes sharp, like a blackbird, Nathan thought, following the underground burrowing of a worm.

"He once told me he had purchased 18,000 acres of virgin land in Kentucky and wished to become a farmer," Nathan confirmed. "I was inclined to be sceptical."

"Well, that is certainly a portion of his holdings, though I believe he has yet to pay for the land in question and I do not expect he will 'turn a clod himself,' as they say in Ireland. But he has laid claim to a great deal more than 18,000 acres. Several hundred thousand would be more accurate, registered in the names of certain surrogates. This does not surprise you, Captain?"

"Not especially," Nathan confessed, who would have been surprised only if Imlay had paid for it out of his own pocket.

"Well, and we now approach the crux of the matter: if the United

States should expand westward, that land will be worth a great deal more than it is now. However, the entire territories west of the Mississippi and north to the Canada border are presently part of the Spanish Empire. And Spain is stubbornly opposed to settlement, fearing to jeopardise its hold on the region. Their agents in Natchez and New Orleans, indeed, all along the Mississippi, have been encouraging the Indians to attack the few settlements that have been established there, which are mainly American of course. And of course, their hold on New Orleans blocks any access to the sea by means of the rivers. But you will know all this from your own experience of the region."

Nathan's mind was racing. True, all this *was* known to him. The mystery was, where it was heading.

"However, we have now learned that certain factions in Madrid are anxious for an accommodation with the Revolutionists in Paris," the banker resumed, "and that in return for peace in Europe they would be prepared to cede the entire region to France. That is, the vast territory west of the Mississippi, from New Orleans to the Canada border and westward to the Pacific Ocean."

He gave Nathan a moment to take this in.

"We need to know if the French and the Spanish have come to an arrangement along these lines," explained Earl Spencer in case he was having difficulty. "That is why we want you to go to Paris."

In the sudden silence Nathan could hear the pigeons coo-carooing on his lordship's windowledge. It sounded to him remarkably like a dry chuckle, the kind the Devil might make, or Gilbert Imlay. He spread his palms in a gesture of helpless confusion. "But how am I to even begin to . . . to . . ."

"You will carry a letter from Imlay introducing you to Madame Tallien as his agent," continued the banker briskly, "in which capacity you will invite her to confide in you concerning the intentions of the French government in North America. Has there been a secret agreement with Spain along the lines I have outlined? What has France agreed in return? And is the United States involved in the deal?"

You could not fault him for clarity, Nathan thought, and as easy as pounds, shillings and pence.

"But why—even if she knows—would she pass on such information to me?" he enquired reasonably. "Even if she thinks I am a friend of Imlay's?"

"Because it could make her the richest woman in Europe."

Another short silence. Even the pigeons appeared attentive.

"If the territory is ceded to France," his lordship expounded, "and the French come to some arrangement with the United States over settlement in the region, then the land Imlay has registered in their names will increase substantially in value. If Madame Tallien knows of this, then she will almost certainly be anxious to purchase more land from the same source. And that will tell us a great deal."

Nathan considered the prospect gloomily. So he was to become a land agent for Gilbert Imlay, while the fellow continued to strut around London, wining and dining in Covent Garden and entertaining his concubine in Charlotte Street.

"Come now," said Spencer, seeing his downcast expression, "from what I have heard, you will find Madame Tallien a charming confidante. She may even invite you to one of her notorious salons. I am told they would shame the courtesans of Venice for indecency and cause even the Hottentots of the Limpopo to consider themselves o'erdressed."

"I cannot wait," murmured Nathan, with something of his lordship's humour.

"Excellent, for there is a vessel waiting for you at Deal, which will transport you across the Channel this very night."

"Tonight?" Nathan was startled.

"I am sorry if that inconveniences you. If you have any more duels outstanding, I am afraid they will have to wait upon your return."

"But what of the *Unicorn*, my lord?"

"Never fear, we will not give her to someone else. I should not think you would be long detained. Indeed, the sooner you bring us news of what the French are plotting with their friends in Madrid, the sooner we will be able to make our own dispositions to counter it."

"Then I had better make my own dispositions, my lord, if I am to leave for Deal before dark." This would not take long. He had one bag to pack and two women to bid farewell—three if you counted Izzy.

"Before you do, there is one more thing." Nathan braced himself. "As Imlay's representative, you will find yourself at the heart of the seraglio that presently governs France and in an excellent position to judge its strengths and weaknesses. It is to be hoped that you will learn a great deal more that will be of use to us. In particular, why the opposition in Paris failed to act during the landings at Quiberon."

"Is that something Madame Tallien might be expected to know, my lord?"

"It is. For her husband has the responsibility for repressing internal dissent—in the Vendée and elsewhere. It is important for us to have more knowledge of the strengths and weaknesses of the opposition in Paris."

Nathan's gloom increased proportionately.

"From what Imlay has told us, Madame Tallien and her friend Rose are not only the greatest trollops in Paris, but also its most notorious gossips. I am persuaded they will be only too happy to babble out their secrets to you and that you will soon become the most intimate of friends. Indeed, I cannot but envy you the opportunity."

"I was only wondering, my lord, why, if he is so trusted, you do not send Imlay himself?"

"Ah. Well, now." His lordship shot a look at the banker. "That is to stray into areas that do not properly concern you. I will only say that while Mr. Imlay has made himself extremely useful to His Majesty's Government from time to time, his paramount loyalties are, we believe, to the United States of America. And of course, to himself. If any conflict of interest were to arise, I do not believe we could rely upon him to put Britain first, whereas in your case, of course, we can."

"And can we be sure that Imlay's recommendation is still to be trusted by his friends in Paris?" Nathan persisted. "For he has been away a long time."

"Oh, I think so. His friends still appear to have every confidence in him. And after all, they have a great deal to gain by it. They have ambitions to buy America. And you, sir, will sell it to them, at a most advantageous rate."

CHAPTER FOURTEEN

Dance Macabre

IT WAS OVER A YEAR since Nathan was last in Paris. In the month of Thermidor: the time of the heat. He had stood pretty much where he was standing now when he had first seen the death carts trundling down the Rue Honoré with their daily quota of flesh and blood for the machine on the Place de la Révolution.

They had been led by a little drummer boy with a face like an angel, beating the step; then came the foot soldiers with fixed bayonets; then a troop of horse; and then the carts. Farm carts with tall sides that the English called tumbrels and the French *charrettes* that were handy for carrying hay and other loose produce of the fields. But on that occasion they had been carrying women. Women from many walks of life and of many different ages, though most were in their twenties or younger. Their hair had been roughly cropped, so roughly as to lacerate the scalp in parts. Their hands had been tied and their chemises torn to expose the nape of the neck and, in some cases, the breasts. Some were praying. Others weeping. A bystander told Nathan they were nuns. Nuns and whores. He did not appear to make a distinction.

The procession had put Nathan in mind of a similar event, in Salem, Massachusetts, where they had once hanged seventeen women for the practice of witchcraft. It had happened long before his birth but it was part of his family history and it had been described to him many times when he was growing up, for one of the condemned had been his great-grandmother, Sarah Good. And many times since had he seen her, in his nightmares, flying across the moon on her broomstick, as witches do in childish dreams, or twisting slowly at the gallows with her face black and her tongue protruding and her eyes staring and the rope creaking. In certain conditions aboard ship, in a gentle swell when there was little else to trouble him, he would hear the creaking of a rope and it would haunt him still, that slowly twisting corpse.

Now he watched a very different procession advancing down the Rue Honoré, or the Rue *Saint*-Honoré, as it was now called, its former sanctity having been restored to it in these more tolerant times. It was led by a number of young men dressed all in black, as if for a funeral, but with long plaits hanging down over their shoulders, like thin coils of rope, or snakes, and their hands thrust insolently into their pockets. They were known as *Muscadins,* Nathan had learned, and their garb distinguished them as men who had been condemned to death in the time of the Terror or who had suffered the loss of at least one close relative to the guillotine. They sauntered, rather than marched, down the centre of the street, those at the rear forced into an indignant scuttle from time to time by the disrespectful horses that followed: six prancing greys pulling a violet-painted carriage with matching curtains. And behind the carriage came a troupe of young women attired in muslin, so thin and so closely aligned to the curves of the female form that its value in preserving the modesty of the wearer was negligible. Indeed, the material appeared to have been soaked in water, or oil, to make it more revealing. These were the *Merveilleuses,* he had heard, an exclusively female order united by their striking physical beauty and a passionate resolve to outrage the rest of society by any means imaginable. Nathan had seen many things in Paris that were not seen in other cities and had thought himself inured to shock, but he did blink a little at this, for he doubted if even Babylon in all its glory could have surpassed so blatant a display of harlotry. And yet there was a kind of almost pastoral innocence about it, a splendid indifference to convention, the creatures dancing with such obvious delight in their own bodies, as if to express their sublime joy of life and expunge the horrors of the past when death had ruled here.

Behind them came four young men of exceptional beauty and muscularity, wearing nothing but a pair of goatskin breeches and playing pan pipes. And behind *them* came a long line of open carriages and cabs carrying the *Jeunesse Dorées*—the Gilded Youth of Paris—in oversized coats with enormous collars and exaggerated cravats that covered not only the neck and breast but most of the chin; flesh-coloured nankeen breeches so tightly moulded to the limbs that they appeared to be wearing nothing below the waist save their gleaming boots: the new *sans culottes* of Paris, following the route to the guillotine.

Nathan had taken much the same route from his hotel: past the studio of the artist Jean-Baptiste Regnault where Sara had studied—and occasionally posed nude if Imlay could be believed; past the old disused priory where the Jacobins had met to debate the cause of Revolution and chart its uncertain course; past the boarded-up doorway of the Duplays' workshop where Robespierre had lodged when he was the greatest man in France and which the mob had anointed with ox-blood for his own final journey to the guillotine. He walked with a head full of memories, ignoring the shop windows with their latest fashions, the leaflets proclaiming the delights of some new dance hall or theatre, the prostitutes who openly accosted him at every step. More than twenty thousand, according to one report, were now operating on the streets of Paris. Where had they been at the time of the Terror when they were not bundled into the death carts; how had they made a living? On into the Place de la Révolution where the guillotine had once stood: an open meadow where sheep and cows now grazed and couples walked arm in arm. Impossible not to think of the blood that had been spilled here and the heads that had rolled. Of Marie

Antoinette, the golden Queen of France, sketched in the tumbrel by the artist David as a toothless, grey-haired crone; and the dignified, if puzzled gentleman who had been its King and was brought here in a closed carriage lest his bearing incite the crowds. Of Charlotte Corday who had stabbed Marat in his bath and Madame Roland who had done nothing very much but speak out of turn and serve sugared water at her salons instead of champagne which was quite enough, according to Danton, to make an end to her. Of Danton himself, who had been the voice of Revolution, and Desmoulins, its stammering scribe. Of the thousands of others, some famous, most not, who had trod these same bloody boards, thinking what to say, or simply struck dumb, wondering how they came to be here and very much wishing they had a smaller part in the drama. But not a sign, not a stain, no statue or memorial stone remained to mark their passing, nothing to remind the strolling couples what had happened here at the time of the Terror: just the grazing cows and the sheep and the wild flowers growing in profusion amongst the sun-bleached grass.

Nathan had been in Paris for three days now and still he could not credit it: the difference from the city he had left a year before in the hothouse summer of '94 when thirty, forty people a day, sometimes more, were butchered by that tireless blade. So many, there had been complaints about the stench of blood and the machine had been moved, temporarily, to the Place du Trône on the far side of the city, where Sara had been sent on the day it ended.

But now the guillotine was put away, like a toy that had out-lived its owner's infancy, and there were new men on the throne of Republican France: widely known as the Thermidorians, after the month of their victory—though as Nathan recalled, every one of them had been a terrorist when it was the thing to be, making their violent speeches in the National Convention and signing war-rants for execution and lining their pockets, when they thought Robespierre wasn't looking.

But now Robespierre was dead and it was business as usual. There were fortunes to be made by those who had access to the men of the moment. And the women.

Nathan was on his way to attend a "soirée" at the home of Madame Tallien on the Champs Elysées, the written invitation having arrived at White's Hotel within a day of sending round his card and the letter of introduction from Imlay to announce his presence in this city of sin and his desire for an audience with its ruling deities. He had been advised to take a cab but felt he owed it to his memories to walk, talking his time, letting the past walk with him, whispering, pointing, wondering, sharing his astonishment. He had walked this way when he had heard the news of Sara's execution, on the very day that Robespierre had been overthrown and the Terror ended. Out of the city and beyond, through the Champs Elysées and along the river, walking all day, scarcely noticing where he was going or what he saw. And walking back in the darkness, wishing he would meet with some footpad or Jacobin on whom to vent his anger and his grief. And shortly afterwards, he had left for England, thinking never to return.

He had no idea what to expect, business or pleasure, though the two seemed inextricably conjoined in the Paris of the Thermidorians. But judging from the procession he had seen heading in the same direction, pleasure was very much on the agenda this evening. He supposed the carriage might have contained Our Lady of Thermidor herself, for he had heard that she travelled in style and with a view to entertainment.

He followed the directions he had been given across the Place de la Révolution and through the woods of the Champs Elysées, dappled green and gold by the light of the setting sun, until he found the little lane leading down towards the river. It was a quiet, secluded place; it might have been buried deep in the countryside, except for a certain, what was it? Artifice? Yes. For there were coloured lanterns among the trees, barely noticeable in the still bright sunlight, and a profusion of flowers that did not seem entirely natural on either side of the lane, and little red-and-white toadstools so preposterous he bent down to examine them more closely and found they were made of waxpaper.

At the end of the lane were wooden gates, entwined with ivy, and two attendants, clad in goatskin breeches and high cloven heels. They eyed him balefully for he was no Gilded Youth—and certainly no faun—but attired like a respectable gentleman of New England, in a beige-coloured coat and matching breeches, with brown-and-black Hessian boots and a brown, wide-brimmed felt hat. Brown? Beige? These were not the colours of the Thermidorian. *And he was on foot.* But his invitation was in order and he spoke a polite, respectable French, so they let him pass, directing him down what appeared to be a rutted farm track with more wild flowers and even bigger toadstools with lights in them. And so, at last, he came to La Chaumière, the fabled home of Our Lady of Thermidor.

It was a thatched cottage, with walls of wood and brick, set among rambling roses and honeysuckle, like a cottage in England inhabited by a modest class of yeomanry. There was even a cabbage patch and unlike the toadstools, the cabbages were real for Nathan could see real butterflies flitting among them and the holes that real caterpillars had made. The door of the cottage was open and two pretty young women awaited him in the porch wearing similar dress to the charmers that had followed the royal carriage, and with the same consideration for decency. They each carried a tray of fluted glasses containing what was almost certainly champagne—for the fashion for sugared water had gone the way of Madame Roland's head. Taking one and murmuring his thanks, Nathan ducked through the low lintel of the open door.

But it was the wrong door.

Or the wrong house. It had to be. He almost stepped out again to make sure.

He had been expecting some bucolic retreat, entirely bogus but in keeping with the rustic artifice of the exterior. Well, here was artifice, sure, but there was nothing of the rustic about it. At first glance the room appeared to be at least double the size of the exterior, its dimensions flattered by a large panorama of woods and fields, vineyards and faraway hills glimpsed between the classical columns that supported the high painted ceiling. So cunning was this *trompe l'oeil* he might have been deceived into thinking the landscape was real and that he had entered some kind of pagoda set in the open air had it not been for the mythological creatures that gambolled about its phony fields: nymphs and satyrs romping with hippogriffs and centaurs under an azure sky where gods and goddesses looked down in benevolent approval from among fluffy clouds. And in the centre of this wonderland a fountain—a real fountain with real water—from which Neptune, armed with a trident, glowered less amiably, rather as Robespierre might, had he been suddenly revived and transported hither, his head stitched back upon his shoulders and a false beard attached to his frosty countenance.

Otherwise, the room was empty.

Nathan looked around carefully to make sure. Yet he cannot have been entirely alone for above the sound of the running water he could hear music and laughter. He touched one of the stone columns tentatively, as if it might disappear or make the walls fall down like a house of cards. It did not do either of these alarming things, though it revealed itself, not entirely to his surprise, to be made of stiffened paper, like the toadstools. He sipped cautiously from his glass but it was, indeed, champagne, and looked about him warily, searching for the human life he knew must be here somewhere: cunningly concealed among the landscapes and the columns. And indeed it was. For between two painted Nubian slaves with Etruscan vases and little else to hide their nudity, he espied another open door, revealing a tantalising glimpse of moving figures beyond. He advanced towards it, half expecting to find more artifice, and emerged on to a stone terrace, crowded with people: real people of flesh and blood, though their authenticity might have been disputed by one who had not observed the cortège upon the Rue Saint-Honoré. *Muscadins* and *Merveilleuses* and other of their kin, were eating and drinking, talking, laughing and dancing, while a large orchestra, dressed as gypsies, played the polka.

Nathan moved through this assembly as if in a dream or fairy tale, murmuring his excuses and retreating shyly when he ventured to brush against a portion of human anatomy not normally exposed to sight or touch. And yet on close acquaintance there was something asexual about these women: something of the macabre, with their short hair and their rouged cheeks and the blood-red ribbons they wore about their necks imitation of the decisive line drawn by the guillotine. Their eyes and smiles were just a little too bright, their complexions a little too sticky with paint and powder, but steely, too, like painted, mechanical dolls designed by a confectioner.

Beyond the terrace was a long meadow sloping gently down to the river. There were people here, too, though spread more thinly on the ground, and white-clothed tables, filled with delicacies and adorned with wild flowers. Nathan was tempted to make the best of it and eat his fill, for he had not had a decent meal since leaving London; there were great food shortages in Paris, or so he had believed until now, but he resolved to seek out his hostess first; she was, after all, his sole purpose in coming here. He had a rough description of her: young, dark-haired, beautiful, a taste for exotic dress . . . He looked about him, his senses reeling. Where was he to find her in such a crowd? And what would he say if he did, for he could scarce talk business on such an occasion?

And then he saw her. She was moving among a circle of admirers, tall as an Amazon; gracious as a queen, and dressed in a Grecian tunic that reached to just above the knee but was slashed to the waist to reveal a glimpse of naked thigh. Her hair was short and tightly curled and there was something about her that was both boyish and brazenly feminine. Nathan thought of Cleopatra—the girl Cleopatra who had seduced Caesar—though he knew immediately, if only from the ornamental dagger she wore at her waist, that this was his hostess, the celebrated Thérésa Tallien, Our Lady of Thermidor.

He watched as she strode through the meadow, just below where he stood upon the terrace, listening to a young man at her side, with the other women trailing behind her like the Queen's wardrobe. She was laughing, or at least showing her teeth which were as near perfect as the rest of her body, for this was no candied doll or automaton. She walked like a ballet dancer or an athlete, and there was a bloom about her, a glow almost, that was part attributable to her youth—for she cannot have been much above twenty—and part to health and sheer exuberance. She wore Grecian sandals tied with thongs almost to the knee and rings on her toes and he remembered that it was widely reported that these were to hide the rat bites she had suffered whilst in prison during the Terror. Though she appeared to be listening attentively, her dark eyes never stopped moving among the crowd and finally she looked up and saw Nathan watching her from the terrace. Though he was by no means the only spectator, she appeared startled. Her glance flickered away, almost shyly, but then returned and held his gaze for a moment with a question in her eyes. She said something into the ear of one of her female attendants, who fixed Nathan with her own stare, quite rudely and almost aggressively, so that he turned and moved away through the crowd—but slowly, feeling their eyes still upon him, pausing to take another glass of champagne from a passing nymph. Then he felt the pressure on his arm.

"*Monsieur*, where are you going? There is one who would speak with you."

She was an older woman than their hostess and dressed more demurely in a long muslin robe, though it hung so low upon her breasts that the word "demure" could only be used by way of a comparison; it seemed that the slightest untoward movement would cause it to drop like a curtain, leaving her entirely exposed. He stared into her eyes with almost desperate fervour lest his own be dragged to the nether regions where they so much desired to be.

She cocked her head to one side and surveyed him curiously.

"You are a stranger, I think, to our little gatherings." She spoke in a gentle lilting voice with a slight lisp.

"I am, madam."

There were probably wittier things he might have said but they did not occur to him instantly. He was relieved that he could make any kind of noise at all, beside a low moan or a bleat.

"Then permit me to introduce myself, for we do not stand upon ceremony here. My name is Marie-Josèphe de Beauharnais."

And she made him a little curtsy, her eyes brimming with humour as if it was all a wonderful joke—him, her, her name, her appearance, this place, Paris, the Revolution . . . even the fanatics who had come so close to killing her, for he knew her now as the woman the banker had spoken of in London: the Creole from Martinique who had shared a prison with General Hoche and escaped the guillotine by a whisker and was now the lover of Barras and the intimate of Our Lady of Thermidor. The woman whom Coney had called Rose.

He took off his hat and bowed, catching her hand and touching it to his lips for he saw that he must play the gallant.

"My name is Turner," he informed her. "Captain Nathaniel Turner, from New York."

The smile did not falter but he noted a sudden sharpness in her eyes, swiftly masked by the long lashes.

"Captain Turner," she repeated softly, as if it were a caress, "and newly arrived in Paris?"

"Is it so obvious?"

"Not at all, but you stand out from the crowd, sir, and you have caught the eye of our hostess. Come, let me introduce you, for she has seen that you are alone and no-one must lack for company at La Chaumière."

And so he was led down the steps from the terrace into the heart of the new Republican court of France and it opened for him as if his fairy godmother guide had waved her magic wand, and he found himself gazing into the appraising, angelic eyes of Our Lady of Thermidor. Rose murmured an introduction. Again, that wary look, swiftly masked.

"Captain Turner, so glad you could join us." Her voice was husky, not as attractive as her friend's, but then she did not need it to be; her voice was irrelevant. She gave him her hand and he lowered his head over its elegant arch, trying not to look too fixedly at the twin peaks beyond. He had not paid court to a queen before and it was disconcerting, for the first time, to find her almost naked.

"You have come directly from New York?"

"Not directly."

"By way of Mars, perhaps?"

"But of course. And now I am in Venus."

Oh la. And the merry laughter. For there was as much artifice in the conversation at La Chaumière as in the décor. Rose, he noted, had bad teeth and raised her hand to her mouth to conceal them. But the eyes remained sharp.

"And we have a mutual friend . . ."

"Indeed."

"He is well, I trust?"

"He is very well and bids me present his most sincere respects."

"He is in America?"

"No. He is in England at present."

The courtiers had drawn back a little, perhaps sensing something more than idle chatter, all bar Rose and the young man, who was looking upon him more shrewdly than Nathan might have expected, though now he shot a glance at Thérésa who mouthed the one word, "Imlay."

"But he has been to America very recently," continued Nathan, "and has news of your mutual interests."

Had he said too much, he wondered, for the eyes clouded slightly and it was the man who answered for her.

"Well, we will be pleased to hear it, will we not, my dear?" With a brilliant smile but without taking his eyes off Nathan's for an instant—and there was something in them, for all their liquid charm, that made Nathan think of Robespierre. "Perhaps we will have an opportunity later, Captain, when you have had a chance to enjoy yourself a little."

Was this a putdown? It could very easily have been, but there was a swift glance to Rose that seemed to contain some unspoken instruction for Nathan felt her hand upon his arm once more and she led him off towards the tables for she felt sure he needed feeding, she lisped.

Indeed he did, and had no objection to being fed by such a one, for there was a supple voluptuousness about her, an overt sensuality that made her even more alluring to his eyes than the other nymphs, with the exception of Thérésa herself. Every movement she made threatened his precarious composure, just as it threatened to dislodge the precarious muslin from her breasts.

"My goodness!" He saw that she was gazing in something like awe at the amount he had heaped upon his plate and he frowned in mortification for he had not really been thinking about it. "You must not eat quite so much," she abjured him, "or you will not be able to move. And you cannot be permitted to leave without dancing at least one polka with me."

A polka? In that dress? It was unimaginable. But perhaps not. All things considered, it was best not to let his mind dwell upon such delightful possibilities, for if it carried to his loins he was lost. She led him to one of the small tables set out under a little grove of trees, hung with lanterns. The natural light had leeched from the sky, transforming it from a part-wiped palette of creams and blues and pinks to a soft, seductive violet not unlike that of the carriage he had seen in the Rue Saint-Honoré. Despite his unease, Nathan felt strangely elated. True, there was the permanent ache, deep in his heart, for Sara—and it would always be there, especially in Paris— but sometimes it felt less intense than at others and this was such a time. It had nothing to do with his charming companion, he told himself, but more with the sheer exhilaration of playing a part, of being behind enemy lines—and finding them occupied by beautiful women with next to nothing on.

But he did not fool himself that he was among friends. Nor that they would smilingly direct him homeward if they saw through his pretence. He was walking upon a tightrope without a safety net, knowing that if he made one false move he would surely die. And he loved it. Well, perhaps love was too strong a word but he was, in his own way, content. Why? Why so much more than being the captain of a ship at sea? Was it the absence of responsibility, the relief of being freed from the burden of command? Or the intoxicating sense of recklessness, while some small but vital part of his brain focused solely and soberly upon the next careful step.

But there were other duties than the burden of command. He was here to gather information. And there was something to be learned right now.

"The gentleman we just met . . ." he began.

"Monsieur Ouvrard. I am sorry, I should have introduced you."

"Not at all. But he seems . . ."

"Confident?"

"Well . . ."

"Arrogant?"

He laughed. "A little of both." Though the word he had avoided saying was "proprietorial." "He has an enviable air of composure, certainly, for someone so young."

"That is possibly because he is one of the richest men in France."

He stared at her curiously, half-smiling. "He cannot be much more than twenty-five or twenty-six," he said.

"He is twenty-three."

"So. He inherited a sugar island?"

Rose shrugged her pretty shoulders. "Much good it would do him if he did, with the blockade. My family own a part of one and I am as poor as a church mouse." She noted his expression. "It is true. Thanks to the British Navy. My fortune is what you see before you."

He said what was expected of him but for once her mind was on other things. She was watching Ouvrard thoughtfully as he bent his head close to Thérésa's. "As a matter of fact, he was an accountant when the Revolution began, working for a grocery shop in Nantes. And Thérésa, as you might know, is the daughter of a banker and a noble. Now look at them."

"Well, I suppose that is what a Revolution is about," Nathan responded lamely, for he detected a note of bitterness in her remark.

"Oh, really," she murmured, "is that why so many died? I am sure if they had known, they would have skipped happily to the guillotine."

"I meant Equality. Or at least, the possibility of advancement in life, even for an accountant in a grocery store."

"And was that what your American Revolution was about? Advancement in life? Getting rich?"

"Partly," he agreed. "Though for appearance sake, we called it the pursuit of happiness."

"Well, I do not know about happy, but certainly it has made a lot of people wealthy, though most of them appear to be bankers."

Nathan looked toward Ouvrard. "So he is a banker now?"

"Did you not know? Yes, he is a banker and a man of business. And, of course, a lover."

"A lover? Is there money in that?"

"Oh a great deal, if you love the right people." She cocked her head in that way she had—contrived, of course, but no less attractive for that. "I wonder why I am talking to you like this? I am usually more circumspect. Is that the word? Perhaps it is because you are an American."

Nathan recalled what Bicknell Coney or Lord Spencer had said about her lack of discretion, but this was too good an opportunity to miss—and had perhaps been presented for that purpose.

"You have known many Americans—besides Imlay?"

"Ah, Imlay. I think there are not many like Imlay. You have met him recently, you say?"

"I met him only last week, in London." She glanced swiftly about her to see that they were not overheard and it reminded him of the time of the Terror, so perhaps things had not changed so much after all: perhaps the artifice was not confined to La Chaumière. "As Americans, of course, we have the privilege of visiting in England and France," he added innocently, "though passing between the two is uncommonly difficult at present."

"And he was in good health, Imlay?"

"Excellent health—and high spirits."

So high, indeed, that Nathan had been inclined to regret his decision to fire wide that morning in Lincoln's Inn Fields for as he was led away by the Watch he had glanced back to see Imlay beaming broadly and speeding him on his way with an amused salute.

"You have known him long?"

"Long enough. We met in New York some years ago."

"New York?" She raised a delicate brow. "Then you are not a frontiersman, Captain?" she teased him.

"No. More a seafaring man."

"So you have not visited the western territories?"

He decided not, for his knowledge of the region was confined to what he knew from Bicknell Coney and the maps he had pored over in London, and they were not very good maps at that. But it would help to have had some experience of the frontier.

"My own explorations have been further south. In the bayous and swamps about New Orleans and the Mississippi Delta."

She shuddered theatrically. "I have always had an aversion for snakes," she said, "and other swamp creatures." He wondered how she could tolerate Imlay. "So you have not been tempted to put your own money in Imlay's ventures?"

"My own money is tied up in shipping," he assured her, which was true in its way. "But I wish I had a thousand or so to spare, for there is a great deal to be made from Imlay's ventures, I think. Especially if there is to be peace between France and Spain."

"Really? Well, you must talk to Monsieur Ouvrard about that," she said, "for I know nothing of investments—or of politics."

Too far, too fast: he felt her draw back while he swayed upon his tightrope, one foot in the air. But then she began to prattle away about La Chaumière and how Thérésa seemed to have started a fashion for the pastoral—as if there was anything remotely pastoral about it; he felt like reminding her that Marie Antoinette had nourished similar conceits and look where it had got her.

She was a puzzle to him, this Rose: a curious mixture of the coquette and the sophisticate. Sometimes her conversation was that of a knowledgeable courtier with her head screwed on; at other times she was exceedingly silly. He wondered what was real and what pretence. Or perhaps she was all pretence, like La Chaumière. A waxpaper toadstool. But he recalled his conversation with Lord Spencer at the Admiralty when Coney had left them.

"You must be careful of Rose. She is not at all what she seems. She has suffered a great deal in her life and is nobody's fool. Her husband accused her of being unfaithful—apparently at the instigation of his mistress—and sent her to a nunnery. She was barely pregnant with his child at the time. Or someone else's."

"She became a nun?"

"I do not believe that was in prospect. She merely lodged there with many others considered to be fallen women, from whom she learned a great deal of her tricks."

"So she is tricky."

"Exceedingly so, according to Imlay. Far trickier than her friend Thérésa who is pure innocence by comparison. But her prime concern, I have been assured, is money. And she is greedy. There lies your advantage."

Well, the information came from Imlay so it had to be taken with a pinch of salt, but one thing Nathan was sure of: Marie-Josèphe de Beauharnais was a survivor. She had survived an idiot husband who was as cruel as he was stupid, and she had survived the prisons of the Revolution, and she was still here and appeared to be enjoying every minute of it.

She was now pointing out people in the crowd.

"The woman over there with the face of a bulldog and the body of a Venus; that is Madame Hamelin. You must not go near her—there are no limits to her indiscretions. She once walked naked down the Champs Elysées for a bet. The woman in the shawl looking as if she is at her First Communion; that is Madame Récamier. Do not be misled. She has had more lovers than Messalina. Her husband is a banker: another who has done well from the Revolution. Oh, and see who has joined her—La Raucourt. You have not heard of her? But of course you are from America. She is an actress, but she would scratch my eyes out if she heard me call her that for she thinks of herself as a great tragedienne; she would make a stoat weep. But do not stare at her so or she will come over and clout you with her stick. You will not have failed to notice the stick."

Nathan had not. She leaned upon it like a country gentleman. Nor had he failed to notice that she was dressed like one. He asked if this was from inclination or amusement.

"Oh inclination, of course. She always dresses like that—except when she is upon the stage and obliged to play the part of a woman. She is entirely impervious to convention and lives with one of our late Queen's ladies-in-waiting. I mean Marie Antoinette," she added, as he was an American.

"Ah, *that* queen," he murmured dryly. "And who is the military gentleman who looks as if he has been fired out of a cannon?"

"Where?" She gazed about the company with interest.

"On the terrace. He has been glaring at us for some minutes."

She found him and looked quickly away. "Oh my God, I cannot believe you said that." She had gone quite red.

"I am sorry," he said, "I did not mean to give offence. Is he a friend of yours?"

"Oh no. Good heavens. But you have got him absolutely. He is even called Captain Cannon—in some circles."

"He is an entertainer?"

"Oh heavens, no! Oh dear." Her delight appeared genuine. "No, it is what Barras calls him. He is a real soldier, if you will believe it. He commanded the artillery when Barras took Toulon and now he is a general. Well, a chief of brigade, which I am told is the lowest form of general, and he is the poorest soldier in the French army."

This was probably an exaggeration but he certainly looked poor, unless he dressed for effect. The shabbiness of his uniform was set off by a large bicorn hat which he wore athwart, as opposed to fore and aft, and his lank hair hung straight down on either side like the ears of a spaniel. But there was nothing of the spaniel in his eyes, at least at the moment, for he wore a scowl as ferocious as any villain in a comic opera.

"Please do not stare at him," Rose begged, "or he will take it amiss. He is an Italian and very passionate. He thinks himself in love with me."

"I am sure that is true of most of the men here," Nathan assured her gallantly.

"No. Really in love," she insisted seriously. "He says he wants to marry me, though he asked Thérésa first, the toad. She thought it very amusing, but I believe she is quite fond of him. He has become quite the little pet but it would not do for you to cross him. Perhaps we had better mingle."

She gazed about her vacantly but they were distracted by a commotion upon the terrace. People were applauding and drawing back to permit the passage of a tall, burly individual in a splendid uniform with epaulettes like wings, a wide blue sash about his chest and black ostrich feathers in his hat. The music stopped and then struck up again with the "Marseillaise" and Rose leapt to her feet with her hand to her mouth.

"Oh, it is Barras!" she exclaimed. She shot Nathan a brief glance but it was clear she had dismissed him entirely from her mind. "You must excuse me," she said, and she was off across the lawn, holding up the hem of her robe and running as lightly as a young girl though even from where he sat Nathan could see how the newcomer goggled at her dancing breasts.

Barras. One of the saviours of Thermidor. Nathan had met him on the night of the coup, with Imlay and the other plotters in the Café Carazzo. Later he had watched as Barras led a contingent of the National Guard to the Hotel de Ville to arrest Robespierre. Now he had replaced the Incorruptible as the leading man in France. There could scarcely have been a greater contrast. Where Robespierre had been every inch the provincial lawyer from Arras, Barras was a former viscount and an officer in the King's army who had fought against the British in India. Notoriously corrupt but efficient, too, from what Nathan had heard tell. He must be in his early forties now, energetic, amorous, indulgent. He had certainly put on weight since Nathan last saw him but he strode across the lawns with all the vigour of a man in his prime. He swept off his hat to Rose, caught her by the waist and planted an enthusiastic kiss on her lips.

But Nathan had stopped taking any further interest in the proceedings, for among the entourage that had followed Barras down the steps of the terrace, attired in all the magnificence of one of the Golden Youths of Paris, was Able Seaman Benjamin Bennett, late of His Britannic Majesty's Navy. And before Nathan could duck under the table, or hide behind a tree, or do one of a dozen things that might later have occurred to him, their eyes met and he saw that Bennett recognised him and was as astonished as he.

CHAPTER FIFTEEN

Secrets and Allies

NATHAN LAY AWAKE staring at the ceiling, listening to the muted sounds of the city as it dragged itself from sleep: a sleep that had evaded him for most of the night as his over-wrought brain struggled to make sense of the events of the previous evening. In particular the astonishing appearance of the man he had last seen running across the sand dunes on the beach of Quiberon.

What the devil was Bennett doing in Paris? And in such company?

And what was he doing now?

Nathan had not stopped to enquire. It seemed sensible to make himself scarce. Now he was not so sure. Perhaps he should have stayed, sought a private audience. Taken him somewhere quiet, down by the river, where he could have demanded an explanation or slit his throat with the midshipman's dirk he carried in his boot and slid the body into the dark waters of the Seine.

But he knew, even in the fantasies of his sleepless mind, that there was no way he could have done that: that it was one thing to kill in the mad slashing rush of a boarding party on the deck of an enemy ship and quite another to cut a man's throat in cold blood at a private party. Not unless you were well practised in the occupation.

But what was he doing in Paris?

Useless to speculate, though it had not stopped Nathan from doing so for most of the night, when he was not thinking about Thérésa Tallien and Rose de Beauharnais and Gabriel Ouvrard and the strange, dark little man they called Captain Cannon.

And Imlay, of course—pulling the strings back in Charlotte Street.

Was this what it was like for him—playing his endless games of pretence and deceit, ever fearful of exposure? Did Imlay lie awake at night, night after night, wondering if he had been found out? Braced for the clatter of marching boots, the thunderous pounding of fists or musket butts upon the door; the sight of the bayonets gleaming in the lamplight when he looked down from his bedroom window. As Nathan did.

It had happened before. The last time he was at White's. Only on that occasion it had been Thomas Paine they had come for. On Christmas Day, during the time of the Terror.

> *I saw three ships come sailing in,*
> *On Christmas Day, on Christmas Day,*
> *I saw three ships come sailing in,*
> *On Christmas Day in the morning.*

He remembered the flushed Toby jug faces of the Americans singing their carols on Christmas Eve at White's Hotel, in defiance of official censure. The gendarmes in the hangover dregs of the middle watch, running up the stairs, pounding on the doors with their terse commands: *Allez, allez! Reveillez-vous!* The Americans, sober now and hurting, peering out of the doors in their nightcaps. And the long, lupine face of Commissioner Gillet of the *Sûreté* with his warrant for the arrest of Thomas Paine, author of *The Rights of Man*, Deputy of the French National Convention, subject of King George, citizen of the United States . . .

Citizen of the world.

But that was in the time of the Terror and the Law of Suspects, when every house was obliged to post the names of its occupants beside the front door and no man in Paris slept sound in his bed, nor woman, for gender was no impediment to the remorseless juggernaut of the State, and police raids were a nightly occurrence. And the candles burned late in the room that had once been the Queen's boudoir in the Palace of the Tuileries, where the Committee of Public Safety met and decided who was to live and who was to die.

It was different now. Or so he had been assured. The Law of Suspects was repealed, the prisons emptied of all but the most hardened criminals, the most recalcitrant dissidents; the trips to the guillotine no longer a daily feature of Paris life.

But the Committee still met. Still signed their warrants for arrest. Still held the power of life and death over every French citizen and every foreigner unwise enough to be drawn into their web. And even if the men who had succeeded Robespierre were too idle, too indulgent, too interested in making money to execute their authority with anything like the same zeal, it was not beyond their powers to do so. For all Nathan knew the warrant was made out already: signed, sealed and delivered to that other Committee who met along the landing—the once-dreaded *Sûreté*. And the gendarmes already despatched.

A clatter of steps upon the cobbles. He tensed, every nerve alert, but it was only a delivery boy, or some other early riser, for the noise faded and there was no thunderous knocking upon the outer door. He dragged himself up, all the same, and went to the window. The sun was rising over the shining rooftops of Paris, the sky tinged with rose. Rose. The thought of whom might have occupied him far more pleasantly through the long hours of darkness, had it not been for Bennett. Bloody Bennett.

What was he doing in Paris?

Useless. He might as well get up.

He was about to turn away from the window when a movement caught his eye at the far end of the little street. Two figures were standing in the shadows, one tall, one quite small. He watched, frowning. A transaction of some sort. Then he saw that the smaller figure was just a boy, a baker's boy with a basket of rolls. But what of the other, who stood there still, having his breakfast? And still apparently watching the hotel at the far end of the street. Nathan let the curtain fall and sat on the edge of his bed. He had been watched before, on his last trip here. It was an unpleasant experience. Not quite as bracing as having a 16-gun broadside trained upon you, but no less discomforting for that. Worse, in a way, because of the uncertainty. The thought that it was all in the mind, while every instinct assured you that it was not.

He dressed carefully, patting his pockets to make sure he had everything he might need if he was obliged to make a sudden decamp or was hauled off to the Châtelet or the Luxembourg or whatever other place of detention and torture they used in Paris these days, for he was sure they would not have been entirely swept away. He ensured that the thin blade was concealed in the specially tailored sheath inside his boot, and that the gold coins sewn into the lining could not be detected by a casual touch. Then he went downstairs to have his own breakfast. It was rather better than he was used to in Paris, consisting of several fresh rolls, still warm, probably from the same baker's boy he had seen in the street, even a small pat of butter and some jam. But no coffee: that was a rare delicacy thanks to the British blockade; they offered small beer instead.

Nathan ate heartily—his worries never seemed to affect his appetite—and made conversation with some of the other guests. They were Americans for the most part: businessmen and shipping agents, making a killing from the war. They talked mainly of prices and food shortages and the continuing problems of the French economy. There was a great scarcity of gold and the paper currency, the *assignat,* was practically worthless. The general opinion was that if the French did not contrive to build up their gold reserves, they would not be able to trade at all. This was of more than passing interest to Nathan, who had contributed significantly to the problem by smuggling millions of fake *assignats* into the country during the time of the Terror. But the greater part of his mind continued to be preoccupied with the problem of Bennett—and the possibly related issue of the figure lingering at the end of the street.

He sat at a table in the window where he could keep an eye on the man. He was at some distance and wore a crown hat with a wide brim—making it impossible to see his features—and, unusually for the time of year, a long greatcoat, reaching almost to the ground. Sometimes he walked up and down but mostly he just leaned against the wall, biting his nails. But several times Nathan would see him looking towards the hotel. Not one practised in the art of surveillance, he decided. Perhaps he was trying to pluck up the courage to come in and ask for work.

This was absurd. There were any number of reasons for someone to be hanging about in the vicinity of the hotel. Nathan tried to put it out of his mind and think about his next move. He needed to renew his acquaintance with the Madonna and the Rose. It was irritating that Bennett's appearance had obliged him to leave early or he felt sure he could have contrived another meeting. Now he would have to think of another way of approaching them. Perhaps he might send some flowers with a note of thanks.

He was still pondering his options when he saw a carriage turn into the street and draw up outside the front door. Quite a splendid carriage with a team of four matching greys and two footmen, also a near match, at the rear. So much for the Revolution, Nathan was thinking, not considering it had anything to do with him. But then as he watched, one of the footmen leaped from his perch and ran to let down the steps, opening the door to reveal the dapper figure and handsome features of the Banker Ouvrard. He glanced up at the hotel, saw Nathan's face in the window, and touched his hand to the brim of his hat in a gesture that was not without irony.

"I felt I should apologise for my abruptness of last night," began the banker promisingly. "I did not wish you to feel put out."

"Not at all," Nathan assured him. "You were right. It was neither the time nor the place."

"I appreciate your understanding. Paris is now much safer than it was for the pursuit of business interests, but it is still necessary to be discreet."

They sat in a quiet corner of the lobby. The same corner, in fact, where Nathan had met Thomas Paine, the evening before his arrest.

"I will come directly to the point," Ouvrard continued briskly. "Gilbert Imlay." He leaned back and regarded Nathan with a secret smile as if they shared some delightful private joke.

"You are acquainted with Mr. Imlay?" Nathan enquired politely.

"I have met him." The smile broadened a little. Whatever the joke, he was clearly enjoying it. "Did he not mention my name to you?"

"Whatever my own failings in the matter, Imlay has a great regard for discretion," Nathan replied. "He named very few of his acquaintance in Paris."

"But Madame Tallien was among them."

There was no point in denying it but Nathan's nod was reserved.

"I am here as the representative of Madame Tallien," the banker assured him, though with a continued amusement that Nathan was beginning to find irritating. "Imagine she is before you." He watched Nathan's countenance with interest. "Difficult, I agree. Perhaps this will assist you." He reached into his pocket and produced a slim violet envelope which he slid over the table. It was addressed to Nathan and contained a single sheet of paper, also violet and heavily scented.

> *Dear Captain Turner,*
>
> *I am pleased to introduce to you Monsieur Ouvrard who has been so good as to advise me on certain matters of business. You may place your complete trust in him, in the sure knowledge that he has all that of*
>
> > *Your good friend, Thérésa Tallien.*

Nathan replaced the letter in the envelope and passed it back. Rather to his surprise Ouvrard took it and put it carefully back in his pocket.

"Good. Now we can talk business," he continued briskly. "As I am sure you are aware, Mr. Imlay made certain investments for Madame

Tallien before I had the honour of advising her on such matters." Did this imply a criticism or degree of doubt? "I take it he has instructed you to report on the progress of those investments."

Nathan dropped his voice. "Imlay is presently in London," he confided, "but he has recently returned from Louisiana where he was able to make an account of the situation in the western territories. Unfortunately the Spanish authorities continue to oppose settlement in the region, actively encouraging the Indian tribes to attack those brave enough to venture west of the Appalachians—apparently with the approval of Madrid." He paused and tried to think how a land agent might put it. "As a consequence of which, land values in the region remain static."

"Static," Ouvrard repeated, as if this was not a word with which he was familiar.

"Neither up nor down," added Nathan, for the sake of clarity.

"So, pretty much at the price Madame Tallien paid for the land," Ouvrard persisted.

"Perhaps a little less." Nathan was beginning to get the hang of this. "At present."

"Not to say worthless."

"On the contrary. It is worth a great deal—to someone with, shall we say, the antennae of a man finely tuned to the political situation. In fact, Imlay feels that now is the time to buy."

Ouvrard raised a quizzical brow. "And may I ask what has led him to such a remarkable conclusion?"

Nathan glanced out of the window. He could no longer see the man at the end of the street but his view was partly obstructed by Ouvrard's coach and four. He leaned forward and adopted a conspiratorial tone. "Because Imlay has learned that an agreement is in prospect between Madrid and Paris. An agreement that would not only bring peace between the two nations but cede the entire region west of the Mississippi to France."

The smile was still on Ouvrard's face but the humour no longer reached to his eyes.

"If that were to happen," Nathan continued, "and the French authorities were to open the region to settlement—as Imlay is persuaded they must, given their close alliance with the United States—then any land purchased now, at the present low price, will increase enormously in value."

"And how confident is Mr. Imlay that this situation will arise?"

"He appeared confident enough," Nathan replied, "when I met him in London."

"Imlay, I am told, invariably appears confident. But how reliable is his information, do you suppose?"

"Well, he may not be privy to state secrets, but he is prepared to stake his reputation upon it."

"His reputation." Ouvrard's tone implied this was worth pretty much the same as the discredited paper currency of France. Or the land west of the Appalachians. "And other people's money."

"He has invested a great deal of his own, I believe," Nathan declared with slight, if affected, umbrage, "and is anxious that his friends in Paris should not think he has taken an unfair advantage."

Ouvrard appeared genuinely amused. "So he wishes Madame Tallien to invest more of her money in this venture."

"Frankly, as much as she can raise."

"Though her previous speculation has failed to return a profit. And is now running, I suspect, at a considerable loss."

"But the potential . . ."

Ouvrard raised his hands. "Please. I think we have heard quite enough about the potential from Imlay. He even wrote a book about it, I recall."

"*A Topographical Description of the Western Territory of North America*." Nathan pronounced the title as grandly as if he were Imlay. "Published by Debrett."

"He also writes fiction, I believe."

"I understand he has turned his hand to fiction on at least one occasion, but to the same purpose—to encourage emigration to the American frontier and beyond. Mr. Imlay believes, as I do, that this is a great country with the potential . . ." He ignored Ouvrard's expression, "to become a new Empire of the West. All it requires is people to farm the land and expand the trade of the region by way of the Mississippi. And whoever owns the land . . ." He leaned back spreading his hands and leaving the banker to imagine the riches that would accrue to them.

"Will very likely dispute the ownership with the Indians for many years to come," Ouvrard concluded dryly. "While the Spaniards control the entire trade of the region from their base in New Orleans."

"That is the point," Nathan insisted. "The Spaniards may no longer control New Orleans. Nor be in a position to encourage the Indians in their resistance."

"And pigs may fly to the moon but I would not advise an investment in lunar husbandry."

Nathan regarded him coldly. "Then you would advise Madame Tallien not to extend her investment in the western territories."

"With respect, sir, you have given me no good reason why I should—apart from some half-baked notion of Imlay's that as the price for peace in Europe, Spain will be willing to hand over the bulk of her possessions in North America."

"Imlay pointed out that Madame Tallien is in a position to make her own informed judgement on that subject."

"Did he indeed?" Ouvrard's voice was soft but his eyes were dangerous. "An informed judgement based upon what?"

Now Nathan smiled, though he felt he had laid his head upon the block. "Based, I imagine, upon the advice she receives from her friends."

"Well, I will pass on your observations to Madame Tallien." Ouvrard took up his hat and prepared to leave. "And her friends in high places."

Was there an implied threat in that? It rather depended on who he meant. In his role on the Committee of Public Safety Tallien probably issued instructions to the *Sûreté*.

They walked to the door together.

"How long do you intend to stay in Paris?" Ouvrard enquired politely.

"Not more than a few days. I have business in other parts of Europe."

"I see. How enviable to be an American," the banker murmured, "and move freely through the warring nations of the continent. So advantageous to business. Among other things." Nathan made no reply. Ouvrard preceded him through the door. The sun had risen high above the rooftops.

"The summer continues," Ouvrard declared, putting on his hat. He glanced at Nathan. "What is the expression you use in America? For when the summer continues into autumn?"

Nathan was unable to enlighten him.

"I am sure Imlay told me. I have it. "*An Indian summer,*'" he said in English. "Because it extends the season of attacks by Indian war parties. An expression much used on the American frontier. I am surprised you have not heard of it."

"Perhaps that is because I am from New York," said Nathan.

Ouvrard laughed. "Of course. Well, we must try to become better acquainted during your stay in Paris. Perhaps you would care to dine with me one evening. I will invite some people along whom you might find entertaining."

"I would be delighted."

The footman held open the door of the carriage. Ouvrard offered his hand.

"Very good. Until then."

Nathan stood watching as the coachman expertly turned the carriage in the narrow courtyard. He had made as much progress as he dared hope, and although Ouvrard had made some sly remarks concerning his business credentials, on the whole he felt he had reason to feel pleased with himself.

Then the carriage swept away and he found himself staring into the face of a young man in a long greatcoat and a battered beaver hat. The man who had been waiting at the end of the street.

"Captain Turner?" he enquired.

Nathan inclined his head in what might have been assent or puzzled consideration.

"My name is Junot," continued his new acquaintance, "and I have the honour of acting for General Buonaparte."

"Acting?" Nathan's sharp response cut across the name which was, in any case, unfamiliar to him. "General who?"

"He considers that you have greatly maligned him, sir, with a lady whose good opinion he very much values and he invites you to name your second."

Nathan stared at him in disbelief. "I am sorry," he said. "I am confused. You are telling me that some man I have never met wishes to fight with me?" Buonaparte. The name meant nothing to him. It sounded Italian. Then he knew. My God! Captain Cannon!

"He will fight you with swords or pistols at any place and time you care to name."

"But this is absurd."

The voice was cold with dislike. "You made several disparaging remarks about the general before a number of witnesses, sir. And he will have satisfaction."

Nathan almost laughed. First Imlay. Now Captain Cannon. He would get himself a reputation. But then he looked into the man's eyes and saw that they were quite serious, or quite mad, and he did not feel like laughing at all.

CHAPTER SIXTEEN

Captain Cannon

"MOST UNFORTUNATE," agreed Gabriel Ouvrard, when Nathan came to his office with news of the general's challenge. His face was grave but his eyes betrayed a lively curiosity. "What exactly did you say?"

"I cannot remember the exact words," Nathan confessed, "but something along the lines of, 'Who is that man over there who looks as if he has been shot from a cannon?'" Ouvrard's lips twitched a little. "And I believe I may have asked if he was an entertainer."

"You said that about General Buonaparte?"

"Is that his name? I did not quite catch it. He is Italian, I believe."

"He is from the island of Corsica, which became French about a year before he was born. He is quite sensitive about his nationality. Indeed, about most things. Fired out of a cannon. Oh dear. You could not have done worse had you tripped him up and kicked him. Ridicule is a powerful weapon in Paris. And a grievous insult."

"But I did not mean to give offence," Nathan protested. "I did not know he was a general. And besides, I am sure I was not overheard. Apart from Madame de Beauharnais, of course, to whom I was talking at the time."

"And who is possibly the most indiscreet woman in Paris."

"Oh God."

"Well, we will have to see what we can do."

"I am sorry to be so importunate, but I know so very few people in Paris—will you act as my second?"

Ouvrard shook his head firmly. "You cannot fight him," he said.

"I would not wish to be thought shy," Nathan insisted warily. "I would gladly apologise but would he accept it?"

"Probably not, but there are other pressures that can be brought to bear. Leave it with me."

Nathan returned to his hotel and spent a restless afternoon cursing his folly. He could not begin to think how he could explain the situation to the First Lord of the Admiralty, if he lived to enjoy that privilege. He was sitting in the lobby nursing a glass of wine when Ouvrard returned, looking even more pleased with himself than usual.

"General Buonaparte begs your pardon," he said, throwing down his hat, "and hopes there are no hard feelings."

"My God, what did you tell him?"

"Well, in the first place I pointed out that you are an American— which of course, answers for a multitude of sins. And then I said that in the United States the expression 'looking as if he has been shot from a cannon' means a bold fellow, a damn-your-eyes fire-eater, a man of great daring and audacity."

Nathan stared at him, torn between admiration for his inventiveness and an uncomfortable feeling that he was being made game of. "Really?"

"No, I did not." Ouvrard laughed. "Though the temptation was strong. I told him that Rose had made it all up—to make him jealous. He liked that. He thinks she is beginning to care for him. I also indicated that your life—and good will—is of extreme importance to the Committee of Public Safety, and if he persisted in this foolishness he would find himself serving in the ranks. He did not like that at all."

"Well, I must thank you, sir. You have saved me a great deal of embarrassment. And I am sorry to have put you to so much trouble."

"No trouble at all. As a matter of fact, I enjoyed it very much. It will make an excellent story for the dinner table. Provided Buonaparte is not there, of course. Oh, and speaking of dinner, he wishes you to join him at the Café Procope in the Cour du Commerce, which is a particular haunt of his, so that he can express his regrets to you personally and in an appropriate manner."

Nathan was startled. What did he mean by appropriate?

"He wants to buy you dinner," Ouvrard explained. "I may have given him a greater sense of your importance than I intended. He probably wants you to put in a good word for him with the Committee."

"But is this wise?"

"It would be less wise to refuse. He would take it extremely amiss and we would be back where we started from. Don't worry. Ask him to tell you how he drove the British out of Toulon and flatter him outrageously. He'll like that."

"What else should I know about him," asked Nathan, "in case I say the wrong thing?"

"What else should you know? I am not sure that I can tell you very much. He is a nobody. However, nobodies have a way of becoming somebodies in France, since the Revolution. Like myself. Let me see . . . His parents were shopkeepers, I think, in Ajaccio. Something like that, anyway. Very Italian. Corsica belonged to Genoa, you know, until the year he was born. Napoleone—that was his name then. I think he has dropped the 'e' since, to sound more French, though if you heard him speak you would never mistake him for a Frenchman. He joined the French Army, I don't know in what capacity, but it was in the artillery, which was easier if you were not a gentleman. Then came the Revolution and he turned up at the Siege of Toulon. The city had gone over to the allies, handed the entire French Mediterranean fleet to the British. Barras was sent down there by the Convention—as *représentative en mission*—to help take it back. The way he tells it, he found Buonaparte in charge of a munitions convoy and put him in charge of the artillery. I don't know if it's true; it might just be one of Barras's stories—but he came up with a plan—Buonaparte that is—to take some strongpoint and bombard the British fleet in the harbour. And it worked. Toulon fell to the Republic—it was the turn of the tide.

"Barras was very generous in his praise, though naturally he took most of the credit for himself. Buonaparte was made a general—a *chef de brigade,* which in the French Army is a little above the rank of colonel—but then came Thermidor and he was accused of being a Jacobin. He was a friend of Robespierre's younger brother, Augustine, I believe. So poor Napoleone was arrested, thrown in prison—the usual story. The Republic has lost more generals to the guillotine than it ever lost to the enemy. But . . . people spoke up for him, Barras included, I think, and instead of giving him the chop they sent him to the Vendée, to command an infantry brigade. He is supposed to be there now but he keeps making excuses. In the meantime he hangs around trying to persuade people to let him invade Italy. Sucking up to whoever he thinks will help him, including me. Oh, and asking women to marry him. I believe it's three at the last count." He counted them off on his fingers . . . "Thérésa, Rose—Oh, and his landlady. Probably because he owes her rent. He lives in some cheap hotel in Montmartre now, I think, with the man he calls his aide de camp, who used to be his sergeant: the one who waylaid you outside White's. Somehow he manages to get himself invited to the right parties. Thérésa takes pity on him, and I think Barras throws him the occasional scrap. He sees him as a kind of pet. It is unfashionable to have a monkey these days. Also, he says he might be useful some day—though I think they've just struck him off the army list for refusing to go to the Vendée. So there you are. You know as much as I do now. The things to steer clear of are Corsica, the Vendée, and the Jacobins. And be careful what you say about Rose. He fancies himself in love with her. And Thérésa." Nathan had covered his face. "Best let him do most of the talking," Ouvrard added sympathetically. "It won't be hard. Oh, and no matter how much he insists, don't let him pick up the check. He would have to put it on the tab and there could be an unpleasant scene. They know he hasn't got any money."

"I feel really relaxed about this," Nathan assured him, ironically.

"You may find it quite interesting," Ouvrard replied, not very convincingly. "I am told he can be quite an entertaining companion, when he is not sulking. And besides, it is surely better than meeting him at dawn in the Champs Elysées." He noted Nathan's expression. "Or perhaps not."

Nathan paused at the entrance to the Cour du Commerce, his head filled with memories. This little cobbled street near the university had once been the crucible of Revolution. Or, as an agent of the police might have put it: a cesspit of malcontents and political agitators. Danton and Desmoulins had lived in the house on the corner. Danton had rehearsed his speeches here; Camille written his tracts. They used to meet Robespierre at the Café Procope. Marat had lived in the street opposite. He was stabbed to death there by Charlotte Corday—in his bath. Nathan remembered coming here in the time of the Terror, to dine with Camille and his wife, and to meet Danton, who was dithering, with uncharacteristic indecision, over whether to make a move against Robespierre. And now they were all dead; the doomed Children of the Revolution.

If they had known what would happen to them, he wondered, all those rabid young idealists—to their friends and families, to their Revolution—would they have been quite so eager for change? Would Camille have stood on that café table in the Palais Royale in the summer of 1789 and urged the mob to storm the B-B-Bastille? Would Danton have roused the rabble to rise up in defence of their liberties: to fight all the kings of Europe and all their armies with nothing but audacity, audacity, and yet more audacity? Would Marat have so ardently desired to see the streets bathed in blood? Or Robespierre striven so hard to oblige him?

Probably. They were ruled by something more than their hearts, or even their heads. Danton would have said it was their Destiny.

And where would it end? In the French Republic of Thermidor ruled by Barras and his courtesans: the seraglio of Paris? Or would the kings come back to claim their own? Or would someone emerge from the shadows: a face yet unknown? A new Robespierre or Danton. It seemed impossible, after all that had happened. There was no passion left. He had the feeling that even the French must have had enough drama for one lifetime. That all they desired was a quiet life, to be ruled by lawyers and bankers, who had a vested interest in peace and stability. As for the demagogues and the warmongers, the hotheads and the prophets of change, they could all go back to starving in garrets, or ranting in cafés and hoping they could find someone else to pick up the check.

The Procope was crowded, the clientèle more numerous, more prosperous-looking than in the older days, better clothed, better fed, even, for all the food queues in the streets. All but one, sitting glowering at a table in the corner, out of the light, nothing to eat or drink, all alone and quite ignored. Captain Cannon.

"General." Nathan strode toward him, swept off his hat, spread his arms in a pantomime of regret and remorse. *What can I say?* Buonaparte looked up, his expression uncertain, stood awkwardly, indicated the chair opposite. A crossfire of stumbling apologies, explanations, clumsy courtesies. Nathan looked for a waiter, desperate for a drink. The waiters ignored them. He sat. Looked about the room, smiling, wondered what in God's name he could say.

"You come here often?"

An unintelligible answer. Delivered in a heavy Italian accent, the eyes darting about the room under heavy brows, the fingers, which were hairy and very dirty, twitching about the grubby tablecloth like spiders' legs, as if he would tear it in pieces or yank it off and fling it across the room in a fit of desperate rage.

It was a disaster. How on earth were they to get through the next hour and a half? The next few minutes even. Food and drink were the only possible solution, but no-one appeared willing to supply it. Finally Nathan stood, excused himself, and under pretext of looking for the washroom collared a waiter, was directed to the head man, collared *him,* would cheerfully have throttled him but forced a smile instead. He was only lately come to Paris, he said, was unsure of the worth of the *assignat* and would they accept coin. Slipping the astonished man two gleaming *louis d'or,* he begged to be excused his ignorance, but murmured that it was better to be refused now rather than wait until the meal was served and cause offence. "Oh but no offence at all, *monsieur,* not at all," sliding the King's head out of sight where it would cause none. "And who is *monsieur* dining with today? Ah." The smile fading somewhat but the coin still warming his pocket if not his heart. "Well, the general is one of our regular customers." Doubtfully. But—a snap of the fingers and waiters emerged, simpering from the woodwork. The general quite taken aback. The best wine, the best glasses. The general frowning, doubtless considering the expense. "Please, you must be my guest," Nathan assured him. "I have had some excellent news today. Profitable news. And to dine with the victor of Toulon! Such an honour. It was all we talked about in New York for months."

Slowly, but perceptibly, the victor of Toulon began to relax. His eyes gleamed with childish delight as dish followed upon dish, bottle upon bottle, the attentive waiters almost lapsing into self-parody. Nathan, too, began to relax, almost to enjoy himself, though he had dined with lovelier companions. Captain Cannon's appearance did not improve upon closer inspection. His eyes were his best feature— sharp and mobile, ever darting this way and that—but as for the rest: his nose was sharp and angular, his cheeks hollow, his complexion pale, almost yellow, and pitted with some skin disease or discolouration which added to the impression that he had not washed for several days. The absurd hat was hanging on the wall behind him like a large dead bat and his spaniel's ears appeared to have been dusted with flea powder. Despite the angularity of his features, his forehead was quite alarmingly broad, as if it had expanded like a balloon with all the knowledge it had absorbed and which its possessor, who had become garrulous, attempted to convey to Nathan with all the enthusiasm of a zealot. His interests were wide and apparently random; his notion of gentlemanly converse to indulge in a series of lengthy monologues on a subject of his choosing. He held forth with equal facility upon philosophy, law, political economics, the classics, astronomy and medicine. When Nathan expressed admiration for such a profundity of knowledge, he admitted that he jotted down all the interesting facts he came upon in a small notebook which he carried about with him on all occasions—he produced it from his pocket and waved it in Nathan's face. It contained everything and anything that might one day be of use to him, he said, and a fact once digested he never forgot.

And did some subjects interest him more than others? Nathan ventured. Ah, yes. The brown eyes gleamed. He was particularly interested in the nature of greatness: of the qualities that contributed to it. Was Nathan aware, for instance, that a surprising number of the great men of history had been found upon their demise to possess three testicles?

Nathan was not so aware. He agreed that this was indeed surprising. He would have thought it had been more widely recognised.

"And what was the purpose of the third testicle, do you think?" he enquired with an interest that was not entirely feigned.

"The purpose, *monsieur*?" The general frowned.

"I mean, what extra virtue might it impart to the bearer? Does it, perhaps, contain the essence of greatness?"

The general confessed that he had long brooded upon this but had come to no significant conclusion, though it might be that it gave the bearer a certain assurance, much as the possession of seven lives imbued a cat with the confidence to take risks that it might otherwise abjure.

"Well, if that is a measure of a man's greatness, then I am destined to remain in obscurity," Nathan admitted cheerfully. He was rewarded with a deeper and more ominous frown. "I do not suppose it is the only measure," he concluded hastily.

"No," the general agreed. He became more sanguine. "I, for instance, have a star."

"A star?" Nathan was perplexed. "You mean . . ."

For a moment the general shared his bemusement. Then it dawned upon him what Nathan meant and he exploded with sudden and violent laughter. His face became a better place. He glanced down into his lap and finding nothing more remarkable than a napkin, lifted it with a comic expression and shook it about, as if a star might fall from its ample folds. The transformation was remarkable, at least to Nathan. It would be too much to say that a glow pervaded their corner of the room but in this new mood he possessed a charisma that transmitted itself to the waiters and several of those dining at the nearby tables.

"No. I am as most men in that regard," he asserted, wiping his eyes with the napkin. "My star is in the usual place: in the heavens. Every man has a star, you know, though mine, alas, has not shone brightly for many a month."

Nathan said he was sorry to hear it.

"It may have abandoned me entirely," the general confessed. The clouds had gathered once more about his brow. "I am what you say in English 'at the seashore.'"

"On the beach," Nathan corrected him instinctively.

Buonaparte leaned forward across the table and dropped his voice. "It is not widely known, but I once applied to join the British Navy."

Nathan expressed his surprise.

"It was when I was in Corsica. I was born there," he confided, as if it was a great secret. Nathan contrived to look astonished. "It had just fallen into the possession of the King of France—it was long before the Revolution, of course—and the people, being of an independent nature and strong-willed, rose in rebellion against him. There was even talk of putting the island under the protection of King George, but it came to nothing."

"And your application?"

"That, too. I wrote to the Admiralty but they did not reply. Otherwise I might have been the captain of a frigate by now."

Nathan allowed this was a great loss to the British Navy, if not to France.

"Well, the French do not seem to think so," Buonaparte replied glumly. "For I have been unemployed now for several months."

"How can that be," Nathan enquired, "with the nation at war?"

A shrug. "They wished me to take the command of a brigade of infantry in the Vendée and I was obliged to come to Paris to make a protest. The War Minister was a man called Aubry. Captain Aubry. Forty-five years old and he had not advanced beyond the rank of captain. He was condescending. I was very young to be a brigadier, he said. 'One ages quickly on the battlefield,' I told him, 'and I have just come from there.' He took it badly. He insisted upon my joining the Army of the West, under General Hoche." He made a face as if he had tasted something unpleasant. "When I persisted in my refusal, I was taken off the army list. I am a general in name alone. And so you see me as I am, a ruined man."

"Would it not have been in your best interests to agree?" Nathan proposed cautiously.

"To serve under Hoche? And in the infantry? Preposterous! I am an artillery officer, you know."

"There is a distinction?"

Buonaparte looked astonished. "Very much so. I was trained at the greatest school of artillery in Europe. This was in the days before the Revolution, when for a man of my background—my family were by no means poor, you understand—it was impossible to serve as an officer in a respected regiment of the line without title or influence. But an officer of artillery needs ability, intelligence, an affinity with mathematics. You have never served in the military?"

"I regret not. I went to sea at an early age. In the merchant marine."

"Ah. Well, for an artillery officer to serve in the infantry—and in the Vendée, against rebels, it is a great insult. And besides, I had other plans. I have still."

Nathan waited for him to expound upon them but unhappily he forbore to do so.

"But I had heard that General Hoche has enjoyed some success in the Vendée," Nathan said, hoping to provoke an indiscretion, "and the situation is now more settled."

"Ha! Well, that is what they say. I would be surprised if it were true. The country will never be settled until we have some victories in the field—and I mean in a foreign field." He lowered his voice. "As it is, I fear the government may not endure. It is only a question of whether it falls to the Jacobins or the Royalists."

"The Jacobins? Are they still a threat?"

The eyes darted to the surrounding tables but no-one appeared to be taking notice. He leaned forward. "On the day I arrived in Paris a mob, inspired by the Jacobins, surrounded the Convention. They shot one of the deputies dead and put his head on a pike. They called for a return to the days of price controls; even a return of the Terror. It was like the last time I was in Paris when the mob attacked the Tuileries."

"So? You were in Paris before?"

"I was, in '92, when they massacred the Swiss Guard. I saw it all. Those good soldiers thrown to the wolves, their bodies mutilated. And yet, I tell you, if the King had mounted upon his horse and shown himself their leader, the day would have been his. The Revolution at an end." He snapped his fingers. "The mob will never stand up to regular infantry. Or artillery," he added thoughtfully, as if he was even now planning the tactics, making the dispositions. "Not with a half decent commander."

"And now?"

"Now? Well, for now they are held in check by the National Guard who are for the most part men of substance, shopkeepers and the like, artisans, respectable bourgeoisie. They do not want a return to the days of the Jacobins, the days of the Terror. But if it were the Royalists and not the Jacobins . . ." He inclined his head in consideration.

"I confess you surprise me," said Nathan. "I had thought the Royalists were finished. At least in Paris."

"Not at all." He looked at Nathan in surprise but he dropped his voice. "There is a great deal of disillusionment with the Revolution, even in Paris. Perhaps especially in Paris. And Paris, you know, is all that matters. No, ideas are all very well, but a Frenchman wishes, above all else, for security—and food in his belly. Food and wine. And to know his job is secure."

Nathan filled his glass.

"When I was sixteen, I would have fought to the death for Rousseau," Buonaparte continued. "Now? I tell you frankly, the man was a fool. A simpleton. A Republic of Virtue, with the morals of the French? Pah! And their vices. Absurd! It is a chimera. The French, they have been infatuated with the idea. But it will pass away, like all other ideas. What they want is glory. Glory and the gratification of their vanity. As for liberty, of that they have no conception. Look at the army. They require a master, sir. And the nation is as the army. It must have a head: a head rendered illustrious by glory and not by theories of government, fine phrases, or the talk of idealists, of which the French understand not a whit. Let them have their toys and they will be satisfied. They will amuse themselves and allow themselves to be led." He frowned in consideration and added, "provided the goal be cleverly disguised."

Nathan chose his words with care. "So you think they would look to a new king?"

"A king or a more natural, a more inspired leader. For I must tell you, frankly, I have no time for kings. But provide the people with a strong leader . . ."

"Like Barras . . . ?"

"Barras! Pah! Have you seen him? Well, I should not be so scornful. He is not without talent but indolent, incredibly indolent, even for a survivor of the old regime. And too inclined to be ruled by his vices—as Paris is ruled by its women. Women, my friend, hold the reins of government and men make fools of themselves for them. Even I." He lapsed into melancholy. "No, it is beyond hope," he brooded. "My career is in ruins. My friends have deserted me, my purse is empty, my personal life . . ." But he sighed and left the details to Nathan's imagination. "Every venture, it appears, is doomed to failure. Indeed, I am become so desperate I am writing a novel."

Nathan expressed polite interest. "On a military subject?"

"Romantic."

"Ah."

"But the hero is a military man, based in part upon myself. It is a tragedy. The tragedy of Eugénie and Clissold. Clissold is me. I think in the end he is going to kill himself." He had become so dejected Nathan was moved to offer solace.

"But a man like you, with so much talent . . ." He floundered. "Surely there is an alternative?"

"To writing?"

"I meant suicide, for I do not scorn writing as a means of consolation, though I am told it often has the opposite effect and it is difficult to make a living from the occupation."

"And what do you think I should do?"

There was a dangerous glint in his eyes and Nathan recalled that he was quite mad.

"Oh I would not presume to give advice," he began, "but as an artillery officer, you must have a great knowledge of mathematics, geometry and the like."

"And how would that advantage me, outside the artillery?"

"Well, I am sure I cannot say, but often something turns up." Nathan struggled for inspiration—and found it in an unlikely quarter. "I once knew a man whose greatest ambition was to build bridges, but no-one would let him, so he turned to writing political tracts, with some success. Many people read his works and found them stimulating. He became a great man in America. France, too, for a while, until they locked him up for sedition. Perhaps you know him, for he is still living in Paris. His name is Thomas Paine."

"I know of him, of course," Buonarparte admitted with a frown, "but I do not think he is the happiest of men, or the most admired."

"No." It occurred to Nathan that Tom Paine was probably not a good example after all. "He served his apprenticeship as a corset maker," he continued, "so he has always had that to fall back upon, which is useful."

"Not in Paris," Buonaparte pointed out. "Not among the women of my acquaintance."

They reflected upon this in a gloomy silence. But another bottle was procured and the wind became more favourable. The general began to talk eagerly and with great knowledge of other generals including Alexander the Great, which subject carried him in turn to Asia Minor, Egypt and India. He was passionate, he said, about the East. He had a great desire to travel. Indeed, he had just had an offer, he said, to go to Turkey.

Nathan blinked a little. "Why Turkey?"

"Why not? They wish me to train their artillery. A man could do worse. I will lead an army into the East. Egypt, Persia, India . . . I am fed up kicking my heels in Paris. I have applied for permission to leave for Istanbul. The moment it is agreed, I am off."

"Well, I would be very sorry," Nathan assured him. "The Republic can ill afford to lose a man of such prodigious talent."

"You think so?" Buonaparte gazed at him soulfully. "Monsieur Ouvrard said you are a great friend to the Republic."

"I hope I am."

"Well, if you have any influence at all, tell them to read my report on the invasion of Italy."

"Of Italy?"

"It is with the War Office at present. They have only to read it. Italy is the answer to all our troubles. Glory, that is what the French need. Glory and gold. And I can give them both, if only they will listen to me. Imagine, if you will, that this is the Alps . . ." He reached for the salt but succeeded only in knocking over his glass of wine. He gazed at the spreading stain in comic dismay. A waiter rushed up with a napkin.

"I fear I am too much in drink," Buonaparte confessed. "We must speak again."

Nathan became aware of a presence at his shoulder. He looked up, expecting to see one of the waiters, but it was the man who had lingered outside his hotel: the general's aide. He looked at the red stain on the tablecloth and then at Nathan as if it was all his fault, which it probably was.

"Ah, here is the good Junot," the general announced. "Come to carry me home."

It appeared that this might be a literal requirement for he staggered to his feet, clutching his chair for support. He flapped a hand in Nathan's direction. "This is Captain, Captain . . ."

"Turner," said Nathan, bowing. "At your service."

"A good man," said the general. "A very good man. I feel renewed, sir, by your faith in me." Nathan was nonplussed. "I have seen my star in your eyes, sir. And it is rising in the East." He squeezed Nathan's arm firmly, but his own gaze was unfocused. He threw his arm around his aide's shoulder. "I believe our fortunes are about to change for the better, my good Junot. But now you must get me to my carriage."

Junot looked confused.

"I speak in jest, fool." He rolled his eyes at Nathan. "Just get me to my lodgings, Junot. The carriage can wait for better days."

Nathan followed them to the door and watched the pair make their way down the street, the general walking unsteadily and discoursing with his aide, doubtless about his plans for the invasion of Italy, or Persia, or wherever his star might guide him. He felt deflated of a sudden with a sense that he was wasting his time in Paris, that Imlay's much-vaunted contacts had led him only to this: lunch with a derelict, washed up on the beach like some half-pay lieutenant, destined to rabbit on endlessly about his ambitions and the injustice of his superiors while his uniform became increasingly threadbare, his speech more incoherent. And then he realised that the general had gone off without his hat. He turned back to retrieve it and walked straight into Benjamin Bennett.

"Well, Captain," said he, softly, "and what brings you to Paris? Still looking for your missing countess? Or is it something else you have lost?"

CHAPTER SEVENTEEN

the Agent Provocateur

IT IS OF SOME ADVANTAGE to be an American in France," Bennett declared as they walked in the gardens of the Luxembourg Palace, "as doubtless you will have discovered."

"More so than being English, assuredly," Nathan conceded.

And Bennett laughed. He seemed remarkably at ease, in the circumstances, though Nathan detected a certain artifice, entirely in harmony with the fashions of the day. He was dressed much as he had been at La Chaumiere, with the addition of a tall beaver hat and a silver-tipped cane. No-one observing him strolling through the Luxembourg Gardens, Nathan thought, could have imagined him swarming up the rigging of a British ship-of-war in the striped jersey of an able-seaman, or skulking in the marches of the Vendée with a band of Chouans. But then nothing in Paris was as it seemed.

The Luxembourg had been built for Marie de Medici, widowed queen of Henri IV, in the style of a fairytale castle of the Renaissance. After the Revolution it had become a prison. Thomas Paine had been interred here, and Danton and Desmoulins during the time of the Terror. And Nathan, too, on his last visit to the city. Now it looked to be empty, most of its windows broken or boarded, though he could still see bars here and there, and it wore the haunted look of tragedy and loss. The gardens were neglected, though still opened to the public, and a riot of brambles and dog roses clawed their rambling way up the walls.

They walked upon a long terrace overlooking the park lake, its fountain long stilled, its waters clouded: Nathan with his hands clasped behind his back, much as he might have walked his own quarterdeck aboard the *Unicorn,* though not with an able-seaman wearing a beaver hat and carrying a silver-tipped cane. At one end, nearest the palace, a number of men sat playing chess on folding tables set out in the open air.

Nathan kept his explanation simple, as befitted the disparity in their rank. It was not for Bennett to question him, who had once been his captain, though he held Nathan's life in his hands. He had become stranded on the beach at Quiberon, he temporised, and finding himself cut off behind enemy lines, had made his way northward in the guise of an American sea captain called Turner. And so at length came to Paris.

"Doubtless thinking to catch a ship here for Dover or Deal," Bennett proposed in his mocking drawl.

"I knew a man in Paris, an American, who I thought might be of assistance," Nathan informed him tersely. "But unfortunately he is away on business."

"Still, you are not without friends, I find," Bennett observed. "Indeed, you appear to move in the most exalted of circles."

"Come now, Bennett," Nathan rebuked him sternly. "We are both in some way of being incognito. And in your case I see the owl has become something of a peacock."

Or a songbird, he added silently, for Bennett's finery did not come cheap and he suspected him of selling his services as an informer and peaching on his former associates among the Chouans. But, as Bennett explained it, things were a lot more complicated than that.

His story was that he had fought with the Royalists on the Quiberon peninsula until, abandoned by the British fleet and running out of powder and shot, they had been obliged to surrender to the forces of General Hoche.

"Hoche was generous," he told Nathan. "At least to begin with. He promised we would be treated leniently and as legitimate prisoners of war. Then Jean-Lambert Tallien returned from Paris—and brought the Terror back with him."

Tallien, it appeared, had been sent to Brittany as a representative of the National Convention, to keep an eye on the military and ensure its efforts were unimpeded by any lack of Revolutionary zeal. According to Bennett, he had initially given his backing to the policy of reconciliation but then had word from his wife, Thérésa, that his enemies were accusing him of indulgence; or worse, of plotting to restore the monarchy. Fearful of suffering the fate of Robespierre and others who had misread the mood of the Convention, he revoked the promise made by Hoche and embarked on a series of savage reprisals. Hundreds of Royalist prisoners were condemned by military tribunal and shot by firing squad in a field just outside Auray. They included over four hundred nobles of the old regime and many of Bennett's comrades among the Chouans. Bennett himself was saved by his accent. When they discovered he was an American they sent him to Paris to be interrogated by agents of the Committee of General Security.

"They locked me up in the Châtelet," he told Nathan, "while they figured out what to do with me."

Nathan was familiar with the Châtelet, the gaunt fortress-prison on the River Seine opposite the île de la Cité. In his previous incarnation as Captain Turner he had seen the insides of three French prisons: the Châtelet being the first, though by no means the worst. It had not been an encouraging start to his career as a British agent and he had no desire to repeat the experience.

"I told them I had been pressed into the British Navy and left on the beach but they knew I had been fighting with the Chouans. I must suppose some of the other prisoners had talked before they were shot. I demanded to see the American ambassador but they said I had forfeited any rights I had as an American citizen by joining the Royalists and fighting against the soldiers of the Republic.

Then one day there was a new interrogator, someone more senior, a *commissaire* of the *Sûreté*. He proposed a deal. I was to be given my liberty—and a passage back to Boston—provided I remained in Paris to spy upon my fellow Americans."

"And you agreed?"

Bennett did not trouble to answer. They were not, after all, walking in the exercise yard of the Châtelet.

"I was set up as a wealthy American come to enjoy the pleasures of the French capital. A Sybarite. You appear surprised but I assure you there are such creatures in the world, though they are not usually from Nantucket. I was provided with an apartment in the Rue de Condé and a servant, who is doubtless in the minor ranks of the police force, and a sum of money to enable me to play the part with conviction."

"I am only surprised the Sûreté takes such an active interest in a few American expatriates," Nathan remarked dryly, "given the friendship between your two countries."

"Oh, the French could never entirely trust a man who speaks English as his native tongue," Bennett declared with his easy grin. "And can you blame them? But after my initial reports, which reached a level of banality that, I pride myself, has never been surpassed in the secret world of intelligence, their interest diminished somewhat. I was required to broaden my studies. I was to use my position in fashionable society—for my natural charisma, aided by my lavish spending of the Committee's funds, had given me a certain standing therein—to become an agent provocateur, eliciting the Royalist inclinations of my fellow Sybarites and encouraging their indiscretions. In short, to add to the Committee's knowledge on the likelihood of a Royalist insurrection in the capital."

Nathan's interest increased. "And is there a possibility of that?"

"Oh yes," replied the American with apparent satisfaction. "Oh indeed yes. And it may happen a great deal sooner than my employers seem to think."

"With any prospect of success?"

"A very good prospect, I would venture. There are a great many Royalist agitators active in the city. Foreign, too. The Austrians, of course, the Venetians and other Italian states who have an interest in knowing which way the wind is blowing. And, I am sure it will surprise you, the British." He regarded Nathan with his easy, if irritating, smile.

"It does not surprise me in the least," replied Nathan evenly. "Though I do not have your advantages. But what have they achieved?"

Bennett looked at him. "How long have you been in Paris?"

"A few days."

"And have you not sensed the anger in the streets?"

Nathan could not say that he had.

"Believe me, you will—and very soon, if I'm not much mistaken. When Barras and his gang got rid of Robespierre they promised the people a new Convention. Only now it turns out the people don't get to choose who is in it. Barras does. He and his toadies. Two thirds of them are to be 'nominated' from among the members of the old Convention."

"So what do you think will happen?"

Bennett looked up at the sky as they continued their promenade along the terrace. "I guess that depends on the weather." He cocked an eye on Nathan. "And the British."

"What can the British do—in Paris?"

"Nothing in Paris. But a new push in Brittany at the right time—and if the weather stays like this . . . It could be a real Indian summer."

Nathan looked at him, startled, recalling his conversation with Ouvrard.

"I gather from this that your own loyalties are unaltered," he proposed, with a hint of irony. In truth, he had never been sure where Bennett's loyalties lay, one way or another. They were certainly not with the British Navy.

"I am an agent provocateur," replied Bennett dryly. "This is how I operate."

Nathan paused at an empty table with an abandoned chess set, the

King in checkmate to a knight and two rooks and the board surrounded by fallen pieces. "My life is in your hands," he said. "As I suppose you must know."

"Oh I do," Bennett assured him. "My masters require constant feeding with information and you would be a dainty dish indeed to set before a commissioner of the *Sûreté*. I find myself in something of a dilemma."

What did he want—money? Somehow Nathan doubted it. But certainly he wanted something.

"You have not thought of seeking help from the American ambassador? Or of using the Committee's funds to contrive your escape from Paris?"

"I considered it. Briefly." Bennett studied the chessboard as if the game was not yet over. "But I am obliged by certain constraints. Certain hostages have been taken—one in particular—who would suffer from such self-regard." He picked up one of the squandered pawns and replaced it on the board, to no particular advantage that Nathan could see. "Besides, I have decided to wait for the counter-Revolution. And then I shall kill Jean-Lambert Tallien."

Nathan studied him carefully. He did not appear to be joking, though it was hard to tell with Bennett.

"For some personal reason, or because of what he did at Auray?"

Bennett turned on him with a sudden flush of anger: an intimation of a different character. "That is not personal enough?"

"You could kill him now," Nathan ventured guardedly.

The mask came down. Bennett studied the chessboard again. "Not so easily. And I would doubtless suffer the consequence, whereas the new regime might consider I had saved them the trouble. However . . ." He toyed with his pawn. "I may need a character reference."

"What, for killing Tallien? I doubt it."

"It is not inconceivable that my activities on behalf of the *Sûreté* will become more widely known. That my masters will, under pressure, name their principal informers." He looked directly at Nathan.

"In which case it would be wise to have someone to speak up for me, someone who has the ear of the Royalist command."

So that was it. Nathan checked his immediate impulse to point out that the Royalist command would scarcely give him the time of day—in Paris, or elsewhere. "Well, if I am around at the time and in a position to do so, I will be pleased to give you all the references you require," he assured him. "Our fates, I comprehend, are intertwined."

They walked on, back towards the city through an avenue of chestnut trees, the spiky fruit heavy upon the bough and beginning to fall.

"This *commissaire* you encountered in the Châtelet," Nathan mused. "Did you ever discover his name?"

"Oh, he made no secret of it. His name is Gillet."

Nathan stopped in his tracks and stared at him. "Gillet?"

"Like the guillotine. Why? Do you know him? Is he another of your Paris acquaintances?"

"No. No, I'm sorry. It was just—just the name. As you say, so like the guillotine."

Bennett was regarding him with a curious smile, either because he knew more than Nathan suspected or because of the shock on Nathan's face. For he did indeed know Gillet. He had first met him at White's Hotel on Christmas Day 1793, when he turned up at the head of a file of gendarmes, sent to arrest Thomas Paine on the orders of the Committee of Public Safety. They had avoided conflict then, if narrowly, but their subsequent encounters had been far more violent. Nathan still bore the scars of the flogging he had received at Gillet's hands in one of the sinister *Maisons d'Arrêt* used by the secret police at the time of the Terror. And the last time they had met had been in the Hôtel de Ville in Paris on the day of Robespierre's downfall. Nathan was convinced that in the confusion of that night, Gillet had fired the shot that carried away Robespierre's jaw. They had exchanged shots themselves as Gillet fled into the night and Nathan was certain he had hit him in the arm. He still saw him sometimes, in his nightmares, swishing that bloody cane as he walked around him, lashing out at his naked thighs and back and buttocks. And the savage smile on his face. He was the only man in the world Nathan had ever vowed to kill on sight. In cold blood or not.

But in those days Gillet had been a committed Jacobin. It was a shock to know he was still alive and at liberty—and, from what Bennett reported, still in his old profession.

"Well, he seems to know *you*," Bennett insisted. "Though he appears to be under the impression that you are an American. He proposed that I should solicit your friendship, win your confidence and discover what you are doing back in Paris. Otherwise, he said, he may be forced to resume his own acquaintance where he was forced to leave it last summer. I formed the impression," he added, watching Nathan's face carefully, "that he had conceived an active dislike for you."

CHAPTER EIGHTEEN

Dining Sans Culottes

NATHAN RETURNED TO THE HOTEL rather more thoughtfully than he had left it, wanting nothing more than to lie down in a darkened room and draw the shades upon Paris and all its uncertainties.

This was not to be.

A familiar carriage was standing in the Passage des Petits Pères, its four immaculate greys champing at the bit, and there was a note waiting for him in reception. Monsieur Ouvrard's compliments and he would very much value Captain Turner's company as soon as it was convenient for him. The carriage was at his disposal.

Nathan consoled himself with the thought that the banker might have the information he required and that he would be able to leave the city at first light, if not before. He felt a greater sense of oppression than at any time since his arrival here, as if Paris were some living, breathing entity: an animal that had sniffed him out, the parasite in its midst, and was hunting him with deliberate menace. He felt it rising from the streets, glaring down at him from the rooftops, just as he had on that thunderous day in Thermidor when Robespierre and his supporters plotted insurrection in the Hotel de Ville and the tocsin rang to summon the people of the sections to rise in their defence. And Sara, unbeknown to him, waited for the death wagons in the sweltering courtyard of the Conciergerie. He longed to be driving westward to the coast. He felt an immense physical longing for the sea, so intense that for a moment he imagined he could smell it on the wind.

But instead he was driven to the place Ouvrard called his office on the Île de Saint Louis, an ancient warehouse smelling of money.

"I have made certain enquiries concerning the subject we discussed earlier," the banker began, when the usual courtesies had been exchanged and they had settled into a pair of large comfortable chairs in his study. "Peace talks between France and Spain have been in progress since late spring—in Basel, in Switzerland. They have been cloaked by parallel talks with the Prussians and the German principalities. A treaty of sorts was agreed at the end of July between François de Barthélemy for the Republic and Domingo d'Yriarte for the Spanish Crown, though it has yet to be ratified by the Convention and the precise details are hard to come by. There are also a number of secret clauses. Now, what I am about to say to you is in the strictest confidence, as I hope you understand." Nathan nodded gravely, his hopes rising. "It appears that the future of Spain's possessions in North America did come under discussion. How Imlay came by that information I do not know—nor do I wish to. A man of business has as much of a right as any man, or government, to keep himself informed in these troubled times. However, it would be dangerous—even for me, with my connections—to admit that I knew of such discussions, and I would be obliged to explain how I came by such information." Nathan nodded again in acknowledgment of the implied threat. "However, Spain appears not unwilling to return New Orleans to France—and with it, all its territories west of the Mississippi River." Nathan allowed his features to betray a degree of natural satisfaction and Ouvrard wagged an admonitory forefinger. "But at a price. In gold. Come in!" A servant entered with coffee on a tray. "Leave it," said Ouvrard, without looking up. "I will see to it myself.

"I regret I am not at liberty to reveal the exact amount," he resumed when the door had closed. "In that respect, I am sworn to secrecy.

However, it is, as you might imagine, significant. And the stipulation
that it must be paid in gold makes it impossible for the Republic to
contemplate such an outlay. It is no secret that the French government is on the verge of bankruptcy. To raise anything like such a
sum the government would have to go cap in hand to the international banking community. And the bankers are by no means eager
to oblige a Republic which has—at least until recently—shown itself
hostile to their interests. Nevertheless, the advantages of securing
such a prize have persuaded Barras to seek advice from those in a
position to assist him."

He poured coffee into two delicate Sèvres cups. "Milk?"

For a brief moment Nathan saw him in the little grocery store in
Nantes. "A little."

"Sugar?"

"One spoon, if you will."

"I think I am the only man in France who does not take sugar,"
the banker revealed composedly. "I like the true bitter taste of the
coffee bean. One spoonful did you say? Well, the main money market in Europe is, of course, London which, for obvious reasons, may
be ruled out of contention. The German and Swiss bankers are far
too cautious to contemplate such a risk. Besides, they do not think
the present government will survive the autumn. Which leaves the
Italians. The Casa di San Giorgio in Genoa has a long history of investment in the New World. It financed the expedition of Columbus
in 1492, did you know?"

Nathan indicated that he did not and expressed polite interest
though it was not the most pressing of his concerns.

"Well, I have reason to believe that the Genovese would not be adverse to funding the venture, *ceteris paribus*. Alas, in the world of finance all things are rarely equal. And here one must weigh a number
of adverse items in the balance." This talk of money made Ouvrard
seem much older of a sudden and for all his youthful good looks
and the profusion of his brown locks, there was something of the
Bicknell Coney about him, even in his voice which took on a dry,

almost gnomic quality. "You must understand that the Casa di San Giorgio and the government of the Republic of Genoa are, to all extents and purposes, one and the same. The present Doge is a director of the bank, as are many of the leading members of his council. I believe this has been the case for several centuries. If it became known that the bank had lent money to the present government of France, it would be regarded as a hostile act by the Allied powers. The British maintain a large fleet in the Mediterranean, with a base close at hand in Corsica from which to sustain a blockade of the port of Genoa, while a large part of the Austrian army is garrisoned in Lombardy and in the Alpine passes. And, of course, the Papacy would undoubtedly pronounce the leading families of Genoa excommunicate, to which, as Italians, they cannot be entirely indifferent."

Nathan concluded that he would not have embarked upon such a detailed exposition if the cause was as hopeless as it appeared. "So where does that leave the western territories of North America?" he enquired.

"On the table, as they say. Negotiations continue. Certain pressures may be brought to bear. You must understand that the Casa di San Giorgio has been controlled by the same families since the Middle Ages and they are not always in agreement; far from it. The Brignole and Spinola are thought to favour the French interest. The Doria and the Grimaldi are much opposed. It is unfortunate that the Convention thought fit to expel the Grimaldis from Monaco where they have been its princes for some hundreds of years. And to make matters worse the daughter-in-law of the last prince was a victim of the guillotine on the last day of the Terror . . . Have I said something to alarm you?" he added, for Nathan had started and was staring at him with a curious expression.

"I am sorry." Nathan took a moment to gather his thoughts. "I had just remembered something."

The last day of the Terror, when he had followed Gillet to the Hôtel de Ville with murder in his heart, ignorant that Sara was even then on her way to the guillotine. Had this woman, this Princess of

Monaco, been with her at the time? His information was that two women had fled from the death carts but one of them had been re-captured and dragged back to the scaffold.

He forced his mind back to the present. "And in the meantime— your advice to Madame Tallien?"

"You are thinking of Imlay's investments, naturally. Well, in the meantime, I am afraid that they, too, must stay 'on the table.' However, I am urged to use what means I can of prolonging your stay in Paris."

He smiled disarmingly but Nathan could not help but wonder if the banker had now become his jailer; surely he would never have taken Nathan into his confidence if there were the slightest chance of his leaving Paris.

"It would be a pleasure," he replied, though he was already won-dering how to contrive his escape from the city; he had, after all, dis-covered all that was asked of him, and with Gillet breathing down his neck he could not afford to push his luck.

Ouvrard stood. "Splendid. We will do our best to make your stay as pleasurable as possible. Indeed, I am instructed to invite you to a late supper at the house of Madame de Beauharnais, if you are not too fatigued."

Nathan groaned inwardly, for it *had* been a fatiguing day and though he would have been ashamed to admit it, the charms of Madame de Beauharnais paled in comparison to a quiet evening at White's Hotel. But he put a brave face on it and mentioned only that he would welcome the opportunity to change his shirt and splash a little water on his face.

"My dear sir, you must avail yourself of my wardrobe. And, my va-let, too. No, I insist. I have shirts of every size and description. I will instruct the good Anton to bring you a selection."

Nathan could not help wondering if Ouvrard had bought a job lot from those obliged to part with them at approximately the same time they had been forced to part with their heads, but they were of good quality and not a trace of blood upon them and so, washed, shaved and made as presentable as the good Anton could contrive in the time available to him, Nathan joined Ouvrard in his carriage for the short journey to the house of Madame de Beauharnais.

"It is a modest little townhouse near the Palais Egalité," Ouvrard informed him, "but quite charming. And perhaps I should warn you that suppers *à la Beauharnais* are apt to be a little, well . . . *theatrical.*"

Nathan eyed him warily. "In what way?" He imagined party games, possibly of a rather lewd nature. He was not far wrong.

"Well, sometimes there is dancing."

"That does not sound too outrageous."

"Upon the table."

"Ah."

"And on the last occasion Madame Tallien took off her clothes."

"I see. All of them?"

"All of them. Though, as you may have noticed, she does not wear a great deal at the best of times. There had been comments on the flimsiness of the fabric and she had a wager with one of the other guests that her entire costume did not weigh more than two silver coins. On the instructions of Madame de Beauharnais scales were brought in by a servant and she stripped before the entire party of thirty or forty people. She won the bet."

"And will Madame Tallien be there tonight?"

"Oh, assuredly. She and Madame de Beauharnais are inseparable."

"And Monsieur Tallien?"

Ouvrard laughed. "I do not think so. Have you ever met him?"

"No, I do not believe I have had that pleasure." In fact, they had met briefly on the evening of Ninth Thermidor, when Tallien was celebrating his success in denouncing Robespierre before the National Convention. But in the subsequent, more violent events of that night he had been notable by his absence. Nathan remembered him as a handsome man but with a slightly vacuous look as if he did not quite believe in his own distinction.

"He has been in the Vendée for some months now, helping to re-press the local peasantry, but I believe he has lately returned to Paris.

However, Madame de Beauharnais cannot stand him and between the two of us I do not believe Madame Tallien can, either. He can be a terrible bore and she tries to keep him away from her friends. Before the Revolution he was a printer's devil, which is to say the apprentice who runs about with the typeface and mixes up the ink. Many of us came from humble origins but his seem to have affected him more than most. He feels obliged to proclaim his virtues in a loud voice, as if he were speaking in the Convention. Then of course someone like Barras feels equally obliged to put him down and he sulks for the rest of the evening."

Nathan was aware that they had been following the route of the death carts from the Palais de Justice and along the Rue Saint-Honoré. They passed through the old Palais Royale, now the Palais Egalité, with its shops and its cafés, strangely quiet for this time of the evening. Looking through the windows of the carriage he could see the towers of the Louvre and the Tuileries, the new administrative centre of the capital where the Convention now met. But there were so few people about. Was this normal? Then they saw the soldiers. Regular soldiers, marching in good order, behind a mounted officer. Ouvrard had seen them, too. He was looking thoughtful.

"They are heading for the Stock Exchange," he said.

"Why the Stock Exchange?"

"I imagine to guard it, rather than to close it down. I trust I am not mistaken. It is in the Le Peletier section where the mob has been especially restive of late. I hope there is not going to be trouble."

"Is it likely?"

"My dear fellow, the city is like a powder keg. It could go up at any time. The people are angry. Also, hungry. They deplore the price of bread. They deplore the extravagance of their new rulers. They wish to restore the monarchy. They have short memories, it appears."

Clearly Ouvrard was not overly impressed with the will of the people.

"Does that not trouble you?" Nathan asked.

The banker smiled. "I expect I will survive," he said.

The carriage turned into a small street off the Rue Saint-Honoré; the Rue Chantereine, another name from the old regime. Nathan saw the heavy street lanterns where the mob used to string up anyone they suspected of being a part of it. In the heyday of the Revolution this had been bandit territory, handy for the agitators in the Palais Royale and the market women from Les Halles with the sharp knives they used for gutting fish and other objects. It was not a part of Paris he knew well. He jerked his head hastily back inside the window as they turned through a narrow archway, almost scraping the sides of the carriage against the crumbling columns, and on into a narrow unpaved lane between high walls and lime trees—Nathan blinked at the rural setting so close to the heart of the city—and finally stopped in a cobbled courtyard. The footman opened the door and let down the steps and Nathan was confronted by stables and a coach house and what appeared to be a neo-Greek pavilion topped by a typical Paris attic with steeply sloping roof.

"Welcome," said Ouvrard dryly, "to *chez Beauharnais.*"

Stone steps led up to the pavilion where their hostess awaited them in a little semi-circular antechamber. She was dressed, as before, in the Greek fashion but this time the muslin covered her entirely from her neck to her ankles, though her nipples were readily discernible through the thin, close-fitting fabric. She wore her hair *en chignon*, with that thin little blood red ribbon at her throat. Nathan kissed her hands, complimented her on her appearance, expressed delight at her charming abode. Such a surprise, tucked away in the centre of the city.

It was very small, she confided, but she was in love with it; she had not long moved in. It was just about adequate to her needs but everything fitted in like a little doll's house, with a kitchen below ground and attic rooms for the children and the servants. The children? Nathan looked about him warily, lest he step on them but they were not in evidence: tucked neatly away in the attic, probably, row upon row of them on mattresses.

There was but one little bedroom, she continued, but that was enough, was it not, for one little girl? With a roguish chuckle, taking his hand and leading him into the salon.

He walked into a blaze of golden sunlight from two large French windows on the opposite wall and took a moment to adjust his eyes to the glare. Then he saw that the room contained five people: two men and three women. Thérésa was one of them: dressed more decorously than before, in a long muslin gown not unlike that of her hostess but in flaming red, her long black hair unbound and falling freely about her shoulders. She was so stunningly beautiful that Nathan felt a constriction about his chest and throat, even while he made the conventional noises of greeting. The others were introduced. Madame Hamelin, the pug with the body of Venus; another woman called Madame de Coligny who would have been ravishing enough if not cast in the shade of La Tallien. And the two men— a dashing officer of Chasseurs with a startling mass of black curls who was introduced as Lieutenant Murat, and an older man with a long patrician nose and a haughty air, introduced simply as Talma; he turned out to be an actor. An intimate little party, as Madame de Beauharnais described it, with a giggle.

There was, Nathan thought, altogether too much giggling for his comfort. Something of the school-girlish, even conspiratorial, in the manner of the four women, as if they were not used to the company of men, which was ridiculous. Ouvrard detected it, he could tell, and was slightly puzzled by it. He looked about him now and again, as if someone might jump out from behind the curtains. Only Talma seemed entirely at his ease, telling a lengthy story about his part in a play: Voltaire's *Brutus* now running at the Théâtre Français. Naturally he was playing the lead, and during the assassination scene, when he had been about to plunge his knife into Caesar's back, he had tripped over his toga and driven the weapon home with far more power than he had intended, causing his victim to cry out "Jesus Christ!" in a loud voice that had the audience howling with laughter and turned the entire tragedy into farce.

The Hamelin looked a little puzzled at this until it was pointed out to her that Jesus Christ had not been born at the time, at which she went into paroxysms of mirth, as if to make up for her ignorance.

Altogether, Nathan thought, he had spent more relaxed evenings as a junior midshipman in the company of his superiors, though lacking the heady proximity of four gorgeous women in thin cheese-cloth. He could barely take his gaze from Thérésa, the tautness of the scarlet fabric drawing his eyes like moths to the flame and with almost as perilous an effect. He ate the first two courses with no clear idea of what they were, spoke nonsense in what seemed to him a stranger's voice and drank far too much wine.

Suddenly he became aware that the four women were standing up.

"And now the surprise," said Madame de Beauharnais.

Was this where they began to dance upon the table? But no, they were leaving the room. Was dinner over? He was sure he had only had two courses and light ones at that. He tried to catch Ouvrard's eye but he was gazing studiously into his glass. Talma began to hold forth again, another long theatrical anecdote, and then he stopped dead and stared towards the door. Nathan followed his glance and he felt his heart leap into his throat and jam there, choking him.

"Tra la!" Thérésa stood there, quite nude, except for her little red ankle boots and the blood-red ribbon about her throat. She waltzed into the room, twisting round to show that she was as naked behind as she was in front and looking back over her shoulder at them to make sure she had their complete attention, which was indeed the case. Nathan had not previously seen her from behind, even clothed. It was better than he could have imagined.

"Tra la!" Their four heads jerked back to the door as the Hamelin entered, similarly attired. She was not as beautiful as Thérésa but her body was far more voluptuous: a walking, curvaceous scandal. Nathan saw Murat as if the mirror of himself, his eyes staring, his mouth open.

"Tra la!" Madame de Coligny had a hard act to follow but she managed it well enough, being almost as well endowed as the Hamelin. And finally . . .

Rose. Or the Queen of Hearts, as she announced herself, for as well as the uniform red ankle boots she wore two little hearts, attached by some mysterious means to her nipples and a larger one covering the mound of Venus. It showed a certain comparative prudery that Nathan would not have anticipated. Murat began tentatively to clap but stopped when he realised he was the only one to do so and that the performance was possibly not yet over. Indeed, it had hardly begun.

The four women orbited the table with little dance steps, finally forming a tableau in the dying light of the sun as it poured in through the wide, half-open windows, the Queen of Hearts seeming somewhat overdressed among her nude companions. But not for long. Resting upon Thérésa's shoulder she pulled off first one boot and then the other. Not a breath, not a sigh. Utter silence in the room. The Hamelin plucked a heart from one nipple, the Coligny the other. And Rose herself performed the final unveiling, removing the heart-shaped design from her loins to reveal the darker fabric beyond.

"Behold," said Our Lady of Thermidor, gravely, "the Queen of Spades."

Nathan felt the beginnings of hysterical laughter. He suppressed it with difficulty. Then Talma, with his fine sense of drama, began to applaud. An overloud noise in the silence. Ouvrard joined in and then Murat and finally Nathan—what else could he do?

But now what? Four fully dressed men, who hardly knew each other, and four naked women. An orgy, for all its appeal in Nathan's fantasies, was actually quite alarming when it presented itself as a genuine prospect. For all the delightfulness of Thérésa, in particular—fully revealed to him in all her nude magnificence—the idea of stripping off his own clothes and cavorting naked with her in the presence of others was really something he had rather not do. And what if it was not Thérésa? What if it was the Hamelin or de Coligny? He would probably cope, a demon voice informed him. But what if it was Rose—the chosen one of Captain Cannon?

If Buonaparte heard as much as a whisper of these proceedings, he would have Nathan's guts for garters.

Fortunately, there was a reprieve. At least, for the time being.

To Nathan's frank astonishment, all four women sat down again, at their original places at the table. Rose rang a little bell, and the servants entered with the next course. Not by a single look or a fumble did they betray that they had noticed anything unusual. Dishes were laid upon the table. Napkins shaken out upon naked laps. Then they retired. Nathan observed that the main dish was some form of fowl, possibly duck.

"Will you carve, sir, being a military man?" Rose requested Captain Murat.

Murat carved. His hands shook a little. The conversation flagged.

"I once played Agamemnon in a loincloth," Talma declared, his voice a little more high pitched than it had been. "It was a little inhibiting at first, but I soon found it quite . . . liberating."

This did not entirely break the tension. The women, having achieved the climax of the evening, as it were, did not appear to know where to take it from here. It would have been better, Nathan thought, to have waited until after pudding.

Thérésa rallied first.

"A glass of wine with you, Captain?"

Nathan, who had looked to Murat, quite forgetting his own rank, realised she was talking to him. He found himself blushing as he fumbled with his glass. Their eyes met. Her expression was unmistakable. My God, he thought, she's going to have me.

Their glasses clinked and then in the silence they heard the sound of a bell.

"Jesus Christ!" said Talma. It was the tocsin. The dread alarum of the commune, not heard since the time of the Terror, calling the people to arms.

In the silence that followed they heard the clatter of hooves in the cobbled courtyard outside. Voices were raised. Boots rang across the outer chamber and the door was flung open to reveal . . .

Paul François Jean Nicolas de Barras. Booted and spurred in his blue uniform and his plumed hat, with a great curved sword at his waist, looking every inch the former vicomte, victor of Toulon, hero of Thermidor. His immense frame seemed to fill the smallish room.

He stared at them in total astonishment.

"Good God!" he said.

Rose was on her feet, her expression one of shock and dismay. Her napkin slipped from her lap. She made a grab for it. Went for the tablecloth instead. Dishes slid to the floor. Murat stood to attention, saluting.

"Do come and join us, Citizen Barras," said Madame Hamelin calmly. "We are having a little duck but there is plenty to go round."

The tocsin rang again. Barras snatched off his hat.

"Do you hear that?" he said. "Do you know what it is? It is the tocsin. Do you know what it means? It is the mob, madam, out upon the streets with their muskets and their pikes and their blood rage, and here you are sitting bare-arsed naked in this, this . . . this bawdy house." He waved his hat about the room. Nathan looked to Rose in sympathy. She was trying to wrap the tablecloth around her but most of it was still on the table, weighed down by dishes. Her eyes were filled with tears. He felt a sudden gush of affection for her, not unmixed with lust.

"They are marching on the Convention," said Barras, quietly now but with deadly earnestness. "Thirty thousand of them, at the very least, from every damned section in the city—and the Garde Parisienne with them. And if we do not stop them they will be marching back with our heads on pikes. So get your clothes on, you whores, and hide yourselves in the stables until it's all over, and pray to God or whatever deity you worship in those tiny brains of yours that you won't be wearing a different red stripe round your throats by the time the night is over."

He glared at Murat who was still standing rigidly at the salute.

"Who are you, you ponce?"

"Sous-Lieutenant Joachim Murat, sir, 21st Regiment of Chasseurs."

"Well, Sous-Lieutenant, get on your fucking horse and join your regiment at the Tuileries. You, too, Ouvrard, if you don't want to end up back in your grocery shop flogging lemons." His eye swept round the table. "As for the rest of you, we need every man we can get, even half a man like you, Talma. If you can't shoot a pistol you can inspire us with your rhetoric." His head jerked round to Murat again.

"Murat, did you say?"

"Yes, sir."

"Weren't you with that cunt Buonaparte at Toulon?"

"No, sir. That would be Sergeant Junot, sir. But I know who you mean. We have met on . . . on several social occasions."

"Have you, indeed? Why does that not surprise me? And do you know where he is now?"

"I . . . I suppose he is in his quarters, sir."

"His quarters? He has been struck off the army list, you whoreson. Where in God's name *are* his quarters?"

"I . . . I don't know, sir."

"I've been trying to find him all day. I expected to see him here," he snarled at Rose de Beauharnais as if it was her fault that he was not.

Nathan opened his mouth, perhaps unwisely. "I believe he lodges at the Hôtel de la Liberté," he offered.

Barras looked at him. If he recognised him from the last time the tocsin had rung in Paris during the month of Thermidor he showed no sign of it.

"Then perhaps you would care to go and fetch him," he proposed icily, "and bring him to the Tuileries. Tell him if he gets there in the next hour, he can have a new uniform and the Army of Italy. If he leaves it any later he can see what he'll get from the Royalists and hope it isn't a firing squad."

And right on cue, from out of the falling darkness, they heard a ragged volley of musket fire and then, as the echoes died away, the steady beat of a drum. It sounded no more than a street away and it was getting closer.

CHAPTER NINETEEN

a Whiff of Grapeshot

THE COUNTER-REVOLUTION COULD hardly have come at a more convenient time, Nathan reflected, as he walked briskly away from the sound of the drum. Unless, of course, one were a committed satyr. He admitted to some regret that he and Madame Tallien had not become better acquainted during the course of the evening and had they been alone he did not deceive himself that he would have remained inviolate. But he had discovered in himself a certain prim reserve when confronted with public lewdity and lubriciousness. Not that he had encountered a great deal of either in his short life, nothing like as much as he had hoped at one stage, but once as a young midshipman he had peered down into the lower depths of a 74 at its mooring in Spithead shortly after a horde of tarts had been let aboard from the bumboats and had been shocked to the core. It had become engraved upon his impressionable mind like one of Gillray's grosser caricatures. Ever since, the prospect of uninhibited mass copulation had possessed little attraction for him. Perhaps it was the Puritan in him, for though you would never have thought it from her own behaviour, his mother came from a long line of Huguenots, imbued with the convictions of John Calvin.

He began to wonder where he thought he was going. He had, of course, no intention of trying to find General Buonaparte, even if he had known where to begin looking, for he had no idea where the Hôtel de la Liberté was situated. When he had left the house, his only thought had been to head in the opposite direction from the advancing drum. His previous experience of Paris induced him to the belief that a drum was the herald of sudden, indiscriminate bloodletting. But now he began to recollect his true character as a British naval officer, in which capacity he had always understood it to be a summons to action stations.

He stopped for a moment, undecided. He did not wish to become involved in a street fight. Especially as it would be difficult to tell at a glance and in the confusion of the moment whose side he would be fighting upon. However, it was his clear duty to offer his services to the Royalists. The trouble was he did not know where to find them. Before he had left London he had been given the name and address of a certain lawyer near the Palais de Justice to whom he could pass on valuable information in the surety that it would make its way to England and who would, if it became necessary, secure Nathan's escape from Paris. He supposed he could try to find him, but it was a little late in the day to be scurrying around looking for lawyers. Besides, he was not entirely sure he wished to risk his life for the Bourbons. It was one thing when you were on a ship-of-war on the high seas, fighting in the company of your fellow countrymen, for the flag; for your family and friends; for your own advancement or survival. Quite another when you were in the streets of Paris fighting for the French—of whatever political allegiance.

Whilst so preoccupied, he had continued striding towards the centre of the city and now he found himself among the arcades of the Palais Egalité—or the Palais Royal as it once was and might shortly be again. The shops were all closed and shuttered but there were a few cafés still open, serving refreshments to those who had nothing better to do than sit around waiting for the next Revolution or counter-Revolution to take place. Nathan was passing such an establishment with his head down when he found himself hailed by a gentleman seated at one of the tables set out upon the walkway. Looking up, he saw to his astonishment that it was Captain Cannon.

He was with his hanger-on Junot, drinking coffee and cognac—surprisingly perhaps, given the amount of liquor he had consumed in the Procope. But he seemed perfectly sober now.

"Come and join us," he said. "We have just come from the theatre."

It was good to know that some aspects of Paris life continued uninterrupted.

He asked Nathan where he was going in such a hurry. Nathan considered. Several conflicting thoughts crossed his mind. Finally he said, "As a matter of fact, I was looking for you."

"Oh." Buonaparte eyed him without much interest. "And why is that? Have you got my hat?"

"No." *His hat?* Then Nathan remembered he had left it behind at the Procope. The general's hair hung greasily about his shoulders, his complexion more jaundiced than ever in the light of the cheap candles. Nathan dropped his voice. "No, but Citizen Barras asked me to look out for you. I have just been having supper with him." He glossed over the true circumstance of the repast, though he had a sudden vision of Rose de Beauharnais attired as the Queen of Hearts, just before her dramatic transformation into the Queen of Spades. He felt himself blushing. If Buonaparte only knew. "He wants you to report to him at the Tuileries."

It could do no harm, after all. Indeed, it might do the Royalist cause some considerable good to have the preposterous Captain Cannon helping to direct the defence against them. And if the counter-Revolution turned into a damp squib, as Nathan half-expected it to, he would have covered himself with Barras.

"What does he expect me to do?" growled the general. "Has he forgot they took me off the army list?"

"Oh, he'll put you back on again," Nathan assured him glibly. "And give you command of the Army of Italy. And a uniform. With a hat."

"He said that?"

"He did."

The general looked at Junot. "What do you think?"

"It must be worse than we thought," said Junot. "He must be desperate."

Not exactly the most diplomatic of responses from the aide de camp to a general, Nathan reflected. But Buonaparte did not appear to notice anything untoward.

"What forces does he have at his command?" he asked Nathan.

"I don't know. He didn't say." Then he remembered Murat. "I think he has the 21st Chasseurs," he added impressively.

The general did not quite spit but he looked as if he would have liked to. "And did he make any estimate of those opposed to him?"

"Thirty thousand or so. But it was just a guess. Most of the sections, the Garde included."

"And he wants us to join him?" Junot sneered.

Nathan shrugged, as if it did not bother him one way or another.

"If the Royalists would place me at their command they would have Barras grovelling at their feet by midnight," declared Buonaparte.

"I was not sent by the Royalists," Nathan felt obliged to inform him.

"You think we're so keen to die for Barras and his cronies?" demanded Junot, who had grown a little heated. "Those terrorists who only rose against Robespierre because he had them on his death list? Would _you_ die for that lot?"

"I am an American," Nathan pointed out. "It has nothing to do with me."

"The Army of Italy," Buonaparte mused.

"And a uniform."

Buonaparte drained his coffee cup and rose to his feet.

Junot looked at him in surprise. "Where are you going?" he said.

"The Tuileries," replied Buonaparte. "You are, too. Finish your coffee."

Junot was astonished. "But why?"

"No-one else is offering me anything," said Buonaparte.

Junot fumbled in his pockets for some change and the two men began to make their way through the tables. After watching them for a moment and for reasons he did not at all understand, either then or later, Nathan followed them.

The Convention was still housed in the old royal theatre of the Tuileries, where it had been in the time of the Terror. The lobby was crowded with civilians, almost certainly members of the Convention, Nathan reckoned, from the noise they were making and the poses they were striking. Junot forced a way through with some difficulty and they found Barras with a group of army officers gathered around a map of the city spread upon a table. He had a brow like thunder and it didn't clear when he looked up and saw Buonaparte standing before him.

"Where have you been?" he demanded. "I've got people all over the city looking for you."

"I'm here now," Buonaparte pointed out.

"Then you can make yourself useful," Barras informed him. "The sections have assembled their forces at the Peletier. Their next step will be to march on the Tuileries. Your job is to defend it. And you had better make a better job of it than the Swiss Guard."

"Very well," said Buonaparte coolly, "but I want absolute command."

"Bollocks," said Barras. He almost laughed in his face. "The members of the Convention have appointed me to the command of the Army of the Interior."

Buonaparte bowed politely. "Then the best of luck to you," he said, turning to leave. "And the members of the Convention."

"Hang on, hang on, hold your horses," Barras growled. "You can be second in command, how's that?"

"And Italy?"

"We can talk about Italy when you've saved Paris."

"How many men have you got?"

"About five thousand."

Buonaparte appeared sceptical. "Regulars?"

"About half of them. The rest are volunteers."

Nathan wondered if they were all from the theatre like Talma. It would not have surprised him. There were a score or so officers gathered about the table, though they didn't seem to be taking much interest in the proceedings. Most were smoking and chatting. He saw that one of them was Murat. He avoided his eye.

"I suppose it could be worse," murmured Buonaparte.

"They've got at least thirty thousand. With Danican commanding."

"Danican couldn't command his own bowel movements."

"You say that about all the generals," Barras said, but his brow had cleared.

"Very well, but I make the dispositions."

"Be my guest," said Barras, standing back from the map.

Buonaparte glanced at it briefly. Then he looked around the table.

"You, sir." He pointed at Murat who regarded him askance.

"Me, sir?"

"Yes, you sir. Where's your horse?"

"My horse, sir?" Murat leaned back, hand on his sword, and looked down his nose. "I imagine he is with my groom, sir."

Some of the officers began to snigger.

"Don't give me that Horse Guards shit, Murat. Your father was an innkeeper. You were drummed out of the army and worked in a candle shop before the Revolution. And you address me as 'my General,' do you understand."

Murat stiffened. "Yes, my General."

"Good. Do you know Les Sablons?" Murat looked blank. Buonaparte stabbed a finger on the map at a point to the west of the city, in Neuilly-sur-Seine. Nathan remembered going to see Imlay there when he had lived with Mary Wollstonecraft. "Where they grow the potatoes."

"Not intimately," replied Murat, with something of his former manner. Then he caught Buonaparte's eyes. "Yes, my General."

"And do you think you can find it in the dark? Without your groom to help you?"

"Yes, my General, but . . ."

"Take two hundred men. You'll find thirty or forty field pieces there, in the park, with horses and men. Bring them back as fast as you can. And if anyone tries to stop you, cut them down with your sabres. You'll enjoy that."

Murat had entirely lost his languor. He saluted. "Yes, my General." And he was gone.

Nathan looked at Buonaparte in total bemusement. Could it be possible that he knew what he was doing?

It appeared that he did. He began by forming the disorderly representatives of the people into a "patriot battalion" which was distributed along the elegant frontage of the building facing towards the Tuileries Gardens. The regular soldiers were formed into two line battalions to defend the more vulnerable approaches from the rear, in the direction of the city. The general himself kept moving, striding about the perimeter, placing men here and there, a brisk little figure in his greatcoat but still without his hat, followed by Junot, in the role of aide de camp, and a train of soldiers and civilians to whom he issued instructions from time to time and sent scurrying with orders to one or other of the posts. As the lobby emptied, Nathan snatched up the map of the city, rolled it up under his arm and followed the general out into the night. Whenever Buonaparte stopped and gazed about him, Nathan unrolled the map for his inspection with a helpful and attentive air. For the first time since his arrival in the city he felt glad there was no-one from the *Unicorn* with him, but he was curious to see what would happen and this was as good a place as any to observe the unfolding events of the counter-Revolution.

Not that it was unfolding at any great pace. They heard drums from time to time from the direction of the Palais Egalité and the river, but of the hordes of which Barras had spoken, not a sign. It had begun to rain and Nathan wondered if they would simply pack up and go home, as they had on 9th Thermidor when the commune had summoned the sections to the defence of Robespierre and the Jacobins. Shortly after midnight they heard the clatter of hooves and iron wheels from down the Rue Saint-Honoré and out of the darkness came Marat and his two hundred sabres with a long train of artillery

behind them. Nathan counted thirty-six guns as they circled round
the appropriately-named Cour du Carousel, mostly 6-pounders with
limbers for powder and shot. They looked impressive enough but he
was at a loss to know what the general was going to do with them, in
the middle of a city. He was not long left in doubt.

"Map!" Nathan hurried up and spread it out on one of the limbers,
holding it down against the wind and driving rain while Junot lifted
a storm lantern for the general to see by while he made his dispositions. Four cannon were placed at each end of the Rue Saint-Nicolas
guarding the approaches from the Palais Egalité and the Louvre; four
more in Port Saint-Nicolas pointing up the quay; six at what used
to be called the Pont Royal—Nathan had no idea what it was called
now—which was the only direct route to the Tuileries from across
the river; two in each of the little side roads leading on to the Rue
Saint-Honoré; and the rest lined up along the elegant frontage of the
building facing out across the gardens of the Tuileries.

Buonaparte personally supervised the positioning of every cannon, poking his long nose into the caissons to make sure the powder was dry and the cartridges were protected from the rain. He
ordered the guns loaded up with grapeshot: canvas bags bulging
with metal slugs and chain links. It would be devastatingly effective at close range—Nathan had witnessed just how effective on the
crowded decks of a man-o'-war—but he had never seen it used on a
crowded street before. For all the violence of the Revolution he knew
of no circumstances in which cannon had been used in the streets of
Paris, not during the storming of the Bastille in '89 or the massacre
on the Champs de Mars when Lafayette had ordered the National
Guard to fire their muskets into the crowd; not during the last attack on the Tuileries when it was still a royal palace, garrisoned by
the King's Swiss Guard who had died, almost to a man, trying to defend it. In fact, he could think of no instance in the history of warfare
where cannon had been used *inside* the walls of a city and he doubted
if they would be now. What general in his right mind would order
French gunners to fire grapeshot into the massed ranks of their own

citizenry, most of whom wore the patriotic blue-and-white uniform of the National Guard? And even if he did, what gunner would obey?

Still, they worked through most of the night, manoeuvring the heavy pieces into position in the cobbled streets while the rain came down in sheets, whipped into their faces by a chill wind. So much for the Indian summer, Nathan thought as he followed the little general from one post to another, wishing he had a tarpaulin to keep him dry. The map had become a soggy pulp in his hands but Buonaparte had no more use for it: the entire perimeter and most of the streets leading to it seemed to be engraved on his brain. Yet Nathan marvelled that anyone took any notice of him for he looked an outlandish, almost impish figure with his sharp features and his long hair plastered to his face by the rain, his clothes more than ever resembling those of a tramp looking for some doorway in which to spend the night. But there was something decisive in his manner that seemed to impress the officers around him and the men toiling at the guns. Certainly, throughout that long night Nathan never heard a single one of his orders questioned and he noticed that men looked towards him with increasing confidence.

Nathan stayed as close to the general as he dared in the hope of finding out what was happening in the rest of the city. He heard that the Royalists had made their headquarters in the old convent of Notre-Dame des Victoires in the Le Peletier section a few blocks to the north of the Tuileries and it occurred to him that he might quite easily find his way there. But he could just as easily get himself shot. And what use would he be? He would stay here, he decided. He might even find an opportunity to knock Buonaparte on the head if at any time he looked like winning. The Royalists had apparently called on Barras to surrender and he had told them to go to hell. The President of the Convention had issued a more poetic rebuttal, instructing his fellow representatives to die fighting and "with the audacity that belongs to the friends of Liberty." As politicians they doubtless found this inspiring.

Nathan heard other rumours, too. That the British had landed at Île d'Yeu, off the coast of the Vendée, with the Comte d'Artois, brother to the French king. If this was true it seemed particularly ill-advised, for it was even further from Paris than Quiberon and it was a mystery to Nathan how the seizure of an island off the French coast could at all aid the Royalist cause in the capital. He would have thought that a landing in the Pas de Calais or even Normandy would have given more encouragement to the men preparing to fight and die in the streets of Paris—but, as would doubtless have been pointed out to him by my lord Spencer or one of his underlings at the Admiralty, he was not paid to think.

The rain stopped shortly before dawn. The men waited by the guns in a restive silence, the only sounds coming from the horses in the rear as they champed on their bits, their hooves clattering on the cobbles. A cold grey light spread over the roofs of the city. Nathan would have killed for a cup of coffee. Then, shortly before five, the attack came.

It was announced by a sudden volley of musketry from the Rue Saint-Nicolas which ran the length of the Tuileries on the side nearest the city. It appeared that a number of men had slipped into the Hôtel de Noailles during the night and opened fire from the upper floors of the building, aiming down into the Cour du Carousel and on to the steps of the Convention. There were no cannon at this particular point but it soon became apparent that Buonaparte's talents were not confined to the artillery. He directed a withering musket fire from the Tuileries and then personally led a contingent of regular infantry in a charge. They were still fighting their way up the stairs, floor by floor, when a runner came with news of an attack on the far side of the palace across the Pont Royal.

When Nathan arrived there with the rest of the general's makeshift "staff," it was to see a column of blue-coated National Guards advancing in good order across the bridge, flags flying and drums beating for all the world like regular infantry. The rising sun, peering warily through the clouds still gathered over the city, glinted on their bayonets. They looked unstoppable. But they were not regulars. They were citizen soldiers. Working men, shopkeepers and artisans, drilling at weekends on the Champs de Mars. Family men, too, for the most part, their uniforms washed and brushed by their loving wives and daughters, their boots and belts polished by their proud sons before they sent them out to fight and, in this case, die.

They were three quarters of the way across the bridge when Buonaparte gave the order to fire.

Six cannon had been placed wheel to wheel at the end of the Quai du Louvre facing directly down the bridge. They fired singly, with a space of about five seconds between each gun and at a range of about fifty yards.

The canvas bags were ripped apart and the grapeshot spread out like shotgun pellets, but with far more lethal effect. It tore through the front ranks hurling them to the ground, each discharge exposing the ranks behind to the fire of the next gun so that to Nathan, watching from the far bank, it was as if a terrible wind had swept along the length of the bridge. The final gun fired. Deafened by the blast, even at a greater distance than he was used to on the deck of a ship, it seemed to Nathan that there was an eerie silence. The drums had stopped beating; the flags were no longer flying. Then he heard the wailing and the screaming.

The cannon were loaded and ready for the next rippling volley but there was no need. The column was broken, shattered into its individual parts, each fighting and struggling with his comrades in a mindless panic to reach the far bank, out of that terrible wind. And left on the bridge, lying where they had fallen, were thirty or forty mangled bodies and as many wounded, crying piteously or crawling away from the still smoking guns, dragging their shattered limbs behind them.

A horseman came galloping up from the palace to report another attack, from the north, this time, on the Rue Saint-Honoré. And so it went on, throughout the morning. Dashing from place to place, fighting fire with fire. And always the little general was there.

"It is necessary to be seen to be in command," Nathan heard him say to Junot at one point. "Or the rogues won't fight for you."

It seemed to work. The rogues seemed more than happy to fight for him. Nathan saw the grins they gave him when he came running up with his long hair flapping about his shoulders, his spaniel's ears. The little corporal, they called him, which puzzled Nathan until Junot explained that a corporal was always in the front line with the men, whereas a general invariably stayed at the rear, giving orders. But it seemed to Nathan that the besiegers lacked any enthusiasm to push their attacks home, especially when they saw the cannon. They had no appetite for grapeshot and he did not blame them. He sometimes wondered if his own men would have faced it on the decks of the *Unicorn,* if there had been anywhere to run to. He sometimes wondered it about himself.

Towards midday he found himself in a little street off the Rue Saint-Honoré, a cul-de-sac with a church at the far end which someone told him was called the Saint-Roch; the Royalists were said to be using it as a stronghold. It looked to Nathan more as if they were using it as a sanctuary or a suitable place to die. Two or three hundred of them were gathered on the church steps, some in the uniform of the National Guard, others in their shirtsleeves or flapping coat-tails. About a hundred men came pouring out of the Convention building, members of the "patriot battalion," representatives for the most part, fired with the expectation of victory. They charged down the narrow cul-de-sac—and came racing back when the enemy opened fire.

When the smoke cleared, Nathan observed a man in a white shirt with a red bandana tied round his head who appeared to be organising the Royalists into ranks on the steps of the church. He seemed vaguely familiar but there was still too much smoke to see him clearly. Then Buonaparte came riding up on a white horse someone had found for him. Nathan remembered what the general had said to him in the Procope: "If the king had mounted upon his horse and shown himself their leader, the day would have been his."

But there were disadvantages in showing oneself too prominently.

Rallied by the man in the red bandana, the dissidents were advancing down the street, firing as they came. Either the horse was hit or it slipped on the cobbles and went down. And Buonaparte with it.

The horse was up in an instant but in a blind panic, running towards the church and the advancing enemy, dragging the little general with it, his boot caught up in the stirrup.

Nathan ran forward. It was the first opportunity he'd had to knock him on the head. Instead, he grabbed the horse by the trailing reins and held it by the bit, doing his best to calm it. He did not know why. Possibly it was instinctive. As he would have helped any man who had fallen off his horse shortly after they had both enjoyed a good dinner. A shot took off his hat and another hit the horse in the head taking it down for good. Then Junot was there with a squad of regular soldiers and the enemy falling back towards the church.

Five minutes later, Buonaparte brought up six cannon and blew them to pieces.

Nathan stood at the end of the little street, watching. It seemed, apart from holding Buonaparte's map and his horse, that this was all he had done during the entire course of the battle. Watching while the Royalist cause was dashed to death on the cobbled streets of Paris. The counter-Revolution, it appeared, was over, the 30,000 men of the sections melting away into the shadows of the city, taking their muskets and their uniforms with them.

The victors were gathering about their hero, patting his shoulders, shaking his hand. He broke free and came over to Nathan, seized him by the ear and pinched it hard. Nathan stared at him in astonishment. Was this an admonition or some strange Corsican ritual? But the general was smiling.

"I told you, you are my lucky star," he said.

He moved on, to better things, more important people.

"All it took" Nathan heard him say, "was a whiff of grapeshot."

Junot came up, also grinning. "A glorious victory," he said.

But to Nathan it was more like a slaughter. He walked towards the little church where the dead and the dying were piled up on the steps. Among them was the man in the red bandana and Nathan saw, with a shock of surprise, that it was Bennett.

The bandana was red from the blood that had soaked into it from a head wound. More serious was the great hole torn in his stomach. He probably had minutes to live but he recognised Nathan when he knelt down beside him and he writhed his mouth into a parody of the familiar mocking grin.

"So you chose the winning side this time," he said. "Unlike me."

He coughed up blood.

"I will find you a doctor," Nathan told him, wondering where he could even begin. Perhaps Buonaparte could help if he could find him.

Bennett moved his head wearily from side to side. "I am a dead man," he said. He seemed quite calm about it. Nathan looked about him, at the bodies piled up on the steps of the church and all along the little cul-de-sac. "Why did you join them?" he asked wonderingly.

"Wrong place, wrong time. I have never been able to say no."

Nathan raised the man's head from the cobbles. He tore off his stock and wiped the blood from his mouth and chin.

"Thank you." Bennett caught Nathan's hand. "There is something I have to tell you. The hostages . . . One of them was your countess."

Nathan did not know what he meant at first. Then he remembered what the American had told him when they were walking in the Luxembourg Gardens: about certain hostages that had been taken at Quiberon who would suffer if he played false with his new masters of the *Sûreté*.

"She escaped. I heard last night. Before all this."

"Escaped?" Nathan stared at him. "From where? The Châtelet?"

"No." Bennett ran his tongue over his dry lips and Nathan wished he had water for him. "From Auray. With some others."

"But how do you know?"

That parody of a smile again but his voice was a rasping saw, a death rattle in his throat. "There are others who love her. Besides you."

"Charette?"

"Charette is dead. By firing squad."

"How can I find her?"

"She will head south. For Provence. Where she came from. She told you that."

How in God's name could he have known that? Was he another of those unhappy men who loved her?

"There is something else . . . Gillet. He will kill you. You have to leave Paris."

He choked and a gush of blood came out of his mouth on to the cobbles. Nathan felt him die in his arms. He laid his head down gently and stood up, wiping his hands on the bloodied stock. Then he saw Ouvrard. The banker had a musket in his hands and a bandolier around his chest, but if he had been in a battle it had not left its mark on him.

"Someone you knew?" he said.

"A fellow American." There was no point in hiding it. "God knows how he got caught up in this."

"Are you all right?"

"Yes. It's not *my* blood." Nathan looked down at the dead man at his feet. "I would like to make sure he gets a decent burial," he said.

"Let him be buried with the men he chose to die with," said Ouvrard. It sounded callous but he was probably right. Besides, how was Nathan to arrange a funeral? "Here." Ouvrard passed him a hipflask. The brandy caught at his throat and he felt its fiery heat reaching deep into his stomach.

"You saved Buonaparte's life," said the banker.

How did he know that? It was not a story Nathan wished to have repeated. "I just stopped his horse from running away with him." He passed the flask back and wiped his mouth. He needed to get away from here. He needed to get away from Paris. He began to walk back towards the Convention building hoping to leave Ouvrard behind him but the banker fell in step beside him.

"It is good to have credit with a great man," he said. "You never know when you might need it."

Nathan smiled grimly. "So he is a great man now?" he said.

The lobby where Nathan had arrived barely twelve hours ago had been turned into a field hospital. Here were plenty of doctors, if a little too late for Bennett; even nurses.

"The wives and daughters of our representatives," Ouvrard informed him. "Come to tend their wounded heroes."

The ones who had not been wounded were already making speeches in the Conference Hall. Buonaparte, looking more ragamuffin than ever, was standing beside Legendre on the Presidium.

"Yesterday they would not even give him a uniform," murmured Ouvrard. "Now he can have anything he wants."

"Barras promised him the Army of Italy," said Nathan.

"Well, he might have to wait a bit for that," said the banker. "There is still some clearing up to be done here in Paris."

"But then?"

"Oh, then I think it is safe to say he will be heading south. And the Genovese may wish they had been more obliging. So, my friend," he clapped Nathan on the shoulder and gave him a shrewd look, "you can go back to London and tell Imlay to buy as much of America as he can afford. Tell him the Republic is back in business and soon we will have money in the bank—even if it is not ours."

PART THREE: THE SACRED CHALICE

CHAPTER TWENTY

the Serene Republic

A LIGHT BREEZE from the west-south-west wafted the frigate *Unicorn* gently along the rocky coast of Genoa under a full spread of sail that should, touching wood, bring her to her rendezvous with the British Mediterranean fleet shortly before nightfall. Almost as satisfyingly, a delightful smell of coffee, bacon and eggs rose from the galley to tease the olfactory senses of her captain who had not eaten, by his own reckoning, which was almost invariably accurate in such matters, for a little over ten hours.

Nathan had been up for the last two of them, pacing the weather side of the quarterdeck or gazing out over the lightening sea towards the distant coast of Liguria which lay under a slight haze off the larboard bow. Twice he had taken his glass aloft for a better view and been rewarded, as the haze lifted, with a glimpse of snow upon the high peaks of the Alps, which swept down almost to the sea at this point, and, at a lesser distance, of a small fishing village with lime-washed houses clinging to the sharply-rising cliffs like so many barnacles. And the sea and the cliffs, the little houses and the mountains beyond, all bathed in the rising sun of a beautiful spring morning. He thought he had never seen such a pleasing or more peaceful coastline.

It was not likely to remain so.

All along the Côte d'Azur, between Saint-Raphael and Nice and up into the foothills of the Alpes-Maritimes, the French Army of Italy was preparing for war. And heading south from Paris to take up his long-awaited command, if the intelligence was correct, was Nathan's impatient young friend, Captain Cannon.

He would not be unopposed. Somewhere among these mountains were 30,000 Austrian and Piedmontese troops, Britain's chief remaining allies in the war against Revolutionary France. And between these two opposing forces—the Serene Republic of Genoa, whose present neutrality in this war would not save it from the consequences.

It was very likely that Buonaparte would find Italy a tougher nut to crack than the Garde Parisienne. If the Allied troops did not beat him, the mountains would. Besides, in Nathan's considered if as yet unsought opinion, the main thrust of the French spring offensive would come much further north and from General Hoche's Army of the Rhine. Captain Cannon and his Army of Italy were small fry: a mere diversion. Not that this would make it any easier for the even smaller fry in their way.

Or for Nathan, whose role in this gathering storm was fraught with the usual complications.

His instructions from the Admiralty were punctuated with numerous caveats and preconditions and references to important if obscure individuals whose good opinion, unlike Nathan's, was very much valued by His Majesty, even if His Majesty was doubtless as much in ignorance of their existence as Nathan had been until his present commission.

A minor star in this galaxy was even now hovering upon the edge of Nathan's vision.

"*Signor Grimaldi, come sta?*" Nathan greeted him, thus exhausting his command of the Italian tongue, though he comforted himself with the thought that in extremis he could probably get by with Latin. Not that it would be necessary in this case, for Grimaldi spoke perfect English, rather better in fact than most of Nathan's officers and crew, and Nathan's greeting had been in the nature of a jocular and faintly ironic welcome to his native land.

It was not as well received as he might have hoped.

"Good morning," replied George Grimaldi, with a thin smile. He was a man of about thirty with saturnine good looks, impeccable dress and a considerable opinion of his own consequence. Though he had been born and raised in Genoa, and spoke fluent Italian, he had spent most of his life in England, where a branch of the Grimaldi family had been established since the reign of James II and where they had the honour—as Nathan had been loftily informed—of being kin to the Lords of Beaufort. Despite such pretensions, he had been groomed for a career in merchant banking, which had been the family business for some several hundred years, and he had been introduced to Nathan in London as a representative of the Casa di San Giorgio and the nephew of Frederico Grimaldi, a present director of the bank. But he had other, less well-defined links with the directors of the Bank of England. Certainly it was the ubiquitous Bicknell Coney who had prevailed upon the Admiralty to ship him to Genoa aboard the *Unicorn*, though the precise nature of his mission there had not thus far been disclosed to her captain.

"Do please join me," Nathan invited him as warmly as he could contrive. "I have been observing your homeland and finding it as delightful as I have read in the books, though admittedly it is still at some distance."

It had been impressed upon Signor Grimaldi by Nathan's officers that when the captain was upon the quarterdeck the weather side was his solitary preserve and admission to this sanctuary was by invitation only, but it was only natural that Grimaldi should wish to gaze upon the land of his birth after so long in exile. However, his expression was not eager. "Where is this?" he enquired after peering myopically into the haze.

"I believe the little port you see there is called Maurizio," Nathan revealed. "Do you know it?"

The banker shook his head, as if there was no reason why he should. The territories of the Serene Republic stretched in a thin crescent between the mountains and the sea, from the French border in the west to the Grand Duchy of Tuscany in the east, though the port of Genoa was the only place of any consequence, certainly in the sophisticated view of the Grimaldi.

Nathan persisted in his enquiries, if only to establish his right to do so. "Were you very young when you left Genoa?"

"I was ten."

"Ah."

A small silence fell between them while Nathan wondered if the Italian had been as morose at the age of ten as he appeared now. There was altogether something of the curmudgeon about George Grimaldi, though he was not much older than Nathan. Possibly it came with the profession: the heavy responsibility of looking after other people's money and so often being forced to admit that they had lost it.

"And you were never back," Nathan broke the silence, "until now."

"I came back in the eighties—briefly."

Nathan was aware of the confidential nature of Grimaldi's business but found his manner irksome at times. He had the air of a man who has been gifted with a particular insight into the innermost secrets of the world and the grublike creatures who crawled upon it: as if he was not merely a banker but a master of the universe descended from upon high for some apocalyptic purpose that must remain secret until it was achieved, and perhaps for all time. This, of course, made it difficult to know precisely what he *had* achieved, which must be useful for bankers at times, Nathan reflected, if not masters of the universe.

Nathan had, of course, been made aware of the importance of the Casa di San Giorgio in the present machinations of His Majesty's Government. Bicknell Coney had spoken of it in terms of awe, quite out of his normal character. It was, he had said, the Holy Grail of Banking.

His choice of words was not accidental. In fact, as he had subsequently explained, the sacred chalice itself was reputedly among the treasures contained in the bank's vaults—which were appropriately known as the *sagrestia,* the sacristy—in the depths of the Palazzo di San Giorgio in the centre of Genoa. Legend had it that the *Sacro Catino* had been hollowed out from a single emerald the size and shape of a man's cupped hands and presented to Solomon by the Queen of Sheba. In later years it had come into the possession of Joseph of Arimathea, a wealthy Sanhedrin from Jerusalem who became a follower of Christ and set it before Him at the Last Supper; and the following day, on the Hill of Golgotha, Joseph had used it to catch the blood that gushed from the Saviour's side as He died upon the cross. Its fate since then was less impressive. During the First Crusade it had been sold to a Genovese adventurer by some Jews in Caesarea who claimed it was the genuine article and it was brought back to Genoa to swell the coffers of the Casa di San Giorgio.

Whilst affecting a proper Protestant suspicion of this legend, Coney had observed that the possession of such a relic could not but add to the bank's credit, at least in the eyes of Papists and other susceptible clients. Certainly that credit had survived the vicissitudes of history for some 400 years. Not only had it provided the funds for Columbus to make his celebrated voyage to the Americas, but it had enabled the Spanish Crown to exploit the resources of the New World for the next two centuries, while the profits of such enterprise had enabled the bank to establish its own empire in the East—a chain of trading posts and colonies rivalling that of the Venetians and stretching across the eastern Mediterranean and the Aegean Sea to the Black Sea and even the Crimea.

As for the Grimaldi, they had been directors of the bank since its inception: merchant adventurers, soldiers, admirals, doges of Genoa and princes of the Church. They had even created their own principality in neighbouring Monaco, though the last prince, Honoré III, had been dispossessed and imprisoned by the French during the time of the Terror, his tiny domain subsumed into the French Republic and renamed Fort-Hercule. Nathan's enquiries about the prince's daughter-in-law and her death at the guillotine had met with a puzzled frown from Coney, who clearly considered it an irrelevance, but his protégé was more forthcoming.

"Her name was Françoise-Thérèse de Choiseul-Stainville," he revealed, "and she was the wife of my cousin Prince Joseph." Then in a surprising gush of confidence, he added: "There is a legend that she cheated the guillotine at the last. It was the day of the coup against Robespierre and the guards were less vigilant than normal, the crowds restive. It is said that she jumped down from the charette and ran into the crowd with another prisoner, a woman. One of them was shot and subsequently beheaded; the other escaped. But if this was indeed the princess, I am at a loss to know why we have not heard of her since."

"And the other woman," Nathan had enquired with an affectation of mild curiosity. "Do you know who she was?"

But this met with an indifferent shrug. "I have not heard that she was of any account," remarked the Grimaldi before relapsing into his habitual reserve.

Gazing now towards the shore, Nathan recalled that Sara's own homeland was in these same mountains, just a few miles above Monaco, and that she had always vowed to return here. If ever they were separated, she had assured him, this was where he would find her, in the little town of Tourettes *"drinking lemonade and eating little cakes made of oranges . . . and waiting for you there."*

He was diverted from these painful thoughts by Gilbert Gabriel who brought the welcome news that breakfast was ready.

Breakfast had become something of a ritual since Nathan's return to the *Unicorn*. He usually invited a small selection of his officers to share it with him in his day cabin and found it a much less formal occasion than dinner and much more conducive to relaxed conversation, even with George Grimaldi in attendance.

There had been a number of changes in the gunroom during his absence. Tully and Holroyd had both passed their examination for lieutenant but had been superseded in authority by a new first, Mr.

Duncan, who had joined the ship in Portsmouth where she had been given a complete refit after her ordeal in the mouth of Morbihan. The sailing master, Mr. Graham, had been taken ill and replaced by an older, calmer man, Mr. Perry, who had served for many years as the master of a Levanter and knew the Mediterranean well. They had also taken aboard three new midshipmen, all sons of men to whom Nathan owed favours of one kind or another, as was the way of the service.

So it was a mix of old and new faces that greeted Nathan for breakfast. There was Tully, of course, a more or less permanent fixture; McLeish, the ship's surgeon, and Midshipman Lamb, both of whom had been with him in the Caribbean; Midshipman Anson, one of the newcomers, a fat little boy of twelve and a great-grandson of the legendary admiral who had sailed round the world and been First Lord of the Admiralty during the Seven Years War. And Duncan, the new first lieutenant. Duncan was an odd fish for the service, having been educated at Saint Paul's School and intended for the law—and doubtless politics in due course, for his father was a wealthy London alderman and his godfather no less a personage than Lord Chancellor Thurlow—until he "ran away to sea" as he put it. He was apt to declaim on subjects which were of little interest to the rest of the company—and was doubtless a great loss to both professions on that account—but he displayed a wry humour at times which Nathan found encouraging and though he was not a natural born seaman, he appeared to be an excellent manager of men and organiser of their duties, which was the most you could expect of a first lieutenant.

The table had been set with Nathan's best white linen and the white-and-blue Delftware that his mother had presented to him when he was first made commander of the brig sloop *Nereus* in 1792, the last year of peace. It was a marvel to Nathan that despite the damage caused to the ship's timbers and rigging, and the murder and mutilation of so many of her crew, this delicate porcelain had survived the intervening years of combat and storm almost intact. And upon the sideboard, the weather being calm, were set a number of pewter dishes containing the best the Angel Gabriel and Nathan's private larder could contrive. There was oatmeal with sweet cream, smoked herrings and sardines with mustard sauce, grilled kidneys, bacon and sausages, fresh eggs provided by the ship's hens and newly-baked bread from the ship's ovens with a choice of spreads including butter, honey, orange marmalade and several jams.

"Do not deny yourself, Mr. Lamb," Nathan instructed the elder of the two midshipmen, unnecessarily judging from the amount already heaped upon his plate. "I doubt you will find it as appetising as your rat suppers but we will do our best to tempt you with our less noble delicacies."

A restrained smile from Mr. Lamb who was watching Mr. Anson carefully to ensure he did not gain any advantage over him in the matter of sausages.

"I am told you are the best rat-catcher aboard the ship, Mr. Lamb," remarked the first lieutenant as he helped himself to the kidneys, "and that you keep them in a cage, like the witch in *Hansel and Gretel,* to fatten them up with weevils for times of famine."

Lamb blushed and shot a fierce glance at his fellow to see if he blushed in turn and revealed himself an informer.

"When I was a midshipman aboard the old *Hermes* I used to serve them spatch-cocked with a bread sauce," remarked Nathan with a distant air. "It was condemned as effeminate by my critics but held by the majority to be superior in every way to the straight, roasted variety cooked upon a spit."

This information reduced the company to a thoughtful silence for a moment until Dr. McLeish diverted them with a discourse on the superiority of rat's meat to rabbit, the latter being confined to eating grass while the rat's diet was usually more varied and when fed upon grain or rice quite delicious.

"I once ate a Spanish dish called a *paella,*" he disclosed, "which was a mess of rice and peas flavoured with *rata de marjal*—which, loosely translated, means rat of the wetlands. I would very much recommend it," he informed Mr. Lamb, "for your next experiment in the culinary arts."

Not to be outdone, Mr. Duncan regaled them with a story of when he had shipped some Russian troops in the Black Sea and observed them scraping the tallow from the bottom of the lanterns and rolling it into small balls which they would swallow and wash down with a drink of vodka.

"They were the dirtiest troops I ever saw," he said. "They would pick the vermin off each other's jackets and eat them quite composedly as if it was the most natural thing in the world."

This led to a discussion on the merits of weevils, which were said to be at their finest when the biscuit which they inhabited was at an advanced age of decay and crumbled into dust when tapped upon the table. The smaller sort were widely held to be easier to digest than the larger variety known as boatmen, their fat white bodies and black heads being somewhat off-putting to the more delicately minded unless, as Mr. Tully observed, you closed your eyes and thought of whelks.

"I have never eaten a weevil," McLeish remarked to great astonishment. "What does it taste like?"

"Cold," replied Mr. Duncan after some consideration. "And bitter."

"But quite succulent," added Mr. Lamb in the interests of accuracy.

"Hence the expression, 'pop goes the weevil,'" contributed McLeish, miming the action of squishing one between finger and thumb.

Nathan saw Signor Grimaldi push aside his oatmeal in distaste but the rest of the company settled down to their feast with every appearance of complacency. He was about to start upon his own when he heard the faint shout of "Sail ho!" from the tops but it was a routine-enough alert in the Mediterranean and Holroyd, who had the watch, would let him know soon enough if it was of any consequence.

"When was you in the Black Sea, Mr. Duncan?" he ventured, being desirous of drawing out the lieutenant whenever the occasion presented itself, for he was still something of an unknown quantity aboard the *Unicorn*. "And how was it that you came to be shipping Russians?"

"I was in the Russian service for a time," replied Duncan, "during the war with the Turk." He clearly enjoyed the sensation this caused. "I was then a lieutenant upon half pay," he explained, when pressed, "and as it was a time of peace I was permitted by the Admiralty to enrol in the Russian Black Sea fleet as a volunteer. I served aboard the flagship *Vladimir* under the American admiral, John Paul Jones, who caused us such mischief during the last war. He had by then transferred his services to the Russians and was a great favourite with the Empress Catherine who declared that he would get her to Constantinople before the year was out. But unfortunately this aroused the antagonism of her lover, Prince Potemkin, who assailed his private character with allegations of sexual misconduct and had him dismissed."

This was all very exotic for the captain's table of the *Unicorn* and the company was reduced to silence for a while, save for the chomping of midshipmen's jaws continuing their remorseless advance.

"And was you ever in action against the Turk?" asked Tully with interest.

A snort from Mr. Anson, who was susceptible to the giggles and for some reason seemed to find this amusing. He pretended to have choked upon a sausage and Mr. Lamb, who was aware of his weakness and encouraged it whenever possible, patted him solicitously upon the back.

"Regrettably I was not," replied Duncan, "being taken with the dysentery off Yevpatoria and I was like to be shite for the kites, as the Khazaks say . . ." a strangled cry from Mr. Anson "had I not been shipped home in an English vessel we encountered off Sevastopol."

Nathan suspected the first lieutenant of playing to the gallery for both young midshipmen were now thoroughly discomposed. He wondered if it was bad for discipline but decided he was getting old. He was contemplating whether he should have a second helping of the bacon and sausage or move directly on to the preserves when young Quinn entered with Mr. Holroyd's compliments and he was very sorry to interrupt the captain's breakfast but thought he should come up on deck to look upon a sail that was giving him cause for concern.

By the time Nathan had climbed into the maintop, Holroyd's concern had become more apparent, even to the naked eye. She was a ship-of-war—Nathan could just make out her topgallants and royals—hull up on the horizon at a distance of between three and four miles to the south-west and bearing down on them with all the sail she could make.

"She changed course even as we first sighted her," the lieutenant reported. "I cannot make out her colours, even with the glass, but I thought it better to be more safe than sorry."

"Quite right," replied Nathan, though his stomach expressed displeasure. He took the glass and steadied it upon her. She was ship-rigged, almost certainly a frigate, and quite a large one. As Holroyd had indicated her colours were quite obscured, if indeed she was flying them, and there was no other clue to her identity. The chances were she was British even so close to the shores of Provence for the French fleet had been well worsted off Genoa no more than a few months since and rarely ventured out of Toulon. But Admiral Jervis kept a loose blockade in the hope of tempting them out again and it was not unknown for the odd cruiser to slip past the few pickets he had placed there.

"What was her course when you first sighted her?" Nathan enquired.

"Nor'-nor'-west," replied Holroyd promptly and with a subtle significance in his tone. "About six points to the wind."

Nathan took his eye from the glass and gave him a searching look, though Holroyd was unlikely to have got it wrong. Even so, six points was about as close to the wind as any square-rigged ship could lie and would only be contemplated if she was involved in a chase or setting a direct course to her destination. And in this case, nor'-nor'-west would take her on a direct course to Nice or possibly

Menton, where Buonaparte was known to have his headquarters.

Still, this did not mean a great deal. She might have been sent by Jervis to look in on either port or clawing her way up the coast and sailing as close to the wind as she dared.

"Break out the ensign and hoist the private code," he said.

Holroyd had already consulted the code book and the flags were bent on to the halyard. Nathan watched as they were run up. The two ships were still at some distance but the signal should be clearly visible with the glass. He raised his own. Nothing. She was still coming on and still he could not see her colours.

"Very well," he said, reluctantly. "Beat to quarters."

His orders were to avoid combat until he had safely delivered Grimaldi to Genoa *unless such combat were unavoidable or could be contemplated without compromising his mission.* Nathan silently cursed whichever underling at the Admiralty—if it was not the First Lord himself—who had added this caveat, for it threw the onus straight back upon him. Clearly it would compromise his mission to engage with a ship of the line, but where did he stand with a ship of the fifth- or sixth-rate? Could he contemplate a fight with a 32-gun frigate, with which the *Unicorn* was equally matched, but not one of 36 guns? Indeed, even an unrated brig or a gunboat might inflict considerable damage in the uncertainty of battle. A lucky shot might carry away the *Unicorn*'s rudder or a mast and she might be driven upon the shore. Or she might catch fire, for it was rumoured that the new Directory in Paris had instructed all their ships to use heated shot. And unless he made his esteemed passenger crouch like a rat on the orlop deck, a stray shot might, heaven forefend, take off his head. Would the Admiralty find the *Unicorn*'s captain culpable in such a circumstance? Without a doubt.

The martial beat of the drum rolled out across the still waters and within seconds the starboard watch was pouring up from below. Nathan's breakfast party disgorged upon the quarterdeck, looking as bloated as he felt. The Angel Gabriel would be in a terrible stew as they cleared the decks for action, the great lumbering oafs crashing about the captain's cabin, taking down the bulkheads, breaking up his table into its several pieces, tearing up his carpet of chequered canvas, the precious porcelain bundled into its straw. And the drum beating and the rumble and squeak of iron upon timber as they ran out the guns. The shouted orders and the scamper of running feet. The scrambling up the ratlines and out along the yards. The heavier clumping tread of the marines in their red coats with their blancoed belts and their polished brass and their muskets. It all seemed so wrong somehow, so utterly alien, on this golden morning, and the two beautiful white ships in their sparkling pool of blue water and the snow upon the distant mountains. And the drum beating.

Nathan looked back at the approaching vessel, still cracking on apace. He could see the gunports now—a surprising number of them for a single-decker . . . He had a moment of deadly suspicion before he raised the glass and then he knew. She was a razee, or to give it the correct French term, a *vaisseau rasé,* a two-decker ship of the line "razeed down" to make a large, single-deck frigate. There were only three such ships in the British Navy—the *Anson,* the *Indefatigable* and the *Magnanime*—and to Nathan's certain knowledge none of them was serving in the Med. There was just a faint possibility she was a Spaniard or a Neapolitan but Nathan very much doubted it. She was a Frenchman; he would stake his shirt on it. He even thought he knew which one, for he knew every ship in the French fleet by heart: her name, her rating, her history, even, in many cases, the name of her captain. He tried to focus on the figure-head at her bows but she was still too distant. He counted the gunports again and nodded to himself in silent confirmation. She was the *Diadème.* No, that was in her previous life. The *Brutus,* she was called now, for she had been born again since the Revolution. She had been launched as a 74-gun ship of the line back in the fifties and seen service in the Seven Years War and the American War; if he was not much mistaken she had fought with De Grasse at the Battle of Chesapeake Bay which had delivered Yorktown to the combined armies of Washington and Lafayette, effectively sealing the fate of the colonies. But in 1792—Year 1 of the Revolution—she had been renamed the *Brutus,* for in Republican circles Brutus was an honourable man, and shortly after razeed to a 42-gun frigate. A brute of a frigate.

The one thing Nathan did not know was the calibre of those guns. As a ship of the line she had mounted twenty-eight 36-pounders on her lower gundeck with thirty 18-pounders and sixteen 8-pounders above. But now he was not sure. He cursed himself for his ignorance for it mattered a great deal. He wondered if any of his officers knew. He looked down to the quarterdeck and saw them staring up at him; those who were not staring out towards the distant frigate on their starboard quarter. But this was a waste of time; he was fooling himself and he knew it. Whatever the size of her guns and for all the ambiguity of his orders he could never persuade himself, much less their lordships, that a fight with a 42-gun razee could be contemplated, to use their own term, without compromising his mission.

For all the anguish it would cause him—and the respect it would lose him with his new officers and those of the crew that had not been with him when he had fought the *Virginie*—he had to run.

He glanced up and around him at the sail he was carrying and then out towards the enemy. He guessed they were fairly matched for speed but little by little she was closing upon them and he thought he knew why. She was sailing large with a quartering wind—perhaps three-and-a-half or a full four points off her quarter—almost certainly her best point of sailing, while the *Unicorn* was sailing parallel to the coast with the wind almost directly astern. If each ship held steady to its present course, the *Brutus* would soon be within firing range and being French she would fire into their rigging with a fair chance of bringing something vital down. Then she would close with them and with her heavier broadside she would have a clear advantage.

Nathan went down the ratlines considerably faster than he had climbed them. If he was to keep ahead of her, and well out of range, he had to alter course, to bring the wind further round on his own beam and run to the north-east. But there was a problem with that. He could see it written on the face of his new sailing master even as he reached the quarterdeck and gave the order and he could see it in his own mind's eye as clearly as if he were looking upon the chart. For five miles ahead, jutting out from the mountains, was the long, jagged spur of Capo Mele and the new course he had set would bring them running down upon it within the hour.

CHAPTER TWENTY-ONE

the Razee

THE *UNICORN* HAD SPREAD HER WINGS. With topmast and topgallant studding sails set on the fore, her spritsail stretching forward along that slender neck of a bowsprit, she might have been taken by some watcher upon the shore for a great white swan, Nathan thought, speeding across the still blue waters of the bay before taking flight to soar over the cliffs of Capo Mele.

If only. For every few minutes brought her another few hundred yards closer to disaster at the foot of that menacing spur: distinct now despite the haze, at a distance of about a mile and a half off their starboard bow. Nathan dragged his eyes away from the line of gently breaking surf and looked back toward their pursuer, at much the same distance in a diagonal line from their stern. That distance had hardly wavered since their change of course. For all his studdingsails and spritsails, for all the other little tricks in his book: lower lifts, braces and trusses hauled as taut as possible, topgallant clewlines set up tight, top-burtons and preventer lifts rigged and the mainsail weather-clewed to take full advantage of that quartering wind, the frigate could not lengthen the distance between them. The *Brutus* clung on grimly, neither gaining nor falling away. The same mythical watcher upon the shore would have imagined her driving the *Unicorn* before her into the deadly enclosure formed by that curving line of coast. Not so much a swan now as a farmyard goose to the slaughter.

But not so helpless. Nathan looked to his guns, the double line of 18-pounders, run out on each side, but manned only upon the starboard: double-crewed, nine men to each gun, and instructed for once to aim high, like a Frenchman, in hopes of bringing down a topmast or spar. He had drilled them at great expense in powder until they could load and fire in a little under two minutes. Not quite the three broadsides in five boasted of a crack frigate but not far short. Still, there was no denying that the *Brutus* was by far their superior in firepower. Even if she had sacrificed the heavy 36-pounders on her lower deck when she was razeed, Nathan was prepared to wager that she carried the same number of 18-pounders as she had during her previous incarnation as a third-rate, plus twelve 8-pounders as secondary armament on quarterdeck and forecastle and half as many carronades—or the mortars favoured by the French marine. A significant advantage, if she could fire them as fast. True, the French were not renowned for their rate of fire. Penned into harbour by the British blockade for months on end, they had precious little opportunity to practise with the long guns. How fast and accurately the *Brutus* could fire would depend on how long she had been out on her recent cruise and, of course, upon the quality of her crew. But for all the prejudices of his fellow captains—and among his own men, for he knew how they talked—Nathan saw no reason for the French to be any better or worse than British seamen, either at sailing the ship or firing the guns.

He caught the eye of Mr. Perry—a more phlegmatic being than either of the two sailing masters who had preceded him—but he sensed the anxiety behind that stoic front, for it was a difficult manoeuvre that Nathan intended and it only needed one serious mistake or a fouled rope or a lucky shot from the *Brutus* to confound them utterly.

Nathan felt a familiar recklessness come over him. "Ready, Mr. Perry?"

He saw the answering glint in the older man's eye.

"Ready as I'll ever be, sir."

Tully was biting his lip thoughtfully as he raised his eyes aloft. He would be worried about those studdingsails. He was a far better seaman than Nathan would ever be and less inclined to take risks, for he knew all the things that could go wrong, especially with this amount of canvas aloft. But then sometimes it was better *not* to know . . .

"Very well, Mr. Perry."

"Port your helm!"

The two helmsmen spun the wheel and Nathan watched tensely as the bow came round to starboard; further, further, but still the frigate stretched her slender neck towards that executioner's block of a headland. He saw the waves breaking lazily over the rocks at the point, launching themselves playfully into the air and falling back.

"Steady the helm! Everything being manned, haul taut!" Above a hundred men, every man that was not at the guns, hauling at the braces and the sailing master peering anxiously aloft, the speaking trumpet raised and lowered, raised and lowered like an automaton. "Clear away the head bowlines! Lay the headyards square! Shift over the headsheets!" The wind now directly aft and the yards braced in. "Haul aboard! Haul out!"

And they were on the starboard tack, heading out into the open sea.

Nathan looked over to the *Brutus* and tried to put himself in the position of her unknown captain. He had two clear choices: he could come round on to the same tack as the *Unicorn* and keep the weather gauge or he could continue on his present course and cross the frigate's stern. He would figure on firing two, possibly three broadsides before she moved out of his range. But he might take just as many from the *Unicorn* on his approach and he could not be sure if the British captain would resume his former course the moment they weathered the cape. No, Nathan was sure the Frenchman would come round upon the same tack. He was counting on it.

She was visibly closer now; she must have gained almost a thousand yards while the Unicorn clawed free of the headland. He could see her figurehead clearly, the noble Roman warrior, helmed and armoured: "the noblest Roman of them all" as Mark Antony had proclaimed, with the bloodied corpse lodged safely at his feet. Brutus. Why did the name trouble him so? Then he remembered the actor Talma at that infamous dinner party and the story he had told about the tragedy by Voltaire. It seemed like a dream now, an absurd flight of fancy. If he had known then that his own Brutus was awaiting him off the coast of Genoa . . .

But he was become as whimsical as Mr. Blake, seeing some divine significance in every trivial coincidence.

Even so, it was an unfortunate, disturbing memory and he wished he had not had it. He stared out across that diminishing stretch of sea and focused on more practical issues. A mile now or less—and still she came on. And with a return of his superstitions he felt a sense of impending doom, as if this was long planned.

A tongue of flame leapt out from the Frenchman's bow—and another, the twin report rolling out over the sea towards him even as he saw the two splashes off his starboard bow. Barely fifty yards short. He looked to the headland. They were almost clear now but there were rocks on the chart for at least another three hundred yards, just below the surface of the water. He must hold his present course for another two or three minutes longer and then . . .

She was coming round! At last the *Brutus* was coming round. He could see the length of her larboard broadside with the guns run out—and something else, too, something he had not seen before: a broad purple stripe running below the gunports. What a strange thing to do, he thought, for purple was the colour of the imperial toga—hardly a Republican gesture. But then he remembered that it was also the colour of Mark Antony's mantle that he had used to cover the corpse of his slain rival, when he found him on the hills above Philippi.

Still, it was a strange thing to do—and a strange thing for Nathan to be thinking about at such a time. But as usual in such critical situations, when Death was at his shoulder, he felt a part of himself floating free, detachedly observing his own actions and feelings, too, as if his soul was taking notes before its imminent release.

Both ships were now running almost parallel at a distance of a little over a mile and heeling slightly to larboard. Nathan felt a moment's exultation, for the *Brutus* carried her guns very close to the waterline—it was an inherent defect of the razee as a class—and on this tack it brought them even closer. It would be difficult, at this range, for her guns to fire high. But then he glanced along his own gundeck and saw that at least half of them were wedged up against the gunports and unable to bear.

"Ease the helm!" he called out. And then to the first lieutenant: "Mr. Duncan, fire as you bear."

But even as he passed on the order, the *Brutus* erupted in a rippling broadside and Nathan steeled himself to stand rigid, unblinking, as a score or so of iron balls with a combined weight of over three hundred pounds came hurtling over the sea towards him. But he had been right. They were falling short—fifty or sixty yards short . . . All but one, the one freak shot that skipped up from the sea and struck the spritsail yard of the *Unicorn* at the exact point it was joined to the bowsprit, bringing it crashing down into the sea on their lee side and the sail with it, where it lay like a sodden white corpse, a great sea anchor dragging them round by the head, unable to bring a single gun to bear and the wind wafting them gently on to the rocks at the foot of Capo Mele.

There were men already rushing forward with axes and knives to hack at the braces and lifts that still attached the shattered spar to the bowsprit, but for the moment the *Unicorn* lay helpless off the point and Nathan looked to the razee, bracing himself for the next shattering broadside for she was closer now and had their range. But to his utter astonishment he saw that she was turning away, luffing round to the south-west as close to the wind as she could lie. He stared at her, uncomprehendingly—and then he heard the cheers and looked

the other way—and saw the line of ships approaching out of the haze
to the north: five, no six ships-of-war emerging from behind the
headland, out of the Bay of Alassio, close-hauled with their guns run
out and the blue ensign of Admiral Jervis streaming proudly at the
stern.

With a rattle of chain and a definitive splash, the *Unicorn's* best
bower anchor plunged into the tranquil, almost transparent waters
of the Bay of Alassio, and a moment later her captain, resplendent
in his full dress uniform, stepped down into his waiting barge for
the short journey to the *Agamemnon,* 64, where he was to report to
the commodore of the British squadron; for this was not, as it transpired, the full Mediterranean fleet under Admiral Jervis but a mere
detachment sent to keep watch upon the port of Genoa. Moored beside the *Agamemnon* in line abreast were two frigates: the *Inconstant,*
36, and the *Tartar,* 28, and a little closer to the coast, the *Speedy* brig,
which appeared to be sending boats ashore. Two more frigates, the
Meleager and the *Blanche* had been sent in pursuit of the *Brutus,*
though with little hope of catching her, in Nathan's opinion, before
she found a safe haven under the guns of Cap Ferrat.

He settled himself into the sternsheets of his barge, carefully positioning his sword so that it did not discomfort either himself or
Signor Grimaldi who sat beside him. He was nervous, for it must
have been clear to every man in the squadron that not only had he
been running from a fight with an enemy only marginally superior
in weight of broadside, at least in the view of the British Navy, but
that he had made a thorough hash of it. He could only hope that the
commodore would form a tolerant view when he had cast his eyes
upon the Admiralty orders lodged in Nathan's breast pocket. He had
also brought the mail out from England—it rested in two large bags
at his feet—which might win him a warmer welcome.

Despite his unease, Nathan studied the *Agamemnon* with keen interest as the barge came round her stern for though she was lightly
armed for a ship of the line, she was one of the fastest ships in the

fleet: it was said that she could outsail anything she could not out-gun and outgun anything she could not outsail. But she appeared to have suffered some damage aloft—she had a spar rigged for a top-mast on main and mizzen—and as they drew closer he saw that her stern gallery was stove in and the starboard gallery entirely carried away. Still, they had let the steps down and dressed them in white rope, out of respect for Signor Grimaldi if not Nathan, and they came aboard to the shrill wail of the boatswain's call and the stamp and crash of a marine guard and the commodore awaiting them on the quarterdeck.

Any satisfaction Nathan might have derived from this courtesy was swiftly dispelled by his opening remark: "Well, sir, I see you have had the misfortune of tripping upon your horn," which was clearly intended to be appreciated by as many that were within earshot and was rewarded with an entirely predictable level of mirth. Although the wretched state of the *Agamemnon*'s stern tempted Nathan to re-spond that at least he had not fallen upon his arse as *they* clearly had, he wisely refrained, confining himself to a bashful grin and thanking the commodore for saving him from further embarrassment.

"Not at all, not at all, glad to be of assistance," said he, in a more kindly manner. Captain Nelson was an odd-looking fellow, Nathan thought: small and slightly built, almost delicate in appearance for one who had the reputation of being an accomplished seaman and fighter. Nathan had read with admiration of his dogged pursuit of the 84-gun *Ça Ira* shortly before the Battle of Genoa, raking her time and again before the admiral called him off for fear he would take on the entire French fleet by himself. He had been made post back in the American War at the age of twenty, astonishingly young for one without influence or title to his name, for though his uncle had also been a captain in the service, his father was a country cler-gyman in Norfolk. He must now be in his late thirties but there was still a youthful, eager look about him: though his appearance was not improved, in Nathan's opinion, by a green eyeshade which he wore under his hat and which cast a sickly pall over his features.

When Nathan introduced Signor Grimaldi, the commodore's look suggested he knew rather more of his occupation than Nathan's discreet signal had conveyed.

"We had better adjourn to my cabin," he proposed, "though I wish it were in a better state to receive you."

This in reference to the shambles that greeted them when they went below—many of the windows boarded up and the rest newly glazed, the frames unpainted, the upholstery stripped, the floorboards exposed and half the cabin curtained off with velvet drapes. He was halfway through repairing the damage caused by a storm, Nelson explained: "The worst storm I have known in the Med, which forced us to run before it on bare poles but had us well pooped before it was done and came pouring through the stern windows." Which information was probably more revealing to Nathan than it was to Signor Grimaldi who nonetheless treated the commodore with an obsequious regard entirely lacking in his manner aboard the *Unicorn*.

They made themselves as comfortable as they could, and Nelson removed his hat and eyeshade to reveal a rather more pleasing countenance than had appeared on the deck when it was coloured green, though he seemed to have a slight cast in one eye. Nathan recalled that he had read something in the *Gazette* about his being wounded while serving ashore at the Siege of Calvi in '94: a cannonball had struck a sandbag and hurled a storm of sand and stones into his face, permanently depriving him of the sight of his right eye. There had been some debate in the service about the incident and whether a naval captain serving ashore was entitled to the rank and remuneration of a brigadier, as Nelson had apparently desired. At any rate, a few months later, he had been appointed an honorary colonel of marines in recognition of this and other services—with the remuneration that came with it—so perhaps he felt it was worth the loss. He still had the other eye and the wound did not appear to have much disfigured him.

Nathan presented his Admiralty orders. "I also have a letter that I

was to give to Admiral Jervis," he said, "or whoever was commanding in his absence."

"That," said Nelson, holding out his hand, "would be me."

He slit open the seal and studied it in silence for a while. Then he
looked at the other document and moved his eye from one to the
other, as if to compare the two.

"Well," he said. "Well, well, well."

There was a knock upon the door and the purser entered with
the rest of his mail.

"If you will excuse me," he said, "I will just take a quick look
through these. I am eager, as you might imagine, for news from
home."

But he skimmed through it with alacrity, setting aside some
bulky packages that appeared to be of a more personal nature
and opening only those that contained the Admiralty seal. While
he applied himself to their contents, Nathan and Grimaldi were
served with port wine and sweetmeats by his steward who addressed them with easy familiarity in a strong Norfolk accent, asking them if they knew Burnham Thorpe. He appeared quite put
out when they confessed they did not. Many of the crew were from
the Norfolk coast, he informed them sociably, having followed "his
worship" to war in high hopes that it would prove more profitable
than smuggling, in which, thus far, they had been disappointed.
The tenor of these remarks finally penetrated the commodore's
consciousness and he looked up sharply and instructed the fellow to be off with him and take his unwanted opinions with him,
which appeared not to dismay the steward in the slightest, for he
favoured Nathan with a broad wink before departing.

"I am afraid I allow the fellow too much latitude," the commodore informed them, "and he takes advantage of it, but I have
known his family since I was a boy." He pushed his correspondence
aside. "So, Signor Grimaldi, I am informed that you are to go into
Genoa."

Nathan wondered if the Admiralty had thought to inform him

rather more comprehensively than they had thought to inform Nathan. It was entirely possible.

"I was there a few months ago," confided the commodore. "Magnificent. Never seen so much marble. Marble everywhere. Superior in many ways to Naples." Grimaldi smiled politely but Nathan wondered privately if he considered this so great a compliment. "Met the Doge," the commodore continued impressively. "Signor Brignole. A worried man. Did my best to reassure him but he's caught between the devil and the deep blue sea, as it were."

"The devil . . . ?" Grimaldi was looking puzzled.

"The French, in this instance. They're crawling all over him. All over the Littoral at any rate. Alassio's full of them. There is said to be above 60,000 of them poised upon the border and they have sent a new general from Paris who sounds as if he means business." He fished among the papers on his desk. "This is what he has been handing out to the troops—in lieu of pay I suppose. Do you read French?" Grimaldi shook his head, still looking bemused, and Nelson read from the document in his hand.

"Soldiers!" he began impressively. But then he stared at it frowning. "My French is much improved of late for I have been taking lessons but I'm damned if I can make out the words."

"I can probably make a fist of it," Nathan offered, "if it is of any help."

Nelson thrust it across the desk. "Read it out aloud, if you will, for the benefit of Signor Grimaldi here."

Nathan cast his eyes over it. It appeared to be a form of printed proclamation, heavily studded with exclamation marks. "*Soldiers!*" he read. "*You are naked and half-starved. The government owes you everything; it can give you nothing! The patience and the courage that have carried you into these mountains do you credit, but provide no adventure, no fame. I will lead you into the most fertile plains in the world where you shall find great towns, rich provinces! Within your grasp Glory, Honour, Riches! Soldiers of Italy! Shall you be found wanting in constancy, in courage?*"

It was signed General Buonaparte, commander-in-chief of the Army of Italy.

"You find it amusing?" remarked the commodore, for Nathan was smiling as he looked it over.

"Well, it is very like him" Nathan's tone was almost fond. He caught himself up. "From what I have heard."

The commodore's glance was shrewd but he contented himself with a grunt. "Well, I wonder if the Doge of Genoa was amused when he read it. Do you know him, sir?"

This to Grimaldi who shrugged as if it was nothing to write home about. "We have met," he admitted, "though he was not then Doge. The Grimaldi and the Brignole do not often agree."

"I am very pleased to hear it," commented Nelson, "for I tell you frankly, I believe he is much inclined to the French. Perhaps he thinks they will let him keep his own riches in recognition of his services to them. Certainly he has an odd notion of neutrality. He permits his vessels to carry supplies to the French army and offers up his ports as havens to French men-of-war." He paused a moment before continuing almost diffidently: "For which reason we have been obliged to place Genoa under blockade."

"Under blockade?" repeated Grimaldi, who had quite lost his composure.

"In response to which he has closed the port to any vessel carrying the British flag, save those that are brought in as prizes by the French." He glowered. "There are three in Genoa as we speak. And when we sent to recover them we were fired upon by the rogues."

"Then how am *I* expected to enter the port?"

"It will be more difficult, I agree. But I thought if we were to land you at night, a little down the coast, it would not be beyond your capacity to walk into Genoa."

"Walk?" Grimaldi appeared stunned.

"Or beg a ride on a cart or something." Nathan looked up sharply and caught the glint of humour in the commodore's good eye. His heart warmed to him. "It is not as if you are on official business,"

Nelson reminded the banker. "Indeed, it might be in keeping with the clandestine nature of the affair."

There was a sudden crash from behind the velvet drapes, followed by a kind of squeal—some child skivvy of the steward's, Nathan thought—but it was followed by the unmistakable sound of a female voice raised in anger, though speaking some foreign tongue, possibly Italian, which he did not comprehend. He glanced in surprise at the commodore but Nelson did not appear to have heard it or found it so unremarkable as to be unworthy of comment.

Signor Grimaldi had his own concerns. "But how am I to communicate with you?" He thought of something else. "And if I am successful, how are we to remove the . . . the cargo?" He made an odd, almost comic gesture with his head towards Nathan.

"I believe we may speak freely before Captain Peake," the commodore proposed briskly, "especially as he may be obliged to assist you in the removal of the said cargo." He addressed Nathan directly: "Signor Grimaldi has been requested to approach the directors of the Casa di San Giorgio with a proposal to take certain of its valuables into the custody of the Bank of England for the duration of hostilities."

Having met Mr. Bicknell Coney, Nathan was not as surprised by this information as he might have been. "An admirable arrangement," he remarked wryly.

"Well, I do not know how we are to accomplish it," complained Grimaldi, "if we cannot sail into Genoa."

"I am sure something may be contrived," replied Nelson. "And *in extremis* I am advised that we should endeavour to recover the most important item in the inventory." He lowered his voice with a swift glance toward the velvet drapes; Nathan looked too, but whatever they concealed was now quiescent. "I am speaking, of course, of the *Sacro Catino*. The Holy Grail. Though I am told it is more in the nature of a dish, which might render the task a little less trying." Grimaldi stared at him as if he had lost his mind and the commodore explained: "I comprehend it is not large in size, nor of any significant weight—in pounds and ounces, I mean."

"Forgive me, Commodore, but it is not a matter of walking into the Palazzo San Giorgio and slipping it into my pocket."

This was more like the Grimaldi Nathan had known aboard the *Unicorn*. He awaited the commodore's response with interest.

"I did not for a moment consider that it was," replied Nelson coldly. "However, I assumed that your esteemed uncle, Signor Frederico Grimaldi, might contrive some more legitimate means of assisting us."

"My uncle is but one of the directors of the Casa di San Giorgio, albeit the most important," Grimaldi retorted. "And the task of persuading the others is now rendered a great deal more imposing by this decision to blockade the port."

"Well, I am sure the Grimaldi will rise to the occasion," Nelson assured him, blithely, "as they always do. And the alternative, of course, is to risk losing the object to the French. I am sure I need hardly remind you of what they have done with their own sacred relics since the Revolution."

There was a brisk knock upon the door and a lieutenant entered.

"Yes, Mr. Berry?"

"I am sorry to interrupt your deliberations, sir, but the *Speedy* has signalled with urgent news from the shore." He paused a moment to give the proper import to the words: "General Buonaparte has crossed the border with a large army and is advancing on two fronts towards Genoa."

"Well, gentlemen," declared the commodore with perfect composure. "It has begun."

CHAPTER TWENTY-TWO

the Price of Glory

FROM A DISTANCE, the port of Genoa did not seem overly concerned with its imminent destruction by hordes of naked and half-starved French soldiers urged on by their eager young general with the promise of riches and whatever else occurred to his fertile imagination. No boatloads of refugees poured out from its ancient harbour. No convoys of loaded wagons headed southward along the winding coast road towards Livorno. No tocsins were rung. Indeed the inhabitants of the port seemed to have lapsed into slumber well in advance of the setting sun, or to have extended their siesta into the middle of the evening. A few early lights glimmered faintly along the waterfront or in the hills beyond, but little movement could be discerned. A church bell rang the quarter hour and the sound of music drifted across the mile or so of still water to where the three British warships lay at their moorings, in clear view of the shore and in the direct path of any vessel that wished to enter or leave the harbour.

"He has made a deal with the French," pronounced the commodore as he leaned upon the larboard rail of the *Agamemnon*, gazing out towards the capital of the Serene Republic. "I am as certain of it as my own name."

Nathan did not need to ask who "he" was any more than he needed to enquire into the circumstances of the commodore's birth and patrimony. Signor Giacomo Maria Brignole, otherwise known as His Serene Highness the Doge of Genoa, was the constant object of the commodore's biting condemnation. Little more than a French lapdog, a traitor to his people and his class, a puppet, a stooge, a mountebank . . . these were just some of the criticisms levelled at him in Nathan's hearing. He was beginning to think there was something personal in it. What had passed between the two men, he wondered, during that singular meeting almost a year ago? What assurances had been given, what resentments planted?

Or perhaps it was just that the commodore resented his own impotence, lying here in the Genoa roads while a young French general led his armies up the coast and through the mountains, out of range of the commodore's guns, seizing the moment, pursuing his destiny. There had to be a scapegoat and the Doge of Genoa lay conveniently to hand.

"He has sold his birthright," Nelson declared, "but then what else do you expect of an Italian? Though I hope he may burn in hell for it."

"But where does that leave Signor Grimaldi?" Nathan enquired diffidently.

They had landed Grimaldi in the early hours of the morning at a small beach to the west of the city, accompanied by an officer of the 69th Regiment of Foot—serving aboard the *Agamemnon* in the capacity of marines—who spoke excellent Latin, the commodore assured the dubious banker, and had, besides, picked up "a little of the local lingo" in previous trips ashore and could "pass for a native." Nathan gathered that there was something of a history to these excursions ashore, though either to provide intelligence or entertainment he had not yet discovered; probably it was a mixture of both. Grimaldi, however, had looked decidedly sorry for himself when they had lowered him into the *Agamemnon*'s cutter and for all his haughty self-regard, Nathan felt responsible for him.

"Oh doubtless he will manage," Nelson remarked carelessly. "He has plenty of relatives in the city and he has Pierson with him. Besides, whenever have you known a banker come to harm?"

Nathan could not immediately recall. "But if the Doge suspects he is working for the English," he began.

"He is not working for the *English*," Nelson corrected him. "He is working for the Bank of England." He caught Nathan's eye. "I am persuaded there is a distinction. These bankers are something of an international community, not unlike the Jews or the Freemasons. They look after their own. One cannot but admire them for it. I doubt the Doge, for all his duplicity would betray him to the French. Though I cannot see him agreeing to the proposals. Still," he sighed, "we have done our best. We have carried out our orders to the letter, what more can they ask? And now here is Captain Fremantle come to join us." For the barge of the frigate *Inconstant* could be seen crossing the darkening waters toward them. An unfortunate name for a ship of war, Nathan reflected, even before it had been corrupted to the Incontinent, as he was assured it had by all but her own crew. "And Tom Allan, if I am not much mistaken, is ready to serve supper."

This proved to be the case and they adjourned to the captain's cabin which had been made a little more presentable than the last time Nathan had seen it, with a chequered canvas nailed to the floor, the long polished table gleaming with candlelight and the commodore's silverware, and—rather more surprisingly—a splendid young woman in a low-cut dress of violet muslin, not quite as revealing as that of Our Lady of Thermidor but not a long way off it, even allowing for the poor light.

"Allow me to present Signora Correglia," the commodore intoned, "who has come from Leghorn to be with her mother. Captain Peake has recently joined us from England, Signora."

Nathan had suffered introductions to several women whose relationship to the introducer had, of necessity, been swathed in ambiguity—"a friend of the family on my father's side" had been his favourite until now—but this sprinted into the lead by a good head. The signora smiled charmingly and Nathan bowed over her hand.

She was a ravishing creature, though a little older than he had first thought, petite and dark-haired with the figure of a pocket Venus and deep, dark eyes. She was afraid she spoke very little of the English, she said, but she seemed perfectly at ease in the capacity of hostess, greeting the other officers as they arrived with a familiarity that persuaded Nathan she was something of a fixture aboard the *Agamemnon*, though whether she came with the ship or had been acquired by her captain in the course of his travels remained to be discovered. Nathan knew nothing of the commodore's marital status, nor did he care, but if he had a lady at home, Signora Correglia stood in for her handsomely. She sat at the opposite end of the table from the commodore, ensuring that everyone had a full glass of wine before him and beaming complacently upon the company, though it was clear from the few compliments that were addressed to her that she barely spoke or understood a word of English.

They had been joined by Mr. Berry, the first lieutenant, Mr. Fellowes, the purser, Mr. Roxburgh, who was introduced as the "principal medical officer," rather than the ship's surgeon, a young gentleman called Hoste and another called Nisbet who turned out to be the commodore's stepson. His mother was alive and well, Nathan ascertained in the course of the evening, and living in Burnham Thorpe with Nelson's father, the clergyman, so what young Nisbet made of the stand-in could only be conjectured, but he smiled upon the lady and was smiled upon in return as amiably as the rest of the company. And finally there was Thomas Fremantle, captain of the *Inconstant*, an affable gentleman in his early thirties, rather on the short side and running to fat but with excellent manners and a ready wit. He and Nelson seemed to be on good terms.

"Not brought your dolly with you?" Nelson had greeted him upon his arrival.

"I thought it more respectful to leave mine behind in Leghorn," replied Fremantle, evenly, "but I am told you are not so troubled by convention."

"Pish. I know very well you've got her stowed aboard," Nelson rebuked him, "but are too much a prig to expose her in company. He hides them away, you know," he informed Nathan. "Shoos them off whenever someone of status appears upon the horizon, like cats."

It was, all things considered, an enjoyable evening: supper aboard the *Agamemnon* clearly fulfilling the function of breakfast on the *Unicorn*.

"I am told that in Paris dinner and supper are become indistinguishable," Fremantle remarked over the Welsh rabbit. "Dinner having been moved back so far into the day as to merge the two."

"Then I hope it is more dinner than supper," remarked the doctor, a man of substance, subjecting his portion of toasted cheese to critical regard.

"I am surprised that the French, who are notoriously considerate of their stomachs, can contemplate such a large gap between breakfast and dinner," Nelson contributed, "or supper or whatever it is they call it."

"Oh, but they have invented a new meal," Fremantle informed him, "which they call lunch. Or to be precise, *la fourchette,* a fork lunch, meaning something more substantial than a sandwich. I am told it is all the rage."

"I am astonished, with so much else to divert them, that the French have either the time or inclination to go to war," mused the first lieutenant, an honest fellow with an open countenance and little time for conversation—or for Captain Fremantle, Nathan gathered from small hints of disapproval.

"Oh, but not many of them do," Fremantle assured him cheerfully. "They send others—conscripts for the most part who have no choice, or fanatics who would die for *La Révolution*."

"And what is Buonaparte of the two? Do you know as much about him as you do about French dinnertime?" Nelson quizzed him.

"I have not made so close a study. But I am told he is a Jacobin, which puts him in the fanatic camp."

"Perhaps Captain Peake can enlighten us," suggested the commodore, "for I believe he has made a study of the particular subject."

All eyes turned upon Nathan, even the signora's, who tended to look brightly upon whoever was addressed by the commodore, when she was not pouring wine.

"He was *once* a Jacobin," Nathan replied, "but I do not believe it was from conviction, the rather to advance his own career, this being the time of Robespierre. He is a Corsican, which is to say more Italian than French."

"Hence the name," Nelson supplied.

"A mercenary then," proposed the first lieutenant.

"Not really." Nathan was moving into dangerous waters but the conversation interested him too much to let it pass. "Not in the financial sense, at least. He is very much attached to glory."

"Ah. *La Gloire*," the commodore pronounced. "There is no word quite like it in English. Mere glory is nothing to it. *La Gloire*. The greatest virtue a man might aspire to—or a nation. A goddess beyond compare." He raised his glass to Signora Correglia at the far end of the table, but with a hint of irony.

"And yet it comes at a price," declared the doctor provocatively. "Like any mercenary. There is always the butcher's bill."

"Ah, there speaks the voice of reason," said the purser, with the suggestion of a sneer.

"We live in an age of reason, I believe," the doctor rebuked him sharply.

"But what have we lost by it?" Nelson mused. "Where is the higher calling? The belief in a man's Destiny? You count the cost, Doctor, in terms of human suffering, but you do not see the credit that is accrued. You have seen too many wounds, too many corpses. But I tell you, a glorious death is to be envied. And life with disgrace is dreadful."

For a moment Nathan thought the doctor was going to come back at him, but he thought better of it and reached for his wine.

A little later, supper being ended, Fremantle invited Nathan to walk with him on the deck and smoke a cigar.

"Well," said he, when they were alone, "what do you make of our gallant commodore?"

"He seems to know his business," Nathan replied cautiously. He thought it an odd question to ask on Nelson's own ship. It occurred to him that Fremantle was drunk.

"Ah yes, he does that. We are good friends, you know."

"So I understand," Nathan acknowledged, wondering if this were a warning or an invitation to speak freely. It could be either.

"And what of the commodore's lady?"

"Signora Correglia?"

"Who else? I saw no other that was present."

"I formed no opinion, not being able to converse with her in her own language. But she appeared to be an amiable hostess."

"Ah yes. *Très agréable,* as they say in France. But you were not surprised to find her in that capacity?"

Nathan did not know what to say. "The commodore tells me she is on her way to see her mother, in Genoa," he ventured.

Fremantle took a step back and surveyed him to see if he was joking.

"He told you that? Tell me he didn't say that."

Nathan could give him no such assurance. Fremantle threw back his head and delivered his mirth to the heavens.

"Oh dear, oh dear." He composed himself. "Well, I suppose it is true in a way. She does have a mother in Genoa—and she does go there from time to time. Nelson says she brings back excellent intelligence."

"Well then?"

"Well then." Fremantle regarded him with continued amusement. "She is a whore, you know, procured by Mr. Udny, the consul at Leghorn. He procures women for all the officers. It is a useful sideline."

"Well, she appears to be a very nice whore," Nathan remarked.

"Oh, she is, she is. I had her before him, you know."

Nathan was beginning to take a dislike of the man. He

acknowledged the claim with a slight bow.

"Well, we all need our consolations." Fremantle appeared mildly defensive. "It is like to be a long war for all the assurances to the contrary. Are you married?"

"No."

"No, nor I. Wouldn't mind it, though, if I met the right woman. But in the meantime, there are always dollies. You should ask Mr. Udny to find you one, if you are ever in Leghorn. He knows the right sort."

Nathan thanked him and said he would remember it.

"Do you go on to join the fleet in Saint Fiorenze," Fremantle pressed him, "or are you stuck with us for a while?"

"I believe I am stuck with you," Nathan replied, forcing a smile. "If not for the duration."

"Well, I hope we can find you some entertainment," Fremantle offered with a small bow. "Nelson has a knack for being in the forefront of the action, wherever it is. You heard about the *Ça Ira?*"

"I read of the encounter in the *Gazette*," Nathan said.

"I was with him, you know. In fact, it was the *Inconstant* that first caught up with her. She had been in collision with another Frenchie and was lagging behind the fleet. This was when they were running for Corsica. She had 84 guns to our 36 and the first few exchanges I kept a healthy distance, I don't mind telling you. But then Nelson comes up in the *Agamemnon*." He paused and when he continued his voice was lower, huskier. "The official report will tell you they exchanged broadsides for above two hours until the arrival of two more Frenchies forced him to veer away. But the truth is the *Ça Ira* was under tow." He saw Nathan's look of surprise. "Yes. Under tow from a frigate. She could not bring her broadside to bear. Nelson hung on to her stern and raked her, time and again, for over two hours. I was there, I saw it. I saw the blood running from her scuppers. Then two other ships came up and the admiral called him off, but the next day we caught up with her again and took her. I was there then, too. I went aboard her when she struck. She was carrying over a thousand troops for the invasion of Corsica. There were hundreds dead, heaped up in the scuppers or lying below. We kept finding them, piled in the cockpit, cabins, cable tiers, wherever they had crawled to die. I have never seen such a shambles and hope never to again."

He fell silent and Nathan thought of the bodies on the steps of the Saint-Roch in Paris when Buonaparte fired upon the people with his cannon. "What are you telling me?" he frowned. "That he should not have done it?"

"Oh no, no, not at all." His protest seemed sincere. "No. What am I saying?" Clearly something bothered him, if it was not plain jealousy. "I suppose I am saying that the doctor is right and that glory has its price. But, of course, you know that. And so does Nelson, though he appears to think it is well worth the expense. Yes. Oh, but I tell you, he is a real fighting captain and I for one am proud to serve under him."

The tenor of this last remark was not necessarily at variance with what had preceded it, but it was uttered in so different a tone that Nathan gazed at him with bemusement until he heard a footfall on the deck and turned to see the commodore emerging from the companionway.

"Well, gentlemen," he greeted them. "Still a quiet night?"

"Not a peep from the port," said Fremantle, "except for the bells ringing ten of the clock. And here is my barge. Right on time, so I regret I must take my leave of you."

They watched the barge of the *Inconstant* draw off into the darkness with her captain safely stowed in the stern.

"Fremantle," mused the commodore, smiling with some affection. "A terrible fellow. Talks a lot of nonsense but he's not a stupid man, far from it. In fact he is surprisingly knowledgeable on a great many subjects. Reads a lot. He has a fine library aboard the *Inconstant*, though it is the very devil to get him to lend you one of his books. Says I'll only ruin it. He livens up the conversation, though, don't you think?"

Nathan agreed that he was, indeed, an entertaining table companion.

"Yes. A great asset when you are at sea." Nelson gazed after the departing barge where they could still make out the upright figure of Fremantle in the stern. "He has his darker moments, though. A sort of brooding melancholy that comes upon him. As I suppose it does upon all of us at times." He laughed awkwardly. "Needs a wife. Do *you* have a wife?"

"No, sir." Nathan's lack of a wife seemed to be the topic for the evening.

"Everyone needs a wife. What is it Paul of Tarsus said? 'Better to marry than to burn.' Quite right. Mind you, no reason why you can't do both."

Nathan nodded wisely in lieu of wise remark.

Nelson looked out at the distant port, the lights of the mole dancing towards them across the still water. "I wonder how he is getting on over there?"

"Signor Grimaldi?"

"Yes. Speaking frankly, I cannot say I was overly impressed. Still, he is a Grimaldi and blood is thicker than water, as they say." He pondered a while, still looking towards the port. "What do you reckon it is worth?"

Nathan was as startled. "I suppose it depends how much gold is in the reserves," he ventured.

"I was thinking of the *Sacro Catino*."

"Ah. Well, given its history . . ."

Nelson looked up at him sharply. "You think it is the real thing? The Holy Grail?"

"Oh, as to that, I am not even sure such an object ever existed."

"Well, He drank from *something* at the Last Supper," the commodore rebuked him tetchily. "I am speaking of Our Lord. '*And He took the cup and gave thanks and gave it to them, saying, "Drink ye all of it, for this is my blood of the new testament, which is shed for many for the remission of sins."*' It is in Matthew I think, though I do not recall the exact chapter and verse."

"Yes, but . . ."

"Is it the same cup?" the commodore finished for him. "I know. The Papists and their relics. I am told there are enough pieces of the Sacred Cross to make a decent-sized frigate. And it is not even a cup, from what we know, more a sort of . . . dish. *And he answered and said, "He that dippeth his hand with me in the dish, the same shall betray me."'* Still, dish or cup, an intriguing story. You have read Sir Thomas Malory?"

"I fear not," Nathan confessed.

"But you know of the quest for the Holy Grail? The Sangreal, as Malory calls it."

"I know of the legend," Nathan replied cautiously.

"Five knights went in quest of the Grail, but to succeed you had to be free of sin. Lancelot was ruled out on account of his adultery." He lapsed into another thoughtful silence. Then: "Even if it is not the real thing—*'Cut from a single emerald, the size of a man's cupped palms.'*" He cupped his own and gazed down upon them speculatively. "And I have small hands. Must be worth a King's ransom."

"Grimaldi said it was priceless."

"Priceless! How I hate that word." The commodore's tone was caustic. "You would have thought that as a banker he would not talk such nonsense, when all you require to know is the exact worth of an object in pounds, shillings and pence—so it might be divided into its quarters and its one-eighths. And then you know where you are with it. Have you took much in the way of prizes, if I do not give offence?"

This was not quite the non sequitur it appeared to be, the captain's share of prize money being one quarter of the value, with one-eighth to the flag officer he happened to be serving under when the prize was took. Nathan did not think it would apply to the Sacred Chalice of Genoa though, in the circumstances.

"Only two," he confessed. "A small hooker off Étaples with a cargo of cider, salt pork and ship's biscuit. And the frigate *Vestale*, off Le Havre. That was when I was commander of the *Nereus*. I might have taken the *Virginie,* too, had she not sunk."

"I remember reading about it in the *Gazette.* Struck upon a reef with the *Unicorn* in hot pursuit." They reflected silently upon this misfortune. "The *Virginie* and the *Vestale,* eh," the commodore remarked at length. "You have an eye for the maidens, I perceive."

"Well, I would settle for something less *virgo intactus,*" replied Nathan with a misguided attempt at humour, "if she were well stacked." He felt his cheeks grow hot as he recalled the commodore's paramour in the cabin below.

"I have not been lucky, either, in the matter of prize money," Nelson confided after a moment. "I have taken enough shot from the French in my time but precious little in the way of their silver, I regret. Or their gold. And I do not suppose I ever will. It would almost persuade a man to quit and go into Parliament."

Nathan made a sound in his throat that might be taken for a laugh.

"Oh, but I am quite serious," the commodore assured him. "I have been asked if I would like to stand for Ipswich in the next election, and I am giving it serious thought. My situation here is intolerable. While the Doge claims to be neutral every damned ship sailing under the Genoese flag is under his protection, even if it is loaded to the gunwales with supplies for the French Army of Italy. We take 'em anyway, of course, where we can, but we can be sued for it by the owners, and will be no doubt, in the course of time. Little wonder I have pains in the chest."

Once more they fell into an uneasy silence, gazing out towards the sleeping city.

"What will he do, do you think?" ventured the commodore at length.

"The Doge?"

"I was thinking of Buonaparte."

"Whatever we do not expect of him," replied Nathan, surprising himself a little by this insight.

"Ah yes. The only way to fight a battle. Or a war. He will not come near Genoa, will he?"

"I believe not," said Nathan, though for the life of him he could not think why he should presume to have an opinion on the matter.

"Because of the Doge and the deal he has made?"

"I do not think he is a great respecter of deals," said Nathan. "No. I think he will go straight for the Austrians. For the jugular."

"Ah yes. Always go for the jugular. A man after my own heart. You care for a coffee?"

"Thank you, I would."

They were about to go below when there was a cry from the lookout and an answering hail from the water, and they turned to observe the cutter emerging out of the darkness and in it, just discernible by the light of the lantern, the huddled figure of Signor Grimaldi in the stern.

"It is gone," announced Grimaldi dramatically, as soon as he stepped aboard.

Nelson led him over to the weather rail where they were granted a little privacy.

"Keep your voice down!" He looked back across the deck and caught the eye of the army lieutenant who had accompanied the banker into Genoa. "Mr. Pierson, would you be so good as to find my steward and tell him to make sure my cabin is clear and do you attend upon us there." He turned back to Grimaldi. "Now what is gone, sir?"

"All of it. The gold of the Casa di San Giorgio. Gone." He was shaking, either from cold or shock or a combination of both.

"What do you mean 'all of it'?"

"All of it. Gone." Clearly this was Grimaldi's word of choice. He seemed to derive some comfort from it. The commodore exchanged a glance with Nathan. If he had possessed two eyes he might have rolled them to the night sky; as it was, he did what he could with the one that was available to him.

"The entire reserves of the Bank of Saint George cannot be gone, sir," he instructed Grimaldi firmly. "This is foolishness."

"Even so. It is gone." They could hear his teeth rattling. It evoked no sympathy in the commodore.

"How do you know it is gone? Did you inspect the vaults?"

"No. But I spoke to those that are in a position to know."

"And how is it gone? Who has taken it? The French?"

But now here was young Nisbet to inform the commodore that his cabin was made ready for him and they led the shivering banker below.

"Now, sir, calm yourself," Nelson instructed him, sitting him down in a chair. Then to his steward: "Do not stand there gawping like an idiot, man. Pour him a brandy and then take yourself off."

They waited impatiently while this was done and Grimaldi had composed himself a little.

"Last month the directors of the bank had a meeting," he said, "and decided the reserves should be removed to a place of safety."

Nelson gazed at him in frank disbelief. "What? But what can be safer than the vaults of a bank?"

Nathan, whose mother had suffered from this delusion, could have named a number of locations, starting with her mattress, without greatly exercising his imagination but he listened patiently for Grimaldi's opinion on the matter.

"It was felt that in the event of an invasion, the vaults would be no more secure than anywhere in Genoa," the banker explained. "That in fact, it would be the first place they would look. So it was decided to remove the reserves to a secret location. Somewhere out of the city."

"And this was achieved?" The banker nodded. "The entire reserves—without being observed or reported?" The commodore remained sceptical.

"It was done at night. Under pretext of removing the furniture from the palace for safekeeping in the event of an invasion."

"And they think the French will believe that?" He sighed. "However, at least they have not got their hands upon it, so far as we know. Was your uncle privy to these discussions?" Another nod.

"So he knows where they have been secreted?"

"I imagine so."

"What do you mean, you imagine so? Did you not speak with him?"

"No." He bowed his head. "My uncle has also gone."

Nelson took a chair and sat down in front of him. He leaned forward with his hands upon his knees and his chin jutting to within a foot of the banker's face. "Your uncle has also gone," he repeated with heavy significance.

Grimaldi looked up. He appeared tearful. "With his entire family."

"Also to a secret location?"

"Possibly."

"Possibly the same secret location?"

The banker saw what he was driving at. "Oh no!" He appeared indignant. "Oh no, there is no connection. The two events are entirely unrelated."

"You expect me to believe that?"

"But I assure you it is true. My uncle did not leave until a few days later. And by sea."

"By sea?" Nelson frowned. "Why?"

Grimaldi reached for the brandy but Nelson laid a hand upon his arm.

"Why?" he repeated.

"It appears that my uncle was concerned that the French, if they came, might oblige him to disclose the location of the treasure."

"I see. This did not occur to the other directors of the bank?"

Grimaldi shook his head. "I am sorry, I have no idea," he said.

"So where is he now, your uncle?"

Grimaldi lowered his head again. "I do not know," he confessed.

"Look at me, sir. What vessel did he sail in—do you know that?"

Another shake of the head. Nelson looked up at the lieutenant who was standing in the shadows with Nathan. "Can you help us with this, Mr. Pierson?"

"I believe it was a small brig, sir. One of the English prizes brought into Genoa: the *Childe of Hale,* of Liverpool."

"What—with an English crew?"

"Not entirely, sir. But I believe there were some English crewmen aboard."

"And where was she headed?"

"I believe for Leghorn, sir. But it was the night of the storm."

"What? The storm that laid us so low?"

"Yes, sir."

"They put out in *that?*"

"It was not then upon them. But sailing a course for Leghorn . . ."

"They would have sailed right into it." Nelson put a hand to his brow and massaged it gently. "Well, I suppose we must send to Leghorn in the hope that she made it but . . ."

"We were forced to run before it, sir," the lieutenant reminded him. "Far to the south-west."

"Thank you, Mr. Pierson, if I ever need a new sailing master . . ." He caught himself up and raised a hand. "I am sorry, sir, I forget myself. Please, pour yourself a brandy and we must get you something to eat." He stilled Pierson's protest and raised his voice: "Allan! Thomas Allan there!"

The steward stuck his long nose through the door.

"You want me now, is it?" he said. But then he saw the look on the commodore's face. "What can I do for your honour?"

"Bring us whatever was left upon the table that you have not already gorged upon, you rogue, and swiftly." The commodore turned back to Grimaldi who still had his head in his hands. "Well, sir, I am sorry you have suffered such ill tidings but I hope we will have better news for you when we have sent to Leghorn." He did not seem confident of it. He hesitated a moment and then added: "But if I may ask . . . the *Sacro Catino*—was it among the other treasures that were removed to this secret location?"

Grimaldi looked up. His face was anguished. "Why do you ask?"

"Why do I ask?" The commodore controlled himself with difficulty. "I ask because it is by far the most valuable item and . . . being so small and of its nature delicate and, of course, *sacred,* it occurs to me that it might have been secreted elsewhere."

It was a shrewd supposition. The banker looked to Pierson, almost beseechingly. Nelson looked too, but with a more commanding eye.

"There is a rumour, sir, that it was taken by the Grimaldis," replied the lieutenant gently. "In the *Childe of Hale.*"

CHAPTER TWENTY-THREE

Spoils of War

THE *UNICORN* LAY UNDER WORKING SAIL off the Rock of Monaco in a sultry evening heat. The sea was calm with just the very lightest of breezes coming off the shore. Nathan could smell pines and, he could have sworn, a hint of oranges. But then oranges had been much on his mind of late, for in the hills above Monaco—perhaps some ten or twelve miles inland—was the little town of Tourettes where Sara had said she would be waiting for him some day, if ever he lost her, sitting at the café in the square, drinking lemonade and eating cakes made of oranges.

It was a melancholy thought. For even if she were still alive, which was doubtful, and had found her way there, which was unlikely, he could never have reached her, for Monaco was now in the hands of the French: its princes in exile or prison, its harbour guarded by French guns, the tricolour flying—or at least drooping—from the masthead high on the fort. It had even been renamed, as was the way of the Revolutionists, and was now known as Fort-Hercule—presumably after the virile giant who had made the world safe for mankind by destroying the monsters that threatened to devour it.

Nathan gazed across the intervening water towards the vast monolith, rising some five hundred feet above the sea. The Rock had been a coveted possession, even in classical times. Perhaps even earlier, for it was said to have been a refuge for the primitive peoples of the distant past. According to legend, the castle on top of the Rock was seized by subterfuge in 1297 by the Genovese Francesco Grimaldi—known as *il Malizia,* the Cunning—with a group of armed men disguised as monks. And the Grimaldi had held it ever since, until the Revolution. It was of interest to Nathan now only because of the Grimaldi inheritance—and the probability that a number of merchant vessels, delivering munitions to the French armies along the coast, were sheltering in its small harbour, safe from his guns.

He had been sent here by Nelson to gather intelligence and disrupt the enemy supply lines, though the French seemed perfectly happy to live off the land, taking all that they needed to eat and drink from the Italian peasantry. Other supplies, such as guns and munitions, were ferried in small vessels that slunk along the line of the shore at night, keeping to the shallows, and sheltering by day in the ports and fishing villages that had been seized all along the coast of Liguria. Nelson had sent to the admiral, asking for small gunboats or brigs that could stand closer in but they were in short supply in the British fleet. In the meantime, his frigates patrolled the hostile coastline, picking up what scraps they could, helpless to affect the clash of Titans in the mountains.

How that clash was going, Nathan had no idea. The fishermen he had encountered along the coast, who were practically his only source of intelligence, appeared to know very little about the movement of armies and to care less. The French and the Austrians were fairly matched for size, at least in Italy, and it seemed to Nathan that they would fight themselves to a standstill in the mountains until the winter brought a plague on both their houses. The only thing he had learned of any interest—and that from a newspaper he had been given by the captain of a Venetian *barca-longa*—was that shortly before he left Paris for the front, General Buonaparte had celebrated his marriage to a widow woman called Marie-Josèphe de Beauharnais.

So Captain Cannon had won his Rose. Or "Josephine" as he apparently preferred to call her. Perhaps the new uniform had made all the difference.

Nathan watched the sun dipping beneath the long promontory of Cap Ferrat, some five miles off their starboard bow. A perfect sunset. But there was a humidity in the air and he did not like the look of the dark clouds gathering to the north, in the mountains above Monaco. There had been light but variable winds for some days now, the seas calm with mild morning mists, typical of the Mediterranean in spring, according to Mr. Perry, the master, but some instinct warned Nathan that this was about to change. He looked aloft but decided it would be over-cautious to take in sail, with no more evidence than an instinct.

A grumbling in his stomach reminded him that it was some hours since he had last eaten. He crossed over to Tully, who had the watch. "I am going below, Mr. Tully," he addressed him formally, and then in a lower voice: "If you have the leisure when the watch is ended, come and join me for supper. I will get some chilled wine sent up from the hold."

It was now quite gloomy in his cabin and the Angel Gabriel followed him in with a taper to light the lanterns.

"What have we got to eat?" Nathan asked him, slumping in a chair and throwing his hat on the table. "Catch any fish?" For there had been a time in the afternoon when they had been becalmed and Gabriel had seized the opportunity to cast a line. He fancied himself a fisherman, having excelled as a poacher in his youth, before he turned to highway robbery and then to cutting throats in the King's name.

"I could grill you up a half-dozen sardines," he offered, "with some fresh lemon and herbs." He was a handy cook, too, when he could be bothered but you could not debate the menu with him or he became recalcitrant. "And there is some potted blubber that is very nice with toast or crusted bread."

"The sardines would be excellent," Nathan assured him, "though you may keep your potted blubber." This was a speciality of the Angel's. A dish of jellyfish that he left to stink to take the toughness out and then boiled up with vinegar and sesame seeds, sealing the resulting mess in a jar with butter. Then, after a short pause: "Are they large sardines, because I have invited Mr. Tully?"

"They'll go round," replied Gabriel shortly. "There's bread and cheese if you're still hungry."

"And perhaps a bottle or two of the *branco* you picked up in Gibraltar?"

Mr. Kerr, the late captain of the *Unicorn* had possessed a fine collection of wines which Nathan had inherited—though this might have been disputed by his family had they known of it—but its bounty had been exhausted during the voyage homeward and Nathan had been forced to purchase some of his own. He was particularly partial to the *branco* which had been delivered packed in straw and ice from the mountains above Gibraltar and was now stored deep in the hold to keep it cool.

When Gabriel had gone Nathan heaved himself up from the chair—the humidity was exhausting—and helped himself to the Madeira on the cabinet by way of an appetiser. He carried it over to the table and studied the chart that was spread there. He was still lost in contemplation when eight bells announced the end of the watch and shortly after he heard Tully's knock upon the door. Nathan invited him to pour himself a glass and join him at the chart.

"I want you to imagine a situation," he proposed when Tully had joined him at the table. "You are standing out from the port of Genoa bound for Leghorn when you are beset by a storm, a most severe storm from the north-east." He remembered what Nelson had said of it. "The worst storm you have ever known in these waters. What do you do?"

"Well, being unable to return to port, I would have no choice but to run before the wind."

"Under bare poles."

"If it were so severe, yes."

"But would you not then run upon the shore—somewhere between Capo Mele and where we are now?"

Tully considered the chart. "I might," he agreed. "Unless I took some action to prevent it."

"Such as?"

"I might contrive to get some canvas aloft. A reefed topsail and perhaps a storm jib to bring my head around if the wind were not too violent."

"They tried that on the *Agamemnon*," Nathan informed him, "and lost their topmast. Came damn near to losing the ship."

Tully nodded thoughtfully. "I take it we are not talking of the *Agamemnon* in this instance," he surmised.

"No." Nathan was sworn to secrecy about the gold of the Casa di San Giorgio, but figured he had some latitude in matters that were peripheral to it. "We are talking of a brig, of about two hundred tons. An English brig called the *Childe of Hale,* taken prize by the French but still with some English in her crew."

Tully looked down again upon the chart. "Well, a brig of that size and a storm of that severity, she might have foundered in deep water, long before she reached the coast."

"I know. But if she did not. What would you do, if you were her master? Say you had tried to bend a sail to the mast and it had been lost, and the mast, too."

"Well . . ." Tully put down his glass and lowered his nose to the chart. He followed the line of the coast like a dog questing for a scent. "Well, I might try to beach her." He stabbed with his finger. "Here at Ventimiglia."

"Just what I was thinking," said Nathan. They caught each other's eye and laughed.

"What are you looking for?" asked Tully, regarding him curiously.

"A needle in a haystack," said Nathan. There was probably a more appropriate metaphor, something with the sea in it, but he was damned if he could think of one. A shell on a beach did not quite do the trick. "Ah, here are our loaves and fishes," he said, as the Angel

Gabriel appeared before them, closely followed by two of the ship's boys bearing their supper.

They had eaten most of the sardines and demolished one of the bottles of wine when they heard the cry of "Sail Ho!" from the deck. A moment later, young Lamb came below with the first lieutenant's compliments and the information that the schooner *Pearl* was bearing down upon them, bound for Gibraltar with mail from the fleet, and if he had any letters for home he might like to prepare them for despatch.

Nathan had letters in progress for both his parents and a note for Alex with some drawings he had made. He scribbled a final word, sealed them in their separate envelopes and hurried up on deck. The *Pearl* was alongside and Signor Grimaldi, having been forewarned, standing by with his servant and his bags.

"Well, sir, I will miss your company," said Nathan insincerely, shaking him by the hand, "but I do not suppose you will be sorry to see England again. I can only regret that your mission was not more successful."

Grimaldi made some grudging reply and Nathan watched him go with relief, for he had not been the easiest of passengers. In exchange, there was a despatch from the commodore and a letter from his mother which the *Pearl* had brought on her voyage out from Gibraltar.

Nathan returned to his cabin and opened the despatch first. It was brief and to the point. Buonaparte had defeated the Austrians at Montenotte, in the mountains north of Genoa, and was pushing northward, with the Allied armies in full flight before him. Nathan was commanded to rendezvous with the rest of the squadron off Voltri in three days' time.

He sat down to read the bulkier message from his mother. No news of any import. The usual tirade against the Ministry and the steps that were being taken to suppress dissent—another one of her friends had been arrested. It was worse than the Inquisition, she said. But then there was something on Mary Wollstonecraft and Imlay which caught his attention.

"*Mary appears well on the road to recovery and sends her regards. She has been seeing some of her old friends, I am glad to say—those that are not imprisoned as a danger to the state—and seems to have put Imlay behind her. As to him, the rogue has not been seen in London for some time and it is believed he has gone to Paris, where he no doubt keeps another woman or two.*"

Nathan was still pondering this news when Mr. Fleetwood appeared with the first lieutenant's respects and he would be obliged if the captain would come up onto the deck as there was a suspicion of a sail moving close to the shore.

"Where away, Mr. Duncan?" Nathan enquired, frowning into the darkness at the foot of the Rock.

"Two points off the larboard bow, sir. It was Mr. Lamb who saw it— or thought he did."

"By God, Mr. Lamb, you would see a black cat in a coal cellar," murmured Nathan, for the clouds had gathered since he had gone below and he was damned if he could see a thing.

"The moon came out for a moment, sir, and I am sure I saw something moving against the cliff."

"Big, small . . . ?"

"About the size of a small brig, moving towards the north-east."

Which was more or less the same course as the *Unicorn*. She had been ploughing her lonely furrow all evening, down to Cap Ferrat and then back up again to Cap Martin; her sentry's beat. And not so much as the hint of a sail. Nor was there now, so far as Nathan was concerned. His eyes had adjusted to the darkness but he still could not see anything moving between the frigate and the shore. One day, he thought, they would be able to fire some kind of a light into the air, like a firework, that floated in the firmament like a star. He had a mind to design one but had not yet resolved the key problem of gravity. The clouds parted briefly and the moon shone through.

"There!" cried Mr. Lamb, throwing out an arm and his voice slipping back into its juvenile state. Nathan followed the line of the pointing finger and saw her—just for an instant, exactly where the midshipman had said she was: a brig under full sail at a distance of about a mile and a half and just about to round the point.

"Mr. Perry!"

"Here, sir," replied the sailing master in his soft voice. He was standing almost at Nathan's shoulder.

"I am sorry, I did not see you there in the dark." Nathan always felt a little awkward with Mr. Perry, like a bumptious young officer instructing an old hand, though there was not more than ten years between them. "How much closer can we go into the shore?" he asked him, though he knew the answer already.

"With the wind as it is, sir, I think we are as close as we may bear."

"What if we were to take her in tow?" They had the boats out already at the stern.

But Mr. Perry was making a mouth and shaking his head. "I would not care to go much closer than we are now, sir, in these waters."

"But the charts show deep water at the foot of the Rock."

"I would not rely too much upon the charts, sir," the master replied diffidently, "not off these shores." This was true. The charts in their possession were mostly of French or Genoese origin and Nathan had been shocked at how bad they were, though this might be deliberate, of course, in the hope of confusing the enemy. Nelson had ordered his captains to take soundings in all the bays, wherever it was possible. "We know the bottom shelves steeply beyond the point," Mr. Perry reminded him, "and there are a great many rocks just under the surface of the water."

"Could we not board her from the boats, sir?" suggested the first lieutenant. "For she cannot be moving more than a couple of knots."

Nathan thought about it. But that one glance had revealed a number of gunports along her side. No more than a half-dozen, he thought, and there was no means of knowing if there were guns behind them or not. But it was a risk. The sky was lighter out to sea and they would almost certainly see the approaching boats, if only by the white splashes made by the oars. He hated to think what half a dozen guns, even small ones, loaded with grape, could do to his boat crews across a mile or so of open water.

"I think if we cannot take them by surprise . . ." he began, but his brain was leaping ahead of him. About two miles along the coast was Cap Martin and beyond that a shallow bay. If he could get there first and send the boats in before the brig rounded the point they could make their attack from inshore, where it would be least expected.

He explained the plan to his officers. "But we must clap on sail to get ahead of her, Mr. Perry," he said. "As much as she will bear."

"Stuns'ls, sir?"

"Stuns'ls, kites and all."

The sailing master cast his eyes aloft. "I do not know about that, sir," he confessed worriedly, "for I think there is a storm coming on."

It was no more than Nathan had been thinking for the past hour or so but he sighed with impatience. "Well, if it does, we will just have to get them in again, Mr. Perry, as fast as you like, but I think it might hold off long enough to achieve our purpose."

And so studding sails and kites it was and they fair flew along, by comparison with their former progress, at a speed of three knots and two fathoms, as Mr. Lamb reported scornfully upon casting the log.

"Not fast enough for you, Mr. Lamb?" Nathan quizzed him dryly. "Well, if Mr. Perry is not much mistaken we will be running a great deal faster before the night is out." And pray God we do not run upon the rocks, he added silently, avoiding Mr. Perry's eye.

"I am going to give Mr. Tully command of the boats," he informed the first lieutenant quietly. He expected a protest and he got one. As first lieutenant it was Mr. Duncan's privilege, no his duty . . . "But you do not speak French," Nathan pointed out, "and Mr. Tully does. If he is challenged and he is able to engage in converse with them it will gain a few vital seconds."

"Then let him serve under me," the first lieutenant replied reasonably.

"That would be to risk losing my two best officers," Nathan argued. "I would be left with Mr. Holroyd as my only lieutenant. I cannot countenance it."

The truth was, he had more confidence in Tully. He knew this could be construed as unfair, as showing favour to a friend, but there it was. He knew in his heart that Duncan was not the man to lead a raiding party off a hostile coast in the dark, whereas to Tully, the ex-smuggler, it was all in a night's work.

"Very well, Mr. Perry, you can take in the stuns'ls," Nathan instructed the master when they had weathered the point, and the words were scarce out of his mouth when the master was off and roaring down the deck.

"Stand by the booms! Stand by to take in t'gallant stuns'ls."

Nathan was confident they must have gained a least a mile on the brig, which had been hugging the shore all around the bay, but the wind had pushed them further out to sea and he fretted away at the weather rail while the seconds ticked by.

"Ease away the outhaul! Clew up!"

His boarding party was assembled in the waist and the master at arms and his lads handing out pikes and cutlasses and whatever other lethal weaponry the crew favoured. Only the officers would carry pistols, to cut down the risk of an accidental discharge that would alert the brig. Tully would take Holroyd and Anson with him, but not Whiteley and his marines. This was not a job for marines.

"Haul tight! Rig in!"

The moment the studding sails were in, they backed the foretopsail to deaden way and let the boarding party down into the boats.

"Good luck, Mr. Tully," Nathan called out to him as he went over the side. "We will do our best to distract him for you."

The boats had barely vanished into the darkness when a sudden gust laid them over almost on their beam ends and threw Nathan sprawling into the scuppers.

"Very well, Mr. Perry," he said, when he had found his feet and wiped the blood from his lip where he had knocked it against one of the quarterdeck carronades. "You may shorten all the sail you like." He grinned bashfully at him, even with the pain in his lip, but the master was already turning away and roaring again.

"Topmen aloft, reef and lay in!"

Nathan was worried for Tully and his boats, bobbing about in the darkness off an unknown shore and a gale coming on. And there was no certainty that the brig had followed them. They had got in the royals and topgallants and were putting the first reef in the courses when Mr. Lamb cried out that he had sighted her, standing out from the point directly off their larboard beam. Nathan still could not see a thing but he took the midshipman's word for it.

"Very well, Mr. Duncan," he said, "run out the guns."

The gun crews were shorthanded with so many hands aloft and the boarding party away, but Nathan only meant to make a show of it. There was no chance of hitting her at this range and in the darkness, but the more attention that was paid to him the less chance they had of noticing what was coming up on their weather side.

He heard the squeal of the trucks as the guns were run out.

"Remember, now, you are to load with cartridge only," Mr. Duncan was fretting in a harsh, low voice, repeating the instruction all along the gundeck, as if he was afraid it might carry to the brig in the darkness off their quarter.

"Where away, Mr. Lamb?" Nathan sang out to the midshipman with the eyes.

"There, sir!" Pointing frantically towards the headland as if he could not believe she had not been seen. "Directly amidships." And at last Nathan saw her . . . Creeping along the foot of the headland, the sly dog, and so close to shore; the charts *must* be wrong. He must be able to go in closer . . . But too late now, he could not be firing upon his own boats. He felt another gust of wind on his cheek, nothing like as bad as the last one, but it was fair warning.

"Ease your helm," Nathan ordered, for the brig had drawn a little ahead of them now. And as they fell off the wind: "Fire at will, Mr. Duncan."

The guns went off at five-second intervals and in the brief flashes Nathan saw the brig's topsails outlined against the cliff. He could not see his boats. They must be right in among the rocks.

"Shall we fire again, sir?" Duncan requested.

"Yes, Mr. Duncan, and keep firing until I instruct you to stop," Nathan commanded him sharply. He supposed the first lieutenant must bemoan the waste of powder, but it was not he who was paying for it. Then, in the pause before they resumed, he saw the flash of small arms on the deck of the brig and heard the sharper crack of pistol shots. Moments later, he saw the light at her stern: the signal that Tully had taken her. A cheer rose from the guncrews and even some of the men aloft.

"Belay there!" the first lieutenant roared but there were grinning faces all round and a few minutes later the brig, ablaze now with lights at stem and stern, came heading towards them across the bay, towing the *Unicorn*'s boats behind her.

"She is the *Bonne Aventure* privateer," Tully informed him when he had come aboard. "Eight guns. Six swivels. Crew of sixty-five."

"Well done, sir," Nathan congratulated him with a broad grin. It was the first prize the *Unicorn* had taken in all her long voyaging back and forth across the Atlantic. "Very well done. And did they put up much of a fight?"

"Not to speak of it, sir, for they did not spot us until we were safe over the side. We have two men wounded, neither of them serious. They lost a half-dozen before they decided to throw up the sponge." For once he sounded almost as excited as Nathan.

"And she is a privateer?"

"Well, the captain has a letter of marque from the French authorities but he is more of a pirate in my opinion. She was making for San Remo, which has been her base for the best part of a year, and most of her crew are Genovese: smugglers, I would say, taken to buccaneering since the war."

"Even so, I would have thought they would have put up a better fight than that."

"Well, I did have my sword at the captain's throat," Tully explained diffidently, "and he may have been anxious not to provoke me."

"That would make a difference," Nathan agreed. "And what condition is she in?"

"Oh in good shape, sir, as far as I can tell, and armed with eight-pounders."

They would almost certainly buy her into the fleet. Nelson had been complaining he did not have enough gunboats that could run close inshore. Nathan began to do sums in his head. He might count on a thousand pounds if he was lucky.

"There is something else I should like to report, sir," said Tully. "In private."

Nathan looked into his face.

"Very well. Let us go below."

When they were in Nathan's cabin, Tully reached into his pocket and took out a velvet purse. He emptied it carefully upon the table. Nathan stared.

"I did not want them rolling about the deck in the dark," said Tully dryly, "or we might have had a riot on our hands."

Nathan picked up one of the stones and held it up to the light between his finger and thumb. It was oval in shape and about the size of his thumbnail, cut into a score or so of facets. "Are they real?" he said wonderingly.

"Well, I am not a jeweller. The captain of the *Bonne Aventure* assures me they are."

"Where did he get them?"

"He did not say. But I think we may take it they are a recent acquisition or he would not have kept them aboard the brig. They took a *barca-longa* off Île de Levent, according to the crew, carrying a Jewish family from Genoa fleeing the war. I would think it came from them."

"And what happened to them?"

But Tully only inclined his head. "I doubt we will ever know," he said.

Nathan looked at the jewels again. He was having trouble keeping his eyes off them. There were ten of them in all. A blue sapphire set in garnets that might have been worn as a brooch, a pair of emerald earrings, a ruby pendant set in silver filigree and the rest diamonds.

"They must be worth a fortune," he said.

"The captain thought so. He offered me half if I would let him keep the rest."

Nathan subjected Tully to serious scrutiny but he did not appear to be speaking in jest.

"He asked to speak with me alone in his cabin. He had them in his desk—knew we would have found them. 'A straight division of the spoils,' he said, 'and you do not speak of it.'"

Nathan grinned at him. "I knew you were too honest to make a decent smuggler." He swept the gems back into their velvet pouch and raised his voice. "Gabriel! Gilbert Gabriel there! We had better get the purser to make a record of this," he said to Tully, "before I am tempted to offer you the same deal."

"I was counting on it," said Tully. "Oh, but there is something else. There was an Irishman among the crew."

Nathan winced. "Hell, Martin, if he has been serving the enemy . . . You know how much I hate to hang a man. I had much rather you had cut his throat."

But Tully was shaking his head. "He says he was pressed into service," he said. "After being shipwrecked." He was smiling as he watched Nathan's face. "On the coast, just west of Monaco—in a brig called the *Childe of Hale*."

"Where is he?"

"I had him brought aboard. I thought you would wish to speak with him. Young Anson has him in charge."

"Ask the purser to come and see me," Nathan instructed Gabriel who was waiting on him at the door. "And ask Mr. Anson to bring down the seaman that is with him."

"Do you wish to speak with him alone?" Tully enquired tactfully.

"No, you might as well stay and hear this," Nathan told him, "as you know so much already."

The seaman's name was Flynn. Matthew Flynn from Dublin. And

a most nervous, garrulous Dubliner he was, too.

"I swear to God, sor," he said, "I would never have raised a hand against a man in the King's Service. You know that, don't you, sor?" He appealed to Tully. "You seen me knock one of them on the head for you. I knocked one of them on the head for him, sor," he assured Nathan, "soon as I knew they was King's men come aboard."

"Very well, Flynn. Tell me the truth and it will not go hard for you."

"I swear to God, sor, every word is the honest truth."

"So what about the *Childe of Hale?*"

"Oh, is it that?" He sounded relieved. "Oh, that was my last ship, sor. Wrecked off the coast hereabout. That is when I fell into the hands of the Frenchies, sor."

"And you had sailed out of Genoa, had you not? Bound for Leghorn."

"We had that, and right into the bitch of a storm, the worst . . ." He gave Nathan a shrewd look. "But how did you know that, sor?"

"Never mind how I knew it. What happened to you? Did you run before it?"

"We did that. And was like to run on Cap Ferrat, so the skipper, he thought to beach her." He scowled. "I tell you, sor, you could not see a blessed thing for waves and spray. I never seen the like. I thought we was done for."

"But you survived."

"Yes, sor. God and the Holy . . ." He recalled that he was among Protestants. "Praise God we did, sor. For he run her close in upon the shore before she went over and we run up along the masts to the shore like rats, we did, and we watched her break up from the shore in the pouring rain, like drownded rats it was."

"And the passengers?"

"Sor?"

"You had passengers aboard, I believe."

"Aye, we did, sor. Two men and two women and two little ones. A boy and a girl they was."

"The Grimaldis."

"Was that their name? I did not catch it, though I knowed they was Italian."

"What happened to them, Flynn? Did they go down with the ship?"

"Oh no, sor. No. I see what you're driving at. No, we got them ashore, sor. We would not save ourselves and leave them in the ship at the mercy of the wind and the waves, Christ Jesus, no."

"You got them ashore."

"Every man jack of them, sor."

"And then what?"

"Sor?"

"Then what did you do?"

"Well, when the rain eased off a bit, like, the skipper thought as we would try to get along the coast 'cos we knowed we was not far from the border. Only the devil of it was the French nabbed us as we was trying to slip past the Rock—a cavalry patrol it was—and locked us up in the fort there and that was when they made me take service on the *Bonne Aventure,* only that they knew I was from Dublin and inclined to think the worse of me for it, but I would never . . ."

"And what of the Grimaldis? Were they taken with you?"

"Oh no, sor. No. I take your meaning. No, they decided to go a different route. Inshore like. The old man, he was not looking so chirpy, do you see, and they said as there was a monastery that would take them in, a few miles up from the coast, run by the Benedictines. They seemed to know it pretty well, from what they was saying to the skipper, that part of the coast and all. I reckon we should have gone with them but the skipper was all for trying to get back over the border, the idyot."

Nathan leaned closer to him.

"Now Flynn," he said. "I want you to tell me the exact truth and don't flannel with me. Did you tell the French this?"

"No, sor, I did not. For whatever else I am, I am no informer. Nor was I ever asked."

"So the French never suspected there was anyone else with you?"

Flynn shook his head.

"And this was what—about three weeks ago?"

"Three weeks to the day, sor, I can tell you straight. No, that is a lie. Three weeks and a day it was."

"Very well, Flynn. But if I find you have been lying to me you will be for the high jump. In the meantime, as you had no violent objection to serving with the French you can attempt to redeem yourself with King George." The seaman closed his eyes. "Come, sir, it is better than hanging and I will cut you in for a share of the prize money for the *Bonne Aventure* as you knocked one of them on the head. I will have you rated ordinary seaman and we will see how you go along."

When Nathan went up on deck the weather was much worse and they were standing out from the cape with the brig close behind under shortened sail.

"I would like to send down the topgallant yards, if you will let me, sir," said Mr. Perry, "and close reef the topsails."

"Very well, Mr. Perry, make it so."

He sought out the first lieutenant. "I am going to give Mr. Tully the *Bonne Aventure* to run up to Voltri," he told him. "But I would like us to stand off Monaco for a day or so, for I may have business ashore."

He saw the look on the lieutenant's face and turned away to hide his own, but then there was a sudden flash of lightning and a cry from one of the lookouts in the tops, quite obscured by the clap of thunder that followed.

"Sail ho!" he cried again when the thunder had stopped rolling off the cliffs. "Three points off the starboard bow."

Nathan's head jerked round and he stared in disbelief, as if there could be another vessel so reckless as to venture so close inshore on such a night. And then the lightning flashed again and he saw it, frozen in his mind's eye like an engraving, bearing down on them about two miles off the Rock of Monaco. And he knew her in an instant.

For she was the *Brutus*.

CHAPTER TWENTY-FOUR

Brutus Redux

A ND NOW THE RAIN came: wind and driving rain straight off the mountains with chips of ice in it like splintered bone. Nathan felt them on his cheek as he stood at the weather rail, his feet braced on the steeply canting deck as the *Unicorn* took the wind on her quarter. It was in his mind to fight for sea room and then he could think of fighting the *Brutus* but with every flash of lightning he could see her bearing down on them, a white phantom off their weather bow, and closing fast. He looked back to the *Bonne Aventure* clinging to his stern and heeling hard over as she came round the point, so hard the gunports on her lee side were almost awash. And he froze at the rail as it came to him, heedless for a moment of the biting wind, remembering the last time he had met the razee off Capo Mele in seas far calmer than this. And yes, he thought, it could be done.

He looked once more to the *Brutus,* seeing only the white water at her bow and the ghost of a sail, but he could divine her captain's intention as clearly as if it were his own. He was planning to cross the *Unicorn*'s stern, cutting between the frigate and the *Bonne Aventure,* and then he would come up on Nathan's lee and run alongside him, out into the open sea, savaging him time and again with the weight of that massive broadside. He would go for the *Unicorn*'s rigging with chain shot and then when she was crippled, pound her with round shot and grape until she struck, or was swept, a dismasted hulk, back onto the rocks of Cap Martin.

"Mr. Perry!" The master came staggering up the sloping deck to him, holding on to his hat with one hand and his speaking trumpet with the other. Nathan brought his mouth to his ear and raised his voice: "Do you bring us two points into the wind, for I am going to try to pass him on his lee side."

The master appeared so much like a gargoyle with his astonished expression and the rain streaming off his hat that Nathan clapped him on the shoulder, grinning. "Go to it, Mr. Perry, and when we have passed him I want you to fall off the wind and come back at him on the same side."

Nathan left him to think about this, for indeed it needed thinking about, and sought out Mr. Duncan to tell him what he intended so that he might pass it on to the rest of the officers and they to the gun crews: he did not want any confusion once they were engaged and could not hear themselves think. Duncan appeared to take it in, when it had been explained to him twice, but Nathan could not help but wish that Tully was still first lieutenant for he would grasp a plan upon the instant and as often as not come up with an improvement.

They ran out the guns, and Nathan forced himself to wait calmly at the rail with his hands clasped behind his back while every atom of his being urged him to be helping heave them into position— and load and fire them too, for his nature was too impatient for this watching, waiting game.

A series of flashes rent the night sky like a rippling broadside and he saw the razee again, barely three or four cables lengths off his starboard bow, and so clearly now he could make out the head of Brutus, staring out at him with his white face, open-mouthed, wide-eyed in consternation—just as her captain might appear as he noted the *Unicorn*'s altered course. But he still had time to fall off the wind. Nathan strained his eyes into the darkness, peering at that white crest at her bow, so close now, so very close. Would he? No. He was coming on, intent on his own plan to cross their stern. And the *Unicorn* was still coming round, taking the wind on her beam now and heeling hard over—Nathan prayed they did not take another gust—and finally he saw the razee's bow swing towards him as she saw her danger; but too late, much too late.

"Fire as you bear, Mr. Duncan!" Nathan roared as he braced himself at the rail. A seemingly endless wait, an unbearable wait, until the first gun fired—and he could have howled with frustration as he saw her bow still coming round, but they passed her so swiftly it was over in a matter of seconds, each gun firing so fast upon its neighbour it was impossible to tell them apart and then they were back in the dark, rushing upon the Rock of Monaco.

"Now, Mr. Perry!" bawled Nathan with all the breath of his being, but the sailing master had the speaking trumpet to his lips and the two helmsmen were heaving hard down upon the wheel, bringing their head out to sea; the hands that were not at the guns heaving at the braces and those that were racing across to the larboard side to heave out the ports. Already they were falling off the wind, further, further; Nathan felt the deck heel hard over as she took it on her larboard quarter. Another flash of lightning, tearing the black shroud of a sky, and he looked for the *Brutus* but could not see her. He could run if he wished, run for the open sea, but he felt a savage lust for battle, for he knew now that he had been right. The razee had fired back at them but only with the guns on her forecastle and quarterdeck. She was heeling much too far to leeward to fire those big 18-pounders on her main gundeck, or even to open the lower gunports. The inherent flaw in the design. And it would do for her yet.

The lightning came again and he saw her. And by God she had lost her foremast! It was down across her starboard side, held on by a tangle of rigging. The darkness again, blacker then ever, and then a sudden rippling flash of gunfire and he saw the little *Bonne Aventure* crossing her stern and raking her with her piddling broadside. Nathan's heart swelled with pride for Holroyd and his crew, but the brig was now directly in their path and it seemed impossible that they would not run upon her in the dark. He glimpsed Mr. Perry's anguished face turned to him imploringly, begging him to veer, but he was damned if he would lose his advantage.

They missed the brig by a whisker. Nathan saw Holroyd's face in the light of the stern lantern and he was grinning, the lunatic, as he brought his hand up to his hat.

And then they were through the gap and there was the razee again, her broken mast dragging her even further to leeward, and they poured another broadside into her as she lay there and Nathan yelled for the master to back the foretopsail and the mizzen, too, so they would not draw ahead of her, and they hit her again and again, firing with round shot now into her hull, double-shotted at point blank range. He thought of Nelson pounding the crippled *Ça Ira*—or Buonaparte, for that matter, bringing his cannon up to slaughter the defeated rabble on the steps of the Saint-Roch. But the *Brutus* was not yet defeated. She was still firing with the higher guns on her quarterdeck and forecastle—and the *Unicorn* was taking punishment. Nathan could see the dead and wounded all along the upper deck and Christ knows what it was like below for, unusually for a Frenchman, she was firing into the frigate's hull. But, of course, they could not raise the guns high enough to do much else. And they were firing from the tops, too, with swivel guns and small arms, concentrating their fire on the quarterdeck. Half the guns there were unmanned, the others reduced to two or three men but still swabbing, loading, ramming, hauling the guns with brute strength back up to the ports. Nathan longed more than ever to help them, if only to take his mind off the target he must make, walking his little fiefdom among the dead and the dying. He saw one of his 18-pounders smashed off its gun carriage, the crew reeling back from it, bloodied and broken. Two gunports smashed into one, the guns silent, the crews dead. But it was nothing to the punishment the *Brutus* was taking.

Nathan did not need the lightning now, for she was lit by the almost continuous discharge of the guns: her foremast a jagged stump cut off just below the top, her main topmast down across her waist and the blood running from her scuppers, staining that purple streak across her side where it showed just above the waterline. But she was still firing, still running on under what sails she could carry, desperately trying to cut across his bow, to come down on his lee and bring her weather guns to bear . . . Or better still to board him, for she had the wind on her side, and if she could only have cut away that hopeless tangle of rigging, she might have achieved it, for Nathan was crowding her as closely as he dared, with just a narrow gap of water between them, pushing her into that other gap, that ever narrowing gap between the onrushing ships and the looming headland of Cap Martin.

"We must bear away, sir, we must bear away!" roared Perry in his ear, hatless now, the rain streaming down his face, mixed with blood from a gash high on his forehead.

And so finally they did. At the last possible minute. And Nathan watched dully as the *Brutus* fought to drag herself clear of the point, knowing she could never make it, not in the condition she was in, not even with the wind on her quarter. And he was right, for the next flash of lightning showed her running straight upon the rocks at the foot of Cap Martin and they heard the terrible sound she made as she died: the long, grinding groan as the rocks stove in her timbers and tore out her keel, even above the triumphant roaring of the waves and the keening of the wind, before the thunder rolled down from the mountains and drowned it out.

CHAPTER TWENTY-FIVE

the Ruined Abbey

A SHORE, SIR?" The first lieutenant stared at Nathan as if he had announced he was off on a brief excursion to the moon. "For a day or two?"

Nathan had been unable to resist this adjunct by way of a provocation.

"But . . ." Duncan looked from his captain to the curving shore, quiescent now and masked by a faint early morning mist. His brain strove to find a hidden clue, a hint of rational judgement in a proposition that appeared, on the surface, to be entirely unhinged. It failed. "But . . . it is French territory, sir."

"I am aware of that, Mr. Duncan. Though the previous owners might dispute it." Nathan was not quite sure where the Principality of Monaco ended and France began, though this was entirely beside the point since the French invasion had abolished any such distinction. "However I am compelled by a higher calling." And then, taking pity on the man and lowering his voice, "I have certain orders, Mr. Duncan, that I regret I am unable to disclose to you for the present. If I am not back by tomorrow sunset . . ." He had better be precise or the poor man would be in an agony of indecision, "shall we say by the end of the last dog watch, then you must sail for the rendezvous. And I mean that, Mr. Duncan. There is to be no hanging on in the hope that we might materialise, like ghosts in the night. Eight bells in the last dog watch and you must crack on to Voltri, is that clear?"

"Very well, sir."

The *Childe of Hale* had left a convenient amount of wreckage strewn along the beach to mark her last landing point. Matthew Flynn did not know the name of the monastery where the Grimaldis had been heading, but according to the map there was only one place it could be: the Abbey of Saint-Sépulcre in the foothills above Monaco.

Nathan took the Angel Gabriel with him and Michael Connor, his self-appointed bodyguard; also Lieutenant Whiteley and two of his marines, dressed in seamen's slops, for he did not want a gaggle of redcoats charging about the countryside. A casual observer might take them for hunters and if they ran into a French patrol it should give them a fighting chance.

They went ashore in the launch and clambered up a steep slope above the little beach. The storm had wrung the sweat from the air, leaving it dry and cold. The wind was now a gentle sigh among the pines and the sea calmer, coiling back in on itself, its claws sheathed. Nathan looked back on it when he paused for a breather, the creamy white foam round the lips of the bay and the two vessels riding peacefully at anchor, the *Unicorn* and her prize, their yards counterbraced and their sails hung out to dry.

Whiteley had the map spread out upon a rock. The monastery lay at the head of its own little valley about two miles inland and there was a road of sorts, or at least a track, leading up from the coast through the pines and scrub. Even over broken ground it should not take them much more than an hour or so to reach it. But they would have to cross the main coast road from Nice to Genoa which, as the marine officer pointed out, must be a major supply route for Buonaparte's army in the mountains. Nathan shrugged. It could not be helped: they could not wait until dark. He thrust his thumbs through the straps of his shoulder pack and led the way.

The coast road turned out to be an unsurfaced track, though

considerably wider than the one they were following inland, and there was plenty of traffic upon it, even so early in the morning. They watched from the shelter of the pines as a squadron of dragoons went by and the dust had scarce settled before a large munitions convoy appeared with more than a dozen heavy wagons pulled by mules. Nathan was thinking it would have made a fine target for a raiding party from the ship when more cavalry came up in its rear. But after that the road seemed clear and he led his little troop across at the run and up into the pines on the far side.

Another stiff climb, bringing out the sweat even in the brisk mountain air, but then the track levelled out and followed a long ridge up to the head of the valley. And there at the far end was the monastery, shrouded in a faint haze of smoke or mist, above terraced slopes of citrus, olive and vine.

The track continued through a pine forest along the side of the valley and though they made good progress they did not see the monastery again until they emerged just a couple of hundred feet below it and saw to their surprise that it was practically a ruin. Windows were broken, part of the roof collapsed, and the front door stood half open on rusted hinges.

They passed cautiously into the dim interior. Birds flitted about the roof beams and there were rat droppings on the stone floors. They went from room to room. Signs of desecration were everywhere. Statues beheaded or otherwise mutilated, religious paintings ripped from the walls and slashed with knives, books lying about the floors with their backs broken and the pages torn; a smell of damp and mould, but also something else . . . something that smelled suspiciously like coffee.

Nathan followed his nose to the chapel. It looked as if someone had used it as a barn or a manger. There was straw and dried dung on the floor and a stack of farm implements in one corner and the smashed windows had been boarded up. The sunlight lanced through the cracks and highlighted the dust circulating in the still air. Dust and a hint of smoke. There were the remains of a fire under the belltower but the ashes were cold. They stood and listened at the foot of the steps. Not a sound. Then Whiteley murmured that he thought the smoke was coming from below.

"Below?"

"There must be a crypt."

They found the steps leading down. Whiteley pointed. In the dust on the bottom step they could see the clear outline of a footprint. Nathan cocked his pistol and remembered to remove the cap. He lifted the latch as silently as he could and kicked the door open, pressing himself back into the wall and aiming the pistol at the length of his arm.

He could see nothing at first in the gloom but he could smell the smoke and the coffee and something else that he remembered from some other time, some other crypt: the smell of candles, hastily extinguished. He looked back up the steps. Whiteley had his rifle at his shoulder, the two marines a step or two behind him with their muskets raised.

"Step out into the light. We know you are in there."

He spoke in French, his words echoing in the darkness of the vault. Silence. Then they came shuffling out of the shadows with their hands raised. A man and two women with two small children, clinging to their skirts. Almost in rags, their faces pinched and dirty. They might have been gypsies or peasants driven off the land.

Nathan lowered his pistol. "Signor Grimaldi?"

"My name is Luigi Caravello," the man said in French with a heavy Italian accent. "We are refugees from the war. Poor peasants from Calvo, *monsieur*."

"Well, I am an English naval officer," said Nathan, also in French, "sent to find the family of Signor Frederico Grimaldi."

The man stared at him. "*Inglese?*" He might have taken them for bandits the way they were dressed and with the weapons they were carrying.

"Yes. My name is Captain Nathaniel Peake. I was sent with Signor George Grimaldi to find you."

"Georgio Grimaldi. He is with you?" He peered past them into the light.

"No. He has gone back to England. We had given up hope of finding you."

"You are English?" It finally dawned on him it was true. "Oh, thank God. Thank God." He turned to the women and spoke a stream of Italian. There was a wail from the older one. She went down on her knees and made the sign of the cross.

"We thought you were the French," said the man. "I am Nicolas Grimaldi. Frederico Grimaldi is my father. But he is ill. He is dying."

He led Nathan deeper into the darkness of the crypt and struggled to light a candle. By its flame Nathan saw an emaciated figure lying on a crude pallet. He looked like a corpse but his eyes were half open and there was a rasp of breath in his throat.

"What is wrong with him?" Nathan asked gently.

"The doctor says it is his heart. And he has the water of the lungs. *Polmonite.*"

"The doctor?"

"From the village. He gave us medicines but he said there was nothing to be done. His heart has given out. I do not think it will be long now."

"We will make a litter for him," Nathan said, "and get him back to the ship."

"You cannot move him," his son insisted passionately, "not in the state he is in. And what of the French?" One of the women addressed him in Italian and after a brief discussion, she let out a shriek and threw herself at Nathan's feet, clasping his legs. The children began to howl and the other woman raised both arms to the vaulted roof and appealed to her chosen deities.

"I have my orders," Nathan persisted but he felt the sweat break out on his brow. "I must get you to a place of safety."

"He will not last more than a few hours," Nicolas Grimaldi implored him, "and then we will bury him here in the crypt. It is a holy place, at least."

Two of Whiteley's marines prised the woman from Nathan's legs and he took Grimaldi's arm and led him up the steps to the chapel where he could hear himself think. In the daylight he saw that he was younger than he had first thought: about thirty or so but with streaks of grey in his hair and a growth of beard.

"This is a difficult situation," Nathan began, "but I cannot risk the lives of my men by waiting here until your father is dead."

"Then leave us. We did not ask you to come."

"We cannot allow you to fall into the hands of the French."

"Well, we must take our chance on that."

Nathan looked up at the sunlight streaming through the smashed windows. It must be mid-morning.

"Who knows you are here?" he asked him. "Besides the doctor."

"The priest, down in the village. I had to get help, when I found the Holy Brothers were not here."

"You did not know it was a ruin?"

"No. I thought they would help us—this is an endowment of the Grimaldi. But it seems they were driven out when the French came, at the time of the Terror."

"So this priest—you trust him?"

"I think so. He is one of those they call the Judas priests—that swore an oath of loyalty to the Republic. But he has given us food and clothing and he found us the doctor. Only . . ." He hesitated.

"Only what?"

"He says the French are looking for us. They have sent someone from Paris—a commissaire of police from the *Sûreté*. And another man, a foreigner. He thinks an Englishman."

"An Englishman?" For one ludicrous moment Nathan thought it might be Bicknell Coney. It would not entirely have surprised him.

"They have been asking about us in Monaco—and in the villages."

"*Signor*, you know why this is, and why they are so anxious to find you?"

Grimaldi looked up at Nathan and shook his head, biting his lip. He was lying.

Nathan spelled it out for him. "If the French come and find your father they will torture him—or rather they will torture you and your family—your mother, your wife, your children—to make him tell them what he knows."

Grimaldi was close to tears. "But what can he tell? What does he know?"

"Of the Casa di San Giorgio."

Grimaldi sank down on the steps of what used to be the altar. "You mean the gold." Nathan nodded. "And that is what you want, also."

For once Nathan wished George Grimaldi were with them. He might have found a better way of putting it.

"I was instructed to make an offer. To take the reserves of the Casa di San Giorgio under the protection of the Bank of England."

Grimaldi stared at him in disbelief for a moment. Then he threw back his head and made a sound in his throat very like laughter.

"Forgive me, *signor,* but I do not see that there is anything to laugh about," Nathan informed him curtly.

"No? Perhaps not," Grimaldi acknowledged. "But some would find it very funny indeed, one of the best jokes in history. For there *are* no reserves of the Casa di San Giorgio. There never have been. Not for half a century at least." He saw the disbelief in Nathan's eye. "Oh, but it is quite true. My father told me. Do you think he would lie to me— on his deathbed?"

"But . . ." Nathan was at a loss. "But it is the Bank of San Giorgio."

"That is the joke. For it is worth nothing. The only thing of value is the name. And that was enough, so long as no-one knew." He was close to tears now. He sat there on the altar and he looked up at Nathan like a supplicant. "The vaults were empty, my friend, quite empty."

Nathan stared at him in disbelief. "But what of the *Sacro Catino?*"

Grimaldi was silent for a moment and when he spoke again it was in a different tone. Drained of emotion, world-weary. "The *Sacro Catino.* So that is what you are looking for." He spoke a sentence in English. "The quest of the Holy Grail."

"*Signor,* I am under orders to offer . . ."

"The protection of the Bank of England. For the Holy Grail. An interesting proposition. But impossible, I am afraid."

"Why impossible?"

"Because someone dropped it."

"Someone *dropped* it?"

"Many years ago. And it shattered into a hundred pieces."

"But I thought it was made of emerald?"

"So it was said. Until someone dropped it—and then it was discovered to be made of glass. You may consider it appropriate. A metaphor for the Casa di San Giorgio."

Nathan put a hand to his brow. "Well, I still have to get you out of here."

Grimaldi stood up and seized his arm. "Let him die," he pleaded. "The priest has given him the last rites. Let him die here and in peace. And then we will go with you."

Nathan looked at the windows again, at the motes of dust swirling in the sunbeams. He sighed.

"Very well. I will give you until tomorrow morning," he said. "I know it is harsh, but then if he is still alive we must take him with us and carry him to the coast."

He told Whiteley what he had decided.

"Well, they have been here three weeks and the French have not found them," offered the marine. "I do not suppose another day will make much difference. Touching wood." Whiteley had been long enough with mariners to share their superstitions.

Nathan told him about the police officer they had sent from Paris. He kept the Englishman to himself. "If they have interrogated the sailors in the fort at Monaco they must know where they landed."

"But they cannot have told them they were making for the abbey," Whiteley pointed out. "Or they would be here by now."

This was true.

"I will post a man in the belltower, all the same," said Whiteley.

"And we might as well make a camp here," he added, looking about the chapel. "Unless you have any objections."

"None at all." Nathan looked up at the wrecked altar. "But there is something else I must do." The lieutenant looked at him enquiringly. "There is someone I must try to find. In a village near here."

Whiteley was puzzled. "The doctor?" he said. "The priest?"

Nathan shook his head. "He has already . . ." But then he stopped himself. It was a gift from the heavens. "Yes," he said. "The priest."

"Do you think that is wise? I mean, with respect, sir, I know the old man is close to death but . . ."

"It is something I have to do," Nathan insisted. "But if I am not back by nightfall, then tomorrow, at crack of dawn, you must leave—with the whole family, and Grimaldi in a litter if needs be. But I must make that an order, Mr. Whiteley, is that clear? If I am not back at first light, you must leave without me."

"Yes, sir." Whiteley's face was stony. As well it might be. If he had placed Nathan under close arrest under armed guard there was not a court martial that would find against him. "But if I might be permitted to observe, sir, it is a reckless piece of work for the sake of a dying man and a Papist priest."

"I know, but there it is."

"And if he is not there?"

"Then I will come straight back." But then he thought again. "Or I will make my own way to the rendezvous. That is why you must not wait for me here."

He took his pack with him but not the map. He left that for Whiteley in case he was not back in time. He knew where he was going for he had looked at it so often on the map it was lodged firmly in his mind. The one certainty in so many imponderables. So many ghosts, so many rumours and conjectures and that one tantalising glimpse of a woman on a white horse riding into the waves. The one fixed point in his life: his lodestar. A village about five miles from here where there was a café in a square where a little girl used to sit with her father on market days and watch the world go by.

CHAPTER TWENTY-SIX

Bitter Oranges

E CUT A STOUT STICK from a tree of myrtle, keeping a
few of the leaves to crush in his hands for the scent. It reminded him of Sara and he wondered if she had used it in
Paris, though he could not have put a name to it then. Perhaps it reminded her of her home in the mountains of Provence for it grew
plentifully here, as it did in the Holy Land. It was a sacred plant in
many religions. The Jews, he recalled, gave it to a bridegroom on his
wedding night, and to a man who did good works, though unversed
in the scriptures.

He made good time at first, following a long winding track that
skirted the valleys, though always climbing. He thought it might be
a goat track but then he came across a roadside shrine—a simple
cross—which had not been made by cloven hooves. He decided it
must be a pilgrim route, possibly connected with the abbey, though
he did not encounter any pilgrims, or indeed any other travellers, in
the course of his own short pilgrimage.

He walked through slopes of scrub and broom and stunted pines
that leaned far out into the valley. Spring flowers grew in abundance
among the grasses and he smelt the strong aroma of herbs. And
everywhere was the sound of running water from mountain streams
swollen by the melting snows. He did not want for refreshment and

the climb was not arduous. He took off his coat, folded it into his pack and strode along in his shirtsleeves and breeches, using his walking stick for rhythm as much as for support. He had the route engraved in his mind and was able to navigate by the sun and the glimpses of sea he caught between the rolling hills. But then he was forced to descend into pine forest and follow a tortuous network of paths and tracks, his footsteps cushioned by a thick layer of pine needles, often veering from his course but always returning to it. He lost the sea as his guide but the sun stayed with him, though he did not care for the speed of its descent towards the hills in the west. He knew he would have difficulty getting back before dark. But at last, emerging from the trees, he saw a small town on a distant hilltop and knew it was Tourettes.

It was one thing to see it; quite another to reach it, for it was set upon a pinnacle of rock at a height above the surrounding country and flanked by a deep river gorge. It took Nathan almost two hours before he reached the town walls and another half hour before he found a way in through an unguarded gate. He began to climb the steep and winding streets, the houses crowding in so closely he could barely glimpse the sky. There were few people about and those he met rewarded him with a hard, curious stare, their eyes darting away from his, though they responded shyly to his amiable greetings and one of them directed him to the town square, which was almost at its highest point where the church tower rose above the surrounding rooftops. He dreaded the sight of a blue uniform and the familiar demand for *"Papiers!"* for though he had brought the *certificat de civisme* that he had used in Paris and the permit allowing him to journey to Le Havre, neither would pass muster here in Provence—and he could hardly claim to have lost his way. His best hope was that if he was stopped, the official could not read, which was not unlikely, and would be fooled by the official police stamp. If not, his story was that he was an American seaman whose ship had put in at Nice and that he had taken the opportunity to walk in the hills and did not know he needed a permit to do so. But far, far better if he was not asked.

Finally he reached the square. And there was the café, directly opposite the church, with a closed sign on the door and the shutters up.

It looked as if it had been closed for a long time. The notice required by the State—listing all the occupants of the dwelling—was still pasted at the side of the door but the ink was bleached to a dull brown and Nathan could not make out the names.

He looked about him. The place was deserted. Perhaps it was siesta time. Then he saw the old man. He was sitting on a bench under the shade of an umbrella pine next to the water trough in the middle of the square. He seemed to be asleep. Nathan went over to him and sat down beside him. The man stirred, gave a loud snore and woke himself up.

"A fine day, *monsieur*," Nathan greeted him politely.

The old man pulled a handkerchief from his pocket and wiped his mouth and whiskers but did not speak. Nathan wondered if he should have called him *Citoyen*.

"Does the café open at all?" Nathan asked, when a few moments had passed in a not quite amicable silence.

"Never," said the old man.

"Never? Ah. That is a pity."

The old man said something he did not catch. Possibly it was the dialect. Also the fact that he spoke very deep in his throat and scarcely moved his lips, like the grumbling of a long dormant volcano or the grunting of a pig, Nathan thought, scavenging for acorns in a forest. Nathan did not share these comparisons with the old man, however, but remarked that he had walked up from the coast and would have welcomed a beer, or even a lemonade.

The old man said nothing.

"Is the water fit to drink?" asked Nathan after another lengthy silence. The man gave another grunt which might have been yes or no. Nathan stood up to work the pump and splashed some water over himself. He pulled his shirt out from his trousers and wiped his face with it and then sat down again.

"That is better," he said. And then, emboldened: "So why is the café never open?"

The old man told him the story. It was so long and told in such an impenetrable *patois* that Nathan lost the thread early on and never took it up, but he gathered it involved a great many deaths for so small a place and much sadness. When he had finished the story, the old man spat in the dust, settling his gnarled hands upon his stick, his chin dropping down upon his chest.

"I knew someone who came here as a child," Nathan prompted him, before he went to sleep again. "With her father. He was an old soldier. A Scot. His name was Seton. Perhaps you knew him."

The old man turned toward him and Nathan saw with a shock that he was blind. He said something that sounded like *"guarda-costa"* which was the name of a small Spanish ship-of-war stationed in the Spanish islands of the Caribbean. Nathan had encountered them in Cuba but he doubted if the old man had. Then Nathan realised he must have said, "La Garde Écossaise"—which was the name of the Scottish Guard, an elite regiment formed by the old Valois kings in the 15th century as their bodyguard.

"That is right," he said. "La Garde Écossaise."

"The *siegneur,*" the old man nodded. "Yes, I knew him. And his daughter, the little girl—what was her name?"

"Sara. Her name was Sara."

"That is right. Little Sara."

Little Sara. This blind, old man is my last contact with her, Nathan thought. This is as near as I am going to get.

"They lived in the *manoir,* the Scottish soldier and his little girl. Yes, I remember. The mother died." He said something else that Nathan did not catch—apart from a word that sounded like *belle.*

"And is it still there, the *manoir?*"

"Oh yes. It is still there. About two kilometres from here, along the river." He took one hand off his stick and lifted it with a great effort, pointing blindly down the hill towards the sun. "But the father died a long time ago. And the little girl, she went away. No-one lives there, since before the Revolution."

And he spat again, into the dust.

Nathan walked down through the steep streets of the town in the direction the old man had indicated. It was only a small detour, he told himself, and then he would begin the long walk back to the ruined abbey. But he wanted to see the place where Sara had been born and where she had lived the first few years of her life. He would tell Alex about it when he next returned home. He wished he had brought his sketchbook with him so he might draw it for him. But perhaps he could do it from memory.

He followed the river, which must be the Vence, for a mile or so until he saw the *manoir* ahead of him. At first glance he thought it was a simple donjon: a fat, round tower with a pointed roof like a witch's hat, but then he saw that there was another tower on the far side, flanked by two wings with smaller, sharper towers at each corner. Not pretty. Too stout, too staunch to be pretty. Too rugged. When he looked upon it he thought more of the old soldier than he thought of Sara. Trees pressed close upon the ivy-clad walls and there were swallows nesting in the eaves. At night there would be bats and owls. It was by no means a ruin, but clearly deserted.

He was about to turn away, for he had little time now to reach the abbey before dark, when he heard something. A sigh in the air, almost like the wind soughing through the pines. And then it came to him that it was singing, and he felt a prickling in his scalp, for it was like the singing of a Siren. He thought of the little girl going into Tourettes with her father in the old carriage they had, singing a country air she had learned. He went closer, as he was meant to, being a sailor, drawn to the Siren's song, on to the rocks. It seemed to come from behind the wall that ran along the rear of the building.

Nathan could hear the words now and it was as if he had heard them before, though he could not think where, for it was a song of Provence. A love song.

> *Je vous aime tant, sans mentir*
> *Qu'on pourrait tarir*
> *La haute mer*
> *Et ses ondes retenir*
> *Avant qu'on puisse me prevenir*
> *De vous aimer.*

He took a run at the wall and hauled himself up by the ivy so he could look over.

And there she was. Hanging out washing upon a line.

She stopped singing and looked up and saw him, peering over the wall at her.

"What are you staring at?" she demanded. "Go away. Shoo!" She flapped a hand at him as if he were a hen. "Shoo! Vagabond!"

He scrambled over the wall and dropped down to the other side.

"How dare you!" she said. "This is private." She raised her voice then and shouted back towards the house. Nathan walked over to her but stopped a yard or so away because he did not know what to do next. He thought she was a ghost and that if he tried to touch her or take her in his arms she would melt into the air, or he would be left hugging a sheet like a lunatic out of Bedlam.

She stared at him for a moment. Then she dropped the basket she was carrying and put her hand to her mouth—and he saw that she had recognised him.

There was a shout from the house.

"Dégage! Va-t'-en! Ou je tire."

Nathan looked up and saw a man in an open window with a gun—a fowling piece—pointing straight at him. He raised his arms hastily aloft and Sara cried out: *"Non, Matthieu, c'est un ami!"* And then Nathan knew it was truly her and not a Siren, not a ghost, but that it was Sara and that at last he had found her.

• • •

They sat on a bench in the garden in the evening sunshine.

"Is it really you?" She touched his face with her hand in several places, almost professionally, like an artist feeling the mouldings of a clay sculpture. "You feel as if you are real," she conceded with a frown.

She looked different. Her hair was cut short and raggedly, like an urchin's, and it was fairer than he remembered it in Paris, almost blonde. And she was thinner than she had been, then, even at the time of the Terror and her face and arms were as tanned as a peasant's. His New York aunts would have recoiled and said she looked like an Indian. Nathan thought she looked beautiful, even more beautiful than when he first saw her in Paris. She smelled of fresh laundry and sunshine.

"I thought you were dead," he said. "I thought they had killed you."

She brushed a hand across her face as if at a fly. "They nearly did. Many times. But you—what are you doing here?"

"I came to find you," he said.

She looked at him wonderingly. Then she laughed. Or at least it was half a laugh.

"But—are we not at war?"

"Yes. And I am the captain of a ship-of-war. It is waiting for us on the coast, a few miles from here."

She shook her head. "This is not real."

"I will take you there and then you will see."

"But—how did you find me?"

"I went to the café, where you said you would be waiting for me."

"It is closed," she said. "It was closed a long time ago."

"I know. An old man told me. He told me about this place, too, but he said no-one lived here."

"He was right. I am a ghost." Her eyes were sad.

"And what about him?" Nathan jerked his head back at the house. "Is he a ghost?"

"Oh, that is Matthieu, the son of one of my father's old servants.

He looks after me and brings me food from the village."

"Then you are not lovers?" He had to ask.

"What? Me and Matthieu?" She chuckled deep in her throat and he remembered it was one of the things that had made him love her.

"So will you come with me?"

"Oh Nathan, I cannot believe it is you." "Nat-'an," she said, as she had in Paris. As her son Alex did. "I had forgotten what you looked like. Until now. I still cannot believe you are real." She touched his face again and his hair. "My beautiful boy that I knew in Paris."

He did not quite like the sound of that. Or the sadness in her voice. She spoke of the past as if it was something she had lost forever.

"I told you in Paris," he said. "You cannot call a man beautiful. It is I who must say that to you."

"Oh, Nathan, so much has happened since then."

"I know," he said.

"I don't think you do," she chided him gently.

He wondered if he should tell her about seeing her on the beach at Quiberon. But perhaps not. They were his men she had been cursing, as they fired on her people. He suddenly felt the huge distance that was between them.

"I want you to come with me," he said. "Back to England."

"To England?"

"To live with me in England."

"You still want me, after all this while?"

"If you will have me."

"Oh, Nathan, I wanted so much to be with you. When we were in Paris. Always."

"But not now."

"Now, it is not possible." *Ce n'est pas possible.*

The phrase tore at his insides, so much sadder and more final than it would have sounded in English, like a line from a tragedy by Corneille. He remembered now, the plays by Corneille that she used to read when he knew her in Paris. He thought she had become too attached to tragedy.

"I cannot leave France." Her voice was quiet but firm.

"Why not? What is in France for you now?" He wanted to shake her out of it, to pull her free from the clutches of Corneille. "There is only sadness for you here." Sadness and memories.

"Alex is here," she said simply. "My son." As if he might have forgotten she had a son. "I have people looking for him in Paris. They will bring him here." He opened his mouth to speak but she put her finger on his lips. "No, Nathan, listen to me. I cannot leave Alex." It came out in a rush. "I cannot go and look for him myself. I am an outlaw. I am wanted by the police. If they catch me they will shoot me, or take off my head on the guillotine. They will put him in an orphanage, and if they ever find out who he is, that he is the Comte de Turenne, then he will never leave it alive."

"He is in England." Nathan finally managed to get a word in. "He is at my home in England. At my father's home in Sussex."

She stared at him and her face lost some of its colour. She shook her head slowly. "No. How can that be?"

"Sara, would I lie to you about such a thing? He is with my father in England. Mary told me to take him there—so he would be safe."

"Alex is safe? In England?" She still seemed doubtful. She clutched at his shirt as if she would shake the truth out of him and he took her hands and held them in both of his.

"*Yes*. So now will you come?"

"Where in England? Is he with Mary?"

"He is with my father in Sussex," Nathan repeated. "At my father's home in the Cuckmere Valley, where I lived when I was a boy. I was playing with him on the shore last summer. Netting for prawns in the rock pools at Cuckmere. He is there, Sara," he insisted. "Waiting for you."

"You took him to England?"

"What else could I do? I thought you were dead. I could not leave him in Paris."

"No." She shook her head but no longer in disbelief. "I am not blaming you. How could I blame you? You have kept him safe for me." She rewarded him with a dazzling smile and there was laughter in her voice. "I cannot believe it. Alex safe in England. And you are here." But then the smile faded and a shadow crossed her face. "But if only I had known. I would have found some way of getting there. I would have come to him. To both of you."

"But I have come for you instead," he said.

"And you still want me?" she repeated wonderingly.

"Of course I want you." He almost laughed, though he was close to tears. "I have always wanted you."

"But I am not the same."

"You are the same to me."

"I cannot believe you have come back for me."

"You said I would find you here, waiting for me. At the little café in the square. Drinking lemonade and eating cakes made of oranges."

"Did I say that?"

"You did. But it was closed. And I have not had my lemonade, or my cakes."

"They did not make the cakes in springtime. They did not make them until the summer, when the oranges were ripe. Otherwise, they would be too bitter. And now nobody makes them."

Then the tears came. He bent forward to kiss them away but she pushed him back.

"I am sorry, Nathan, but so much has happened. So many people have died. And . . . And I have tasted so much that is bitter to me."

He nodded. "It is all right," he said tenderly. "I will make it all right. We will leave together and I will take you to my ship and we will sail for England—to be reunited with your son."

"Leave here?" She looked about her helplessly.

"Yes. If you can bear it."

"When?" She wiped the tears away almost fiercely with the back of her hand.

He looked towards the setting sun. Impossible to walk through the hills at night. "Tomorrow at first light. We have to be at the coast by sunset, or the ship will leave without us."

She looked back at him and he saw that she had decided. "I will make up a bed for you," she said. "In my father's room."

It was not quite how he would have planned it, but at least she was coming back with him, if only because of Alex.

And so he slept in her father's bed and halfway through the night she came to him. She climbed in next to him and he put his arms around her at last. Her cheeks were wet with tears.

"I never thought I would see you again," she said. "When I was in the death-cart I thought of you and it was too painful for me. I could not bear it."

"I am here now," he said, and this time she let him kiss away her tears.

He lay awake until dawn, afraid to sleep in case he missed it, and when he saw the first pale light in the sky he gently shook her awake.

"We must go now," he said, "or we will miss the ship."

They went by way of the abbey. It was somewhat of a diversion but he had to make sure Whiteley was not still there, waiting for him, in spite of his orders. He could not contemplate turning up with Sara on the beach and telling Duncan he had left his shipmates behind.

She wore men's clothes and an old straw hat but no-one would have taken her for a man, save at a great distance. She had bundled a few things into a pack and he saw her put a small pistol in with them. And she took a wicked little knife which she strapped to her left arm under her sleeve. Nathan wondered at this but said nothing.

It was easier on the return journey for it was mostly downhill and Sara walked almost as fast as he could have walked if he were alone.

"I am used to walking," she said. "We went mostly by foot in the Vendée. In the *marais* and in the forest. It was not often that we rode."

It was the only time she had mentioned the Chouans and he did not press her.

"And then I walked all the way from Brittany." She smiled at him then and it was like the sun coming out, like the Sara he had known in Paris. "So you would find me here."

They made good time but it was still almost noon before they reached the abbey. It appeared deserted. Nathan looked up at the belltower but could see no sentry there.

"They must have left," he said. He was a little disappointed even though he had given a direct order. "But we will catch up with them sooner or later."

He spoke confidently but he knew they had little time to spare. He wondered if the old man had died during the night or whether Whiteley had been forced to take him with them in a litter. He had to find out for sure before they moved on.

"I need to look for something," he said. "In the crypt. You can wait for me here."

But she would not let him leave her. "I will come with you," she said. "I do not like this place."

He hesitated. Perhaps he should not tarry. They were obviously not here. But he needed to know if Grimaldi was alive or dead.

"Very well," he said, taking her hand. "It will not take a moment."

They were crossing the floor of the chapel when he heard the sound of a horse stamping in the yard. Nathan turned to run but there was a man standing in the doorway they had just come through: a man he knew—and it was this that stopped him in his tracks as much as the pistol in his hand, for it was Commissaire Gillet.

CHAPTER TWENTY-SEVEN

the Sacred Chalice

SARA BACKED AWAY from the man in the door, her eyes searching the small chapel for a line of retreat. Finding none, she let out a sob and sank to the floor with her face in her hands, but Nathan saw her fingers feel for the hidden knife in her sleeve.

"No!" he commanded her urgently, though he had acknowledged a long time ago she was not his to command.

"I confess I am as surprised to see you here, Mr. Turner, as you must be to see me." Gillet arched his brows in affectation. "Delighted, of course, but amazed. And the countess, too, though I would hardly have recognised her, had we not been so well acquainted in the past." He favoured her with a bow. "But doubtless all will become clear, in the course of time."

He advanced towards them and Nathan saw the empty sleeve pinned to his breast. "You remember the night of the coup," Gillet prompted him. "In the rain at the Hôtel de Ville? But I have learned to shoot as well with my left arm. Better, perhaps. For I recall that I missed that night, whereas you did not."

He was not alone. Three soldiers had entered the chapel behind him—and another: a civilian in a black suit, slouch hat and Hessian boots, less immaculately polished than was usually the case.

"Another surprise for you," said Gillet. "I believe Mr. Imlay is an old acquaintance."

Nathan swore an oath, but in truth it was not as great a surprise as meeting Gillet. Imlay had a way of turning up when he was least expected, and the possibility had been in Nathan's mind ever since he had heard of the foreigner sent from Paris to find the Grimaldis, though he had told himself it was impossible.

In fact Imlay looked more shocked than Nathan. "What in God's name are you doing here?" he demanded with an exasperation that in other circumstances might have been amusing.

"There will be plenty of time for us to find out about Mr. Turner," Gillet assured him crisply. "The priority at present is to find Signor Grimaldi." He looked enquiringly into Nathan's face. "A name that is familiar to you, perhaps." Nathan made a play of looking puzzled. "Oh come now. You know how persuasive I can be when there is something I need to know."

Nathan knew. He had hung in chains before him, naked, in the House of Arrest while Gillet strode up and down and round and around with a long, thin cane, picking his spot. He could hear the swish before it struck. He could see the look on his face as he watched the pain he caused; not unlike the look that was there now.

Imlay spoke sharply to him. "Citizen, a word, if you please?"

Gillet looked into Nathan's eyes for a moment longer before he responded, his voice ironic. "Of course, Citizen, I am at your disposal."

The two men went into a huddle in a corner of the chapel. Nathan watched them carefully. They seemed to be arguing, though their voices were too low for him to hear. He doubted if Imlay commanded here, but you could never be sure with such a man. He noted the position of the three guards: two at the door of the chapel, the other standing to one side under a window with the sunlight behind him. Dragoons—booted and spurred and armed with carbines. But not Gillet's own thugs. And Imlay's loyalties were still a matter of conjecture.

The two men had finished talking. Gillet turned away. He did not look amused. Imlay walked to the door, catching Nathan's eye and indicating that he was to follow him.

"Go with them," Gillet instructed the corporal of dragoons. "And remember," he said to Nathan, indicating Sara with a jerk of his head, "what you have left here."

Nathan walked deliberately up to him, ignoring the pistol levelled at his chest.

"Touch her, go anywhere near her and I will kill you," he said. "I have the authority of General Buonaparte and I will do it."

He saw the astonishment in Gillet's eyes and then he turned and followed Imlay to the door.

"What was that all about?" Imlay said to him in English when they were outside the chapel.

"What?"

"About General Buonaparte?"

"He is a friend of mine. He will do anything for me."

"So I heard in Paris. But what is this about having his authority? Authority for what?"

"That is not for me to say."

Imlay eyed him warily. "Please do not trifle with me, Nathan. The only authority you have is from the British Admiralty. And they sent you to Genoa—with George Grimaldi."

So he knew that much. And how much more?

"So why are *you* here?" Nathan demanded. "And whose authority do *you* have?"

Imlay lowered his voice, though it could be assumed the dragoon did not speak English. "I imagine you were informed about the deal that George Grimaldi was sent to broker in Genoa?"

Nathan kept his expression blank.

"The reserves of the Casa di San Giorgio?" Imlay pressed him. "Come now, what else would bring you here?"

"I've no idea what you're talking about" Nathan told him. He was surprised how relaxed his voice sounded. "I came here for Sara. I found her in Tourettes where she said she would wait for me, and we stopped here on our way to the coast, for refreshment."

Imlay stared at him as if he was mad. "For refreshment?" he repeated faintly. He gazed around the ruined abbey in bemusement and then back at Nathan. "Do you take me for a fool?"

Nathan shrugged. "Believe what you like," he said. "But it is the truth."

Imlay took off his hat and stood for a moment as if in prayer. Then, very deliberately, he said: "Look, I cannot be entirely frank with you but I will tell you this: I need to know what has happened to the gold of the Casa di San Giorgio. That is why I came here from Paris. A great deal depends upon it and . . ."

"Your investments in America, I suppose?"

"That is a part of it, yes. But the gold of the Casa di San Giorgio will purchase a great deal more than that. It will buy the future of my country. And I will stop at nothing, do you understand me, to secure that."

"So now you are working for the Americans?"

Imlay did not reply.

"Do the British know that? Does Bicknell Coney or Spencer? Do the French? Does that man in there?"

"If you do not tell me what I need to know, that man in there will tear it out of you with whatever means occur to his sadistic mind. Do you understand that much, at least?"

"I told you. I came here for Sara."

"And I do not believe you. Look, I know what your mission was. I know that the gold was removed from the vaults of the bank and I know that shortly afterwards, Frederico Grimaldi fled with his family and was shipwrecked on the coast not far from here. I know he was probably here at the abbey—until quite recently. And so does Gillet. All we need to know is where he is now. Then, as far as I am concerned, you can go back to your ship with Sara."

"What about Gillet? You think he will let us go, just like that?"

"You may leave Gillet to me."

"Oh yes? Well, I am sorry. That is all I have to say to you."

"Then I must leave you to him." Imlay turned away.

"Wait." Nathan tried another tack. "What if I were to tell you there is no gold?"

Imlay turned back and laughed in his face.

"It is true," Nathan insisted. "Frederico Grimaldi told me. Before he died."

The laughter died in Imlay's throat. "What do you mean, 'before he died'?"

"We found him here, close to death, and we took him back to the *Unicorn* but we could do nothing for him. He had pneumonia. Then I came back for Sara."

Imlay regarded him carefully for a long moment. When he spoke it was with heavy patience, as to a child. "Either you are lying or Frederico Grimaldi was. The Casa di San Giorgio is one of the richest banks in the world. Almost as rich as the Bank of England."

"Then pity the Bank of England. There are no reserves. No gold. There has not been for many years. It was all a sham. When the French invaded, the Grimaldis knew they would be found out, so they pretended they had hidden it."

"And what of the Sacred Chalice?"

"Ah. So you know about that?"

"Yes, I know about that. And now I want to know where it is."

Nathan repeated what he had been told by Nicolas Grimaldi. "Someone dropped it. And it shattered in a thousand pieces."

"Someone dropped it," Imlay repeated flatly. He thrust his face closer to Nathan's. "Do you find this amusing?" He was close to losing his temper. He waved a hand back towards the chapel. "Do you know what that man is ready to do to you—and to Sara?"

"It was made of glass," Nathan assured him. "Or you could say sand, like all the treasure of the Casa di San Giorgio."

There was still doubt in Imlay's eyes but then they heard Gillet calling him urgently from within. The chapel was empty but the door to the crypt stood open and Nathan followed Imlay down the steps, the corporal at his heels. Gillet had lit a lamp and was peering at one of the stones in the floor. Nathan looked for Sara and saw her sitting with her back to the wall, head down with her knees drawn up to her chest and her hands clasped round them.

"They were here," Gillet said to Imlay. "There is bedding in the corner and someone made a fire: the ashes are still warm. And this stone has been moved." He pointed. "See the marks on the side. Someone has levered it up."

He strode over to the far side of the crypt and stooped down over something on the floor. When he came back Nathan saw that he was holding a crowbar.

"They must have used this." He thrust it at the corporal who inserted it into the crack and levered the stone up a fraction until the other two dragoons could grip it with their hands and pull it back. Nathan eased the dirk out of his boot and held it behind his thigh.

Gillet peered down into the vault. "It's a body," he said.

"Well, this *is* a crypt," Imlay informed him dryly.

"But he has just been buried. Look. No more than a few hours ago, I would think."

Nathan took a step forward and by the light of Gillet's lantern he saw the waxen face of Frederico Grimaldi.

"Is this who I think it is?" Imlay asked him.

Nathan said nothing. He stepped back into the shadows, with the knife in his hand. Gillet crossed over to where Sara was sitting and levelled his pistol at her head, cocking the hammer.

"It is Grimaldi," Nathan told him. He looked back at Imlay. "He died just after we got here—and we buried him."

"And the gold?"

"I keep telling you, there *was* no gold. There *is* no gold."

Gillet gestured with his pistol at Sara. "Strip her," he ordered the corporal.

The corporal looked astonished. "Strip her? Me?"

"You heard me. Now do it!"

"Gillet!" growled Imlay warningly.

"Shut up! I command here."

The corporal looked to Imlay uncertainly. Gillet reached out and grabbed a handful of Sara's hair. Then he reeled back with a cry, his hand to his neck and Nathan saw the knife in her hand and the blood. Nathan was already moving, but he could never have moved fast enough. Gillet had the pistol cocked and aimed. The gunshot was thunderous in the confined space.

But it was Imlay who had fired and Gillet who fell.

Nathan changed direction and ran at the corporal, stabbing him in the stomach and wrenching the carbine from his hands. Another loud report, almost in his ear, and he saw that Imlay had shot one of the other dragoons. Then through the smoke he saw the third trooper running to pick up his carbine from where he had left it at the foot of the stairs. Nathan fired from the hip and saw him go down.

Then there was silence. It seemed to go on for a long time compared to what had happened in the three or four seconds before. Nathan stood, stunned, half-deafened by the explosions in that confined space, the smoke hanging heavy in the candlelight and the acrid smell of gunpowder in his nostrils and his throat.

Then Imlay crossed over to Gillet, picked up his. pistol, and shot the corporal in the head.

Nathan stared at him in shocked disbelief. He saw his lips move but he could not make out a word he said. Then Imlay spoke again and this time Nathan did hear him.

"Don't look at me like that," Imlay said. "This is all your fault."

Nathan looked down at Gillet. He lay on his back in a spreading pool of blood with half of his face shot away.

Imlay was helping Sara up. "I'm sorry," he said. "I could not allow that."

"So now what?" Nathan heard his own voice but it seemed to be coming from a great distance.

"Now what?" Imlay repeated wearily. He looked about the smoking vault. "You tell me."

Nathan still had the knife in his hand.

"Whose side are you on?" he said. Even after what had happened he still did not know.

"Oh, for Christ's sake," said Imlay. "Get out of here and take her with you."

"What about you?"

"Me? It is a little late in the day for you to start worrying about me." Imlay looked about him again, at the four bodies. "I expect I will blame it all on you," he said. "I usually do."

Nathan reached out a hand for Sara but Imlay grabbed him by the wrist.

"Tell me, is it true—about the gold?"

Nathan sighed. "All I know is that is what the Grimaldis told me." How many more would die, he wondered, before it was believed.

Imlay looked down at Frederico's corpse. "Well, he didn't take it with him," he remarked composedly. "I suppose you had better help me cover him up again." But then he frowned and peered down into the darkness. "What is this?" He stooped and gingerly removed something from beside Grimaldi's head. A small silver casket, richly engraved.

He looked up at Nathan enquiringly. Nathan shook his head.

Imlay took a clasp knife from his pocket and slid the blade under the lid and worked away at it until he had wrenched the casket open. He stared for a moment at what it contained. Then he set it hastily down on the floor and stood up, taking a step back, as if it might explode.

"Christ Almighty!" he exclaimed. "Is that what I think it is?"

Nathan peered into the casket. It was filled with broken glass.

"I think it might be," he said.

"Dear God." Imlay made the sign of the cross though he was not, as far as Nathan knew, a Papist. He had seen him like this once before, in the catacombs under Paris, when they had entered the crypt under the Luxembourg Palace and seen the Devil—and the figure of Christ hanging upside down from the cross.

"What will you do with it?" Nathan asked him.

"What will *I* do with it?" Imlay looked down at the object at his feet. "I want nothing to do with it," he said.

"But that is what you were looking for." Nathan's tone was ironic. "The Holy Grail. The last reserves of the Casa di San Giorgio."

Imlay lifted it up and placed it gingerly back where he had found it, at the head of Frederico Grimaldi. Then together they slid the stone back into place.

CHAPTER TWENTY-EIGHT

the Sea

THEY FOUND THE CAVALRY MOUNTS tethered in the courtyard at the rear of the abbey—five of them, of a mountain
breed similar to English fell ponies. Nathan was tempted. It
would make them more conspicuous if they rode down to the sea
but they would make much better time and there was not a great
deal of it left. The sun was alarmingly low in the sky and the floor of
the valley already in deep shadow. He had told Duncan to leave for
the rendezvous at sunset and the first lieutenant was not the man to
disobey a direct order. He decided to take the risk.

They followed the track in single file along the side of the valley,
the ponies picking their way almost delicately among the roots of the
trees, their hooves muffled by a thick carpet of pine needles. Nathan
had his pistols ready loaded in the holsters on each side of the saddle, for Imlay had told them there were patrols out looking for the
Grimaldis, and he strained his ears for the slightest sound of horses
coming up the track toward them. But they made good time and
within the hour they had emerged on to the ridge running down to
the cliffs above the sea. And there in the distance were the two men-
of-war, hove to in the light of the setting sun. Nathan reined in for a
moment, for he was confident now that they would reach the shore
long before eight bells in the second dog watch and he was perfectly

assured that Duncan would not leave a moment sooner.

"There is my ship—the *Unicorn*. The bigger of the two, a little further out to sea." He pointed her out to Sara, not without a note of pride, for she had been a little too fond of referring to him as a boy when they were in Paris, and he still had thoughts of the Chouan leader, Charette, in his mind. It would do no harm to remind her that he was the captain of a frigate.

"The *Unicorn*," she mused. "I like that. That is a good name for a ship. And the other?"

"That is the *Bonne Aventure*. A privateer we took from the French."

"That is a good name, too," she acknowledged. Then, after a moment: "Do you know it means a love affair as well as an adventure?"

"I did not," he admitted. "But that is how I will think of it in future." He was about to move on when he saw the boat. It had just come into view from below the cliffs and he recognised it as the launch from the *Unicorn*, pulling back to the ship. And though he was too far to say with any certainty, he thought he could see two women in the stern. Whiteley's party from the abbey? He stood up in the stirrups, took off his hat and waved furiously, though there was little chance of being spotted at such a distance.

"Have we missed them?" Sara called out to him.

"Yes, but they will come back for us," he reassured her. "Still, we had better crack on." Then he saw something else. A cloud of dust approaching along the coast road, about half a mile below them. And among it, the glint of steel.

He led the ponies swiftly off the ridge, hoping to lie low among the scrub and the pines until the danger was past. But he realised almost at once that it would not do. There was no time. The sun was just about to slip below the western horizon—he saw its dying light gleaming on the dragoon helmets and the carbines. Their only hope was to cross the road ahead of them and race for the shore.

He let Sara take the lead and they rode the ponies as fast as they dared down the slope of the ridge. The dragoons must have seen them, for several of them had pushed ahead of the main troop and were riding just as hard to cut them off. Nathan reached for one of the pistols in the saddle holster and then thought better of it as the pony almost lost its footing on the sandy track. The only thing to do now was to ride.

They hit the road about a hundred yards ahead of the leading horsemen and plunged into the broom and the rocks on the far side. There was still a track of sorts but it was difficult to follow at any pace and the dragoons were firing at them now from above. Splinters flew up from the rocks and pines and Nathan's mount stumbled and fell. They were both up at once but Nathan had lost the rein and the horse plunged away from him through the brush. He let it go and sprinted after Sara who was trying to turn her own horse back for him. Nathan caught it by the bit and ran with it for a while but the slope was too steep and all three of them went over. They reached the shore in an avalanche of earth and stones but miraculously without breaking their necks. Nathan ran to Sara and picked her up and they both ran together to the sea. He could see men pointing to them from the stern of the brig and they were swinging a boat out from the yards. But it would never reach them in time.

"Can you swim?" he called out to Sara.

"I can swim in a river," she said doubtfully. "But I have never tried the sea."

"It is just the same," he assured her. "But you will have to take off your boots."

He looked back up the slope and saw the first of the dragoons burst through the pines further back along the shore.

"Is it cold, the sea?" Sara asked him as she struggled with her footwear. He admired her composure, though forced to curb the first ignoble retort that sprang to mind.

"No, not at all," he replied, as if it they were about to take a leisurely paddle in Cuckmere Haven. "Not in the Mediterranean."

A shot smashed into the shingle, sending up a shower of stones and he felt a sting on his cheek and the warm flowing blood. He grabbed her by the arm and hustled her towards the water's edge.

She let out a yell when the first wave broke over her.

"You lied!"

"Wait until you are in Sussex," he said. "That is what you might call cold. Now swim," he shouted, as a fusillade of shots echoed around the little bay and the dragoons urged their horses towards them across the sloping shingle.

And they struck out together for the *Bonne Aventure*.

HISTORY

In writing *The Price of Glory* I've combined fiction with historical fact, inasmuch as it is known, and readers might like to know where the battle lines are drawn.

The events on the Quiberon Peninsula and in the Gulf of Morbihan are based on various accounts of the Royalist landings of 1795, though in real life the frigate *Unicorn* was not involved in the expedition. However, the campaign does seem to have been as chaotic and ill-planned as I have described. The divisions in the Royalist command, the failure to reinforce Auray and the collapse of the proposed uprising in Paris are all well documented. It is also true that William Pitt released over a thousand Republican prisoners to swell the meagre ranks of the émigrés, and that these men defected almost as soon as they were put ashore, betraying the defences of Fort Penthièvre to the enemy. The account of the gun brig *Conquest* accidentally firing on the column of refugees is based on a similar incident involving the corvette *Lively*.

The events in London during Part Two are based in part on the love letters of Mary Wollstonecraft to Gilbert Imlay, though I have juggled a little with the dates. Celebrated as a pioneer feminist and the author of *A Vindication of the Rights of Women*, Mary went to France in 1792 to write about the Revolution. Here she met the American writer, Gilbert Imlay, and fell in love. They were married by the US ambassador—in a ceremony of dubious legality—and in May, 1794, Mary gave birth to their daughter, Fanny. Imlay then left her in Le Havre to pursue various interests in England and else-where, but when she joined him in London the following spring she found he was having an affair with an actress. She tried to kill her-self by taking an overdose of laudanum; Imlay came back in time to save her.

Despite her entreaties, however, he continued to see his actress and she made another attempt on her life, which I have described in the book—with some added details of my own, William Blake being one of them. Blake did, in fact, work with Mary on a book of fairytales—she wrote the copy, he did the illustrations—but I made up the story of his seeing her on the waterfront shortly before she jumped off Putney Bridge. And, of course, the presence of Nathan and his mother is entirely fictitious. But the rest of the story is based on the known facts—she *was* saved by a member of the newly created Royal Humane Society who happened to be at the pub at the time and had just learned how to perform artificial resuscitation. The suicide letter I quote is the real one she left at her lodgings.

As for Imlay, I made up quite a lot about him, but then he made up quite a lot about himself. History knows him as an officer in Washington's army during the American War of Independence, an explorer of the American frontier and the writer of *A Topographical Description of the Western Territory of North America* as well as a novel, *The Emigrants*. But he was much more than that. His own family thought he was a traitor—a British agent—but there is reason to suppose he was working secretly for General Washington: what we would now call a double agent.

After the war, Imlay became involved in various land specula-tions on the frontier. Then he disappeared for a while. Some believe he fled to the Spanish territory in the south-east to avoid his credi-tors; others that he became a Spanish agent in the Floridas and New Orleans. He may even have been continuing to work undercover for Washington, now President, who maintained his own secret service, answerable only to himself. I have seen documents in the National Archive in Havana including a confidential report from the Spanish governor of New Orleans to his superiors in Madrid.

Then on the eve of the French Revolution, Imlay turned up in Paris. With France at war with most of Europe, he operated as a shipping agent, running goods past the British blockade—but he seems to have had many other interests. In the Paris Archives des Affaires Étrangères, Louisiane et Florides 1792-1803, there are two documents entitled "Observations du Capitain Imlay" and "Memoire sur la Louisiane" relating Imlay's plans for the invasion and conquest of Spanish Louisiana and New Orleans, written during the time of the Terror and submitted to Lazarre Carnot, the military expert on the Committee of Public Safety. (This forms the basis for the plot of *The Tide of War*.)

In the summer and early autumn of 1795, Imlay was definitely in London because we have the evidence of Mary's letters to him there, but after that, he disappears again. His appearance in Provence in the spring of 1796 is, I am afraid, pure invention but it would not have surprised anyone who knew him. He had fingers in a lot of pies— in France, England, Scandinavia, Kentucky and Louisiana, Florida, New England and the Caribbean. He is buried, for some reason, in Jersey, on the Channel Islands. Or at least there is a grave there with his name on it.

The activities of Napoleone Buonaparte in Paris in 1795 are almost as incredible, but most of what I have written is based on contemporary accounts. He arrived in the French capital, broke and unemployed, in the spring of that year and embarked on a series of bizarre adventures mainly directed towards finding a job and a wife. In the course of these endeavours he wrote a romantic novel and kept a notebook with his peculiar jottings—including the observations about great men with three testicles. The scandalous adventures of Thérésa, Rose and Fortune Hamelin are also well documented, though I have to admit there is a strong suggestion of the prurient about the accounts of their more outrageous activities—especially in the memoirs of Paul Barras. You could say the same for what I've written here, but in my defence it *is* a novel and

I hope my admiration for all three women comes through strong and clear. Good luck to them. I wish they'd been more like Mary Wollstonecraft in their politics but you can't have everything and they probably had a lot more fun.

Which brings us to Nelson. The account of his relationship with Adelaide Correglia is recorded in detail by Thomas Fremantle in his diaries including the surprising information that she went to sea with him and acted as his hostess. Fremantle called her "Nelson's dolly." The fact that she doesn't appear in most accounts of Nelson's life is probably because she was overshadowed by his affair with Emma Hamilton—which was so public it could not be hidden. Also, I suppose if historians had included Signora Correglia in the story of Nelson's rise to greatness, he might have come over as a serial philanderer, which would not have suited the Victorians at all. In fact, he was no better or worse than most naval officers of the time. Nelson's "band of brothers" reflected the social and sexual mores of the Age of Scandal—but they were "cleaned up" for the more guarded, less open, period that followed. Significantly Fremantle's diary was destroyed in the middle of the 19th century, when Nelson's status as a national hero was positively godlike, but a copy had been made of part of it—and in any case the *Signora* is mentioned in despatches—or at least, letters, from Admiral Jervis.

The remarkable story of the Casa di San Giorgio is based on various documentary sources. The bank played a secretive but key role in many of the events of early modern Europe, funding Columbus's expedition to the Americas, the Spanish Armada, and much of the expansion of the Spanish Empire. In the process it established its control over the Republic of Genoa and built its own empire through the eastern Mediterranean, the Aegean and the Black Sea, even establishing colonies in the Crimea: an early example of a bank controlling a sovereign state. Certainly it was too big to fail and when it did, it brought down the Republic of Genoa with it. When Buonaparte occupied the city in 1797 the vaults were, indeed, found to be empty, but I have taken liberties with the story of the chalice.

I have used an accurate account of its reputed history as the Holy Grail—it was found by Genoese soldiers during the First Crusade and belonged to the bank for many years—but it was taken from Genoa by the French much earlier. They were forced to restore it after Napoleon's defeat but someone dropped it while packing it up for transport and it was discovered to be made of glass, not emerald. It was put together again, bound in silver filigree, and is now displayed in the Cathedral of Genoa.

The story of the secret talks between France and Spain over the future of North America is true. The vast territories of Spanish Louisiana—the whole of the present-day USA west of the Mississippi and from Canada to Mexico (828,000 square miles) were ceded to the French but when Napoleon sent an army to take possession in 1801, it was defeated by a series of intrigues by Anglo-US agents (probably Imlay again). So Napoleon cut his losses and sold the whole area to the US for $22 million in 1802. Known as the Louisiana Purchase it was the biggest real-estate deal in history and now comprises fourteen US states and two Canadian provinces.

The End